OUTSTANDING PRAISE FOR THE ROMANCES
OF REXANNE BECNEL

Heart of the Storm

"Great characters, a riveting plot and loads of sensuality
. . . A fabulous book. I couldn't put it down!"

—Joan Johnston, author of *Maverick Heart*

"Destined to be a bestseller from a star of the genre!"

—*Romantic Times*

"Well-written a *Weekly*

"Tempestuous a exanne
Becnel will enthⁿst."

—*mswept*

Where Magic Dwells

"A passionate, compelling story filled with engaging
characters."

—*Library Journal*

"Rich settings always bring Becnel's medieval novels to
life."

—*Publishers Weekly*

"Enthralling . . . Another irresistible medieval ro-
mance from one of the best."

—*Medieval Chronicle*

Dove at Midnight

"Rexanne Becnel understands the medieval mind-set,
and her beguiling characters' passions and adventures
will hold you enthralled . . . She is a master of her
craft."

—*Romantic Times*

My Gallant Enemy

"A love story of old to thrill and delight. Much intrigue
and an awesome, arrogant, but lovable hero and the
lady who turned his heart upside down."

—*Affaire de Coeur*

The Maiden Bride

Rexanne Becnel

St. Martin's Paperbacks

THE MAIDEN BRIDE

Copyright © 1996 by Rexanne Becnel.

ISBN: 0-312-95978-8

Printed in the United States of America

St. Martin's Paperbacks edition/September 1996

10 9 8 7 6 5 4

For Dot
Dorothy Madeleine Knobloch Becnel
1913–1996

The
Maiden
Bride

Prologue: Aborning

"Teach each child to ask blessing,
    serve God and to church;
Then blesse as a mother,
    else blesse him with birch."

—Tusser (1513)

"The second child must die."

A small gasp came from the woman lying in the great bed beside them, but neither Edgar de Valcourt nor his mother, the Lady Harriet, noticed. The midwife worked silently, cleaning her newly delivered mistress of the after leavings of the lengthy birth. A pair of maids had bathed the two tiny infants, then wrapped them in linen cloths. The firstborn already lay in the cradle prepared for it.

The second babe had no cradle, however, and it was her fate Sir Edgar and Lady Harriet now debated.

"You would have my daughter killed?" he asked disbelievingly. "You would order it done so easily as that?"

"To save this family I would do anything," the old woman vowed, not in the least cowed by her son's angry tone. " 'Tis known by one and all that babes like these, born of the same confinement, are cursed with but one soul between them. In an earlier age, both of them would have been drowned. Shouldst be glad I do not hold to such a pagan practice. Nay, but I am of a more enlightened mind." She peered up at him, daring him to contradict her in this, a domestic matter he had no knowledge of. "Since the first babe hath received all the goodness of the soul they share, 'tis reasonable to spare her. She will be a bless-

3

ing on Maidenstone Castle—mark my words on it—and a comfort to you in your old age. But the second one—" She broke off and sent such a frigid glare toward the tiny infant that the maid who held the child fell back a step. "The second one, 'tis cursed with a black and shriveled soul. Do you doubt me, ask the priest." She turned her unflinching stare back on her son. "There is no other choice. You do the child and your family a boon to destroy it this very day."

"But . . . but it goes against God's law to kill a child . . . And against the code of knightly behavior—"

"Doth tell me, my son, that you have killed neither woman nor child in duty to King Stephen and to God?"

"Yea, of course I have. But that is different. That was war."

"And this is not? This is a holy war, a war against the devil himself!" She snatched up the holy beads that hung from her waist and shook them in his face as if they were a divine weapon she wielded. It had the effect of making him drop back a pace from her. "You do but kill the devil's spawn in that evil child." Then her nostrils flared in disdain. "If you have not the stomach for it, then will I see it done!"

"No!"

Though his wife's cry was weak, Edgar turned to her in relief. In matters of war and land and politics he was adept. He made hard decisions without hesitation and dealt with the consequences, no matter what they might be. It was that strength of purpose that had pitted him with Stephen against old King Henry's daughter, Matilda, and thereby won him Maidenstone Castle and the vast demesne it controlled. He'd profited well as Stephen's man, having married a beautiful heiress and fathered two sons already. But this matter of twin daughters was something else entirely.

"Edgar, please," Lady Ella pleaded with her husband in a voice little more than a faint breath in the dim and overheated chamber. He turned to her, anything to avoid his mother's disapproving expression.

4

" 'Tis for the best," he murmured, taking her limp hand in his. "we will keep the good twin—"

"I would keep them both. Do not let her destroy my child. Please . . . I beg you . . . do not let her . . ."

Tears overflowed her eyes, making a wet trail down her pale face, to be lost in her fair hair. She was a beauty, his Ella, and he would do almost anything to make her smile. He'd long speculated that if he had not loved his wife so much, his mother might have liked her better.

"Calm yourself, my wife. You need your rest if you are to tend the child—"

"The children. Not one, but two," she insisted. "We are twice blessed, Edgar, to have them both. Tell me, how do they look?"

"They look . . . like babies," he said with a shrug, for he had not given them more than a passing glance once he'd learned they were not sons.

"Bring them to me," she implored, clutching his hand. "Let me see my daughters."

"Only bring the one," Lady Harriet ordered, staying the maid who yet held the second child in her arms.

"No, both," Ella pleaded, staring up into Edgar's uncertain face. "I have already given you two sons," she reminded him in a whisper only he could hear. "How can you deny me my two daughters?"

For a moment he wavered. The Church would not approve of killing a baby—although he *could* just abandon it in the forest. Still, that would practically be the same as killing it. Then Ella's weak hold on his hand strengthened.

"I will give you more sons after this, my husband. I will fill your hall with strong sons. Only you must give me my daughters."

Her eyes burned up into his, and her slender fingers moved along his wrist. At once his body reacted to her touch, for it had been weeks since she'd shared his bed. If he did not do this for her, she would grieve a long time, as she had when she'd lost their very first child. A girl, as he recalled. It had taken nearly a year for her to respond to him as she always had before, a year of frustration and unsatisfying nights which he did not wish to repeat.

"You will have both your daughters," he promised her on impulse. When she smiled in trembling gratitude and tears of joy filled her eyes, his chest swelled with pride. Anything to keep his lady wife happy.

His mother let out an indecipherable curse, but he ignored it as he mentally calculated how long he must wait before he could bring Ella back to his bed. At his signal both infants were brought to their mother's side, and as she bared her breasts to suckle them, he felt an urgent need that could not wait even a fortnight for her.

But as he left the birthing chamber, pleased with himself and intent on finding one of the dairy maids—the one who in figure and hair color most resembled his beauteous Ella—he was accosted by his mother.

"Art a fool to let her lead you by that mindless rod which rears between your legs!"

"She is my wife," he growled, not eager to be caught once again between his wife and his mother.

"She is your wife," she echoed contemptuously. "And her accursed child shall be your undoing some day!"

"I have made my decision! Begone from here!" he roared, shoving past her as all the pleasure he'd been filled with fled.

But Lady Harriet had never feared her son's temper, nor did she now. "At the very least mark it. So alike they are, you must needs have some mark to set them apart. Mark the second babe, so we can know which of them to fear!"

He was later to regret what he did then, but in the years that followed he never once confessed to it. He swore the maids to silence with one threatening look, and if Ella ever suspected anything, she never confronted him about it.

He stormed back into the birthing chamber and bid the nursemaids bring both babies to him while his wife slept unknowing in her bed. The one babe, the first one whom his wife had named Beatrix, he examined thoroughly, noting every aspect of her appearance: tiny chin, full cheeks, dark eyes, and a faint fuzz of light hair.

The second one, as yet unnamed, was identical in every way, even to the arch of her fair brows and the creases in her tiny ears. So, unable to tell them apart, Sir Edgar did as his mother had demanded. Angry and frustrated, he heated his signet ring over a candle, and when the metal glowed hot, he pressed it to the second baby's tender flesh.

She jerked and screamed, a startlingly loud cry that jolted the other baby awake and started her crying too. But Edgar de Valcourt did not flinch in what he did. Only when the smell of burned flesh assaulted his nostrils did he pull the ring away and view the damage he had wrought.

A smoking, purple scar now marred the perfect skin of the newborn's leg, and that, coupled with the two babies' hysterical crying, overwhelmed him with images of charred souls, writhing in the eternal fires of hell, screaming in endless agony. A shudder of horror ripped through him, and for a moment he contemplated just doing as his mother had originally demanded: ridding himself of the child completely, just in case there was any truth to her superstitions.

Then his wife shifted restlessly in her bed and once more he changed his mind. Ella would never forgive him. She would grieve and she would never forgive him for killing her daughter.

He handed the inconsolable baby back to the wide-eyed nurse with a furious warning glare. Then he turned and quit the chamber.

He'd given both his wife and his mother what they wanted. If that didn't please them he'd give both of them the back of his hand.

Just see if he wouldn't.

Ascencioun

Chapter 1

She knew the castle could not hold out for long. Too many soldiers came over the hill. They poured in an unending wave, following the fluttering red pennant that depicted two black bears battling.

But in spite of that, Linnea de Valcourt spat defiantly past the solid stone crenellation, denying the frightening possibility of anything but a quick, decisive victory for the castle.

"The fools. They but waste their time—and their blood," she stated, with a confidence she did not entirely feel. "Henry of Anjou cannot take Maidenstone Castle, nor any of Wessex. Nor any part of Britain," she added with youthful defiance.

"They've already taken much of Wessex," Sir Hugh, her father's captain of the guard, muttered as he glared at the never-ending horde.

"But they won't take Maidenstone," Linnea vowed. Then her bravery wilted a bit, and in a more hesitant voice she added, "Will they?"

Sir Hugh did not take his eyes from the army that almost reached the village now. A steady stream of panicked village folk fled toward the castle, carrying their children and what few provisions they were able to gather in the scant

11

hour since the alarm had sounded. Linnea saw his jaw tighten and flex, once, twice, and then again.

"Raise the bridge," he growled at the soldier who stood at his side.

"No! Not yet!" Linnea cried without thinking.

But Sir Hugh's murderous glare cut off any further protest from her. "Get yourself away from my battlements, lest ye curse what little there is left of us!" When the censorious gaze of the other soldiers around him joined Sir Hugh's, Linnea fell back a pace, shattered by his words.

Sir Hugh must have spied the stricken look on her face, for his harsh features softened ever so slightly. "Go join your sister in the hall," he ordered gruffly. "And tell your grandmother I'll send word as soon as there's anything to tell."

Linnea nodded, gathering her plain plunkett cloth skirt in one hand as she turned to the steep steps that led down into the bailey. He hadn't meant it about the curse. She knew he hadn't. It was only that he was tense due to the attack. Sir Hugh had never been like so many of the others, staring at her with wary, suspicious eyes. He'd never crossed himself for protection if she came upon him unexpectedly. It was just this damnable war between King Stephen and that Norman usurper, Henry Plantagenet. First his mother, Matilda, now the son. Why couldn't these warring magnates leave the people of Wessex in peace? she wondered, even as the grate of gears and creaking of the chains signaled the slow rise of Maidenstone's newly constructed bridge.

A cry from the villagers stranded outside the walls rose up, a frightened, desperate wail accompanied by the first sting of acrid smoke on the wind. They were firing the village, she realized in alarm. The barbarians were putting the innocent village of Maidenstone to the torch!

"I curse you all to hell!" Linnea muttered as both fury and abject sorrow washed over her. "I curse you to hell, you of the black bear pennant!" she cried, wishing more than anything that she had the abilities so many attributed to her. For if she could curse all those invaders to hell, she would do so without a qualm. She would send them to burn in the fires of eternity, and thereby save her home and her people.

And her people would love her for it, she thought, imagining for one fanciful moment how things would change if she could only do something truly noble to prove herself to the people of Maidenstone—

"Get out of the way," a crude voice demanded, bringing her abruptly back to reality.

She hurried down the last flight of steps, one of the castle guards hot on her heels. He'd not mistaken her for her sister Beatrix, but then, Linnea's plain garb had always set her apart from Beatrix in her finer garments. Besides, Beatrix would not be outside in the midst of battle preparations. Only Linnea would do something so foolish. Beatrix would be in the hall, settling the frightened villagers, or organizing the kitchen, or some other necessary domestic task.

In the bailey Linnea paused, not certain where to position herself during the coming siege. Across the now crowded yard she spied her grandmother standing on the top step that led into the great hall, leaning on her walking stick with one hand while she waved orders with her other.

She would not go to the hall, Linnea decided on the instant. Her grandmother, the Lady Harriet, could barely stand the sight of her younger granddaughter under the best of conditions. Today her acid temper would not be bound by the normal limits good manners dictated.

Then Linnea heard her father's hoarse shout, and after searching the seething throng a few frantic minutes, she spied him striding along the east parapet walk, calling orders and gesturing to his men as he assumed control of the castle's defenses.

He was dressed in a leather jack today, emblazoned with the Valcourt family crest, a blue field with a golden griffin rampant. A short blue cape fluttered behind him and a heavy gold-encrusted belt spanned his generous girth, giving him the look of a powerful knight, much as legend made him. A man unparalleled in bravery, cunning, and

13

strength. If she saw him as a man given more to food and drink than to battles and strategy, it was only because during the past ten years that was the only thing required of him. She did not remember the years when he'd fought for Stephen, helping him wrest the crown from the old king's bastard daughter. She'd heard the stories of his daring, however, stories told and retold in the long evenings of winter. How he'd been knighted by King Stephen himself, though long before Stephen had become a king. And how he'd fought in Stephen's elite guard. How he'd been rewarded for his loyalty with marriage to Stephen's second cousin, Ella, the most beautiful woman in the land. How he'd taken Maidenstone Castle in the days just after the old king's death and held it firm against every one of Matilda's attempts to win it and the crown back from Stephen.

Today, however, it seemed Matilda's son and his followers were making a more forceful attempt than ever.

Linnea shrank back into a sheltered corner, where one wall of the stone kitchen met the palisades fence that surrounded the herb garden. The bailey was thronged with people and dogs and nervous cattle. Above the mad crowd a churning cloud of dust eddied, choking her throat and making her eyes tear. But she nevertheless kept her gaze locked upon her father.

If only Maynard were here, she fretted, as her father limped to Sir Hugh's side and they stared together out toward the fast-approaching enemy. Her brother was a cruel and obnoxious oaf at times, but he was as brave as ever his father had been, and a knight and warrior of considerable skill.

Maynard was in Melcombe Regis, however, with the bulk of their army of knights, archers, and foot soldiers. Maidenstone was defended only by the castle guard and what villagers had made it safely inside before the drawbridge had been raised.

A shiver of fear shimmied down Linnea's spine and she hugged herself. Maidenstone could not hope to win, she thought once more, and it was a terrible thing to admit.

They could not hope to win; therefore they must expect to lose.

At once she shoved away from her hiding place. It did not matter about her grandmother's temper any longer. Linnea needed to find Beatrix, to be there with her in the event the unthinkable occurred. Beatrix would need someone to protect her and, as always, Linnea would do anything for her beloved sister.

Hiking her coarse skirt up in a manner far from ladylike, she dashed across the bailey, dodging frantic villagers and frightened children. The smell of smoke was stronger now, as was the wailing from both inside and outside the besieged castle.

Surely the world was coming to an end, she feared as the panic and confusion around her began to seep into her too. Surely this was hell and the black bear outside their door was the devil himself come to call.

Axton de la Manse sat astride his mighty destrier just beyond the village gates, staring up at Maidenstone's sheer stone walls. Black plumes of billowing smoke turned the sky gray and made his boyhood home a perfect picture of hell. But it was only barns and outbuildings he'd fired, and an occasional shop or storage building in a strategic location. Still, as the acrid stench curled up and drifted from the village to swirl around the castle walls, it was enough to terrorize the hapless villagers—and enough to strike fear into the heart of Edgar de Valcourt and his family of two-legged leeches.

"The villagers are trapped between us and the moat," said Sir Reynold, Axton's captain and most trusted man.

Axton nodded. "Keep the fires going until the bridge is lowered and the gate raised. And bring de Valcourt's son to the front."

"He has fainted and is barely alive."

Axton shrugged. "He fought a good fight—for a de Valcourt. If he should die, so be it. But it will not alter the outcome of this day's work." That he felt a savage satisfaction at having struck the disabling blow to Maynard de

Valcourt's arm did not have to be stated. Axton and Reynold had fought many a battle together and they'd lost many a valiant compatriot in the process. But that was a knight's lot in life. To fight a good fight and then die from your wounds on the field of honor was as much as Axton and Reynold had ever expected of life. As much as they'd ever hoped for.

Until now.

Now he wanted to live to a ripe old age, to put away the tempered steel of sword and dagger and the forged iron of mace and spear. He meant to win back his home this day, and though there would always be service to give his king—or scutage to pay in its place—he meant to settle down at Maidenstone, to bring what little remained of his family back to this place, and to regain everything they'd lost so many years ago.

Only they could not regain *everything*.

His leather-clad fist tightened on the reins and his warhorse danced in a nervous circle. Christ's blood, but his father should be here at this moment, to savor the victory that had been so long in coming. Likewise his brothers William and Yves deserved to be here to share in this triumph.

But they weren't here. He was the only man left in the family. That meant he must savor the victory for all of them, he told himself as the cart bearing the younger de Valcourt rumbled forward. Four times over he would savor his victory this day, once for himself and three times for his father and older brothers. Four times the drinking. Four times the feasting. Four times the wenching.

He smiled grimly at that. He'd been weeks without a woman. If he weren't so accursedly weary he'd call for four wenches in his bed tonight, all at one time.

He stared up at the castle-walls. Soon they must surrender. It was just a matter of time, and that knowledge banished all thoughts of having any women in his bed. The time was at hand. His victory—and de Valcourt's fall.

* * *

16

"He has Sir Maynard—"

"He holds the young lord—"

"Sir Maynard has fallen into the enemy's vile clutches—"

The rumor spread from ramparts to bailey and through the terrified crush into the hall where Lady Harriet barked orders from her place on the raised platform nearest the hearth. Sir Maynard was wounded—dying, being tortured—just outside the moat, lying in an open cart for all to witness his downfall.

They had only to lower the drawbridge—and surrender the castle—to regain their hero and be allowed to tend his wounds.

Linnea heard the rumors just as the others did, and her reaction was much the same. What little hope she'd had disappeared entirely. Without her brother and his army, there was no chance they might hold back the ravenous horde beyond the outer walls of the castle. As long as he was fighting somewhere on King Stephen's behalf there had been a chance, slim though it might be, that Sir Maynard might somehow hear of their plight and come to their aid. They could have held out against a siege for a couple of weeks at least, if they'd had reason to hope.

But now their last hope lay crushed and broken in a cart outside the wall.

"Poor Maynard," Linnea whispered as she clutched her sister's hand.

"We must pray for him," Beatrix whispered back, and dutifully Linnea followed her lead, bowing her head and praying for the older brother who'd never paid either of them the slightest attention, except when he wanted to blame his "accursed sister," as he'd called Linnea, for something that was actually his fault. He'd been very good at that as a child, and she'd suffered many a beating or other punishment for something he'd accused her of.

But that didn't matter today, Linnea reminded herself as she tried to concentrate on the litany of softly worded entreaties Beatrix directed heavenward. "Please, God, save our beloved brother. Save our home and family and people from the vile beast who assaults us now. Please, God, help us, your humble servants, in our hour of need . . ."

It went on and on, as did a hundred other similar pleadings, filling the tapestry-hung hall with a rising and falling hum until the double doors flew open with a crash. Then Sir Edgar himself staggered into the packed chamber and the prayers fell away to an absolute silence.

Had Linnea been frightened before? As she stared round-eyed at her father's haggard expression, her fears increased tenfold. She'd seen her father angry; she'd seen him heartbroken, too. She'd seen him cruel and unbending, and she'd seen him recklessly drunk. But she'd never before seen him afraid. Never.

And she'd never seen him defeated.

"Clear a path for my lord. Clear a path!" the seneschal, Sir John, shouted, shoving and kicking people aside so that Sir Edgar could make his way to his family on the raised dais. A pall hung over the place, a chill broken only by the thrum of fear from beyond the solid walls of the stout keep.

Linnea and Beatrix clung together, just to the left of their grandmother. She still stood, leaning on her cane, as she watched her only son's faltering approach.

For a moment Linnea was actually able to admire her grandmother. Lady Harriet had tormented her all her life. Linnea had never received a kind look or word from her father's mother. Lady Harriet had lavished all her affection upon Maynard, and to a lesser degree, Beatrix. But there had been no affection whatsoever for Linnea.

Still, Lady Harriet's steely temperament stood her in good stead this day. As mother and son faced one another, it was clear to Linnea who was the stronger of the pair.

"They have him . . . Maynard," Sir Edgar confirmed in a whisper laced with agony. "They have him and he is broken. . . . Carried in a pig cart for all to see—"

His voice caught, and he covered his eyes with a hand that shook. Linnea's insides turned to pudding in the face of her father's emotional display and tears burned in her eyes.

"Poor Maynard. Poor Maynard," Beatrix repeated, clutching Linnea's hand with painful intensity.

It was Lady Harriet who stood tall and strong. "Who is this vile emissary from Henry's decadent court that doth assault us in our own home? Who is this spawn of Satan that wouldst kill our sons and rape our daughters?"

Sir Edgar's hand fell away from his eyes and he lifted his haggard features to meet his mother's outraged face. Linnea strained forward to hear, not that she expected to know the name of their attacker. She and Beatrix were kept ignorant of all but the most benign aspects of any matters that dealt with politics. Anything Linnea knew, she'd gleaned from the castle folk or those villagers she'd come to meet during the few times she managed to steal away from her chores.

So when Sir Edgar said, "It is de la Manse—de la Manse—I saw the pennants," she did not at once recognize the name.

"De la Manse!" Her grandmother's eyes grew large and her gnarled fingers tightened on her carved walking stick. "De la Manse," she repeated, spitting the name out as if it were a curse. Only then did Linnea recall where she'd heard it before.

De la Manse. The family that had made their home at Maidenstone Castle before King Stephen bestowed it upon her father for his loyalty. De la Manse, the family that had supported Matilda's claim to the throne all these years while living in Normandy. The family that would, no doubt, fight more viciously than any other family to reclaim Maidenstone for themselves.

"De la Manse." The name raced through the rest of the hall, like fire rushing through a dry field. "De la Manse."

"Silence!" Lady Harriet screeched, stamping her stick on the floor the way she always did when her furious temper overcame her. She glared down at the frightened people of Maidenstone, stilling them with the force of her personality. There was not a one of them who hadn't borne the brunt of that temper at one time or another, and they all knew to heed her most carefully.

" 'Tis imperative we save Maynard," she stated, speaking to her son. "Come to my solar."

When he did not at once respond, but only stared at her with a bewildered expression, she impatiently yanked at his sleeve. "Come along, Edgar!"

Linnea watched them depart, her grandmother leaning on her carved stick, but as rigid and determined as ever, her father slumped in defeat already. Behind them Sir John followed, wringing his hands in worry.

While she could sympathize with her father's distress in the face of this disaster, there was something in her that wanted him to stiffen his spine, to show even half the mettle and fortitude of his aging mother.

"We must pray all the harder," Beatrix whispered when the trio disappeared up the steep, shadowed stairway. But Linnea was of a different mind, and she easily disentangled her hand from Beatrix's.

"I want to see," she replied to her sister, slipping past the seneschal's elderly wife and crippled son. She leaped down from the dais and picked her way across the now noisy crowd, heading toward the door to the yard.

"Wait!" Beatrix called out to her. "Wait for me!" But as Beatrix started across the hall, she was delayed at every step by the good people of Maidenstone.

"What is to become of us, milady?"

"Shall Lord Edgar save us?"

"Will our Sir Maynard live?"

At every interruption Beatrix stopped and tried to answer and placate the asker. No such questions had been thrown at Linnea. Though she was relieved at that, for she had no answers to give, a familiar longing nonetheless crept over her. A familiar loneliness. No one ever directed that sort of attention at her, only at Beatrix. Beatrix, who was beautiful and sweet and gentle with one and all. Beatrix, whose soul was purer than that of the normal person—because Linnea's was blacker. As blessed with goodness as Beatrix was, Linnea was cursed with evil. And though she'd long ago become accustomed to her place in the family—with her lot in life—there were times, like now, when the hurt sprang unexpectedly over her.

Still, she could not blame her sister, for it was no more Beatrix's fault for being born first than it was her own for being born second. God had ordained it that way, and she must resign herself to it—and fight all the harder against the dark urges that sometimes gripped her soul. Some were easier to contain than others. She could walk when she'd rather skip; she could concentrate on her chores when she'd rather daydream in the garden or learn to play the lute.

At times, however, it was nigh on to impossible for her to repress her true nature, like right now, when she knew she should stay here in the hall and help, but no force on earth could prevent her from creeping back up to the wall-walk.

With a last glance back at her sister, and a regretful half-smile, Linnea pushed open one of the immense oak doors and slipped out into the yard.

The smoke was worse than ever, an angry cloud that circled and settled, only to rise once more like a living creature, never quite content. Likewise a worse sort of panic now seemed to have descended over both the villagers and the castle guard. No doubt it was her father's defeated attitude that had affected them so. But once Linnea clambered up a ladder to the eastern wall, then scurried toward the north tower, she saw the real reason for everyone's despair, *especially* her father's.

In the open ground between the castle's narrow moat and the nearest buildings of the village a vast army had gathered. The supply carts that always trailed armies were now rolling up, and even as she watched, a showy tent of pure white canvas was raised with pennants flying from each of the four corners.

It was their leader's tent, of course, this de la Manse. He made himself comfortable while he burned down the village behind him!

The poor villagers who had been left outside the castle were herded tightly together in a silent throng just below her perch. They were guarded by two mounted knights and several well-armed foot soldiers, but the mix of men, women, and children did not seem inclined to try escaping their captors. Linnea couldn't blame them for that. Where would they go if they did manage to escape? How would they live?

But where was Maynard? she wondered. She leaned out between two stone merlons, searching the chaotic scene below. Maybe her father was wrong; maybe it was only a rumor—a false rumor.

Then her eyes locked upon a small, stake-sided cart, the sort of vehicle that livestock or produce might be hauled in, and she froze. Someone lay within the cart, a man sprawled on his back.

It could be someone else, she told herself, though her heart had begun painfully to pound. The fact that he was wrapped in the blue cape of the de Valcourts meant nothing.

Then the man stirred, rolling his head to the side, and even through the shifting gray of the smoke, Linnea could see his hair, his bright golden hair, so like her mother's—and her own.

Her heart stopped in her chest. It *was* Maynard. Dear God, but it was true.

"You should not be up here!"

Linnea did not even turn at Sir Hugh's harsh accusation. "He's still alive!" she cried. "Do they mean to let him die there in front of us without helping him? Won't they let us see to his wounds?"

Sir Hugh moved up beside her and squinted wearily at the unreal scene spread before them. "He is their negotiating point. We must surrender if his life is to be spared."

Linnea swallowed hard and stared up at him. "And *will* we surrender?"

The answer came not from her father's longtime captain, but from one of the pages who rushed up, skidding to a halt before Sir Hugh. "Milady says—" He paused to catch his breath from his fast climb up to the wall-walk. "I mean, Lord *Edgar* says to unfurl the white cloth."

Linnea watched with widened eyes as Sir Hugh nodded, then signaled to a pair of guards who promptly hoisted a length of canvas cloth over the rough stone wall. She could not see it fall, opening as it went. But she could picture it, like the shroud around a dead body, unfurling to expose the corpse. Only it was her family's life at Maidenstone which was dying and being buried this day.

At the sight of the cloth, an unsettling sound rose up from beyond the castle walls—half sob of relief from the captured villagers, half cheer from the marauders themselves. A rider burst away from near the pennanted tent, a youth urging his spirited horse through the other soldiers, carrying the de la Manse banner like a trophy before him. The red cloth seemed almost to glow in the premature dusk of the smoky sky. The black bears, rearing on their hind legs facing one another, appeared to move and claw each other as the fabric rippled above the nightmarish scene.

The boy rode up to the moat, then circled on his handsome steed, back and forth as the bridge slowly creaked down. At that moment Linnea was so consumed with anger and fear that she prayed the horrible lad would tumble off his horse—that he would fall into the moat and drown. The arrogant brat!

But though her tumultuous emotions focused on the boy, she knew he was not the one they must fear. Somewhere beyond him was this de la Manse. Somewhere preparing to enter his former home was a man who must despise them all.

She stared at the white pavillion and tried to picture him, this man her father had bested eighteen years ago. It had happened before she'd even been born, yet she knew that one event was having repercussions in her life still. It would change her life forever.

A shiver of fear snaked up her backbone. The bridge was almost down. The smoke had begun to clear. Best that she join her sister and father now. Best that they all stand together while their lives fell apart around them.

Chapter 2

"They're like dogs with their tails tucked 'tween their legs."

Despite the conflicting emotions that roiled in his own chest, Axton couldn't help but smile at Peter's words. His younger brother's excitement was palpable. This was the lad's first experience with war, his first time away from home as his older brother's squire. By rights he should have been fostered elsewhere, trained in his knightly skills and duties by someone else. But their mother had feared so for him. She'd not wanted him to become a knight at all, not since she'd already lost a husband and two sons to war.

But Peter was set on becoming a knight and he'd worn their mother down. Still, she'd prevailed in her choice of knights to teach him. To her mind, her youngest son would be best trained—and best watched over—by his only living brother, Axton.

Though an unorthodox approach, after almost a year with Peter as his squire, Axton was well pleased. The fact was, his younger brother was far better suited to a life of war than William or Yves had ever been. He was quicker and more decisive, and already displayed considerable skill with both sword and lance. Added to that, he possessed an uncanny ability with horses, from palfrey to destrier.

It had seemed only right for Peter to accompany him on their siege of Maidenstone Castle, the very place the lad *should* have been raised. And it had struck Axton as particularly fitting for Peter to act as negotiator for the surrender of the castle today. He was the only one of the four de la Manse brothers who'd never set foot in their ancestral home, for he'd been born during their forced exile in Normandy. More than that, however, Axton had known it would humiliate de Valcourt to negotiate with a mere lad, a lowly squire at that.

Axton squinted now at the red and black banner waving

jauntily back and forth before the lowering gate. De Valcourt would suffer many more humiliations than this, he vowed. He, himself, would see to it.

Unfortunately, he could not kill the man or his son now, unless presented with no other choice. Henry had ordered it so. All was fair during the heat of battle. But de Valcourt's quick surrender of the castle had abruptly changed the rules. Once they surrendered to him, they had come under his protection—and thereby, the Duke of Normandy's. Axton clenched his fists at the irony of it. His worst enemy within his grasp, and he was bound to uphold Henry's orders to ensure peace in the land!

Of course, the son might still die of his wounds. Axton was amazed he yet clung to life. As for the father, Axton could not in good faith raise a weapon against the man now—unless the old man challenged him.

A just God would see the old bastard do that very thing!

But there was no justice, and it was unlikely that would ever happen. He was honor bound to oblige his liege lord's wishes. How often had the Empress Matilda told her son Henry—and he told the lords who supported him—to kill the sons in battle, marry the daughters in peace, and leave the land in good repair? No pillaging or indiscriminate ravaging of the countryside, save what was absolutely necessary to subdue the populace.

Accordingly, Axton had burned only enough of the village to strike terror into the heart of its people, though in truth he would have acted no differently without Henry's orders. This was his home, despite the fact that he'd been torn from it when only a lad of nine.

When old King Henry had died, Allan de la Manse and his wife and three sons had all been in Normandy, attending the king's daughter, Matilda, and his young grandson, Henry. Matilda's absence from Britain gave her cousin, Stephen, the opportunity to usurp the crown and his men had taken over all the king's strongholds before Matilda could react.

Edgar de Valcourt had found few men to oppose his takeover of Maidenstone Castle, and Stephen had turned a deaf ear to Allan de la Manse's appeals for justice. Their family had been stranded in Normandy, made homeless by both Stephen and de Valcourt. But during the eighteen long years on the mainland, Maidenstone had remained Axton's home, at least in his mind and that of his parents. He had no intention now of burning it to the ground, nor of salting the land, tumbling the castle walls, or slaughtering either villagers or beasts.

Maidenstone was finally his, and the thump of the lowered bridge upon the great stone that buttressed the edge of the moat proved it. He had only to enter his home and take possession of it. De Valcourt could have his crippled son back, for he was no longer a threat. Even if the man lived, he would never fight again. His sword arm was too badly mutilated.

But Axton nonetheless meant still to wed the eldest daughter, if there was one. He would wed the wench, whether young or old, fair or hideous. Then he would get her with child as swiftly as he could. Only then would he be sure that no one could ever again dispute his claim to Maidenstone.

No one at all.

The boy with the banner led the procession across the bridge, through the gatehouse, and into the castle yard. Linnea and Beatrix peered down into the bailey from the hide-covered window of the solar they shared. The lad was a sturdy, dark-haired youth, with curls falling over his brow and an arrogant grin that Linnea detested on sight. Who was this jackanapes stripling that led an army as if he had the right? No doubt the son of de la Manse.

The door flew open with a crash, startling them both. But it was only their grandmother and her maid Ida, not a pair of murderous soldiers.

"Move aside, girl. Let me see," Lady Harriet demanded. She grabbed Linnea's upper arm in her pincer grasp and pushed her to the side.

Linnea backed away, not bothering to rub her arm, though she was certain a bruise would rise there. She'd had a continuing series of bruises from her grandmother for as long as she could remember. Not that she'd ever been truly hurt. They'd only been surface hurts and swift to heal. But Beatrix was never treated so.

Lady Harriet moved up beside Beatrix, sharing the window view, and even clutching her other granddaughter's hand reassuringly.

"Art bringing Maynard within. I saw from my solar. Look, there arrives the cart now."

Linnea inched forward, and standing on tiptoe, tried to catch a glimpse of her wounded brother. But all she could see were the tops of the wagon's side stakes.

"A pox on de la Manse!" Lady Harriet cursed with a vehemence that startled both younger women. "May he be damned unto hell—and all his family with him. Especially that boy!"

For once Linnea was in complete accord with her grandmother. Yes, especially that boy. Beatrix tried to console her grandmother who was visibly shaking, so violent were her emotions. "It is not the boy who is our concern—"

"Be not a fool! That **boy** *is* a de la Manse, son to Allan de la Manse. He above *all* is our concern! Agh, had I but a way to be rid of him." She slapped the stone windowsill and turned away, her mouth pulled down in a bitter expression. "He should be the one carted around, broken and bleeding." Then her icy gaze landed on Linnea and her expression grew grimmer still.

Linnea shrank back instinctively, for she knew that look. It was the reason she avoided her grandmother as much as possible. But she couldn't avoid her now.

"The blame lies with the devil amongst us," Lady Harriet hissed. "Once again am I proven right. First did we lose your oldest brother to the fever. Then your mother and nigh onto half our people. And now, once again, does your accursed soul, black as the depths of hell itself, visit disaster upon this family!"

Had Linnea not leaped safely beyond the reach of Lady Harriet's walking stick, her grandmother would have struck her with the heavy end of it. But that was another lesson she'd learned early. Always stay well out of her grandmother's striking distance. Now, as Linnea kept a wary eye on her grandmother, Beatrix wrung her hands in agitation. Ida made a sign of the cross to protect her from Linnea's wickedness. But whether a violent outburst like Lady Harriet's, or a passive warding off of evil as so many at Maidenstone were wont to do in her presence, both symbolized the suspicion and rejection that were such a pervasive part of Linnea's life. And both hurt just as badly.

Linnea would never let anyone see her pain, though. Least of all her grandmother.

As always, it was Beatrix who came between them. She caught her grandmother's arm and stayed the stick in its place. "This avails us of naught. We must see to Maynard's wounds. Will they let us see him now? Is he to be brought to his own chamber?"

"I don't know what they plan," Lady Harriet snapped. "They are heathens, no matter what Father Martin may say." But her anger petered out against Beatrix's overwhelming goodness. The older woman sighed as if exhausted. "My Edgar awaits them in the hall e'en as we speak. He will receive their terms. Then will we have our questions answered. But do not expect any leniency from them."

Her eyes were fixed on Beatrix now, and for a moment the old woman's voice wavered. "We must protect you from them, Beatrix. For once they lay eyes upon your beauty, there will be no preventing the horrors that will surely follow."

"Horrors?" Beatrix's milky white face paled even further. "What do you mean, horrors?"

"Rape," the old woman's harsh voice grated out. "Ever do armies rape. Still, your beauty and innocence may save us. Even Henry, boy king that he styles himself, must know an heiress with your dowry is better—"

She broke off and her face froze in sick realization. Linnea realized it too. Henry would know that a beautiful virgin with a handsome dowry was more valuable pure than ruined. But Beatrix would no longer possess such a dowry, not if de la Manse took everything—which there was no reason not to expect. She would no longer be a valuable heiress. Linnea moved up beside her sister and laid a comforting arm around her shoulder. "Perhaps we can escape," she whispered, staring hopefully at her grandmother.

Lady Harriet's nostrils flared, as if Linnea's suggestion were so pitiful as to be beneath contempt. But before she could make some biting rejoinder, the twins' longtime nurse, Norma, burst into the room.

"Milord . . . Milord Edgar bids you come to him in the hall, milady." Her color was high and her breathing labored. Clearly she'd run up the two flights of stairs, no easy feat for a woman of her age and girth. It frightened Linnea all the more, and Beatrix as well.

"What of Beatrix?" Lady Harriet asked. "Doth he make mention of her?"

"He said I am to accompany her to the stillroom and collect whatever she needs. Then we are to see to Maynard. The poor lad is to be put in the barracks."

Lady Harriet did not hesitate. It was as if this call to duty had somehow restored her. She unfastened the loop of household keys that hung from her girdle and thrust them into Beatrix's hands. Then she grabbed Beatrix's arms and steered her to the door. "I will join you at Maynard's bedside once my counsel is no longer needed. Agh! The barracks, for he who shouldst be lord here." She spat. "A curse on the lot of them." Then she fixed her cold gaze on Linnea.

"You. Stay out of my sight. You have caused enough misery for one day. Agh, but Edgar should have listened to me—"

She whirled around and departed, leaving them only with the rhythm of her stick clicking on the hard, cold floor. Once that disappeared, however, Linnea could hear nothing but the roar of blood in her ears, and the silent condemnation she'd lived with all her life—only today it was far, far worse.

She knew what her grandmother meant. She should

have been killed at the moment of her birth, so that the evil intrinsic to her soul would be denied an outlet on this earth, and her family would be spared the certain misery that must befall it. Well, that misery was here now, and it *was* her fault. She closed her eyes and swayed, so overcome was she with the horror of her own existence.

Then a steadying hand clasped her elbow, and the black shadow over her dissipated a little.

"The fault does not lie with you," Beatrix whispered fervently in her ear.

Linnea shuddered. Dear, sweet Beatrix. If not for her sister's deep and abiding faith in her, Linnea would never have survived all these years. While there had been very little Beatrix could do to change others' harsh views of the second twin, just knowing that Beatrix didn't believe the worst of her meant everything to Linnea. They shared a bond no one else understood. Beatrix was the only one who loved Linnea, and Linnea loved her back with a ferocity that was sometimes frightening.

Now, that touch on her arm and the whispered words of reassurance were precisely what Linnea needed to rebuild her confidence. She looked into her sister's beautiful sea green eyes and stroked her softly rounded cheek. "Thank you, Bea. Thank you. But no matter whose fault this is, we are nevertheless in dire straits indeed."

Beatrix nodded, then touched her forehead to Linnea's, the way they'd always done when they were children. Linnea felt a closeness to her sister that she hadn't felt in a long time, and her need to protect this most beloved of her family from any harm swelled to even greater proportions.

Beatrix was the first to pull back. "I must go to Maynard—"

"No! No," Linnea countered, holding onto her sister's arm. "You shouldn't go out into the bailey alone, not with all those men."

"Norma will be with me." Beatrix looked over at their nurse who had lowered herself to a bench and was still breathing hard.

"No, Norma will go with me," Linnea stated.

"But you heard what grandmother said. *You're* to stay here. *I'm* to go to Maynard."

But Linnea was determined. As terrified as she was of what she would find outside—both the bloodthirsty invaders as well as her brother's physical condition—she was even more terrified of the thought of Beatrix having to deal with them. "Maynard will be bleeding," she said, speaking quickly before she lost her nerve. "You know I'm much less squeamish than you. 'Tis better if I go." *Besides, this is my only chance to show grandmother that it's not my fault. If I can save Maynard . . .*

"But what if he dies?" Beatrix asked in a trembling whisper, somehow knowing Linnea's thoughts.

Linnea didn't want to think about that. "Come with me, Norma. We must hurry. Quick, Bea. Change gowns with me, then lock yourself inside here and do not open that door save for one of your family."

Beatrix hesitated a moment, and Linnea knew why. They'd not switched identities in many a year—not since their mother had died and their grandmother had forbidden the childish prank. The one time since then that they'd done it, they'd been severely punished—or at least Linnea had been. But finally Beatrix nodded, afraid, but willing as ever to go along with one of Linnea's outrageous plans.

It had always been thus. Linnea reckless and daring; Beatrix cautious and trusting. Linnea didn't truly mind the punishments she earned when they were for some disobedience on her part—and she didn't mind when Beatrix never suffered such punishments, for she knew Beatrix only came along because Linnea coerced her. No, it was only the unfair punishments she resented: being ostracized from her own family; not being loved as much; never having any of the fineries Beatrix was given.

Linnea peeled off her own plain kirtle of faded plunkett cloth. It boasted neither braid nor embroidered trim. The gown she received from Beatrix, however, was bias cut from a fine weave of double twill kersey in a rich forest green. Gold braid circled the neck hole and ran partway down the front of the bodice. A narrow leather girdle worked in a continuing design of Celtic knots and mythical beasts went around her waist. She slipped the beautiful garment over her coarse chemise, for a moment forgetting the circumstances that forced them to chance this exchange of identities. She could almost believe she was the first daughter when she wore such a lovely gown—and it was far from the finest of Beatrix's gowns. But Beatrix's meanest gown was better than Linnea's best.

Linnea smoothed her hands down the skirt, then looped the girdle around her waist. Only when she pulled her thick plait out of the neck hole and looked over at Beatrix did reality once more intrude.

Was that how she looked in her plain garments? No, it could not be and for a moment she feared her ruse would fail. For even in such drab work clothes, Beatrix was still beautiful. Everyone would see through their deception.

"Lord, ha' mercy," Norma muttered just then, staring from one to the other of her charges. "If it weren't for that birthmark setting the two of you apart . . ."

She trailed off, but Linnea felt better for her words. Maybe the differences between her and her sister were not as obvious to others as they were to her.

"Don't be forgettin' the keys," Norma said, but in a whisper, as if she feared the walls would reveal their deception. Did she dread Lady Harriet's wrath, or that of de la Manse, Linnea wondered. A shiver of misgiving slid up her own spine. She could as well ask that question of herself.

"Be careful, dear sister," Beatrix pleaded, catching Linnea close in a fierce hug. "Tell our brother that I pray for him. And hurry back."

Linnea and Norma descended the curving stone stairs, holding hands for mutual support. There was something profoundly different about Maidenstone Castle in the air. Even if the scent of smoke had not lingered and Linnea had witnessed none of this day's dreadful events, she would yet sense the change in her home. Some tension thrummed through the very walls. Some terrible anxiety. And the

32

sounds—they were all wrong. Too many male voices. No female ones.

Where were all the women?

They slowed even more as they rounded the last few steps. Norma hung back, unable to disguise her fear. Linnea wanted to hang back too. But just the thought of Maynard suffering more with every moment she delayed was enough to propel her forward, dragging the reluctant Norma along through the low stone arch that led into the great hall.

She spied the boy first, that damnable de la Manse stripling. He stood with three other men, brawny knights all, and looked the dwarf by comparison. Linnea's nostrils flared with dislike. Who was he to steal their very home from them?

As if he felt the pure venom in her glare, the boy twisted his head, and across the room their gazes met in fiery collision.

A pox on you and all of your line, she silently cursed him.

But his response was to unexpectedly grin, then tug on the sleeve of the tallest of the three knights. When the knight bent slightly down to hear the boy's words, Linnea felt a new frisson of fear. The group of them had been speaking to her father, she could now see, and her grandmother stood just beyond them too. But now everyone's attention was focused on her. Though she could not hear the exchange between man and boy, Linnea knew it concerned her—or rather who she appeared to be. It was only the reminder that she might be saving Beatrix from unwonted attention that gave her the courage to carry on with her charade.

"We'd best hurry," she muttered to Norma. They turned to the left, sidling along the rough stone wall toward the door that led to the kitchen and the stillroom beyond the herb garden. But before they could reach the steel-banded door and freedom, they were blocked by the boy and the huge wolfhound he held by its collar.

"Beatrix de Valcourt?" he asked with more hauteur than

the king himself could possibly possess. "Are you Edgar de Valcourt's daughter?"

Linnea drew herself up. Her heart thudded with both fear and hatred, but she did not at once reply. She could not. She was too frantically searching her mind for the right thing to say.

She must lie, of course. That was the whole point of her disguise, to protect Beatrix from these horrible men who'd invaded their home. But between her debilitating fear of them and her outrage, she could hardly think what best to say.

What she wanted to tell the impertinent pup was to go eat pig dung and then hang himself from the gate tower. But would Beatrix say that? Beatrix would never call him a spindly legged bastard, or vow to cut off his ballocks while he slept. No, Beatrix would be cool and aloof, and always behave as a lady, far too grand for the mere likes of him.

"Well?" he demanded, taunting her now. "Swallowed your tongue, have you?"

I'll cut yours out and feed it to that dog of yours, she thought. But outwardly she only lifted her chin a notch. "I am Lady Beatrix," she stated in the frostiest tone she could manage. She looked down her nose at him, as if he were no more than a disgusting hearth beetle she debated stepping upon.

"Lady Beatrix," he repeated. But he stretched it out in a drawl that made it sound more an insult. "Well, Lady Beatrix, if you would be so good as to join us." He indicated the waiting cluster of people with an exaggerated sweep of his arm.

Without replying to him, Linnea turned to face the little group. Elsewhere in the hall, the milling crowd had gone still and silent. Though the villagers had been herded out, most of the castle folk remained, grouped together in anxious knots. And everywhere the heavily armed de la Manse army lent an unrealistic look to the hall.

Her father stared at her with an expression she could not decipher. Defeated? Hopeful? Old, she decided. He looked old, older even than his own mother.

34

Lady Harriet stared too, but her expression was easier to read. She was consumed by wrath at what was happening to them. But she was also proud of her granddaughter. The old woman raised her chin to a haughty angle, as if to send Linnea a signal, and Linnea responded with the same gesture.

It worked! She thinks I'm Beatrix too. They all do! That knowledge gave Linnea more courage than anything else. She would make them proud of her. Just see if she didn't.

She stalked across the hall, her head high and her spine straight, aware that every eye followed her progress. But it was her grandmother she kept her gaze upon and drew strength from. Hard and superstitious she might be, but she had the bravery of ten men. And so would Linnea.

"My lord," the boy began, addressing the tall knight he'd spoken to before. "I present to you the Lady Beatrix de Valcourt." His imp's grin swung from the towering, sober-faced warrior to her. "This is Axton de la Manse—son of Allan de la Manse—now restored to his rightful title as lord of Maidenstone Castle."

Lord of Maidenstone Castle? Linnea's eyes widened as she stared up at the man. He would be lord here, not this arrogant boy? Somehow that made their situation even more desperate. Axton de la Manse was a man of war, proclaimed as much by the great sword that hung at his hip as by his fierce visage and ruthless expression. God have mercy, but this boded ill. He looked as lief to crush them as anything else.

In truth his appearance was no different from that of the two men who flanked him. But even though all three of them scrutinized her with gazes cold and assessing, it was his eyes she felt. Only his. Cold and gray, they were. Hard as the stone walls of Maidenstone itself. They moved over her, head to toe, with a slow thoroughness that was completely unnerving, and entirely too bold. She knew what that look meant, and it brought a hot blush to her cheeks. But that served, fortunately, to send a jolt of pure fury through her.

Impudent knave!

"Lady Beatrix. Your eldest daughter?" He directed this at her father.

"Aye, Beatrix is my daughter . . ."

"And yet unmarried?" de la Manse interrupted, his voice pitched low. But that deep rumble commanded every ear in the hall, and every eye watched as he turned back to study Linnea once more.

No one answered his question. That was answer enough, though, judging by the smirk that spread over the boy's face. He must be a younger brother, Linnea realized, finding it easier to look at him than at the formidable knight. But she knew that Axton de la Manse was her real enemy here, not this boy.

And there was only one reason he would inquire about her marital state. She drew her shattered nerves around her as best she could.

"Faith, sir, but I would see to my brother. If it please you," she added in a cool tone that she prayed hid the panic that threatened to overwhelm her. He wondered if she were married because if not, he would quickly arrange a marriage for her—that is, for Beatrix. And most likely to himself!

He did not bother to answer her request, but only shrugged and turned back to her father and his previous conversation.

Impudent knave! she thought again. Craven varlet, to imply what he did, then dismiss her so rudely! At the same time, however, Linnea was so overcome with relief not to be the focus of his attention that she could not move. She let out the breath she'd held and her gaze darted to her grandmother's face. But the reassurance she sought was not to be found there. For her grandmother's expression was almost as stricken as her father's.

Lady Harriet knew as well as everyone else in the hall precisely what that inquiry meant, and her fear confirmed it for Linnea. That man meant to marry Beatrix—that man who'd helped defeat Stephen's army and had crushed Maynard's forces. He meant to strengthen his claim to Maidenstone by marrying poor Beatrix, the eldest daughter.

It was Norma's sharp tug on her trailing sleeve that finally started Linnea moving again. With the maid pulling her along, they made their stumbling way through the tense crowd of onlookers. Only when the door closed with a dull thud behind them and they had reached the relative shelter of the little stillroom, did Linnea allow herself to even think the unthinkable.

He meant to marry her—that is, he meant to marry Beatrix.

Thank God she was not really Beatrix!

But that swift surge of relief just as swiftly turned into guilt. Poor Beatrix.

"What will we be needin'?" Norma asked. "Sorrel, of course. And camphor?"

Linnea frowned and beat down her fears for both herself and her twin. "Yes, and willow bark and linden ointment to keep the wounds clean. And perhaps Maybush to calm him. Oh, and we'll need shepherd's knot to make a cleansing wash."

They gathered up the appropriate vials and jugs and pouches while Linnea tried to anticipate everything they might need, including a needle and cord to stitch any gaping wounds closed. There was a comfort to be had in the familiarity of the stillroom—the narrow shelves of supplies; the dusty smell of the small locked room.

But there was no time to linger in the respite it offered. Though the outside world had turned upside down, Linnea knew she could not avoid it. She must see to Maynard first, then she would deal with Beatrix and the terrible fate that awaited her sister. She simply could not think about Beatrix's plight right now, not and keep her wits about her too.

They found Maynard in a corner of the barracks, lying on a hard pallet on the ground, with only his squire and the stable marshal beside him. The boy had fetched water already and the marshal had cut Maynard's clothing away from his wounds. But beyond that, and offering him some water to drink, nothing had been done for him.

Blood caked his body in black and muddied crusts. Flies

droned in the open barracks, only waved off her brother's brutalized body by the vacant-eyed squire.

"Move aside," Norma ordered the two men as she set their basket of supplies down. Then she looked over at Linnea, her normally placid face grim. " 'Tis bad," she whispered, as if to hide the fact from the battered man who lay senseless between them.

It *was* bad, Linnea agreed. Near unto being hopeless. But he yet lived. His chest rose in a shallow and uneven rhythm, and any bleeding had been temporarily halted by the thick crusts of dried blood.

Unfortunately, that dirty crust had to be washed away.

"Hold his legs, in the event he flails around," Linnea ordered the stable marshal as she tried to think how best to proceed. She'd always had an affinity for healing, but never had she dealt with such severe wounds alone. She looked at the squire whose eyes were round as saucers. "Frayne, you sit at his head," she told the lad. Then she and Norma began their gruesome task.

His right arm was broken, horribly so. The two bones of his forearm jutted right out through the skin, but at least it was not a killing wound. In addition, a huge bruise blackened his brow and one of his eyes had swollen shut. With a head wound she knew you could never be certain. Prayers and a poultice for the swelling were her only choice there.

But the horrendous gash in his right side . . .

"Took a lance, right through his mail. Unhorsed him," the squire said in short mutters. His lips thinned and trembled, as if the battle replayed itself in his mind's eye.

Linnea pressed her own lips together, trying to ignore the hideous picture that rose in her mind. Fighting. Cursing. Blood and screams of unimaginable pain. Men falling and dying.

She had never liked her brother, but he had fought for them this day, for all of them, including her. She refused to let him die. She would make him live!

But the horror of it all threatened to undo her. In desperation she searched for the strength she knew only anger would bring.

"Who did this to him? Did you see it happen? Can you identify the villain who has mutilated him so?"

"Oh, aye. 'Twas himself. The new lord."

Linnea looked up, and her hands stilled at their painstaking task of cleaning Maynard's torn chest. The new lord. Axton de la Manse. That meant the sword that had hung at his hip . . . A shudder of horror rushed over her. He'd almost killed Maynard. Now he would wed Beatrix. Surely God would not allow this to happen!

Then she pinned the squire with a cold stare, for he seemed almost in awe of the man who had tried to kill his lord. "The day will come when Maynard shall have his revenge," she swore, hot for vengeance herself. "He shall strike that blackguard down—"

"Beg pardon, Lady Beatrix, but that 'un, he's powerful strong. 'Tisn't likely *any* of Maidenstone's knights could unseat him."

If it weren't for the fact that Maynard jerked—she'd cleaned past the filthy crust, down to the torn flesh itself—Linnea would have boxed Frayne's ears. How dare he extol that pitiless monster's skills! How dare he speak of the man as if he actually admired the marauding knave!

For the next few minutes they were far too busy to talk. Maynard was not awake, not in the truest sense of the word. But he was not asleep either, and the four of them had all they could do to hold him steady while Linnea tended to his wounds. She swabbed his side with the wash of shepherd's knot, then smeared the ointment of willow and linden on it before binding the whole of it with cloth. She would stitch it later. For now it was enough to clean him and stop the bleeding.

His poor, mutilated arm was next, and Linnea had to fight down an overpowering urge to retch as she studied it. Norma cleaned the torn skin and removed splinters of bone while Linnea tried to think out what they must do.

To remove the arm was out of the question. She simply could not do such a thing. Besides it could heal. Couldn't it?

She set her jaw against any hint of uncertainty. "Norma

and Frayne, you two must hold his shoulder still. Sit on him if you must, but keep him still. Marshal, you must pull his wrist—no matter how he screams in pain. You must pull straight out while I position the ends of the bones back together again."

Simple to say, but it was an ungodly task they'd been given. Maynard screamed. He lurched up on the pallet as if jerked upward by a rope. Norma and young Frayne, both with tears of fright streaming down their faces, fought him back down onto the floor, while the marshal pulled, curses and prayers spitting one after another from his mouth.

Everything inside Linnea revolted against what she did to Maynard. But she forced herself beyond her limits to do it anyway. Blood poured anew from the aggravated wound, covering her hands and making her fingers slick. But still she tugged his skin up and forced the bones back into his arm. Her fingers were inside his very flesh and yet she refused to stop. If she stopped she would never be able to start again. If she paused even a fraction of a second, she would fall completely to pieces.

Then the bone fragments met with a little click that she felt, more than heard. She slid one finger around that bone, feeling the hard, uneven crack. By the grace of God the second bone was easier. She knew, however, that his arm would never be perfect, for pieces of the bones were gone. But it was the best she could do, she told herself.

As she carefully removed her fingers, folding the torn muscle and skin back into place, she suddenly realized he'd stopped screaming. She heard Frayne's soft sobs and the stable marshal's labored breathing. Norma was muttering under her breath, *"Pater noster, que es in coelis . . ."* the only prayer she knew in Latin. But Maynard was as still as death.

"He's fainted," Norma said when Linnea's fingers paused uncertainly. "Best we hurry now."

How they managed the rest Linnea could not say. While the marshal and Norma put a splint on the arm to keep the bones fixed in place, Linnea stitched the skin closed and smeared more of the ointment on it. Then they removed the wrappings that covered his chest wound and she stitched it closed too.

Through it all, Maynard remained insensible, breathing shallowly and none too regularly. But he *did* breathe. Finally they rebound his chest with fresh cloth packed with more of the ointment.

His broken head was last, for Linnea knew there was precious little she would be able to do for that. There was a small depression in the bone just above his left eye, near to his temple. Swelling hid any other damage, however. The few stitches she took in his brow might make for a prettier scar than if she left it to heal on its own. But Linnea feared that scars were the least of her brother's worries.

Needles of pain sliced up and down her back by the time her task was completed, and she was filthy with blood and straw and her own sweat when she finally stood up. For a blinding moment she swayed, and only Frayne's quick hold on her arm saved her from keeling over in front of them all.

"Well done, milady," the boy said. This time the awe in his voice was for her.

"Aye, well done, indeed," the stable marshal echoed.

Linnea wanted to believe so. But she knew enough of healing to know that her neat stitches ensured nothing. He might live. But the awful truth was that he would more likely die.

Norma covered Maynard with a length of sheeting as well as a blanket, then approached Linnea. "We'd best return to the hall. Lady Beatrix," she added.

Linnea blinked. Oh, yes. She was Beatrix. She'd almost forgotten. Yes, they'd better return to the solar where the real Beatrix awaited them.

But before they could depart, a commotion started farther down the long barracks building.

"Where is he?" Lady Harriet's voice carried angrily to them. Then she and Sir Edgar burst into their little circle, followed by Father Martin, Ida, and the seneschal Sir John. Four-men-at-arms, unsmiling and wearing the device of de la Manse, followed behind them.

41

Linnea drew back as her grandmother and father fell to their knees beside the pale form of Maynard.

"He lives. He lives," Lady Harriet repeated over and over. "He lives!"

"Milady Beatrix has saved our young lord," the stable marshal said. "She has repaired his arm and stitched his wounds—"

"His sword arm," Sir Edgar muttered. "Will he ever fight again?" He looked up at Linnea.

She shook her head. "I don't know, Father. I don't know. I can't even promise that he will live," she added in the barest whisper.

"Oh, he'll live. He'll live," Lady Harriet vowed. The look she gave Linnea was fierce, but it was also sure. And proud. Proud of Linnea!

The old woman rose slowly, holding hard onto Ida's sturdy arm. But her hawklike gaze remained on her grand-daughter. "Ever have I known that you were blessed. From the moment of your birth have I known it. And now, this day, you have saved Maynard."

She opened her arms to her granddaughter, and though Linnea hesitated, she was not strong enough to resist—nor to confess.

She was not Beatrix, but oh, how she wished she was as she went into her grandmother's arms. To be so loved. To be so valued!

Then, ashamed of her envy and her fears—and of how much she needed her grandmother's approval—she burst into tears.

Chapter 3

Axton de la Manse sat in the ornately carved lord's chair and surveyed Maidenstone's great hall. He remembered it as much larger—longer, wider, and with towering ceilings held up by massive beams. He remembered a sea of long plank tables and stoutly made benches. He and William had fought many a battle across those tables, as well as under them. Some had been long-simmering battles, fought with mock weapons against imaginary enemies. Others had been brief but intense brawls, brother pitted against brother for some insult or slight or other childish infraction.

He'd never bested William. Not back then, anyway. William had been a head taller, two stone heavier, and four years wiser. Yves had also been older and taller. But he'd never been much of a fighter, even as a boy. How many times had Yves retreated up the stairs to the nursery while William and Axton raged at one another?

Axton winced at the thought. Yves had been given few chances during his short life. He'd have made a better scribe than soldier, a better priest or seneschal. But when Stephen had stolen Britain from Matilda—and de Valcourt had stolen Maidenstone from Allan de la Manse, Yves' choices had narrowed down to one. He must fight as they'd all had to fight. Fight for their queen. Fight for their country. Fight for their home.

Yves had been the first to die. Then Allan de la Manse, followed shortly thereafter by William. Axton and Peter were all that were left of their family—them and their mother.

But the fighting had ended this day, Axton reminded himself.

He stared blindly across the hall that had managed to shrink during the eighteen years since he'd last set foot in it. The fighting was over, for the de la Manses had returned, and he would never loose his hold on Maidenstone Castle. Never.

A clatter of hard-soled shoes on the stairs drew his gaze. He was not surprised when Peter bounded down the last steps, the wolfhound, Moor, at his heels.

"Why can I not have a chamber in the keep?" the boy began without preamble. "Four chambers there are above stairs. Two upon each level. And a broad hall that serves as an antechamber where Moor could stand guard."

"You sleep with the other squires unless I require your

services. Then you sleep in the antechamber—standing guard," he added as he eyed his younger brother sternly. Perhaps he should not have allowed the boy so many liberties today—bearing the de la Manse standard; negotiating for the surrender of the castle; riding at the head of the column as they entered the home they'd finally reclaimed. At the time it had seemed fitting, since Peter had been denied any access to Maidenstone Castle since long before his birth. Unfortunately, the day's events seemed to have gone to the rascal's head.

But Axton knew well enough how to remedy that. "If you've time for exploring, then it's apparent you have too little to do. Clear out the lord's chamber and have my belongings moved in there. I'll want my red and black tunic brushed to wear at dinner. Also see to it that these de Valcourt pennants are removed and replaced by ours." He gestured to the hangings that decorated the hall.

"Won't Mother be pleased to know we've taken her home back for her," Peter said, unfazed by the time-consuming tasks his brother had set for him. "Shall we send word to her in Normandy?"

"I've already composed the letter. But I want everything in order when she arrives. That means you've no time for sitting and gloating over our enemies. Get to your tasks," he added in a less than brotherly tone.

While Peter was not averse to testing his older brother, he knew better than to actually cross him. With a few grumbling complaints he went off to do as he'd been ordered, the massive hound trailing like an overgrown pup at his heels.

Axton remained as he was, sprawled back in the heavy oak chair in the middle of the dais, staring gloomily over his restored domain.

Whence came this discontent? He should be elated, drinking and celebrating with his men who'd been so loyal these long years, searching out a toothsome wench eager to win favor with the new lord of Maidenstone. Instead he'd sent everyone off to one task or another, clearing the hall save for the servants who now set up the trestle tables for this evening's victory feast. Sir Reynold was reorganizing the castle guard, installing their own men in all the key positions and determining who would swear fealty to the new lord and who would only cause trouble.

Sir Maurice was meeting with the seneschal, Sir John, to determine how the household functioned. Axton's mother would take over that task once she arrived, of course.

Or should he trust that task to the new wife he meant to take?

Axton had not thought of Lady Beatrix since their brief introduction. He'd put her completely and deliberately out of his mind. But now, with no reason preventing it, he allowed himself to picture her in that first moment when their eyes had met.

She was a beauty. No use pretending otherwise. Young and fair, with eyes the color of the sea, wild and tumultuous, and hair as vivid as an autumn sunset. Tall, slender—and haughty—in appearance she'd been more than he could have hoped for. In truth, following Henry's admonition to marry the eldest daughter—in this case, the only daughter—would not be the hardship he envisioned. But she was still a de Valcourt.

Her father had been horrified when Axton had stated his intention. The man's hands had clenched and his arms had quivered with his rage. But it had been impotent rage, for the man knew he'd been defeated.

If only the coward would have challenged him. To kill de Valcourt in battle would surely have brought him the satisfaction he still sought.

But that was not going to happen, he realized, as his restless gaze once again swept the hall. Though a blood lust yet burned in his veins, there would be no outlet for it this day. And mayhap never. He would have to take his bitter satisfaction in banishing the man from Maidenstone, and from knowing his son would never fight again—assuming he yet lived.

"God's bones!" He swore and slammed a fist down upon the table. His empty goblet rattled on the heavy board surface and a serving wench appeared at once to refill it with ale, then disappear.

But it was not ale he sought. No, only revenge would assuage this thirst. To banish de Valcourt and see the son a cripple was far from enough to douse the fires that eighteen years of rage had fueled. He needed more. He needed some enemy to fight, but they gave him none.

The women of the family offered more resistance than did the men. The old crone would murder him in his sleep, should he allow her the opportunity. And the young one . . .

The young one would be his wife soon enough. He would wed her and bed her on the morrow.

He shifted in the chair. Just the thought of lying with the haughty little wench caused blood to rush to his loins. Perhaps he would have his satisfaction from her pretty hide, he mused. There was something in those stormy green eyes that bespoke a fiery temperament. Perhaps in the struggle to bring her to heel and make of her a meek and tractable wife, he would find the release he needed.

Yes, he was long overdue some pleasure of this place. That de Valcourt's daughter should be the one to provide it seemed especially fitting.

"We could poison him. 'Twould take very little of belladonna or bittersweet to kill him and all the other spineless bastards who do follow him." Lady Harriet paced the solar back and forth, her metal-tipped stick beating a furious rhythm across the plank floor. "Perchance in his ale. A cruel tonic that will see him suffer before he dies, that will make him retch and burn, and twitch on the floor—"

Linnea and Beatrix huddled together as their grandmother ranted on and on. They were perched in the window alcove, Linnea still garbed in her sister's now-stained finery. There had been no time to exchange clothes again and return to their own identities, and now neither of them considered doing it. Lady Harriet was in a towering rage. Even their father shrank away from her when she was like this.

"At least Maynard shall live, blessed be." Lady Harriet stared at Linnea—whom she mistook for Beatrix. " 'Tis well you did, to repair his wounds. But then I should not be so amazed. You have ever been a blessing upon this family."

Linnea sat there stunned, not knowing how to react. When her grandmother's piercing stare slid to Beatrix, however, and darkened with her habitual dislike, Linnea cringed, and her hand tightened on her sister's.

Fortunately Lady Harriet's fury was too focused on Axton de la Manse to bother with the second of her granddaughters. She stalked once more across the room, then fixed her son with her narrowed glare. "Have you nothing to say? No ideas on how we might rid ourselves of Henry's pestilence?"

"What would you have me do?" Sir Edgar muttered, though without any real show of spirit. "Maynard lies at death's door. And you saw his arm—his *sword* arm. Even healed it will never be as strong as it was."

" 'Tis the very reason I propose poison! Beatrix, what say you? Belladonna or bittersweet?"

Beside her, Linnea felt Beatrix stir. But a quick tug on her sleeve stopped her from answering. It was Linnea who responded. "Bittersweet would work, but it has a distinctive taste and would be hard to disguise. And we have no belladonna."

"Ach! Accursed man! There must be something else we can use."

"Perhaps it would be better to wait until after he weds Beatrix," their father suggested.

"After! After? And let him ruin her?" Lady Harriet cried, shaking her stick at him as if he were insane. In truth, it was she who looked more than a little mad at that moment, with her hair springing loose around her face in hanks of wiry gray. The flickering lights of the torchères painted her gold and red, with grim shadows lining her ancient face.

Linnea was so caught up in the exchange between her

father and grandmother that she did not anticipate her sister's reaction to this news.

"He wishes that we be *wed*?" Beatrix gasped when the full impact of her grandmother's words struck her.

Lady Harriet shot her a venomous glare. "Not you, fool. 'Tis Beatrix he would wed. Why would he wish to marry *you*—"

She stopped abruptly. So did Linnea's heartbeat. She knew. Somehow, that easily, their grandmother had deduced the truth.

As the old woman made her way toward the two of them, one ominous click at a time, the sisters sat frozen, side by side in the window. The one was garbed in plain plunkett cloth, her hair wrapped in a head cloth no better than that worn by the indoor servants. The other wore the softest kersey, albeit soiled, with gold braid winking back the flickering of the smoky torchères. When Lady Harriet stopped before them, her eyes flitted back and forth, from Beatrix's flushed face to Linnea's, which had gone as pale as death.

She surely was in for it now, she feared, and she braced herself for the thrashing she expected. To impersonate her sister was bad enough; to deceive her grandmother and thereby make a fool of her—would bring all of the Lady Harriet's considerable wrath down upon her head with a vengeance.

The old woman grasped Linnea's chin with gnarled fingers that were unexpectedly strong and tilted her face toward the uncertain light, searching it for a clue—any clue. Linnea sent a furtive glance toward her father, but it was clear that he did not care about what was happening. His daughters had always been of far less value to him than his sons. He'd lost young Edgar almost ten years ago, and soon after, his beloved wife. After that everything had been for Maynard. He had never loved Beatrix as much as his mother did, nor had he despised Linnea as strongly. And now, when the greatest drama of his daughters' lives was being played out, his primary reaction was disinterest.

Lady Harriet's searching glare went back and forth between the twins again, then settled on the real Beatrix. "Which one are you?" she demanded to know. "You look to be Linnea, but—"

Again she broke off. With a swift yank she jerked up the plain gown Beatrix wore, so that her legs were exposed. Then she let out a guttural cry and whirled to face Linnea.

"You!" She jerked up Linnea's dress—Beatrix's dress it was, but draping Linnea's legs. She grabbed Linnea's ankle and twisted the leg without any regard for her granddaughter's pain. "You devil!" she screamed when she spied the red birthmark on Linnea's leg, the only mark that distinguished the two from one another. "How dare you deceive me! How dare you pretend to be your sister!"

She swung her hand, but the brutal slap did not find its target, for Beatrix grabbed her grandmother's arm before it could, and hung on like a terrier. "She did it for me! To protect me! You cannot in good conscience punish her for that!"

"She had no right to pretend to be you—to trick us all. Agh! She says it is to protect you but I know better. She is filled with deception, that one. Now unhand me," she finished, glaring at Beatrix with the vicious expression more normally reserved for Linnea.

"You do her a grave disservice, Grandmother."

"And you have ever been too forgiving of her!"

Linnea did not know what to do. Beatrix had always shown her love and support in quiet ways, helping Linnea with a chore, sneaking a sweet treat to her—but when their grandmother was not in sight, of course. This overt opposition, however, was something new. Linnea did not know whether to be pleased for herself or worried for Beatrix.

"She has corrupted you," Lady Harriet fumed. She turned to her son, her face livid with her anger. "She has corrupted Beatrix! I told you this would happen, witless man! I warned you that she would one day cause the downfall of this family!"

"There was no harm done," Sir Edgar said in the placating tone he so often adopted with his mother.

"No harm? No harm? What of your son? Did she do him no harm? Do you truly expect him to recover—"

"You said she did well," Beatrix countered. "When you thought she was me, you said she'd done well with Maynard—"

A sharp slap from Lady Harriet cut off Beatrix's words. In the awful silence that followed, Linnea finally found her tongue.

"Do not punish her. It was my idea and . . . and I thought only to protect her from the horror of our brother's suffering."

Lady Harriet turned toward her as if to slap her too. But Linnea stood her ground, her fists clenched in determination. "I healed Maynard, as well as anyone could, given the brutality inflicted upon him by de la Manse. I saved him," she added, with a confidence she did not feel. "And . . . and if you would keep Beatrix from this dreadful man who has overrun us, well . . . I can save her from him too."

Linnea hesitated. She must be mad to suggest such a thing! Yet to protect her beloved twin sister—and to earn the gratitude and appreciation of her grandmother and father, and all the beleaguered souls of Maidenstone Castle—she would do anything, she realized. Anything.

"Let me wed him—as Beatrix. It will weaken his claim to Maidenstone—"

"No, Linnea!" Beatrix cried. She grabbed her sister's arms and swung her around to face her. "I cannot allow you to do such a thing."

"Be quiet, Beatrix." Lady Harriet pushed Beatrix back from Linnea, then stared at her younger granddaughter with eyes that had narrowed to slits. "You would marry this man who invades our home. Why?" She grabbed Linnea's face with a hand that felt like pincers. "What do you hope to gain?"

Linnea was at a loss for words. How could she ever explain to this woman who refused to believe anything but the worst of her? "I love my sister," she began.

"You love your sister," the old woman sneered. "Better to say you love the idea of becoming mistress here."

"No! No, I do this for Beatrix, not myself."

Lady Harriet snorted in disbelief. But before the old woman could speak again, Sir Edgar did.

" 'Tis a good idea," he admitted. Linnea had not expected any support from him, but she was glad to have it. " 'Tis better for all of us that she wed de la Manse," he continued. "We must save Beatrix for a more worthy man."

Lady Harriet shot him a contemptuous look. Then abruptly, her expression turned crafty. Linnea shivered when the old woman's hard eyes fastened upon her.

"If *she* marries him and keeps him happily occupied while Maynard heals . . . or else dies . . ." The old woman ignored Edgar's strangled gasp at that and continued on. "We will still have the ability to find a suitable husband for Beatrix—a strong knight who can then challenge de la Manse's weakened claim to Maidenstone, and win it back for us." Lady Harriet smiled, only it did not reassure Linnea at all. She nodded her ancient head. "Yes, Linnea is the last in line to inherit Maidenstone. If de la Manse marries her, his claim will not be so strong. And it will purchase for us the time to plot against him. Besides," she added, "if he weds her as Beatrix, they will not truly be wed. We can later petition to have the marriage annulled."

Linnea stared fearfully at her grandmother. Her grandmother's sudden glee at this idea had a sobering effect. What had she said? Keep him happily occupied? It struck her now precisely what she'd proposed. Wed this man who'd nearly killed her brother. Share a bed with that towering knight who'd stared at her so coldly, who'd inquired whether she was unmarried. Be a wife to the very beast who sought to steal her home.

A crushing wave of panic made her legs go weak. If Beatrix had not taken her arm, her knees surely would have buckled.

"You cannot do this, Linnea. I have benefited so long from being the firstborn of us, and you have suffered for being second. You cannot now step in to take this responsibility that is mine and mine alone."

"Why can't she?" Lady Harriet challenged. "This is her

opportunity finally to do something good for this family. To make penance for her corrupt soul. To prove herself once and for all," she added, as the idea took hold in her mind.

Beatrix started to protest again, but Linnea cut her off with a searching look. She did not want to take Beatrix's place. Not really. The very thought terrified her. But how much worse it would be to let Beatrix go through with it. She knew that she herself could bear it; she wasn't as certain about her sister. And then there was her grandmother's point. She could finally prove herself to them. To *all* of them.

"Grandmother is right," Linnea told Beatrix. "Though my suggestion was impulsive, now that Father has explained it all, I'm more determined than ever to go through with it."

"But he will—" though Beatrix broke off, Linnea knew what she meant.

She clenched her teeth. "To share their husband's bed is something women have borne through the ages. I will bear it."

"But . . . but what if you have his child?"

"There are ways to prevent that," Lady Harriet answered brusquely. "Besides, what will it matter if she has a child? Its father will be dead. There will be no need for an annulment and the child can be gotten rid of—sent away," she amended with an offhanded shrug. "But enough of this debate. There is much we must do if we are to succeed."

Without admitting Linnea's idea was a good one, or that her son's plan for restoring Maidenstone to their family was sound, Lady Harriet took over the planning of their deception. No one else was to know—save perhaps Norma and Ida. Linnea was to assume Beatrix's role in everything, while Beatrix was to disappear. They would dress Beatrix as a serving girl, covering her bright hair and dirtying her lovely face. They would employ Father Martin to help remove her from the castle, perhaps to Romsey Abbey on the road to Winchester.

"Father Martin will not believe that you wish to spirit Linnea away from here," Linnea pointed out. Though it was strange to think of herself in the third person, it seemed the only logical thing to do. She must become Beatrix now, in what she said and how she behaved. She must be quiet and calm—demure, though it would be nearly impossible.

Lady Harriet stared at her, dislike still evident in her lined face. "Father Martin is of no moment. Leave him to me."

So it was agreed. As they prepared for the coming confrontation with Axton de la Manse, Linnea immersed herself in the details of their plot. She would continue to nurse Maynard—as Beatrix. She would meet the new lord of Maidenstone as Lady Beatrix, his soon-to-be-bride. She would take her vows to him as Beatrix, and she would go to her marriage bed with Axton de la Manse as Beatrix.

She could take some pleasure from the rest of the deception, some satisfaction at deceiving her family's vengeful enemy. But to lie with him as his wife . . . Linnea could feel her heart's pace increase and her palms grow damp.

No matter how well she played the role of Beatrix, the fact was, the woman who went to his bed would be Linnea.

Only Linnea.

Chapter 4

There was no dinner in the hall the first night, at least not for the de Valcourts and their personal retainers. They kept to their chambers—or rather, they were locked in the two chambers on the top floor of the keep. Sir Edgar, Sir John, and her father's manservant, Kelvin, occupied the west chamber. Lady Harriet, Norma, Ida, Linnea, and Beatrix crowded into the other chamber. Beatrix had been well disguised as one of Lady Harriet's personal maids. Sir Reynold, de la Manse's captain of the guard, had not questioned them at all about her. He'd simply had the rooms searched for weapons, assigned a pair of guards to the top of the stairs, and left. Bread, ale, and a vegetable soup had been provided for them. Then they'd been forgotten.

Below stairs the conquerors celebrated. Linnea could hear the drunken shouts, the raucous laughter. From the window she could see the spillover into the bailey. The villagers had gladly fled back to their homes, and now a veritable army camped in the bailey.

How did the castle folk fare? Linnea wondered. She'd heard tales of war all her life, how the victors robbed and raped whomsoever crossed their paths. Was that happening down there somewhere beyond her view? Was Hilda from the dairy being raped this very minute? Or Mary and Anna, the alewife's budding young daughters?

She squinted hard into the darkened yard lit here and there with a torch or lantern. But though she searched for signs of violence and mayhem, she saw only soldiers. Drinking; telling tall tales of their exploits; relieving themselves in the shadows; and, as the evening progressed, vomiting in their hastily prepared beds. But she saw no rape and only a scuffle or two among the men themselves.

When she finally slept lying in the window enclosure with her head pillowed on her arms, dawn was already approaching. And when the first streaks of mauve-gold light fell across her face, she came instantly awake and recalled at once everything that had happened the previous day.

So did Lady Harriet, it appeared, for she was already up as well, sitting in a plain oak chair, staring out at nothing. Plotting, no doubt.

"Guard!" she called out, startling Linnea and jerking the others into an uneasy wakefulness. "Guard!"

A bleary-eyed young giant and an older grizzled fellow burst into the room. "What? What is it?"

" 'Tis my wish to see my grandson. I would tend his wounds and pray over him. See you obtain an escort for me."

The older guard scowled at her. "Sir Axton said ye are to stay put."

"And verily I say that I have much to do this day. Say me

54

this. Does he order his men to practice their superior fighting skills upon old women? Do you slay a one such as me should she choose to visit her dying grandchild?"

Linnea blinked and stared at her grandmother. Her voice still rang with authority, but she also managed to look older than ever—and completely harmless, despite her sarcasm. The guard muttered a moment to his compatriot. Then the younger man left and the remaining guard said, "If milord Axton says you may go, you may go. Otherwise you stay here."

The young man was back in less than a minute. That must mean Axton de la Manse was nearby—probably ensconced in the lord's chamber, immediately below this one. Linnea stared down at the well-worn floorboards. Such a very short distance away, sleeping in the bed she must soon share with him.

She swallowed hard and began nervously to finger comb her tangled hair. It had been *her* idea to marry him, she told herself. It was no more than most women put up with anyway: marriage to a man not of her own choosing, with no right to say no, no power to change her fate.

At least she had chosen to marry him, if this could be termed choosing. Still, that thought brought her no comfort at all.

"He says you may go. I'm to take you meself."

Lady Harriet nodded like a gracious, though feeble, matriarch. "Come, Beatrix. Come, Norma and Ida . . . and Dorcas," she said, using the name they'd given to the real Beatrix. "You too shall attend us."

"Now hold a minute! You just said you," the guard protested. "You didn't say nothin' about *five* of you!"

Lady Harriet fixed him with a benign smile. "The Lady Beatrix is healer here. You see in me merely an old woman who would pray over her grandchild. As for the others, had you been raised in a better household, you would know that a lady does not travel without several servants or retainers, even within her own household. Norma, Ida, and Dorcas we take to attend us."

55

The fellow scratched his head a moment and frowned. "I dunno."

"Well, then, why not send down to your master. Again," Linnea threw in, hoping her voice did not carry too strong a note of hauteur, and hoping also that the man would not want to disturb his liege from his bed another time.

"I dunno," the older man muttered once more. "What d'you think, Fergie?"

The younger man's brows raised high. "If you want to ask him, *you'll* have to do it. *I'll* not be the one aknockin' on his door again."

Linnea stifled a smile. Even Lady Harriet seemed marginally pleased when the two men conferred a moment, then waved them forward.

" 'Tis my wish to have the priest join with us as well," Lady Harriet informed the much aggravated guard as they followed him single file down the two curving flights of stairs. "Have a boy fetch Father Martin. Most likely will he be in his quarters next the chapel at this hour, preparing for morning mass."

There was no conversation after that, only a few indecipherable mutters from the unshaven fellow, and the soft pad of their leather-soled feet on the cold stone steps. Lady Harriet led the way with the real Beatrix close on her heels. Then came Ida, with Linnea and Norma behind. When they passed the second floor, the others hurried by. Not one of them, even Lady Harriet, wished an encounter with Axton de la Manse. Only Linnea paused, just long enough to peek beyond the dim antechamber toward the solid door that gave the lord's chamber privacy.

He was in there, whether alone or with some poor woman unlucky enough to catch his eye, she could not say. Soon enough, however, *she* would be the unlucky woman—

"Move along, Linnea—I mean Lady Beatrix," Norma swiftly corrected herself.

Linnea did not need to be told twice. But before they could begin the descent to the main floor, the door to the lord's chamber flung wide, and her demon bridegroom emerged.

He was buckling on a wide leather girdle over a red knee-length tunic, so he did not at first see them. When Norma nudged Linnea, however, and they both hurried to catch the others, he looked up sharply.

That was all the glimpse Linnea had of him before the solid walls mercifully blocked her view. But as they flew down the steep steps, then weaved carefully through the throng of soldiers sleeping off the night's excess in the hall and hurried to the barracks, that one brief glimpse of Axton de la Manse stayed fixed in Linnea's mind.

Yesterday when she'd first laid eyes on him, he'd been weary and dirty, his cropped hair sweaty and plastered to his skull, his expression triumphant yet nonetheless grim. This morning, however, he was clean and refreshed. His night-dark hair had glinted in the erratic light of the wall-mounted torches. His eyes had been clear and bright.

He was a reasonably handsome man, she grudgingly admitted. Comely in the hard way some men were wont to be. But he possessed a hardness beyond that even of Maynard. It had sent a shiver of awareness through her that yet lingered in the pit of her stomach. For he had looked precisely as he proclaimed himself to be: Lord of Maidenstone.

And he'd looked at her, in that fleeting exchange, with the confidence of a man who ruled all he saw. Including her.

Especially her.

As if he'd seen beyond her wrinkled gown and inadequate ablutions, he'd marked her with those ice-cold eyes as his. God help her, but before this day was done it would be so!

Her limbs were awkward with fear as she scuttled along the dim barracks corridor behind Lady Harriet. What if he had confronted her then? What if he had addressed her as Beatrix, the woman he meant to wed? With only that one piercing glance he'd left her petrified. What if she had collapsed in fear and admitted the truth?

Linnea paused outside the curtained off area that served as Maynard's sickroom. *You must collect your wits,* she told herself. *You make more of him than he is. After all, he is only a mortal man.* And she was the only chance her family had to hold onto its home. The only chance Beatrix had to keep her safe from that giant of a knight who would use her to guarantee his position at Maidenstone. She, Linnea, the reviled second twin, had been given this opportunity. She was the sole hope of her people now, and she could not let something as paltry as fear sway her in her mission!

"Beatrix. What gains you this delay? Your ailing brother awaits."

Linnea was slow to respond to her grandmother's sharp words, for her thoughts were so tangled up in her fear. When Beatrix—that is, Dorcas—tugged at her sleeve, however, she realized with a start that her grandmother was calling to *her*, the new Beatrix. The Beatrix who must learn to respond faster when addressed by that name.

"Yes, Grandmother. I am here."

"He lies insensible still. What gave you him that he lies the night through in such a stupor?"

Linnea bent over her brother. Maynard's eyes were closed, one of them swollen and dark with ugly bruises. As she removed the compress from his head, she could feel the heat that consumed him. "I'll need water—several buckets—to bathe and cool his body." As if awaiting any excuse to be away from such depressing surroundings, the squire Frayne, who'd stayed the whole night at his liege lord's side, jumped from his place in the corner to do her bidding. Linnea began then to check Maynard's wounded side, but before she could do much, her grandmother's hand clamped down on her shoulder like a bony claw. "Will he live?"

Linnea looked up from her crouched position next to Maynard. "I hope so," she said, not nearly as sure as she'd been yesterday. "But he will need our prayers," she admitted.

It was not the answer the old woman sought, but the timely entrance of Father Martin diverted her attention from Linnea.

Linnea instructed Norma to begin bathing Maynard, exposing only one limb at a time, while she checked his mutilated arm. But she listened as Lady Harriet dealt with the parish priest.

"We are in sore need of your intercession, good Father," she began. "After you pray over our beloved Maynard, I would have you pray with me in the chapel. Overrun we may be with heathens, but still will I hear my daily mass."

Father Martin stared at her a long moment. It was clear he sensed some undercurrent in their exchange, but just as clear that he couldn't determine what it meant. When he spoke, it was slowly, as if he chose his words with care. He was just as unwilling to cross the Lady Harriet as anyone else at Maidenstone.

"As you wish, milady. But . . . but if I might make a suggestion. Though you do not value her skills as a healer, Linnea might be better—"

"Yes, but she is not here, is she?" Lady Harriet cut him off. She had placed her hand on the priest's arm, and now she tightened her grip. "Say your prayers anon, then will I accompany you to the chapel. Dorcas, attend me."

He opened his mouth as if to question her, then abruptly closed it. The guard who'd accompanied them from the keep stood just beyond him, along with two others wearing the red and black of de la Manse. With a carefully blank expression, the priest moved up beside Maynard and placed his hand on the unconscious man's head.

"In Nomine Patris, et Filii, et Spiritus Santi . . ."

While Maidenstone's longtime priest prayed over the castle's fallen son, Linnea concentrated on the task at hand. But even as she worked, drawing some comfort from the familiar, droning prayer, she chanced a sidelong glance around the small, ill-lit space. Aside from her and Norma, the others in their party had all bowed their heads in prayer, even Frayne. But the soldiers only watched, the three of them staring unblinkingly at her.

Because they think I am Beatrix. Because they know their lord will soon marry me—and bed me.

Her eyes turned in renewed panic toward her sister. Then an even crueler reality struck her. This was the last time she would see her for only God knew how long. Beatrix, whom she'd never been separated from before. Beatrix, who was her sole support, the only person who had ever truly cared for her.

As Father Martin ended his prayer and all the bowed heads raised, an even worse sort of panic seized her.

Don't go! she wanted to cry. *Please, Beatrix, don't leave me!*

As if she heard her sister's silent plea, the expression on Beatrix's dirty face mirrored Linnea's. They were being torn apart and they'd have no chance to say a proper goodbye.

Linnea started to rise, to go to her, but Lady Harriet must have anticipated just such a possibility, for she stepped between the pair, blocking their view of one another. "Whilst you see to our Maynard's physical needs, Beatrix, Father Martin and I will see to his spiritual ones. Once finished here, come attend me in my chamber." Then she turned away, and leaning on the maid Dorcas for support, she made her way regally toward the chapel.

Were it possible, the morning proved to be even worse than the day before, Linnea thought as she gathered up the dirty cloths that had bound her brother's injuries. Yesterday they'd labored under the dark cloud of fear and uncertainty. Today they were immersed in a storm of despair. Linnea could almost envy Maynard his oblivion.

At once she willed her self-pitying thoughts away. To envy poor Maynard! How selfish of her to think her misery worse than his! At least she was healthy and unharmed.

Thank the Lord that his wounds had not festered. But Linnea could take little comfort from that, for he yet remained in a deep sleep. He was also far too warm despite their efforts to cool him. She feared he was more likely to die than to live, though she would admit as much to no one. Mayhap her grandmother's prayers and Beatrix's would pull him through.

Where was Beatrix right now? she wondered.

She stretched her back and rolled her aching neck from

side to side. Maybe her grandmother would know. "Stay with him at all times, and send for me should he awaken or begin to sweat," she told Frayne. "I'll come back later, though I hope to prevail upon this de la Manse to allow Maynard to be nursed in his own bed."

Frayne did not reply but only glanced warily at the two men who guarded his master. No doubt she should have held her tongue as well, Linnea castigated herself as she and Norma made their way back to the keep. She was three times a fool to speak her mind too plainly in front of *his* men. But she was too tired and too cross to be cautious.

" 'Tis more as it should be out here," Norma remarked as they came into the bailey. Indeed, as they stared about them it was true. Most of the army and its accoutrements no longer filled the yard to overflowing, though their presence was plainly felt. Still, Iron James worked in the open shed of the armory, sharpening swords and other weapons as he often did. A pair of knights instructed several squires in hand-to-hand combat, and the laundress and her helpers worked over their large wash kettles. A half-grown pup romped good-naturedly behind a furiously hissing cat.

Linnea rubbed her tired eyes. It was almost as if nothing had happened here yesterday. As if her life had not been shattered apart in one tense afternoon.

Would that it had all been a dream.

But it was no dream. Rather it was a nightmare come fully to life, she realized. For striding along the wall-walk toward the gatehouse was none other than the author of this disaster. Axton de la Manse. He of the two clawing bears. And now he and that awful boy, trailing him like a flea-bitten bear cub, were up there inspecting *her* family's castle, with Sir Hugh and two other men accompanying them.

It was an outrage! Worse, though, there was nothing she could do about it—at least not at the moment.

But in the end, once Beatrix was wed to someone willing to challenge de la Manse . . .

"St. Joseph's bones," Norma murmured. "He makes

himself quickly to home, doesn't he? Oh, milady, 'tis hard to think that you and he—"

Linnea cut her off with an impatient oath. "Then don't think about it. And for mercy's sake, don't speak of it, least of all to me!"

Then Linnea sighed. She was behaving like her grandmother, blaming everyone around her for things not within their control. "Forgive me, Norma. You're in no way to blame for this and I've no call to be so sharp with you. Please, let's just find the Lady Harriet. I won't feel better until I know Bea—till I know *Dorcas* is safely away from here."

Lady Harriet and Lord Edgar sat at an empty trestle table in the hall, taking a late morning meal alone while the servants prepared for the midday meal. When Linnea and Norma joined them, Lady Harriet gestured impatiently for Norma to take some food and then leave. Linnea she drew to sit beside her on the bench.

"He shames us before our own people!" the old woman hissed, though not loud enough for it to carry. "Eating here, below the salt!"

"Is Dorcas well away from here?"

"Father Martin journeys to Romsey Abbey tomorrow. The maid will accompany him," Lady Harriet confirmed.

"Thanks be to God," Linnea breathed.

"Yes, and thanks be to me for devising such an escape for her."

" 'Tis a very good plan," Linnea agreed. That her grandmother did not give Linnea credit for the idea galled her, but she buried any resentment beneath her relief that her sister was safe.

"Now," Lady Harriet said. "We must be agreed. Should word of another daughter of de Valcourt be raised, we will say she has deserted her family during the attack. That Linnea has ever been a curse upon this family and has abandoned us. They *must* believe that you are Beatrix." She fixed Linnea with her stony stare. "He may not hear of the second sister, but happens that he does, we must all of us adhere to the same tale. Linnea has ever been wild and uncontrollable. None among us is surprised that she has gone off on her own."

Linnea tried to be as hard and callous as her grandmother, as thick-skinned and insensitive. But in the face of such cruelty she could not remain firm. Must she paint her own self as disloyal to her family? A coward who would run from duty? A woman who would abandon her family at the first sign of trouble?

Aching inside, she sought her father's support. But when she met his gaze it was to find him already staring at her, a wrinkle of bewilderment on his weary face.

"You are Linnea?" he asked disbelievingly. "I can hardly credit it—"

"Don't be a fool, Edgar!" Lady Harriet cowed him with her vicious tone, and even the several servants across the hall looked up in alarm. "Don't be a fool," she repeated more quietly. "Speak not that name out loud. Never. She is Beatrix now, until such time as we decide to expose our deception. Beatrix, I say."

He nodded and wiped a hand across his brow. Again the thought occurred to Linnea that he looked even older than his mother, and much less able to cope with the abrupt change in their circumstances.

But she was given no time to contemplate her father's quick decline, for her grandmother pinched her arm, demanding her complete attention.

"How fares Maynard?"

Linnea sighed. "Much the same. Once I have eaten I will return to him. Do you think there is any hope that he will allow Maynard to be brought into the keep?"

Lady Harriet's fingers drummed restlessly on the tabletop. There was no need explaining to her which *he* Linnea referred to. "Mayhap . . . mayhap if he is well pleased with you this evening, he would grant that favor to you."

"Well pleased?" Linnea asked, unaccountably remembering that quick, appraising look he'd sent her this morning. "How am I to please him tonight?"

Lady Harriet gave her a shrewd look. "He will wed you this very evening. He reasons that there is no cause for

63

delay. Methinks he finds you comely in that garb of Beatrix. So if you behave with him as a loving and dutiful wife would—"

"Loving! Dutiful!"

Once more the several people in the hall glanced over at them. But Linnea did not care. It was bad enough to marry the man and suffer the groping that surely must follow. But to appear to relish it—for that was clearly her grandmother's implication. To appear to relish it was simply too much to ask!

She rose from the bench—or tried to. But Lady Harriet grabbed her trailing sleeve and jerked her back down.

"You said unto me that you would save your sister," the old woman hissed, her faded eyes slitted with fiery emotion. "You said you would save your family. But I ken what truly you wish, wretched girl. You wish only to prove me wrong. You wish to prove your miserable existence of some worth. Well, this is your chance. This is the only chance you ever will have. Do it, and do it well. Else, tell me now that you be unequal to the task—and that I have been right about you these seventeen years and more!"

She let go of Linnea's arm as if it disgusted her to even touch so loathsome a creature. But though Linnea was free to run away from the bitter old woman and her hateful words, she found that she could not do so.

That *was* her goal: to prove her grandmother wrong. To prove them all wrong, but especially her grandmother. If she were as pure of heart as Beatrix, she would only care about saving her loved ones. But she was selfish and she'd let herself become caught up in the glory she might gain for herself.

She bowed her head, ashamed of herself. She must do this for her family—and for the right reasons. If she must wed this man . . . if she must subjugate herself to him, though it degrade her body beyond imagination, then that was what she would do. After all, hadn't Maynard done as much? He'd used his body in defense of his family, and suffered terribly for it. But he'd done it just the same. Could she do any less?

Linnea thought of Maynard lying near to death. She would keep that image of him tucked away in her mind as the source of her courage. If cruel, mean-spirited Maynard could be so noble, surely she could do as much.

"I will do it," she said, then took a slow, shaky breath. She raised her head and met her grandmother's narrowed stare. "I will do it, but . . ."

"But what?"

"But I . . ." She swallowed hard and shot an embarrassed glance toward her silent father. "But I do not know what . . . what . . . how to be a loving and . . . dutiful wife."

Her father cleared his throat and looked away. But Lady Harriet, far from becoming uncomfortable with Linnea's question, began instead to laugh. "You do not know the way of it? All the time you have stolen away to the village and your coarse friends, 'twould seem you would know all there is to know of it by now."

Linnea drew back, aghast that her grandmother could think such a thing. Her outrage, however, was met with equal portions of pain. No matter what she did, somehow her grandmother always made it look wrong. Even her innocence—something that should prove she was not so sinful as everyone believed—appeared a shortcoming now.

"Leave us, Edgar." Lady Harriet waved him away with her bony hand. "I would speak with your daughter, to make certain she plays her part well tonight."

He needed no more encouragement than that. But as he made his slow way up to his chamber, Linnea saw a guard follow behind.

They were but prisoners in their own home, free to move about, but only under the watchful eye of their captors. And so would she be a prisoner of her husband, at least until the truth could be revealed.

"Now then, listen close, girl," her grandmother began. "When he takes you upstairs this evening, you must needs be attentive to his mood. Some men want a woman afraid. Cowed. They would take her roughly and relish her tears as fuel for their lust. Since he sees you as his enemy, he is very likely to use you thus. 'Tis rape, plain and simple, but within the bounds of marriage, and so permissible."

Lady Harriet's mouth thinned in distaste, and despite Linnea's anger at her, and horror at the picture she painted, she felt a faint connection between them. Not that of grandmother to granddaughter, but of woman to woman. Women were too often misused by men. Though Linnea had never considered it before, now she wondered about her grandfather who'd died long before she'd been born. Maybe he'd used his lady wife roughly too.

"On the other hand," the old woman continued, "some men there are who want a woman eager for them and willing to partake eagerly in their bed sport."

"But how will I know which he is?" Linnea asked when her grandmother did not elaborate.

"If he throws you down, lifts your skirts, and begins to rut like some randy destrier, you will know. If that is the case, you need not hide your fear nor withhold your tears, for he will want to see them. To enjoy them.

"But should he woo you with kisses and soft touches, that will be your sign that he wants as much of you. 'Tis very simple. If he be cruel, then you may crumple. If he be gentle, then you must appear well pleased and willing."

But it was not simple to Linnea. "How . . . how do I appear willing?" she whispered.

Lady Harriet shifted on the hard bench. It was plain that they'd gone deeper into this subject than she was comfortable with. "Simpleton! Just do whatever he asks of you—and smile! Keep your eyes half-closed, your lips half-parted, and smile. And be certain to act impressed when he reveals himself to you," she added.

"Reveals himself?"

"His manroot," she hissed impatiently. "His arousal. He will want to push it inside you. That's the whole point, girl. He will grow it long and hard, then will he push it inside you so that he can spill his seed. Have you never seen the hounds?"

Linnea pulled back in disbelief. Like the hounds? Dear God! He meant to do *that* to her?

"He may want to see you naked, or even to touch you all over," her grandmother continued, a distasteful expression pulling her lips down. "Especially your breasts."

Linnea hunched over at that, crossing her arms protectively over her chest. Her breasts? She couldn't imagine letting him touch her there—or do the other thing either.

As if she sensed Linnea's resistance, Lady Harriet leaned closer and caught Linnea's chin in her hand. "You *will* let him do that, and more, girl. That and anything else he asks. Nor will you consider yourself ill-used for it either. 'Tis our lot in life as women. He may think you are Beatrix, and you may yet consider avoiding this night's events by revealing the truth to him. But remember you this. Whether him or another, you will someday be wed. Fail us tonight, girl, and I promise by everything I hold dear that I will then see you wed to the vilest, cruelest man I can find.

"You will not fail us tonight, Linnea. You will wed him and bed him and make him content. Or you will be sorry I did not drown you on the day of your birth!"

Chapter 5

The few bites Linnea had eaten settled now like a cold stone in her stomach. Her grandmother had departed after her brief and terrifying description of what faced Linnea this evening, stomping away with the shuffle and click of leather shoes and metal-tipped walking stick so unique to her. But Linnea had not been able to move. She could not, for fear made her legs weak. Fear made her stomach rebel and shut down the workings of her mind.

But even with that fear, she still would have tried to flee the dreadful future that awaited her. Shame, however, was her ultimate undoing. If she ran, then Beatrix would suffer. If she ran, she would confirm all their beliefs about her.

If she ran, they would be right.

She closed her eyes and bowed her head, sinking into the shudder that rippled through her. Would he treat her cruelly, or kindly? Would he want her to cringe and weep, or to cry out in passion?

Which would be worse?

At least she would not have to pretend to fear. But passion . . . She would not be able to pretend she felt passion!

Consumed as she was by utter misery, she did not hear the noisy entrance of several men. Her brow was creased in worry as she tried to determine which saint she should direct her desperate prayers to. Sebastian? No, he was the patron saint of archers. Paula? No, she was widows. Not Bartholomew or St. Lucy either.

St. Jude. His name came to her at once. St. Jude, patron saint to the hopeless and to lost causes. If ever a poor soul was hopeless, she prayed with eyes tightly closed and hands clenched in her lap, it was she. *Please, St. Jude. Hear my prayer and rescue me.* Please, she silently beseeched. *Save me.*

"Lady Beatrix?"

Linnea jumped in alarm. St. Jude had heard her prayer? He was answering her—

Even before her startled gaze met with that of Axton de la Manse, she realized her mistake. Stupid girl, to think a saint would speak directly to her!

Stupid girl, to sit alone in the hall where Axton de la Manse himself could find her!

Never had Linnea felt so vulnerable as she did in that moment. Never had she felt so alone.

She looked up at him, up the towering length of this forbidding man who meant to take her to wife, and the last of her paltry courage fled. He was immense and he held total control over her and everyone else in this castle. He had all the power, both physical and political, and they had none at all.

Her eyes locked with his, unable to pull away, even though she would rather look any place but at him. In just such a manner did the snake mesmerize the rodent, the vague thought tumbled through her head. So did the owl hypnotize the hare.

"Lady Beatrix." He spoke the name again without any hint of emotion. "I would have you join me at the lord's table."

This time he held a hand out to her as if it were not a cold command he'd given her, but a courtly request. And perhaps to him it was. For Linnea, however, he might as well have asked her to leap from between the crenels into the fetid water of the moat. To take his hand—the hand of her enemy who would be her husband—was to put it all into motion, right here and now. Never mind that the vows would not be said until after vespers. Never mind that she would not be prepared even then. He was here now. Unexpectedly. And he held out his hand, with no reason to believe she would not do whatever he should ask of her.

"Do you refuse me?"

Linnea swallowed hard and felt again the cold lump in her stomach. "I . . . I have other duties—"

"Your duty is to me." His eyes, hard as the pale stone walls that encircled the castle, bored into hers. Then he seemed almost to force himself to a gentler mien. "Come, Lady Beatrix. I will not bite you."

Yet.

He had left off yet, Linnea thought as bitterness lent her strength. He would not bite her yet, but if she balked any longer he would.

Using every bit of her willpower, she lifted her trembling hand to him. It would not be forever, she told herself, as if it were an incantation against him. It would not be forever. Just long enough for Beatrix to escape. Just long enough for her family to raise a legitimate challenge to this man. She could survive until the day came when she could reveal her true identity.

Then his hand closed over hers, and even that faint hope began to unravel. For Axton de la Manse's hands were large and strong, and in enveloping hers, seemed to signal a greater strength than merely the physical.

He gave off some power, almost like a heat, that she felt in every portion of her. He touched only her fingers, yet her arm and chest and even her legs felt the shock of it. The shock of him.

"St. Jude," she whispered. "Be with me now."

Axton heard that involuntary plea and knew at once its meaning. She was resigned to her fate. But she was desperately hopeful just the same, that St. Jude might still intercede on her behalf.

Grim satisfaction settled over him. Yes, let her be reduced to prayers alone for her salvation. He knew from bitter experience how unreliable was the answer prayers would give. Hadn't he prayed ten years and more for the chance to right the wrong done his family? Hadn't he prayed for the means to restore his family to property and power? It was only when he'd stopped praying and begun to fight that the tide had begun to shift in their favor.

The deaths of his father and brothers in the defense of Matilda had brought the de la Manse family an estate near Caen. Now he was here, in his rightful home, with his bride beside him, trembling as lief to faint—and no saints to be thanked for it either. Yes, let her pray to her St. Jude, for it would change nothing at all. He would wed her this very evening, and bed her promptly thereafter—and repeat the act daily until she was safely with child. He would hold his home against all claims, even if it meant joining with his worst enemy's daughter. And perhaps he would have from her the satisfaction he had yet to receive from either her father or her brother.

He guided her from the rough trestle table and bench toward the low dais, acutely aware of her nearness. She was taller than average for a woman, and slender of build. But she appeared shapely beneath her rumpled gown. No perfumes clung to her, save perhaps a medicinal fragrance, as of shepherd's knot, and of soft, boiled soap. No powder on her face either, and no jewels, save the few upon her girdle. Was she not vain, or did de Valcourt not gift his daughter with the rings and bracelets and other jewels more common to women of her station?

"Had you another to whom you were betrothed?" he

70

inquired as he pulled back the lady's chair for her and gestured for her to sit.

She did not meet his gaze, but she sat as he indicated, though warily. "I turned down the suit of Sir Clarence of Mercer," she stated after a lengthy pause.

He stared intently at her profile as he seated himself. Her features were as perfect as a man could hope for: straight, slender nose; full, curving lips; small chin and skin that looked as soft as a child's. The unwarranted desire to see her eyes again caught him by surprise. But why? To see if they were as deep an aqua-green as they'd seemed in the brief moment she'd looked up at him. That was all.

Or maybe it was more. Lust? He gave a mental shrug. What if it was? And not only her eyes, he wanted to see her hair unbound, to test its length and feel its texture.

"Why did you turn him down? Why did your father allow you such an indulgence?"

He watched her full lips tighten, but still she kept her face averted. "He was a pig of a man. He still is."

Axton laughed out loud at that unexpectedly candid remark, and as a reward had her wide-set eyes turned finally upon him. Ah, yes. Aqua-green, and turbulent as the sea in a storm. He seized on the moment. "A pig of a man? Pray tell why you call him that. Does he like his dinner too well? Or is it that he has insufficient wealth to tempt you?"

Anger roiled in her stormy gaze. "He had wealth enough to decide he needed nothing else to satisfy a wife. Neither cleanliness, nor manners, nor good humor."

And neither do you, the silent accusation rose between them.

Once more he laughed. Particular little wench, wasn't she? Spoiled by a father who'd stolen everything he'd ever given her. It occurred to Axton that he now owned everything she thought *she* possessed, including her gown and girdle and veil.

For the first time this day he felt a glimmer of real satisfaction for his victory. What father and son could not supply him, she might. Beneath her fair appearance Beatrix de Valcourt had spirit. No doubt on that. Despite her trembling fear which she could not bury beneath her show of bravado, no matter how she tried, she was no coward. Perhaps the fury that yet twisted in his gut could be exhausted upon her. After all, she would be his wife. She was comely, easy to look upon and designed to fit a man's hand—and other portions of him too.

Of a sudden he was eager for this evening's sport and glad he'd not spent himself on castle wenches this night just past.

"Had your father no other swains to tempt you with?" he prodded, wanting to test her mettle further.

She looked away. "He negotiated with others," she answered in a cool, detached voice. "Until your Henry thought to attack us. Of late my father has had other concerns," she pointed out, a trace of sarcasm rising in her voice.

"Yes, no doubt he has," Axton commented dryly. He lolled back in the lord's chair, conscious of the fact that she had probably never seen anyone sit in it save her father. But he was lord now, and she'd come to understand very soon everything that implied. "You've been told that we wed this evening?"

Her chin quivered—or at least he thought it did. But she nodded once, and he was not entirely sure. He decided to find out. "No doubt you see me as a pig of a man—or worse." Then he leaned nearer her and his voice lowered to a husky, intimate whisper. "I trust, my fair bride, that e'er morning next arrives, you will feel more kindly disposed toward me."

She swallowed this time. Hard. There was no hiding her reaction or the fear it revealed to him. That served, however, only to urge him on. He needed to see her completely vulnerable to him. "Since there is none to commend me save myself, I say to you, fair Beatrix, that I take to heart the knightly code. I keep myself clean, maintain an even temperament, and enjoy a great good humor—unless angered by one unwise enough to provoke me."

When she did not respond, but only held herself stiff and kept her eyes averted, he reached out a hand to finger the braided edge of her nearest trailing sleeve. "And I am robust in the manly arts. You need not fear that I will not satisfy my husbandly duties to you, Beatrix."

She flinched, as he knew she would. But this time when her eyes darted fearfully to him, he caught her chin in his hand and held her face steady.

Such a pretty face, with flawless skin and high color. Loose tendrils of reddish gold hair curled astray beyond the confines of her veil, and he had a momentary vision of that selfsame hair loose and cascading around her. Around *him*.

"Deuce take me," he muttered, then sat back, releasing her as an unseemly urge gripped him. Time enough for that this coming night. He was no randy lad, unable to control the beast residing in his braies. A comely wife was a welcome thing, but he would not forget that she was de Valcourt's spawn. He would not forget that she had lived at Maidenstone these eighteen years past and that every one of her luxuries had been bought at the cost of his father's and his brothers' lives.

And he would *not* be led around by his unruly cods.

A boisterous call drew his attention momentarily away from her, and he welcomed the interruption.

Linnea too welcomed the interruption and she could not escape fast enough from his presence. He'd taken much pleasure in tormenting her, and she, fool that she was, had granted him the right, speaking of the suitors her sister had declined.

But she'd been so afraid, especially when he'd spoken of his husbandly duties to her.

She pushed back her chair now, as quietly as she could manage, all the while keeping a careful watch on him. St. Jude had heard her prayer and interceded on her behalf when he'd sent a pair of knights into the hall. One of them, a muscular fellow with dark red whiskers, had glanced uneasily at her before speaking, then turned his steady gaze back upon his liege lord. De la Manse had understood his hesitation at once. So had Linnea. The other men did not wish their conversation to be held within the full hearing of their enemy, even if that very enemy was to be settled in the lord's bed within a matter of hours.

De la Manse had made some pretty excuse as he left her side, as if he thought she dreaded his departure. Vainglorious fool! Now his attention was wholly absorbed by the other men's words and she had her opportunity. But although she silently mocked him, Linnea was nonetheless mindful of the terrible chance she took deceiving a man like him. When he eventually learned who she *really* was . . . A cold shiver ran down her spine. She did not want to think about that right now.

She slipped behind the chair, then glanced over to her left. The pantler's chamber was shielded from the hall by a heavy curtain, and it was there she headed. But as she pushed blindly past the curtain, her foot met a hard, yielding form and she lost her balance. A yelp alerted her to some sleeping hound's presence. But when she could not right herself and fell awkwardly onto the animal, its startled cry changed to a fierce growl.

"Be still e'er he snaps your head clean off your shoulders," a youthful voice ordered. Linnea instantly obeyed. But it was bitterly done, for she realized without seeing him, that the voice belonged to *that* boy. No other lad of the castle would dare to speak in such lordly tones to her. Only Peter de la Manse, brother to her dreaded bridegroom, would do so. Who else came and went with such a huge hound ever at his side? Who else seemed to live to taunt her, the ill-mannered whelp?

"To calm, Moor. To calm," he ordered in his half-boy, half-man's croak of a voice. " 'Tis only a minor aggravation, not worthy of our attention."

The animal had shrugged Linnea off as if she were, indeed, only some minor weight thrown heedlessly upon him and shed just as heedlessly. But though she lay crumpled ignominiously against the rough wall of the pantry, the dog stood over her as if to attack, his huge head lowered, his hackles raised. His great yellow teeth bared.

"To calm," the boy spoke once more, though there was less of command and more of hilarity in his tone. But at least he gripped the beast's studded collar now, affording Linnea the faintest reprieve from her fear of being eaten alive.

"Is it your wont to barrel unannounced through shielded passages? Methinks a bell to chime at your neck would serve us all a good warning."

Linnea pushed herself upright, but slowly. Her veil had come loose during her fall and hung askew, so she pulled it off and knotted it in her angry fists. Her tumbled hair she thrust carelessly behind her shoulder as she faced the snarling hound and its grinning master.

"If you would let me pass," she muttered, curbing her tongue though the effort came close to choking her.

"Go back the way you came," he said with a smug moue. "Unless you do flee from something—or somebody. My brother's body?" he added with the coarse innuendo too common to youthful males. Before this day Linnea had understood little of the vulgar implications, save that they *were* somehow vulgar. But after her grandmother's unsettling explanation of what men and women did together, followed by Axton de la Manse's disturbing hints and now this boy's crude words, she understood far more than she wanted to.

"Your brother is occupied with one of his men," she bit out.

"One of his men? Ah, but you could not be more wrong. He is not of so perverse a nature—nor am I," he ended on a boastful note.

Linnea glared at him. Was she to make sense of that? She chose not to even try, for she'd had enough of male coarseness for this day. "Let me pass. Boy," she added, as fury got the better of common sense. She gathered her unfamiliarly heavy skirts in one hand and started forward as if to push past him in the narrow passage. But the dog lunged forward and she leaped back, and all the while the boy hooted in derision.

"Boy, you say? Man enough to control this mighty beast, and man enough to control you as well."

Sweet Mary, but that was the very last straw. First his

huge oaf of a brother threatening her with his husbandly rights. Now him, with his nasty smirk and vicious pet. "Know you how easy it is to fell one such as he?" she hissed, too angry to guard her words any longer. "To paint a joint of mutton with oil of belladonna and feed it to this thing you call a dog would be no difficult task for me." She drew herself up in the face of his startled expression. "Best you and he stay well out of my way."

Then, afraid to push past him, but more afraid to go back into the hall and chance meeting his brother, she stepped firmly toward the boy, though passing on the side away from the animal he held so tightly to him.

Thankfully he let her go and she did not dally in the short passageway that connected the hall to the castle offices. Through the chamber she hurried. But she noted the disorder in the office, the ledgers spread open on the table, the money box also open—and empty.

A curse upon them all, she swore. They were thieves who robbed her family of right and respect and belongings.

Once beyond the offices, however, she hesitated yet again. Where to fly, now that there was no solace to be found anywhere within these heavy stone walls? Sister gone. Father useless. Grandmother more torment than comfort.

The chapel bell tolled sext, and it was as if it called an answer to her desperation—or once again St. Jude did. Linnea knew that Father Martin was to aid in Beatrix's escape. Maybe she was hidden in the chapel. Even if she weren't, the priest might have some word of her for Linnea. Or he might agree to carry a message to her.

Father Martin was in the small apse opposite the altar where the lord's family worshipped, but so was her grandmother. They prayed—or conferred—heads close and whispers low. No solace to be found here, Linnea told herself, backing away before they noted her presence. A wary search of the priest's private solar and nearby storerooms did not reveal Beatrix's whereabouts either. And so it was with heavy heart and slow tread that Linnea made her way back to the barracks. She could at least sit with Maynard a while and pray for him—for *all* of them. St. Jude, don't abandon us, she sent her silent plea aloft. *Do not abandon us.*

To her surprise, someone was already praying over Maynard, a slight, bowed figure that started in alarm at Linnea's entrance.

"What do you here?" Linnea demanded, fearing for her brother's safety. Where was that squire, anyway?

"'Tis all right, sister," came the response. "'Tis only . . . 'Tis only Linnea," she said, glancing warningly at the prone figure on the floor.

Thank God! Linnea flew to Beatrix's side, enveloping her in a grateful embrace. "Oh, but I have feared for you—"

"Beatrix." The rusty voice was that of Maynard, though a weak, cracking version of it. Both sisters looked down at him, Beatrix beaming with joy, Linnea filled only with relief.

"Beatrix," he repeated. "I am hurt . . . My head . . . Why am I in this . . . this mean place?"

"The new lord does order it so," Beatrix began.

"I spoke to Beatrix!" Maynard cut her off. Even in his suffering he did not forget which sister was firstborn—and which one was not.

The twins shared a look and an understanding. Beatrix stepped back and Linnea, wearing her sister's rumpled finery, knelt beside their brother. He was weak and dazed, but yet possessed of the same unpleasant disposition as ever. "You are grievously injured but, God grant it, you shall survive. Only you must rest and allow yourself to heal."

He stared up at her and in his eyes she saw both pain and bewilderment. She'd seen mockery in his gaze many times, and devilment. Also fury and cruelty. But never the vulnerability that was there now. He was but human, she realized, much like their father. But also a bully, she reminded herself. Like the boy Peter.

Maynard was in her power now, as Peter de la Manse had been in the fleeting moments following her threat to poison his dog. How gratifying was this feeling of power, she thought as she pressed a palm to Maynard's head, testing him for the fever. No wonder men clawed and fought for power, and struggled ever to retain it. When compared to helplessness, there was no contest.

"I will tend your needs, brother," she reassured him.

"And I will pray for you," Beatrix murmured from her place just beyond them.

"Get thee gone!" Maynard gasped, his eyes darting accusingly at the disguised Beatrix. " 'Tis your curse that has brought us to this pass—and laid me low. Agh, but my arm. My arm!"

Harsh sobs wracked him as he mourned his ruined arm. But Linnea's sympathy lay more with her sister—and by association herself. Even in this worst crisis their family had ever faced, they would, all of them, blame an innocent person for their troubles. They would accuse Linnea—or whomever they mistook to be Linnea—for their fall.

She turned to find her sister's face as white as a cold winter sky. Never had Beatrix appeared so stricken. She was not used to the scorn Linnea had grown inured to. On impulse Linnea reached for her and hugged her close. "Go now," she whispered to her beloved sister. "Be safe and know my love stays ever with you."

"I cannot leave you," Beatrix sobbed, breaking down in her arms. " 'Tis wrong of me, and wrong of the others to demand it."

" 'Tis right," Linnea countered, restored by this unexpected moment with her twin. " 'Tis right and . . . and everything shall come out for the best."

Beatrix looked doubtful, but finally she nodded, drying her tears on her sleeve.

"Go now," Linnea instructed her, though to keep her sister close by was what she desired more than anything.

"I shall endeavor to be there, at the chapel this evening," Beatrix whispered. "And I will pray the whole night through for you." Then with a last kiss, she was gone, pushed away before Linnea could change her mind and beg her to stay.

Tears spilled down Linnea's cheeks as she turned, heavy-hearted, to her brother. If he so much as said a word of derision to the sister he mistook for herself, Linnea would never be able to control her righteous anger.

But St. Jude interceded once more on her behalf, as he had in small ways repeatedly this long and endless day. For Maynard had subsided into a fitful repose. While she checked his injuries, he tossed restlessly and muttered unintelligible snatches, but nothing of his sisters, God be praised.

When Frayne reappeared, a silent, guilty wraith in the shadows, Linnea was too drained to take him to task for his absence. Maynard was better. It seemed he might mend. Perhaps she should leave his care to her grand-mother now, for she had troubles enough of her own.

"Dribble this medicine between his lips and make sure it goes down," she warned Frayne, giving him the small stop-pered vial of sundew. "Also this, for pain. Then try to give him at least a dipper full of water every hour or so. And call me should he grow feverish or restless."

The boy nodded, staring at her with round eyes in a dirty face. "What if you are . . ." He faltered and looked away. "Beg pardon, my Lady Beatrix, but I have heard the tale that you and the new lord . . ."

When his curious gaze turned cautiously back to her, it was Linnea's turn to look away. Everyone knew. Every-one's hopes for a peaceful future of one sort or another resided on her—and on how well she performed her wifely duties this evening.

"Perhaps it would be more prudent for you to rouse my grandmother than to send for me," she admitted in an embarrassed mutter.

"Lady Harriet?" His brows rose in consternation. "I was thinking, well, that your sister would be a better choice."

"No! Not . . . not Linnea. She is gone from here now and never to be spoken of again. Do you mind my words, Frayne? You must *never* mention her again, not if you value your position!"

Abruptly she halted her speech, dismayed by her shrill

tone and rising hysteria. She pressed her fingertips to her eyes and willed her trembling to cease. Only when she felt a modicum of control return did she speak again.

"Nothing of Maidenstone is as we have been accustomed to. Our lives have been turned upside down and now we must attempt as best we can to cope. My sister is lost to us. It would be better to pretend she had never existed."

Chapter 6

Darkness rushed over the rolling lands of Wessex, heralded by a violent storm that lashed the castle, the village, and the fields beyond. The ancient ash forest that stood sentinel along the ridge bowed and swayed in fearful homage to the tempest. Sheep huddled beneath trees or in the lean-to sheds spotted around the valley. Wheat stalks lay down in the face of wind and rain, and nary a villager ventured outside the stucco walls and thatched roofs of their cottages.

Only in the castle did activity continue unabated, for the wedding would go forth, storm or no.

Linnea stood in the middle of the third floor solar, surrounded by three maids, as well as Norma and Ida. Her grandmother watched as they dressed her, scowling from her place in a tall chair cushioned with rugs and positioned beside the wall hearth. Though the blaze threw a commendable heat into the chamber, cold yet hung over the place. It was not caused by the storm.

"You have not forgotten my instructions," Lady Harriet said. It was more statement than question.

"No, Grandmother. I have not forgotten. I have thought of little else this day," Linnea said.

One of the maids began to weep, not great sobs, but soft, heartfelt ones that touched Linnea to the core. Yet even amidst her fear and sorrow, she was cognizant that the girl wept for Beatrix, not Linnea. Would she weep if she knew the truth? Or would she rejoice in the deception, as Lady Harriet did, never caring that an innocent girl would be sacrificed this night all the same?

Linnea sought Norma's gaze. Dear Norma who was tired and old, and who, though favoring Beatrix, had never been intentionally cruel to Linnea. Norma's eyes were red-rimmed but she did not cry. Nor did she smile. Of all the servants, only she and Ida knew the truth. The other maids had not been present when Linnea bathed. Only when her shift was on and her hose pulled up and gartered over her birthmark, had they been brought in to dress her hair and arrange her clothing.

Now Linnea stood arrayed in her sister's finest gown and costliest jewels. Her hair was washed and dried, scented with lavender oil and brushed until it gleamed like a rich, golden mantle. Her head was bare, save for the silken cord that circled her brow. Otherwise her heavy hair rippled loose, past her shoulders and arms to hang in living curls about her hips.

The gown was exquisite, but one Linnea had not been allowed to work on. It had been intended for Beatrix's eventual wedding, and both Lady Harriet and Dagmar, the head seamstress, had deemed it bad luck for the second twin to even touch it.

Linnea stared down at the aqua flurt-silke, falling as gently as a waterfall, clinging to her waist, flowing over her hips, and pooling in luxurious waves around her ankles. She fingered the heavily embroidered hem of the left sleeve. She'd sewn every seed pearl on that hem herself. Beatrix had insisted on it. By moonlight she'd sat in the window and sewed them on, not caring that her back ached and her eyes burned. Beatrix had known how deeply hurt Linnea had been by her grandmother's orders, and so, in the quietly determined manner she had, Beatrix had found a way to oppose Lady Harriet.

Linnea swallowed the lump in her throat. *Oh, Beatrix. You and you alone have cared for me. I will not fail you in this. I will wed this man, and bed him, and deceive him as long as is necessary for you to find a husband to challenge his rights to Maidenstone Castle.*

And when the truth was finally revealed, Beatrix and her husband would take their place as lord and lady of Maidenstone, and they would honor Linnea for what she'd done. Everyone would finally accept her, and life would be good.

"Turn, milady, if you please," the maid who'd been weeping asked in a soft voice. She placed a white silk girdle around Linnea's hips, looping it twice, then fastening it with a heavy gold brooch encrusted with amethysts and aquamarines.

"Your bridegroom has sent you a key, Beatrix."

Linnea looked over at her grandmother, perched in the chair like a gaunt, black bird, dressed more for mourning than for a wedding. Linnea wished she could wear black so blamelessly. She'd attended funerals with more enthusiasm than this marriage ceremony that awaited her. But she could not dress for mourning, not and please her husband as was her duty.

"Here." Lady Harriet tossed the key carelessly to her, then cackled with laughter when Linnea made no move to catch it. " 'Tis the key to his heart, methinks."

With a grunt of effort Norma bent her great bulk down to retrieve the key, then offered it to Linnea. " 'Tis for the end of your girdle," she explained. "A symbol of the power you shall wield as wife to the lord. As lady of the castle."

Lady of the castle.

Linnea reached out a hand, taking the cold bit of metal in her palm without being conscious of her action. Lady of the castle. Her grandmother had ever held that position, even when their father married—or so castle talk would have it. But the new lord was not likely to allow that to continue. No, with this marriage, Linnea would assume that role.

She lifted her gaze slowly to her grandmother, her mind spinning with this new realization. She felt again the same unfamiliar sense of power she'd had when she threatened that boy, and later, when she stood over Maynard and real-

82

ized her ability to either heal him, or allow him to die. It was wonderful and terrifying. A sense of independence and freedom, but also of responsibility.

If *she* were lady of the castle, her grandmother would no longer exert a power over her; it would be the other way around.

As if she read Linnea's very thoughts, Lady Harriet's grim expression tightened into a warning scowl. "Leave us," she snapped to the serving women, though her hard stare never left Linnea's face. Once the five maids were gone, she raised her walking stick and pointed it at her granddaughter.

"Beware any foolish temptation to forget your place, girl." The stick wavered in her skinny hand, but still it managed to pin Linnea to her spot. "Beware any foolish thoughts of remaining Beatrix de Valcourt—of remaining lady of Maidenstone. That title is mine and mine alone—until such time as I relinquish it to either Beatrix or a suitable wife for Maynard. You—" She lowered the stick with a threatening crack of its metal tip against the unadorned plank floor. "You are your sister's proxy only, until such time as the charade is no longer necessary. 'Tis a way for you to earn your family's respect—if indeed you *can.*"

Then she stood, and though she leaned heavily on her stick to rise, her physical infirmity in no wise lessened the aura of cruel power she exuded. "Remember, girl, that I can expose your true identity at any time. Think you that de la Manse will condone such a deception? To be rid of the wrong wife—*you*," she emphasized. "He might elect murder over the slower process of annulment. Then he would have Beatrix and all of this would be for naught. Think on it, girl. Best that you play your part and keep your silence. And never think, e'en for a moment, that you could wield power at Maidenstone Castle. I would as lief let him kill you as let that come to pass!"

Then the old woman gestured to the door. " 'Tis time. Your bridegroom awaits, and I would see my plan underway."

Linnea had stood still, with her head bowed under the onslaught of the old woman's hateful words. Now she started forward on wooden limbs. It was an automatic response, for all her life she'd obeyed her grandmother's orders, whether terrified, furious, or sick at heart, as she now was. When she reached the door, however, Lady Harriet stayed her, blocking her path with the stick that seemed an extension of her arm. "You know your duty, girl. Do it."

Linnea nodded, steeling herself against any display of emotion, especially tears. She would do her duty though it meant submitting to her enemy—though it meant allowing him to rape her and use her as he willed. But she did not do it because of her grandmother's threat, nor even as duty to her family. No, she did this for Beatrix, no one else. Only for Beatrix.

It was hardly the way she'd imagined approaching her marriage, not that she'd thought much on that subject. Maynard's marriage had always been important to the family, and Beatrix's. But hers had never been discussed. Not once.

When she'd thought about her future, she'd always imagined life with an ordinary man, a tradesman or foot soldier who would marry her for herself, not because he expected to gain anything from the match. There would be no gain from marrying the second twin of Maidenstone, neither dowry nor even goodwill. Only herself would she bring to the marriage bed of her husband.

But even that was denied her now.

She took the stairs slowly, descending behind her grandmother, one halting step at a time. She was marrying as Beatrix, giving her enemy her body, but as Beatrix's body. The only thing of value she possessed—her purity—was to be sacrificed this day and she would be left with nothing of value to give to her real husband. Nothing whatsoever.

The stair hall was dark, but light crept along its curving outer wall as they neared the hall. Light and sound as well. In truth, the warm, well-lit hall should seem a merry respite from the storm that battered the world outside the stout walls. But Linnea shivered as if from a bitter wind, and the torches that cast golden flickering light to the very rafters seemed to illuminate the dark passageway to hell.

When Lady Harriet entered, the hum of voices altered. When Linnea came into view, the voices stopped altogether. She stood on the last step, staring at the sea of faces, frozen somewhere between going forward and fleeing. Someone shifted near her—it was her father, dressed in the sapphire and argent of de Valcourt, his finest attire. But he looked an imitation of a great lord, she vaguely noticed. His rich garments proclaimed him a man of consequence. His posture and his expression revealed a man defeated. Even this sacrifice she made to gain them time to mount a counterattack was not enough to restore his courage.

Linnea closed her eyes, not wanting to see or acknowledge that fact. Then someone stepped forward—she sensed it, somehow—and she opened her eyes to *him*.

Axton de la Manse dressed not so finely as her father. At least the colors did not shout so boldly. But everything about him announced his dominance. He was lord here. Only a fool would deny it. And only a fool would oppose him, Linnea admitted, trying to swallow past the painful lump in her throat.

He crossed half the distance between them, then stopped. He was the very picture of masculine virility and confidence. Strong of body, well-formed, and beautiful in the harsh manner of a man, he waited there, forcing her to come the rest of the way to him.

How she willed herself to it she could not say. But she took the last step down, then proceeded, one slow pace at a time toward him.

His head was bare and his close-cropped hair, though black as his ebony tunic, yet gleamed in the brilliant light. His brows were two dark slashes; his eyes a pale color in his sun-browned face.

Linnea swallowed again, hard. He was to be her husband, this expressionless man who watched her as if he saw all the way through her. She wanted to look away, so unnerving was his relentless stare. Like a predator's. But as if

85

he compelled her, she could not turn her head nor avert her eyes. She moved forward, conscious of everything, the silence, the movement of her heavy skirt against her thighs, the patterns of air in the drafty hall, first cool on her hot cheeks, then warm. Even the smell, smoky with pitch, pungent with ale, fragrant with a whole roasted boar, imprinted itself on her mind.

But mostly it was him, so dark, so unknown, so threatening, that filled her senses. When she halted before him, a mere arm's length away, she feared she had exhausted the last of her strength. She feared she would faint before him, crumple to the floor. He would defeat her before the struggle between them had fairly begun.

"Was ever a man so fortunate as I," he said in a tone she might have taken for sincere, had his mouth not curved up on one side in a mocking half-smile. All the company leaned forward, straining to hear what word he had uttered to his reluctant bride. "I am in my own home again, after eighteen long and difficult years, and I am to be wed to as beautiful a maiden as a man's eye could ever hope to behold."

Now he mocked her outright! Linnea stiffened in opposition to him, but he paid her no mind. He took hold of her hand and tucked it firmly into the crook of his elbow. When she tried to tug it free, he only looked down into her face, a warning expression in his frosty stare.

"Let us greet our guests, Lady Beatrix, all those who would wish us well in our union."

Then, as if her resistance were of no consequence at all, he steered her in a slow parade around the hall, displaying her to the people—*his* people now.

What did he hope to gain by making such an insincere compliment to her, she fumed as she was forced to accompany him in their farcical promenade. Bad enough that her arm must rest in his, that she must endure the disturbing heat and threatening strength of so intimate a touch. But he also made her pause before various of the retainers. His captain, Sir Reynold, and again before Sir John and Sir Maurice.

"My bride, Lady Beatrix of Maidenstone." He made the formal introduction in each case. "May I present my brother, Peter de la Manse," he said when they halted before the stripling lad she'd despised on sight.

"Welcome to the family," the boy said, a properly solemn expression on his imp's face.

Though he was every bit her height, Linnea lifted her chin and looked down her nose at him, determined that he would know her disdain and believe her threat.

"Come give your new sister a kiss," Axton demanded of his brother, drawing him nearer with an arm on the lad's shoulder.

Linnea saw the resistance spark in the boy's blue eyes, and she took a perverse pleasure in his reluctance. She had frightened him. Good.

It was easy to make her expression cold and threatening when she faced him. "Let us *bury* our animosity," she said to the boy with deliberate emphasis. She turned her cheek to accept his hasty kiss. "Perhaps you will introduce me to your pet on the morrow. I'll bring him a tasty morsel to tempt his friendship."

The boy stepped away from her as if stung, but anger showed through his fear. He would not take her threats easily, she recognized. He would fight back. But Linnea actually welcomed him as a foe. Him she could compete with. Him she could defeat. His brother, however . . .

Her bridegroom's hand moved to the small of her back, a touch far too possessive for Linnea's peace of mind. She tried to step away faster, enough to make his condescending guidance unnecessary. But then she spied a familiar face lurking in the shadows of the pantler's cabinet, a familiar, dirty face partially hidden by a deep cowl, and she stopped.

Beatrix had come!

"The priest awaits." Her bridegroom's voice was close enough that his breath moved her hair. His hand once again circled her waist, and this time rested on the upper swell of her opposite hip.

But Linnea's panic was less this time, for Beatrix's gaze

held with hers, imparting love and giving strength. She stared at her sister just a moment longer. Then, though it killed her to do so, she tore her eyes away. She dared not alert de la Manse or any of his men to the importance of that slight figure in the shadows.

Still, Beatrix was there, and Linnea felt infinitely restored.

She turned toward the priest and accompanied her enemy to the clearing outlined in the center of the hall by a scattering of rose petals and dried herbs. The time had come. She'd made her decision, and though terrified of the consequences, she would not turn back. She would not betray her sister or her family name.

"Introibo ad altare Dei," Father Martin began, facing the marrying couple.

It was much like a mass in many ways, save that it was not in the chapel. Norma had told her the new lord wished to marry in view of as many of his people as possible. Had the weather permitted, they would have wed on the outside steps of the chapel. Instead, all of the castle folk and many of the villagers crowded into the hall to witness the ceremony.

It was not until the priest began the epistle that Linnea began actually to listen to his words. ". . . let wives be subject to their husbands as to the Lord: because a husband is head of the wife just as Christ is head of the Church. And the two shall become as one flesh joined . . ."

One flesh joined.

Marriage was a holy sacrament, blessed by God. Even the joining of the flesh which would occur later tonight, was blessed by the Lord. Yet Linnea felt an unholy fear of what was to come. Bad enough the deception she played with this man, this great dark bear of a man to whom she would now be subject. But she made this vow before God—and God knew she lied.

"Oh, St. Jude," she prayed, bowing her head as the enormity of her sin began to sink in.

"St. Jude cannot help you."

Linnea jerked her head around and met Axton de la Manse's taunting face. Father Martin stumbled over his words at the charged exchange between the two, but he quickly recovered.

"Do you, Beatrix de Valcourt, take this man to be your lawful husband . . ."

Linnea's eyes were trapped by her tormentor's vivid gaze. She did not notice when the good priest paused, waiting for her response.

"Your answer, Beatrix," de la Manse prompted her. "Do you agree to marry me, to pledge yourself to me before God and this company?"

In the unearthly silence of the great hall his voice was not loud, and yet she knew they all could hear his every word. Linnea's heart thumped so violently under his piercing stare that she was certain the watching multitude heard it too.

"My lady?" Father Martin whispered, a worried look on his lined face.

Abruptly Linnea came out of her frozen state. She had no real choice, she reminded herself. She must do this. "I will," she muttered softly, though those two simple words burned like gall in her throat.

The priest heaved a sharp sigh of relief. "And do you, Axton de la Manse, Lord of Maidenstone, take this woman to be your wife . . ."

"I will," he answered, his eyes still fixed upon hers. The remainder of the service she did not hear. Not the closing prayer nor the final blessing. When they knelt side by side, the only words that registered were, "By the grace of God the Father, I pronounce you man and wife."

Then she was hauled up from her knees and drawn against a chest solid and broad, until she had no place to look but up into her husband's ice gray eyes.

"Well enough, wife. Give us a kiss."

A hum began just behind them, then raced like a living thing from one end of the hall to the other. A kiss.

A kiss.

He demands a kiss.

So it must be, Linnea told herself. A kiss now, but much more to come later, she feared. His face hovered just above hers. His hands, strong and with long fingers, were wrapped around her arms, holding her steady before him.

"A wedding kiss for my . . . for my husband," Linnea murmured, though where she found the words she could not say. She met his hard gaze and saw none of the emotions a newly married man should have. Then again, perhaps triumph and possessiveness and a smugness about the mouth were precisely what men felt when they wed.

She closed her eyes. It was the only way she could manage it. Then she pressed up on her toes until her mouth touched his.

For a moment it was not so very bad. His lips were softer than she would have thought, given how hard the rest of him was, and he smelled clean and fresh.

Then his hands tightened and without warning she was crushed against him. She gasped in surprise and at once the kiss changed. His lips forced hers apart and she felt the heat of his breath.

And of his tongue.

Mother Mary, but it was like nothing she could have foreseen. His tongue plunged deeply into her mouth, rubbing the inside of her lips in the most disturbing manner, touching her tongue and stealing her senses completely away! He kissed her as if he meant to consume her, and for a dizzying moment she thought she would faint.

Then he broke off the kiss as abruptly as he'd begun it, and drew back just far enough to stare into her face again. He wore an expression she'd never seen before, and yet instinctively she understood it. He hungered for her. He lusted after her. His eyes burned with an unholy light.

But worse than that, he'd ignited a distressing little flame inside her. She'd heard enough sermons on the sin of lust to know what this feeling must be, and the very idea that *he* could inspire it in her was terrifying! *Dear God. Mother Mary. Please, St. Jude, but this cannot be true!*

But it was. When he'd kissed her, some deep and sinful part of her had felt the tiniest burst of wicked lust. And somehow he knew it, for he smiled then, the first true smile he'd given her.

Linnea could not withstand the searing probe of his eyes, so she dropped her gaze. But it landed upon his mouth, and that brought a rush of shameful heat into her cheeks. That mouth . . . What feelings he managed to conjure in her with that mouth. Strong white teeth. Soft mobile lips. Clever, knowing tongue.

As if he knew the direction of her thoughts, he chuckled. That made things even worse, for Linnea could feel the rumbling movement of his chest against her breasts, and it managed to further fuel the wicked fire within her. "Sweet, sweet tasting wife. Your father promised me that you are an innocent, and your kiss would seem to proclaim it. But your reaction . . . If you heat so swiftly from just one kiss, I wonder what other delights await me in our marriage bed this evening."

Someone nearby who'd overheard his comment guffawed. The hum began once more, carrying the new lord's remarks on his wife's reaction to their kiss. But Linnea had no time for so paltry a reaction as anger. Shame was the greater of her emotions at that moment, greater even than fear.

What other delights indeed—and how wantonly would she react?

He turned her then, and with a hand at her waist, drew her close against his side. "My wife, the Lady Beatrix," he announced to one and all.

But I am Linnea, she thought as she searched in rising confusion for a glimpse of her sister amidst the cheering throng. *I am the wicked sister who can lust after a man who is my mortal enemy and who I am sworn to bring to defeat.* She was sick at heart to discover such an awful truth about herself, and needed just the touch of her sister's eyes upon her to reassure herself and give her strength.

Beatrix was not there, however. And she never would be again, Linnea admitted as panic flooded her. She was alone now, with this man as her husband, and with the first

91

cruel realization that perhaps her grandmother had been right about the blackness of her soul.

He guided her to the dais, still holding her close. She was conscious of his heavy arm, his powerful chest, and the strength of his muscular legs, for they rubbed against her with every step.

"Let us be swift in our meal," he said, his words a hot, disturbing breath against her ear as he seated her.

Her startled gaze flew to his to see that hungry look again, as if a great black bear prepared to feast upon her.

"Yes," he said, reading her expression again, as if her very thoughts were written there for him to see. He traced her lower lip with the pad of his thumb. "I've the same hunger as you, though not for swan or dumplings. You, my sweet bird. 'Tis you I would feast on this evening, and all the hours until dawn. And I will."

Chapter 7

Linnea ate too little and drank too much. Her father and grandmother sat at the high table, though not in the lord and lady's chairs as had been their place before. Linnea and her husband—her husband!—occupied those exalted positions, while Sir Edgar and Lady Harriet sat farther down the table. Linnea could see them only if she bent to peer past her husband's large form, which she refused to do. She would not seek comfort from them for that would reveal weakness to the new lord—something she would not do. Besides, what comfort could *they* give her?

At first the wedding feast was subdued. To have the new lord as well as the old one seated before them just one day after the surrender was confusing for both the people of Maidenstone and the victorious army. But as both the wine and ale began to flow, the tone of the gathering altered. Voices grew louder, laughter erupted, and the coarse jesting common to a wedding feast began to reach the high table.

"Shall she surrender as easily as her sire?" a soldier of de la Manse laughed.

"Methinks e'en faster."

"No, no. Sir Axton will at least break into a sweat in the mastering of the daughter. 'Twas not the case in the mastering of the father!"

Linnea gulped red wine from the goblet she shared with Axton de la Manse, then set the vessel down with a thud. How dare they speak so boldly of her father's defeat? This time she did lean forward to see if her father had heard. But her husband moved deliberately to block her view.

"He is a man—or so 'tis said of him. Let his mother protect him if he cannot protect himself. He is no longer your concern."

She met his taunting gaze with murder in her eyes. "He is my father, no matter that I am forced to wed with you. And he is your father-by-marriage now," she added. "Had you even a shred of honor in you, you would not allow him to be insulted so!"

"And had you a shred of sense in your head, you would not defend him to me," he replied with a fierceness that caught her unaware.

Linnea recoiled in alarm, then caught herself before she could further succumb to fear. "What a fine marriage we shall make then. You without honor, and me without sense."

That last was spoken in a room gone silent save for her shrill voice. Her chest heaved with emotion, both anger and a sick dread of how he must respond to her insult. She waited, as did the rest of the watching company.

For a moment he was still, and so quiet she began to hope he might let it pass. Then he reached forward and caressed her lower lip with the back of one of his knuckles. "I will see this reckless temper of yours exhausted another way, Beatrix."

Her head was all the way against the back of her chair, so she could not avoid his touch. Though it was light, it was worse than an angry slap would have been. By his very control, Axton de la Manse managed to threaten her more effectively than if he had erupted in fury.

"Have more of the venison frumenty," he offered, watching her with his predator's gaze.

"I have had enough," she snapped, though her voice had lost much of its vehemence.

"Good." He sat back, a smile on his face, while everyone else strained forward in their seats, trying to hear their exchange. "Peter," he called to his brother whom she now knew served as his squire. "Escort my bride to the lord's chamber."

A murmur began at the lower tables, but Linnea heard only the rush of blood in her ears. *No, not yet. Not yet!*

He smiled. "I will be up directly, my dear. Do not worry yourself on that score."

She wasn't sure how she came to be on her feet. The boy had pulled back her chair while her husband just lolled back in his, studying her with the smug, possessive expression he might bestow on a newly acquired falcon or steed. Or wench.

"Come along," the boy demanded in an impatient tone.

With an effort Linnea tore her eyes away from the mocking grin of the man who was now her husband. Her gaze swept the hall, searching for help anywhere she could find it. But her father was staring past her, above her head toward the wall hanging that displayed the two bears of de la Manse. Her grandmother was glaring at the new lord, hatred and a trace of dread on her ancient face. They could neither of them help her now.

In desperation, Linnea turned a stricken face toward the boy.

His dislike was plainly written on his youthful countenance. But faced with her obvious distress, he did not gloat as she might have expected. "Come along," he repeated, but more civilly. " 'Twill do you no good to oppose him."

"Heed him, wife." The new lord stood, lifting his goblet, and the rest of the company scrambled to their feet as well. "To my wife, Beatrix de la Manse."

"To Lady Beatrix—"

"—Beatrix de la Manse."

"Hear, hear."

The toasts echoed in her ears, but there was no reassurance in them. Instead, they started a panic that raced throughout her body.

The boy took her hand and would have led her away. But they were both stopped by her new husband.

"No need of a maid for us this evening. I will see to you without aid of maids or relatives, or any others within our private chambers. No one," he added, sweeping the rest of his people, and especially his knights, with a warning gaze. "No need of a guard either, save for two men at the bottom of the stairs. All the other chambers above floors shall remain empty this night." Then he stared straight into Linnea's eyes, and though he lowered his voice, it yet carried clearly throughout the hall. "We may well have need of all those chambers during the next few days."

Linnea fled after that. There was no other way to describe her graceless exit. The boy did not lead her; she led him. She fled up the stairs, even though it led only to her doom. What other choice did she have? Only when she reached the second level and was faced with the solid door to the lord's chamber awaiting her across the antechamber, did she freeze in indecision.

"Go on in. He'll be up soon enough."

Linnea swallowed hard. She could not do it. Though she knew she must, she simply could not.

"Go on," the boy repeated, giving her a slight shove.

"Don't touch me!" she snapped, reacting to him as she should have reacted to his hulking older brother. But that could have done her no good, she told herself. Still, it felt good to release her fury on the boy; and he was, after all, a de la Manse.

He scowled at her. " 'Tis more than glad I am not to touch you, witch that you be. When I wed—*if* I wed—'twill be to a gentlewoman, not to one as lief to scratch your eyes out as anything else."

They stared at one another a long, distrustful moment. "Go away," Linnea ordered him, though morosely, as hopelessness descended over her. "Just go away and leave me be."

He started to do just that. But then he paused and studied her with renewed interest. "He will not hurt you, if that's what you fear. He won't hurt you—unless, of course, you fight him, which only a fool would do."

Linnea's chin came up a notch. "I scarcely think you knowledgeable about the pains men inflict on women—especially women they consider their enemy. You are still a boy, after all."

He bristled at that, as she knew he would. But instead of trading insults with her, he gave her an arch look. "You are not entirely hideous, you know. To my mind, were you to smile and greet my brother with welcome instead of hatred, you would find him a fair-minded man. He would not hurt you," he reiterated.

"And you tell me this to ease my mind, am I right?" she sneered, wrapping her arms around her.

The look he gave her was almost as cold as his brother's. "Be a fool and ignore my words. It matters nothing to me." Then he turned on his heel and crossed to the stairs.

Linnea did not stop him, although she dearly wanted to call him back. But she couldn't, despite the fact that his company was preferable to being left alone. The clatter of his steps on the stairs faded away. Now she was alone with nothing to do but fear what was to come. Arguing with Peter de la Manse had at least been a diversion.

She took a deep breath, then another, trying to calm herself. But it was a futile effort. To avoid panicking, she removed the circlet on her brow, then looked around. The antechamber was much as it had always been, save that the de Valcourt coat of arms above the door to the lord's chamber was gone. A pale shadow in the shape of a shield showed where it had hung for as long as Linnea could remember.

Nervously she approached the stout door she hadn't passed through since the day her mother had died, eight years previously. It scarcely squeaked when she pushed it open. Inside all was neat and orderly. The big bed with its heavy curtains still dominated the room. A fire burned low and steady in the hearth, throwing off just enough heat to keep any chill at bay. Two braces of candles sitting on a pair of narrow tables flanking the door bathed the room in a soft golden light. Did he think to·set the scene for her seduction so easily?

She stepped farther into the room. A trunk, two painted chairs, and a tall carved cupboard occupied the far end of the room, and pegs along one wall held several tunics— garments that were not her father's, and therefore must be Axton's.

Axton. Was she already thinking of him by his Christian name? No, he would be de la Manse to her. Or my lord. Or husband.

No, not husband either, for in God's eyes they could not be truly wed, not when she pretended to be Beatrix and he believed her. Not when she took her vows under the guise of a lie.

But Linnea did not want to think about her lie right now, nor of her awful sin. So what was she to think of?

Her eyes swept the room again, restless. Nervous. Then they landed on the folded stack of his warrior's garb— hauberk, gauntlets, and coif. Surely there would be weapons among his possessions. A dagger or a quetyll which she might easily hide and claim for her own.

She crossed to the cupboard and began to search past clean, folded braies, stockings, and linen shirts. She did not intend to use such a weapon save in self-defense, she told herself. She would submit to his husbandly demands because she must. But if he tried to harm her . . .

Her hand touched cold steel and she instinctively recoiled. Then her fingers closed over a short-bladed dagger, and she drew it out.

In the light the blade had a dull gleam. But the edge was anything but dull, she realized when she gingerly tested it against her thumb.

Where to hide it? she wondered, staring about the chamber. Someplace near to where she was most likely to need it.

She stared at the huge bed. Someplace within reach of the bed, she decided with a shudder of dread.

As she closed the cupboard and crossed to that threatening item of furniture, however, a voice and the sound of footsteps beyond the door set off alarm bells of panic inside her. He was here!

Without pausing to think, she shoved the dagger down between the pelt-covered mattress and the carved headboard. Then she whirled around just as the door flew open, and came face-to-face with her new husband.

"Well, wife," he said, just standing in the doorway, filling it and the whole of the chamber with his presence. "We are at last alone."

Linnea instinctively stepped back, only to come up against the high bed. Her heart pounded so violently that she feared it would burst from the confines of her chest. They were alone. There was no escaping him now.

He stepped into the room, graceful as a predator who knew its prey was well and truly trapped, and closed the door behind him.

He did not latch it, she noticed.

But then, he did not have to.

"Tell me, Beatrix," he began, moving slowly toward her. "How much has your grandmother explained to you of your wifely duties? 'Tis my experience that English maidens are kept far more ignorant of their duties than are French maidens." He stopped just before her, waiting for her answer.

Linnea lifted her head, determined to meet his gaze—and somehow hide her fear. "She has explained enough to me."

"Ah." His eyes roamed over her face. "Well, then. Let us begin."

Linnea stood there, waiting. She wanted to close her eyes and thereby shut out what would happen. But their gazes were caught together and she would not be the first of them to look away.

When he made no move, however, she felt a line of nervous perspiration trickle down between her breasts.

"Well?" he demanded. "Begin, wife. Do your duty to your husband."

Her duty? But how was she to begin? What was she to do first? She had thought her duty was merely to submit but . . . but she must be wrong. In desperation she searched her mind, nervously licking her lips. When his eyes fixed on that small motion, however, she had the first glimmer of an answer.

Kiss him. Begin with a kiss.

Accordingly, she steeled herself, leaned forward, and stretching up on her toes, arched up to kiss him. He was too tall, though, and he did not lean down as he should have.

Angry at this farce he played with her, Linnea snaked a hand around his neck and angrily pulled his head down to hers.

Their mouths met roughly, but she determinedly pressed her lips against his. Almost at once one of his arms circled her waist and hauled her flat up against him so that she felt the entire imprint of his body against hers. But she also felt his mouth stretched into a smile over hers, and she could not mistake the undeniable shake of his laughter.

He was laughing at her!

As if stung, she twisted her head away. But when she would have pulled free of him, his implacable grip kept her still against him.

"My, you are the eager bride. But have a thought, wife. 'Twould be easier by far if first we removed our clothing. Did your grandmother neglect to tell you that such is usually the first step?"

When he released her she stumbled backward, her face red with shame. She knew he mocked her, yet still it flustered her to think how foolish she must appear to him.

"Perhaps I should instruct you, Beatrix, so that there will be no misunderstanding between us. Come here," he said, gesturing to her to follow him as he crossed to sit in one of the heavy chairs near the window. He settled in the chair, his legs stretched carelessly before him, his elbows on the chair arms, his hands loosely woven on his stomach.

"I require but three duties of you." He held up a finger. "First you must care for my clothes personally. Mend them, see them cleaned, and kept in good order."

He held up another finger. "Second. You and you alone will prepare and minister my bath. See that a large enough tub is kept in here before the fire, and good soaps as well. Third," he said, and his expression altered. "Third. You will share my bed—or any other surface I would have you upon—willingly, and often.

"These three things and no others, save that you keep yourself clean and sweet smelling. Can you do as I demand? Willingly?" he added, piercing her with his granite-hard gaze.

Some men want a woman willing, her grandmother had warned her. And so it seemed that was to be her lot, Linnea realized. She must pretend to be willing—to *convincingly* pretend to desire what he would have them do together.

She should be pleased he would not treat her cruelly. But somehow what he demanded of her was even more frightening than the threat of violence. She began to tremble under his unwavering stare. Only the reminder that she did this for her beloved sister—and the rest of her family—gave her the strength to respond to him.

"I can," she vowed, hating the tremble in her voice.

He studied her another long moment, then leaned back even farther in the chair. "Well enough, then. 'Tis no cause for alarm that you know nothing beyond kissing. You will learn the rest in goodly time."

He stretched out his booted feet and gestured her nearer. "Come stand before me, wife, that I may begin your lessons."

Was there ever so difficult a course for Linnea to traverse than the short walk across the lord's chamber? She feared at first she could not do it. But then she recalled Maynard and the wounds he'd suffered for his family, and somewhere she unearthed the courage. Seven steps it took. She stopped just beyond his reach.

A mocking half-smile lifted one side of his mouth. "Closer, wife. Come closer."

She took another step, albeit a short one. It brought her within the span of his large, booted feet. "Shall I remove your buskins?" she asked, wanting to keep her distance from him as long as she possibly could. It was a hopeless and foolish whim, she knew, for what was to come was inevitable. But she couldn't help it.

"If that is where you wish to start, then do so. You remove my boots, then I'll remove something of yours—say, your gown." One of his dark brows slanted up as if in question. But it was no question and she knew it. He was tormenting her, plain and simple. And she must endure it.

"We'll proceed in that manner," he continued. "Each removing the other's clothing until both of us are naked. Then we'll move on to the next lesson."

Linnea knelt on the floor. She hated him in that moment, more completely than she'd ever hated anyone in her life. But she feared him just as much. The next lesson. She couldn't bear to think about that.

Her hands shook as she grabbed the low heel of one dark brown boot. It was warm, but she ignored that. She pulled hard, without any regard for his comfort. She just wanted it off as fast as possible so that she could back away from him.

Once both boots were off, however, he wiggled his feet. "The stockings, wife. Remove my stockings too."

She wanted to spit on him, but she didn't. She peeled off his stockings instead, relieved that they came off easily. But the sight of his bare calves and ankles, so strongly muscled and dusted with dark hairs, sent a strange jolt of mixed-up emotions through her. Though she should not, she felt an obscene curiosity about him. About men in general, she corrected herself. Men were hairier than women. Would he have hair . . . everywhere? A stain of hot color rose in her cheeks at the thought.

"Now 'tis my turn," he said. He leaned forward, and with a hand on each of her arms, he drew her to stand before him. Then he stood also and without warning lifted

101

her completely off her feet. As if she were as light as a down pillow, he turned and deposited her on the chair. He kept his hands on her waist, but now he looked up at her, not down.

" 'Tis my turn," he repeated to her shocked face. Then his gaze lowered from her eyes to her lips, and then farther, to her breasts.

Beneath her heavy gown and whisper-light kirtle Linnea's entire body tautened in fearful anticipation of what was to come. No! her mind protested. She tried to pull away, but she was trapped on the chair.

"I'll take this girdle first," he said, unfastening the brooch that held the silk cording around her hips. "Now the gown." His eyes raised back to hers while his hands found the lacings at her sides and made short shrift of them.

He must have felt how she trembled, for he paused a moment and looked up at her face once more. "You said you were willing," he reminded her. "Have you changed your mind?"

Linnea clenched her teeth. She would not be a coward. "I have not changed my mind, but . . ." She looked away, unable to meet his astute gaze.

"But you are untried and afraid," he furnished for her.

When she refused to answer, his eyes narrowed. "I wonder," he said after a moment or two, "exactly how willing you will be." His hands began to slide up and down her sides, a burning sensation that was not dampened at all by the heavy gown that yet shrouded her body. "Methinks you plan to lie still as a corpse beneath me in the bed, not recoiling, but not responding either. But I say to you that to behave so is not to be considered willing. So, let me explain better what I expect from you."

He reached down and began to draw her gown up, past her knees and thighs, baring her hips and belly and breasts in the nearly sheer kirtle. He pulled the gown over her head, then tossed it unceremoniously aside and returned his hands to her waist.

Linnea feared she might faint. When he began lightly to

stroke her hips and down her thighs, then up again, approaching her breasts, she began to tremble as violently as if the cruel wind outside did buffet her.

"No doubt you will resist me. A daughter of Edgar de Valcourt could do no less. But you are de la Manse now, whether either of us would have chosen to make it so. I will conquer you, Beatrix de la Manse. I will crush all your resistance and rouse you to a desire that you may very well hate. But I *will* make you willing. And I will make you revel in your own wantonness."

His hands curved around to cup her buttocks and he hauled her up against him. Her belly crushed against his chest. His face pressed into the softness of her breasts.

"No!" she gasped, clutching his shoulders and trying to shove him away. But he had her caught and in her struggles she managed only to fit them more intimately together.

"Be still, sweet wife," he ordered, nuzzling his face between her breasts.

"This . . . this is not . . . not seemly," Linnea gasped.

"Between a husband and wife everything is seemly. Tell me the truth, bonny wench. Do you like this?" He rubbed one of his broad palms beneath her buttocks and she flinched in shame.

"Or perhaps this will rouse you better." He began to kiss her breasts through the linen, wetting the nipples with his tongue. She shoved again at him, but he was stronger. When his teeth found her taut nipple in a soft bite, then he sucked it fully into his mouth, she let out a groan of dismay. His palm continued its wanton motion against her bottom and his mouth tortured her pebbled nipples until her fear and anger were muddied by an even more powerful emotion. He was doing something to her. She knew not what— No, she knew. It was like the wedding kiss when his tongue had roused a tiny, wicked part of her. He was doing that again now—and she was letting him.

With a mighty effort she wrenched free of his ungodly embrace. She toppled backward, but he caught her before she fell, and in an instant she was lifted high in his grasp.

One of his arms supported her back; the other held her beneath the knees. Her kirtle billowed beneath her, exposing her legs and much more for anyone to see.

But Axton was the only one there to see. When he laid her down on the black fur pelt that covered the bed, then stepped back and ripped first his tunic, then his chainse from his body, she knew she was foolish to deny him anything. He would take it anyway.

Linnea struggled for control as he disrobed. But the sight of his wide chest and powerful torso was too much. She scrambled backward on the thick bear pelt until she was up against the headboard, her knees at her chest, her arms wrapped protectively around them. When he removed his braies, she closed her eyes too. She didn't want to see.

A chuckle broke the silence, then the bed dipped as he sat on it. "This must go," he said, tugging at her kirtle. Like a stone carving she sat there, eyes clenched shut, allowing him to lift this arm, straighten that leg—whatever was necessary to remove the last of her garments.

Only when she felt his fingers in her hair, spreading it over her bare shoulders and arms, did she at last lift her lashes to view him.

"I will not begrudge you your maidenly fears," he murmured, surprising her with the seriousness of his expression. He separated one long, golden strand from the rest and wove it between his fingers. "But I will not allow my wife to stand with my enemy. I will make you mine in every way, Beatrix, bring you to heel—break your spirit, if I must. Do not think to oppose me," he warned. "For you will not like the consequences.

"Now," he said, tugging slightly on the tendril. "I will teach you the pleasures of the bed."

She would not fight him, she told herself when he gripped her ankles and slowly pulled her down the bed. Beneath her naked flesh the great bearskin caressed her skin with an obscene sort of pleasure. Above her his eyes did the same. She twisted to one side, ashamed to be seen so. But he rolled her onto her back, then held himself above her, poised on his knees and outstretched arms.

"This first time will hurt," he said as he nudged her legs apart. "But we dispense with that now so that you may more quickly find the pleasure of it."

So saying he sat back on his heels and began to run his hands up her legs to her hips and stomach. It was very odd to have him touch her so. A part of her was outraged; another part terrified. But a different part of her admitted that his touch was . . . it was interesting. He gentled her as she might do to a nervous cat or a restless pony.

Her eyes moved over him again, venturing past the pronounced planes of his face and down to his incredible chest with its pattern of dark hair and his hard-ridged stomach with its ripples of muscles. Then her eyes halted in horrified fascination at the straining muscle that reared between his legs.

He will grow it larger, her grandmother had warned her. But *that* large? she wondered, her eyes round with shock.

Before she could react, one of his hands moved down to the place between her legs, where that was meant to lodge. He stroked something and her eyes jerked back to his. He stroked it again, and Linnea felt as if a long banked fire inside her had suddenly been blown into flame.

A small flame, to be sure. But when his finger then slipped deeper and right up into her body, she nearly came off the bed.

"No! Don't!" She tried to clamp her legs together but his knees blocked her efforts. She tried to scramble backward, but one of his hands held her hips steadily in place.

"The first time I will do it fast," he told her, moving over her once more. "Just hold on and it will be done. Then afterward . . ."

Linnea did not hear what he said afterward, for that huge part of him fell heavy onto her belly, like a burning log might fall onto the hearth. He pushed back a little. Then she felt the thick tip prodding her where his finger had been.

"Wait—No!" she began as panic drove away all thoughts but of escape. "You have the wrong—"

"I have the right of it," he countered hoarsely in her ear, halting her before she could confess, in her panic, to her true identity. Then he pushed himself wholly into her.

He did it fast, as he'd said he would. But it hurt just the same. It tore and bled and burned. She would not cry out, however. She refused to. She would not give up what little of her pride she yet retained. Any tears she shed were lost in her hair or in the black bearskin.

While she fought for breath and control, he began a rocking rhythm of penetration and withdrawal, of a stretching discomfort and a momentary reprieve.

When finally he looked into her face, Linnea at once turned away, clenching her teeth in determination. She would survive this, she told herself. She would survive.

And as his movements grew faster and his breathing more labored, she found with relief that the pain had begun to ease. He pulled almost all the way out, then broke his pace and eased more slowly into her.

"Oh," she gasped, then immediately clamped her mouth closed. When he did the same thing again, instead of it feeling like a hot log ramming into her, it felt more like a stroke of hard, wet velvet.

"St. Jude," she whispered, as a tremor of unwonted pleasure washed over her.

Axton slid all the way in, then out. "Is it St. Jude answering your prayers, wife? Or is it your husband?"

This time when he began to move faster, Linnea found herself unwillingly caught up in the frenzy of it. And when he began to thrust inside her at a furious pace, she could not hold back her own panting response.

Of a sudden he jerked against her as if he'd been struck. She felt the sweaty quiver of his thighs, and beneath her fingers his arms tensed almost to steel.

When had her hands begun to cling to him?

He thrust again, once, twice. Then the full weight of him came down upon her, and his only movement was the great heaving breaths he took.

Linnea did not know what to do. She pulled her hands from the slackened muscles of his arms, but that didn't change the awkward, restless feeling that had come over her.

He'd aroused her—or he'd aroused that sinful part of her that she fought so hard to bury. Clearly he was finished—and he had not lied to her about what it would be like. Now, though, the feel of his warrior's body bearing down on hers created the strangest feelings inside her, as if he'd begun something that was still not complete. But he was clearly finished.

So what was to happen now?

As his breathing came slowly back to normal, she began to think he might have fallen asleep. She shifted beneath him, or tried to. At once he moved, lifting up on one elbow to stare down at her.

"Well, wife. The worst of it is done with."

Linnea looked up at him; there was no way to avoid it. The fact that they lay intertwined, with that male portion of him still resting inside her, was an act of such intimacy she could scarcely believe it. But to meet his astute gaze at the same time was almost unbearable. How could she hope to keep her secret from him now? He had but to look long enough into her eyes to see the truth.

Somehow she closed her eyes. She would have turned her face away too, but he caught her chin in his hand to prevent it.

"Look at me," he demanded. His voice held neither amusement, nor even tolerance.

Linnea complied at once, for she recognized the anger implicit in his controlled tone, even though she did not understand its source. Hadn't she done everything he'd demanded of her? But his eyes were hard as stone and narrowed into slits, and his body had gone tense.

"You will not turn away from me, Beatrix, or shut me out. Eighteen years has your family shut me and mine away from what was rightfully ours. But that has changed now and Maidenstone is mine again. I will not be shut out, not by your father nor by you. I will have my satisfaction from *you*, wife, here in this bed—"

So saying, he forced her legs wide and pushed himself deeper inside her. He'd become hard again, but though it did not hurt her this time, Linnea was even more frightened than before. He was angry this time. He did it now to punish her for her father's transgressions. She knew little enough of the dealings between men and their wives, but she knew this was not the way it was supposed to be, a punishment.

"No! You can't— Stop!" She twisted and flailed, then when that did not help, she struck out at him, hitting his arms and shoulders and finally his head.

But he was like a stone carving, impervious to her blows. That only made Linnea more desperate, though. Before it had been bad enough, but at least he'd not intended to be cruel. Now, though—

Her fist struck him hard on the ear. But with one hand he shrugged off the blow and her hand hit the headboard with bruising pain. In the midst of her panic, however, it reminded her of the dagger.

The dagger!

He began the same rhythm as before, but Linnea was too overwrought to succumb to the pleasure it could bring her. He did it to hurt her. That changed everything.

Her fingers clawed between the mattress and wood, searching frantically for the weapon. She would stab him with it. She would find it and make him stop.

Then she felt the cold metal and bone handle. She grabbed it with her left hand and struck out wildly. Anything to make him stop!

"God's bones!" He jerked to the side almost before the blade struck. Almost. Before Linnea could react again, though, her wrist was caught in a merciless grip that forced both fist and dagger down into the fur.

"You bitch!" He glared down at her with murder in his eyes. Linnea knew she was dead. He would kill her for what she'd done. But he would make her suffer first, she feared. Heartless bastard that he was, he would make certain she suffered long and hard for daring to oppose him.

She tried to glare right back at him. But the sting of tears heralded her complete failure. Unwanted, they nonetheless welled up, blurring her vision even when she tried to blink them away.

"Tears hold no sway with me," he growled. "They will no more save you from your punishment than did your puny weapon."

" 'Tis your weapon that is so puny," she responded, not caring anymore if she angered him. All she knew was that she must contradict him. She was already doomed.

"My weapon? Puny?"

He sounded so outraged that Linnea goaded him further. "Yes. Puny. And you are a fool to leave it in your cupboard for me to find."

He stared down at her. Then, without warning and for no reason she could discern, he began to laugh. First he chuckled, then it grew to a great shout of laughter that shook her and the entire bed.

"Puny weapon," he kept repeating between the waves of guffaws. "Puny weapon!"

Was he mad? Had ever a man been so perverse as he? Linnea could only gape at him, not understanding, but relieved that he did not mean to strangle her—at least not right away.

When he calmed, however, not much had really changed. He still lay upon her, pinning her to the bed with his greater weight and strength. He still gripped her wrist and she still held the dagger. The only difference was that a streak of deep red blood trickled from his right shoulder, all the way down his arm to his elbow.

"What shall you do now?" Linnea asked, unable to bear the suspense any longer.

"Now? Now we will see how effective is my puny weapon."

Linnea's heart lurched. St. Jude, but her situation had never been more hopeless.

But when he rolled off of her—still holding tight to her

wrist—it was only to pull her over and on top of him. He made her straddle him over his groin, so that his aroused male flesh lay just between them.

"Mount me," he demanded. He pulled her hand closer to his face and kissed first her wrist and then her fingers that wrapped around the bone handle of his dagger. But his eyes remained locked with hers. "Do as I say, wife. Find your pleasure upon my puny weapon."

He was a madman, Linnea decided. Then he flexed his manhood and comprehension struck her. His puny weapon? *That* immense thing?

He started to laugh again and pulled her upward just enough to allow him entrance to her. "If it is puny, 'tis only that of late it has had no exercise. But you will change all that, wife."

So saying, he grabbed her waist and steadily forced her down until she sat fully upon him and he was sheathed within her. Then he began to kiss her wrist and hand again, bringing the dagger perilously close to his neck and the vein of life that pounded there.

Could she kill him? Linnea wondered. Could she move fast enough? Did she have the nerve to even try?

But he was moving inside her, up and down, and he was forcing her to a slow, bouncing rhythm that distracted her far too much to think about murder. He stroked her with the full length of his manly weapon while he played erotic patterns on her wrist with his lips and tongue. And his eyes stroked the rest of her, her breasts and belly and face.

Her hair fell over them both, half-shrouding them, half-revealing. It was like some dark, dangerous game they played together. They each had their weapons, and yet it was not pain or fear that held Linnea in its grip. He did not claim her body in anger any longer, but in a strange sort of testing manner. She was in control, after a fashion. She reared over him and she held a dagger very near his throat.

Even though she knew he could shift the balance of power at any moment, for the present their situation was not entirely unpleasant. Indeed, the fire that flared between them brought an undeniable wave of pleasure that grew every time she moved over him. As she began to move faster, she realized that she controlled this wonderful, terrible pleasure.

By the time he released her wrist and gripped her hips with both hands, she had forgotten the dagger. She leaned over him, urged to a frantic pace by his demanding grip. Faster and harder, until something broke inside her. Something burst and erupted and she cried out in helpless surrender to it.

But he didn't stop. He forced her on and on, until the pleasure of it was very nearly a pain, until with a great cry of his own, he jerked over and over, spilling his warmth into her. Flooding her with his fire.

Linnea collapsed over him, gasping for breath. Beneath her his pulse pounded a mad race, and he labored for breath. It was not those details she noticed, however, but him. He was all she was aware of.

She was aware of his hand, rolling her onto the mattress. She was aware that they faced one another, that their legs were still locked together and their bellies still touched. She felt his breath on her skin and smelled the sharp scent of sex.

But she was unaware that she had let go of the dagger. She did not note its loss nor hear the thud of steel and bone on the wood plank floor. She did not notice the candles that guttered in their holders or the velvet darkness that enveloped the room.

Most certainly, as her eyes closed and her body relaxed in the exhausted sleep of fulfillment, she was unaware of the confused expression that clouded her new husband's face.

Chapter 8

Axton came awake with a start. But his first instinct—to reach for his weapon—was quashed when he recognized the familiar surroundings. A bed. A woman.

He took a deep breath and slowly exhaled, willing himself to relax again. Then he recalled the rest of it. The bed was in the lord's chamber of Maidenstone Castle. The woman was the daughter of Edgar de Valcourt.

And she was his wife.

He lay in the dim shadows of the false dawn, conscious of her sleeping form. One of her feet was tucked against his calf. Her derrière fitted against his hip and a strand of her hair was caught in the bend of his arm.

He should have punished her last night, he rebuked himself as he remembered everything that had happened between them. Something swift and harsh. He should have made it clear that to cross him was something she could never do again. And to draw his blood . . .

But instead he'd done just the opposite. He'd made love to her as if she were the only woman on earth and last night his one and only chance at her.

That she, a virgin, had found such a shuddering completion had astounded him. That he should care, bothered him more than a little.

That he wanted her now, all over again, made absolutely no sense at all.

But the insistent arousal between his legs silenced any mental arguments. She was his wife and he wanted her. There was no need for excuses or explanations. He could do as he pleased with her and no one would say him nay.

Least of all her, he thought with a smug certainty.

He shifted to his side and drew back the heavy pelt that covered them both. He'd meant to get his satisfaction from her, and he had—albeit not precisely in the manner he'd expected. He'd thought to exhaust his rage upon her and at the same time satisfy his sexual frustration.

But his rage had not lasted.

When she'd closed her eyes to him and tried to shut him out, he'd been furious. More than furious. And when she'd drawn that dagger and cut him, he could easily have murdered her.

But something—her courage, her tears, her ridiculous

reference to his puny weapon—had turned his anger to passion.

His hand ran down the line of her back. Her alabaster skin prickled with goose bumps. He could feel them. She smelled of woman and mating, and he grew harder with each dark whiff of their joining.

His finger slid down to the cleft between her rounded buttocks. Two soft dimples marked the upper curves of the sweet, womanly flesh. If he wasn't careful, he'd soon find her leading him around by his cods, so intense was the desire she roused in him.

Axton frowned and pulled his hand away. He must make her know who was her master. If not by fear, then he would do it with passion. After all, intimidation was intimidation. The secret to success in any battle was to recognize your foe's weakness and attack him there. It had worked with her father; it would work with her. She was clearly a woman of intense passions, so it was there he would attack.

He pushed his hair back from his brow as the idea took hold in his mind. He would bind her to him with passion. With the raw power of sex. He would make her a slave to it so that she could not do the same to him. He would master her in the bed—and any other place where he might come upon her.

He grinned at that thought. Should he find her in the kitchen or the laundry—or even in the herb garden—he would send everyone away, and he would make free with her body. Let everyone in the entire castle know the pleasure he took of her—and the pleasure she received from him.

It would be the ultimate disloyalty to her father and would go far in giving Axton the satisfaction he craved. He would bind his reluctant wife to him. Mayhap he would even cause her to love him.

Awash with triumph already, Axton drew her onto her back and viewed the soft, sleeping form of his wife. Tangled hair like golden silk. Pale skin as flawless as pearl. Sweetly rounded she was, with a narrow waist and full breasts. He would begin with those breasts and their dusky rose peaks . . .

Linnea came awake to sensations she could never put a name to. Like sunlight heating her from the inside out, though it was yet night. Like the juicy fullness of ripe peaches flooding sweetly through her. Like lightning, terrifying and exhilarating.

She arched up, more exhilarated than terrified, lifted as all the secret places of her body seemed to soar upward. Such a succulent feeling, as if *she* were that sweet, juicy peach.

A hand moved down her body in a heated stroke, and Linnea felt the first quiver of alarm. But she was distracted with the wet tug on her nipple by a pair of very clever lips—

"Oh, no!" She lurched away. Or tried to. But an impossibly large form pressed her down into the bed. Not *her* bed. Certainly not *her* thick bear pelt.

Her eyes popped open and though the room was dark, she knew. Axton de la Manse. Her husband.

"St. Jude . . . St. Jude . . ." she murmured over and over when the exquisite caress of both her breasts continued. He wasn't supposed to do this so often. She wasn't supposed to succumb this easily.

But she was, and he knew it.

When he held both her breasts in his large hands, then moved his kiss back and forth between the two, she was lost. His kiss had started a fire in her belly; the tug of his teeth, the subtle threat of it, made her burn all over.

This was forbidden. It must be. But that didn't change one thing about her reaction. When he slid his heavy arousal into her, she pressed up eagerly for it. When he caught her face between his hands, she had no choice but to stare up into this shadowed face. Their eyes met and held, and with every long, deliberate stroke, she felt her barriers crumbling to him.

The connection of their bodies was intimate beyond anything she'd ever imagined. But the connection of the eyes . . .

She felt it beginning, the hot, slow climb that had culminated in that strange, rippling explosion inside her. He fueled it with the leashed power in his warrior's body and the clear purpose in his unblinking gaze.

Linnea closed her eyes, for his scrutiny was unbearable. But she knew he watched her still and that he saw everything. The hot flood of color in her face. The restless tossing. The panting that sped up as she came closer and closer.

Then the cessation of all breathing as she arched and cried out.

He reacted too, with a shudder and a muffled shout. Then he abruptly rolled off her.

They lay like that, occupying the same bed, but far apart despite it. They were both hot and sweaty, but a cold chasm separated them. From unbearable intimacy to this . . . this inexplicable loneliness. Linnea shivered and was suddenly ashamed of her nakedness.

"Wait," he ordered when she moved away and sat up in the bed. He caught her by the wrist and rolled to his side and studied her. Though the room was dark and her heavy curtain of hair shielded her back and derriere from him, Linnea nonetheless felt completely exposed.

"I needs must visit the . . . the . . ." She could not say garderobe to him, for it was too personal a revelation. Surely he must know what she meant. To her relief he let go of her hand.

"Come back to bed afterward. I am not done with you."

She jerked her head around to look back at him. "Not done? But . . . but . . ." *But surely he must be done!* "But dawn approaches," she whispered.

He smirked. " 'Tis even more pleasurable in the light of day. I'll be better able to view my wife's very pretty body."

Linnea slid off the bed at that and snatched up her discarded kirtle. "I should think you would have had enough of . . . of *that*."

"A man never has enough of . . . of *that*," he said, mimicking her. "Especially when his wife is as delectable in form as mine. You are perfectly made for a man's touch, wife. Soft skin. Full breasts. Hair like silk, and though tight as a virgin should be, you have a fiery nature I would not have expected of a de Valcourt."

Every part of her had responded to his appreciative words. Her skin tingled. Her breasts tightened. Even her hair seemed to move and writhe under his words of praise. Most certainly did the place between her legs vibrate in both remembrance and anticipation. But the reference to her family name doused all her other reactions like cold winter rain on an open fire.

Any other de Valcourt would not be so susceptible to him, so receptive and responsive. Most certainly Beatrix would never have succumbed so easily to his unholy wooing. But she was not really Beatrix. She was the second twin. The bad one. Had she known that this would happen, that she would respond to his overtures with such passion, she would never have suggested such an insane deception.

But it was far too late to back out now.

"I have other duties to attend to this day," she managed to say as she slipped into her kirtle.

"Your duty is to me. To my needs. To my desires."

"But . . . but someone must see to the kitchen."

"Your grandmother can do it."

"But . . . what of my brother? I should check his wounds." She stared at him, desperate to be away from the influence of his steady gaze—and gloriously naked body. Even in the faint light that crept through the thick glass in the two windows of the lord's chamber, she could make out more of his body than was proper. Broad chest with its streak of dark hair. Lean hips and powerfully muscled thighs. And that insatiable thing between his legs, that insistent . . . weapon, she thought, recalling last night. *Puny* was hardly the word she'd apply to it, for it was his most powerful weapon in his dealings with her.

When she realized where she was staring, she jerked her gaze back to his face. He was grinning now, as if he knew exactly what she'd been thinking.

"Well?" she demanded, hoping to steer their conversation elsewhere. "May I go see to my brother?"

He considered a moment. Then to her surprise, he nodded. "But hasten back to me, my lady wife. I have a hunger that I would assuage again e'er I break my fast in the hall."

Hot color stung Linnea's chest and face, but she somehow managed to cling to her wits. If he desired her so much, mayhap he would agree to moving Maynard to a better place. "If . . . if I may be so bold, Axton," she added, hoping to please him with her agreeable nature. "Might I have my brother removed from the barracks?" She caught her breath as she awaited his response.

The smile disappeared from his face. "You may remove him from the barracks—and place him in the barn," he finished coldly.

"Oh, please," she blurted out. She crossed to the bed, wringing her hands together. "He needs a clean, quiet place where he might better heal."

Axton sat up and swung his feet to the ground. He was plainly unconcerned by his lack of clothing as he studied her. "If you mean to convince me, I suggest you find a better inducement than that. Why should I care that he heals? Would suit me far better if he should die."

At her look of horror, he gave her a calculated smile. " 'Tis not my plan to kill him, Beatrix. Did I plan that, 'twould already be done."

Linnea released a shaky breath. Thank God for that. But she still must get him to agree to move Maynard. She stared at him consideringly. He wanted her to convince him—or at least to try to.

What would Beatrix do?

Linnea forced what she hoped was a sweet and imploring expression onto her face. "I thank you most gratefully for allowing him to live." *Though 'twas you who caused his terrible injuries.* "If you will grant me this one request on his behalf, I promise to you that I will be a good wife—"

"You've already promised me that. Before God and the Church and every least soul at Maidenstone Castle you promised me that."

Linnea had to set her teeth to stifle the sharp retort that rose to her lips. Instead she advanced a step toward him, her hands knotted nervously. "Please . . . husband. As a wedding gift to me?" she ventured, though she knew she took a chance with such a ploy.

"As a wedding gift." He repeated her words and studied her a long, nerve-wracking moment. Then he smiled. "Now that we speak on it, I have a wedding gift for you. Come here."

Linnea froze. A wedding gift? If this was some coarse male jest and he referred to his . . . that weapon thing of his . . .

To her surprise he reached down and retrieved his tunic from the floor. "Come here," he repeated.

He held a small velvet pouch in his hand when he straightened up. Though Linnea was leery of approaching him lest he grab her and beguile her again with his mind-stealing caresses, she reluctantly complied. When she stood directly before him he loosened the pouch and spilled a delicate gold necklace into his palm.

It was exquisite. Even in the pale light of the solar Linnea could see that much. A gold chain of impossible delicacy, it was interspersed with fiery red jewels. And it was for her. She'd never possessed any jewelry of her own. Even Beatrix had not owned anything as fine as this.

Linnea's gaze rose from the long chain up to his face. "It's beautiful."

"Yes, it is." His eyes glittered. "Lift up your skirts."

"What?" Linnea's eyes went from misty with confusing emotion to wide with shock—then turned hard with fury. "How—how dare you!" she sputtered. "I am no whore to earn jewels in such a way! Is this how the men of your line do deal with women? With their wives?"

To her horror, he began to laugh. That only galvanized her outrage, however. "Spineless cur! Did you learn this at your father's knee? Did he treat your mother so!"

That killed his humor. But Linnea was not pleased with the emotion that took its place, for his expression turned as hard and unyielding as granite. "I will cure you of your venomous tongue yet, woman. Heed my words. Speak no ill of my father nor my mother. Not to me or anyone else if you do value your pretty hide. I will not abide it!"

He glared at her, daring her to contradict him. "Now, lift up your skirts."

When she did not do it—because she was too stunned by the vehemence of his threat, not because she meant to oppose him—he yanked up the linen himself. Linnea heard something rip and she nearly toppled over. But she refused to flinch. Let him do his worst upon her. Indeed, she told herself as he bared her legs and belly to his view, she would prefer he take her cruelly than evoke any feelings of desire from her ever again. It would make it even easier to hate him!

But he did not force himself on her. Instead, as she braced herself for his assault, she felt only his implacable grasp on her hips and the cool slide of delicate metal against her skin. He was fastening the chain around her waist!

A lump formed in Linnea's throat. That was all he'd meant to do, fasten the jeweled chain around her waist. His wedding gift to her, she realized with an unwelcome rush of guilt. And she'd insulted him.

His head was bent as he fastened the chain and on impulse Linnea stroked his dark hair. He looked up sharply at her touch, and Linnea saw the anger in every hard line of his face.

"I . . . I didn't realize . . ." she began, then trailed off. He was still her enemy. She should not apologize to him. Yet she did not like to be cruel when there was no reason for it, not even to him. She'd been on the opposite side of that coin often enough to know how it felt.

"Even if I'd meant to use you thus, and pay you in jewels, it would have been your duty to oblige me. Wife, whore, and everything in-between will you be to me, Beatrix. Best you remember that and never oppose me again." Then he reached between her legs and drew another length of the chain around from the back to fasten at her waist.

Linnea looked down past the kirtle knotted in her left

119

hand to see one gold and ruby chain circling her waist. From somewhere in the back a second chain looped down, passing over her derriere, between her legs, then up again and over her belly to fasten to the first chain. The second chain now dangled between her legs, a loop that hung half the way to her knees.

She raised her eyes back to his, confused and vaguely distressed. There was something disturbingly erotic about the feel of the cool metal and stones warming to the touch of her skin, and rubbing against the tender flesh of her inner thighs.

He met her gaze with eyes as dark and hard as obsidian. "You will wear my gift always, Beatrix. 'Tis but two matching necklaces. However, they are put to a far better use worn thus."

One of his fingers began to trace the path of the first chain. Along her waist, slanting down across her hipbone and low on her belly it slid. Then he followed the other chain lower, past the tight golden curls and along her inner thigh.

Linnea had no breath left in her body when his fingertip stilled. How did he manage to do this to her? some fragment of her mind wailed. How? But the rest of her was too completely in thrall to the erotic spell he'd woven to care. He did it. That was enough for her to know.

When he suddenly stood up and yanked down the kirtle she was trembling like a green sapling in December's gales.

"See to your brother. Put him wherever you would, but not in this keep. I'll not have him here. And, Beatrix," he added, staring hard at her, then letting his stone gray eyes roam slowly down, past her mouth and breasts and belly to stop at the place where the chain dangled beneath the cover of thin linen, "Think of me whenever you feel my chain upon you. It may chafe you at times, but it will also remind you of the pleasure I can bring you to."

He met her wide-eyed stare again and there was challenge and seductive power and all the knowledge in the world in his face.

See to your brother, he'd said. And so she did. She

snatched up gown and slippers and backed from the room. But she watched him as she went, watched the incredibly virile form that was now her husband.

Only in the antechamber, when she could no longer see him, did she begin to breathe again.

Dear God. Sweet Mary. St. Jude, but she was in serious trouble!

She managed somehow to don the gown and pull the laces tight. She thrust her feet into the soft dyed slippers without benefit of stockings. Her hair was an impossible tangle, and she was a sight in her wedding gown, come straight from her wedding bed. Servants would stare. People would talk.

But Linnea didn't care. She didn't spare even a thought for that. As she scurried down the stairs, across the hall, and straight for the barracks and her brother, she was aware of only one thing: the slender chain that swayed against her inner thighs with every step she took. The wedding gift that stroked and caressed her with every movement.

Oh, but she was the worst sort of sinner to be so aroused by such a thing—by such a man. She was the worst sinner that ever there was.

And she'd just been wed to the devil himself!

Chapter 9

Each day was proving to be more trying than the previous one, Linnea thought not an hour later. One day the castle fell to an invading army and she assumed the identity of her sister. The next day she succumbed to another sort of invasion, from a man who was also her enemy. It would seem nothing worse could happen to her. But Linnea had the distinct and uneasy feeling that her travails had only just begun.

She had found Maynard weak with fever again. A very bad sign. It made it only more urgent that she move him to more comfortable circumstances, a place where she could tend him continuously. Though there was no filial affection between her and her older brother, he had become a symbol for her. It was not enough that she had saved her sister from Axton. She must also save her brother. And today he did not look good.

She'd enlisted Frayne and Norma and two of the menservants to move him into Father Martin's chamber just off the chapel. She'd cleaned his wounds and given instructions that he be fed a vegetable broth and bread soaked in goat's milk, if he could swallow it.

But in the midst of her labors Linnea could not escape the ruby-studded chain.

Axton himself might have been there beside her, running the edge of his fingernail along her skin, so profound was the impact of the fragile length of jewelry. She wanted to forget about it and the husband she was bound to, and focus all her energy on Maynard. She wanted to yank it off, to break it into a hundred separate pieces and fling it into the moat.

No, she should disperse the fragments of it to the poorest of their people and let them reap at least some benefit of their new lord's perversions. They could sell the gold links and the ruby stones, and buy new shoes or new pots from the itinerant merchants who occasionally came through Maidenstone village. Or they could visit the fair held at Romsey each spring. She smiled to think of the two young shepherds, Osborn and Siward, sporting sturdy new boots and sucking on hard candies as they watched jugglers and acrobats and fire-eaters perform.

But her pleasant fantasy could not hold. The fact was, she would not dare to remove her husband's wedding gift, no matter how much she despised it. And she *did* despise it, she told herself as she carefully tucked a blanket around Maynard's damaged arm.

"Don't touch me!" he muttered in feverish complaint, then groaned at the pain speaking caused him. "Christ's blood!"

"What is this?" Lady Harriet's sharp voice caused Linnea to jump in alarm. "Why is Maynard put here, next the chapel?"

" 'Tis warm here and more comfortable than the barracks," Linnea began, backing away as she'd always done to keep out of her grandmother's striking range. But if Linnea was forgetting her role as Beatrix now, Lady Harriet apparently was not.

"Why is he not in the keep?" the old woman demanded. "In his rightful chamber?"

Behind his mother, Linnea's father stood, silent and shrunken. Though Lady Harriet glared at Linnea, her father refused to look at her at all.

'Tis because I am ruined, Linnea glumly realized. She was not honestly wed to Axton de la Manse, therefore she was a ruined woman. A fallen woman.

And if they but knew all the things that had passed between her and Axton . . . She shifted and felt the ruby and gold chain, like a thin streak of fire burning her leg.

"Well?" Lady Harriet stamped her stick imperiously. "What say you, girl? Is this the best you can coax of your husband? The priest's chamber? Did you not please him as I told you to do?"

"Grandmother, please," Linnea begged, humiliated to the depths of her being. She could not raise her eyes and face the curious stares of her family and their servants.

"Agh!" Lady Harriet limped up to Maynard's pallet and stared down at him. "How fare you?"

"I . . . I am dying," he croaked, then groaned in agony. Tears squeezed past his tightly clenched eyelids.

"Is this true?" This the old woman directed toward Linnea.

"No. No, I do not believe so," Linnea answered, praying she was right. "But . . . well, he'll be a long time healing."

"And the arm?"

Linnea looked up at her father's words. To a man of war, the loss of his sword arm was the cruelest blow that could befall him. To a knight, death on the field of honor was infinitely preferable to living as a useless cripple.

"I do not believe he shall ever wield a broad sword again." She stared apologetically at her father and then down at her brother. It was not her fault. Rationally she knew that. But she was overwhelmed by guilt all the same. Perhaps if she'd been more careful, set the bones more accurately. But even now, despite the misshapen swelling of his arm, she could tell it would never heal straight. Nor strong.

Maynard had fought his last battle as a knight and lost it. It fell to Beatrix now to marry a man who could return the de Valcourt family to power at Maidenstone. And it fell to Linnea to sustain their deception long enough for that to happen.

"Could I cast that man to the devil, verily I would!" Lady Harriet raged. She began to pace the small chamber, scattering the several servants as she went.

Linnea waved the servants away. Once the chamber was shed of all but immediate family, she faced her grandmother. "Tell me about Bea—" She broke off and glanced down at Maynard. He appeared to have fallen into a fitful sleep, but she nevertheless did not want to reveal anything to him that he might repeat in feverish ramblings. "Tell me what news you have of . . . her."

Lady Harriet gave her a searching look. "She is safe; 'tis enough for you to know that. As for our other plans, suffice it to say that we have begun the steps necessary to find an appropriate husband for her. Now, you tell me. How fared you in your marriage bed? Did he use you roughly or no?"

"I . . . he . . ." Linnea stammered then stumbled to a halt, her face scarlet under her grandmother's avid stare. "I . . ." she began again, only to falter when she met her father's pained expression.

"Leave us, Edgar," barked Lady Harriet. "This is women's talk." Then Maynard groaned aloud in his fitful sleep, and the old woman relented. "No, you stay here with your dying son whilst my granddaughter and I speak privately. Come along," she added, yanking Linnea's sleeve.

They sat in the chapel of all places, with Jesus on his

cross and the Holy Mother in her wall niche staring down at them. "Well?" Lady Harriet demanded. "Tell me what has passed between you. What have you learned of him? Where is his weakness?"

"He . . . he has no weaknesses," Linnea mumbled, unable to meet her grandmother's sharp gaze.

"Was he cruel?"

"No. Well, partly." Linnea swallowed hard. Must she describe what happened in complete detail?

"Did he hurt you?"

There was an odd tone in the older woman's voice, almost a note of empathy. Linnea could hardly believe it. She lifted her head. "He does not like to be opposed. He does not like me to say him nay. So long as I was agreeable, he was not . . . unkind."

The older woman digested that for a moment. Then her expression grew cunning. "Is he a good lover? Big, strong bull he may be, but there are men who do not, shall we say, measure up."

Linnea stared at her blankly. Measure up?

Oh!

Her eyes grew round. She wanted to know about that? "He . . . he is a . . . a big man," she stammered, blushing furiously.

"Aha." Lady Harriet nodded. "And did he take pleasure of you? Did he enjoy it—Did he do the deed more than once?"

Linnea could bear no more. She lurched to her feet. "I cannot speak of this. It is not . . . proper."

Lady Harriet did not stir from the priest's bench. "Your marriage is not proper either. Remember that, girl. 'Tis all part of our plan, as is the way he feels for you. I say again to you. Did he enjoy it?"

"Yes!" Linnea cried. "Yes! He enjoyed it three times!"

And so, God help me, did I!

The length of gold and bloodred stone burned against Linnea's skin, and she was consumed by the mad notion that her grandmother knew all about the wedding gift he'd given her—where it lay, how he'd put it there, and precisely how it affected her. When the old woman began to laugh, a harsh, knowing cackle, Linnea feared she would be sick from the shame of it.

"Three times! 'Tis a wonder he has allowed you to escape him this morning if he is so smitten. What does he now?"

Linnea felt naked before the woman's probing, and resigned too. She stared at the bare wooden floor. It needed to be swept. "I left him in his chamber."

"I see. And where go you from here?"

Linnea's voice grew very small. "Back to him."

The cackling laughter rose again, filling the chapel with a sound surely foreign to so hallowed a place. "Then go to him, girl. Spread your legs for him and make him forget everything but the pleasure he may have of you."

Then as abruptly as her laughter had begun, it stopped. She grabbed Linnea's chin in a brutal grip that brought them face-to-face. "Give him what he wants, *Linnea*, but do not forget what it is that *you* want. Prove you are more than the worthless soul we have known you to be. Prove your value to your family."

She released Linnea's chin then stood up and leaned upon her stick. "Go to him and make him believe you are his in all ways. But never forget the truth of who you are."

Linnea did not linger. She fled the chapel on legs that trembled, only to halt just past the door, unsure where she should go. Her husband awaited her and duty to her family demanded that she return to him. But she needed to be somewhere else, away from everyone, at least for a little while. She needed to reflect on the staggering changes in her life, and to gather her meager resources around her.

She stared at the steps that descended to the bailey, then up a nearby ladder that led to the wall-walk. Perhaps she could find a place on the wall where no one would bother her, at least for a little while. If she could just turn her face up to the sky, close her eyes, and let the wind blow over her, she might be able to think and find a tiny piece of calm amid the tumult that swirled around her.

In the bailey the everyday tasks of castle life had resumed as if no takeover had ever occurred. Three knights practiced with backswords in the tilting yard. Two children lugged a heavily laden basket toward the kitchen. A dog barked at a wood cart pulled by a solid pony and led by a man bent over with kindling. An ordinary scene, but today it seemed unreal.

She slipped down the steps, then scurried up the ladder, hoping she would not be unduly noticed. As Linnea she would not have been. But she was Beatrix now. She still wore the magnificent gown she'd been wed in. Her hair waved in hip-length streamers of gold across her shoulders and down her back. Not a soul in the yard did not pause to mark her passage. By the time she reached the wall-walk, the bailey was silent and she felt the touch of every eye.

Dear God, was she never to know a moment of privacy again? Not that she'd known much before. But this feeling of being forever scrutinized . . . It was worse than being ignored, and almost as bad as being despised.

She found a place in the southwest corner between two merlons. The embrasure formed between them was narrower on the inner side of the wall, but it broadened along the outer edge, creating a precarious perch that nonetheless was just her size. She squeezed into the irregularly shaped spot and sat with her back to one stone merlon. Then she wrapped her arms around her bent knees and stared out at the land that spread south to the sea.

Forests and fields as far as she could see. Sky of heavy, lowering clouds. It was an immense world, and she knew little of it. But still, it appeared far safer to her than did this new world she now inhabited.

She closed her eyes to the view and lowered her head to her knees. She would not cry; that was not her intent. But tears stung her eyes anyway and she had to fight them back.

What was she to do?

The answer was as obvious to her as was the rough stone at her back. She must play the role she'd assumed and wait for Beatrix's return.

But how was she to manage? How was she to retain her

wits when Axton de la Manse unnerved her so? How was she to function at all with that damnable chain reminding her with every movement of the things he'd done to her—and would do again? She could feel it even now, though she sat as still as if she were a part of the castle wall. Its delicate length was alive against her skin, as if it were his hand resting there, just pausing a moment before it caressed her again.

It moved along her thigh in a slow, sultry pattern—

With a panicked cry Linnea jerked her head up. It was him, not her imagination! No chain at all, but his finger touching her in places and ways that would have seen him flogged but one day ago. But this was a new day, and she was his to do with what he would.

Their eyes locked. If the look on his face was any indication, he meant to do it here and now.

Her heart pounded frantically against her ribs, for fear, shame, and anticipation battled for dominance inside her. Worst of all, anticipation was winning . . .

Axton could not tear his gaze away from his wife's flushed, upturned face. Her eyes were wide with fear, and dark with emotion. Her lips were parted and her breath came in short, shallow breaths.

As it had when she'd lain beneath him.

On impulse he leaned farther into the embrasure. He'd found her only because one of his men had pointed mutely toward the ladder. Had it been so obvious that he was searching for her? He'd planned to make a noisy scene when he found her, to order her back to their chamber in a manner designed to ensure that the entire population of the castle would take note. He needed, in some perverse way that he did not rightly understand, to prove his mastery over her. He needed her at his beck and call, and completely in thrall to him. And he needed everyone to know that she was his—that everything at Maidenstone was his.

But he had not expected to find her huddled on the precipice of the castle wall, a sheer drop below her to the foul waters of the moat. Her dejection was a blow to his pride that he had not anticipated. Hadn't he made certain she found her pleasure? Hadn't he heard her cries of rapture and felt her spasms of passion unleashed?

What right had she to be dejected after the night he'd just given her?

He was angry as he drew the gown up her thigh, angry at her disloyalty, and angry at himself for so stupidly expecting loyalty from *her,* de Valcourt's daughter. When she would have stopped him by blocking his hand and trying to tug her skirts down, he stilled her with a single word.

"Don't."

She stared up at him, a vulnerable creature trapped by a stronger, more crafty hunter. Stone walls on two sides, the open air beyond, and him, come to take of her whatever he wanted. He felt the wind, cool and erratic. It pushed the clouds across the sky and hissed over the crenellation that capped the walls. An occasional voice rose from within the castle, but for the most part they were alone. Surrounded by people, visible to both earth and sky, yet completely alone.

He pushed the heavy skirts up, past her bent knees so that the rich fabric pooled in her lap yet left her legs bare to his touch and his gaze.

This was even better than finding her in the bailey, he realized as desire rushed with an almost painful speed over him. He'd planned to take her by the wrist and haul her straight back to their bed, warning one and all not to disturb them. But he would do it here instead—or at least he would do it to her. No one would be able to see what he did as he bent between the merlons. But there would be speculation and there would be talk, and it would be clear to anyone who yet might harbor a loyalty to de Valcourt that de Valcourt's daughter was his, and so was everything else the man had ever claimed to own. It was all his, to do with as he pleased, and it pleased him to see her faint with desire for him here and now.

He leaned against the stone merlon, just barely restraining the urge to grind his aching arousal against the unyielding blocks.

"Oh, no . . . no—" She caught his hand when he slid it between her warm and silky thighs. "No," she pleaded, staring up at him with eyes as dark as the sea. "I'll come back with you. I just . . . I just needed a moment alone—"

"I would not have you unhappy to be my wife, Beatrix."

She shuddered at his words and turned her face away to stare bleakly at the vast stretch of land beyond them. But a tear spilled from the corner of her eye. He saw it and it infuriated him. Had he mistreated her he could understand her tears. But he'd been patient and attentive, far more so than any other man would have been.

He parted her thighs and shoved his hand roughly down to cup her woman's place. She was all warm skin and soft curls—and slow, hot tears. But the sight of her tears managed only to spur him on. He would make them stop, damn her. Just see if he didn't turn her sobs of sorrow into gasps of pleasure!

He slid a finger in her, all the way in, and felt a satisfaction in the soft gasp that escaped her lips. She was wet, and so hot that it made a lie of her tears. She could not cry tears of sorrow and yet be so ready for him.

He began a rhythm of stroking her, slow and then gradually faster, until he felt the muscles of her thighs relax their resistance and saw the heaving breaths that lifted her lovely breasts in so appealing a fashion. Could he fit himself in the skinny opening between the merlons he would have taken those breasts in his mouth; he would have bitten them and teased them until any reluctance or resistance would have become but a shadow of a memory in the deepest recesses of her mind. But he could fit only one shoulder and arm into the narrow space, so he pressed on with renewed vigor.

When her head fell back against the stone and her eyes sought his, he felt an arousal so acute he groaned. Damn her for doing this to him!. But he would turn it to his advantage.

He moved his finger to the taut bud protected by the sensitive folds of her female flesh. Yes, she was ready.

Within a matter of moments he knew he would have her, for she was moaning out loud now. Her hands gripped the stone merlon above her head. Her right foot slipped over the edge of the wall and dangled in space as she strained up against his hand.

Then she cried out and jerked in violent reaction. He caught her by the waist, for she was dangerously close to tumbling over the edge. But that swift movement brought his hard member squarely against the corner of the merlon.

"God's bones!" he exploded, seeing stars, it hurt so badly. Jesus God, but he wanted to double over at the excruciating pain. But he held on to her instead, until he could breathe again and stand upright.

"Didn't I tell you to return to our chamber?" he barked, hauling her toward the narrow opening and forcing her through it. "Was I not clear enough in my expectations of you?"

She pressed back against the stone wall, trapped by his arms on either side of her. Her cheeks were stained with hot color, her eyes still glazed from the scarcely dissipated passion that had gripped her. She could hardly speak for she yet gasped for breath.

If she was beautiful under lesser circumstances, she was ravishing now. The pain in his cods was swiftly forgotten as he grew hard once more. He could have taken the wench where they stood, and died happy—except that now everyone *would* be able to see what he was about. He did not care that the castle folk *speculated* about the goings-on between their lord and lady. That happened in all castles. But he was not going to take her within their view, like some camp whore. She was his wife, no matter the circumstances, and she would be mother to his children. He would not have her publicly demeaned. Still, he had to have her. Now.

"Get you to our chamber. Strip bare of all your clothing. Lay on your stomach across the bear pelt, and wait for me."

Then he made himself pull away from her and walk

toward the gatehouse as if he were not more aroused in this moment than he'd ever been in his life. He would give her five minutes, not a moment longer. He could not endure waiting any longer than that.

Linnea stared at Axton's retreating back. She did not know whether to rail at him, or beg him to return; whether to laugh at this ludicrous situation, or burst into tears. She had wed herself to a madman who seemed both to hate her and desire her in the same breath!

She slumped against the wall. Yes, a madman. But she must be mad too, for in the midst of her fear, she melted to his touch. Despite her shame, she quivered with unholy desire.

He wanted her naked upon that bear pelt. *Dear God. Mother Mary. St. Jude, help me.* She watched him stride down the wall-walk and disappear into the gatehouse, but his image yet remained in her head. Mad he might be, but he knew how to use every portion of his warrior's strength and cunning to lay siege to her body. She had no defenses against him. Worse, she actually enjoyed it. In the midst of his physical dominance of her, she found an incredible freedom, a wild and reckless abandonment of all caution and all fear.

Had he not held on to her, she surely would have leaped out into the air, for she'd felt already that she was flying. He'd flung her high into air so brilliant that it had pained her even to breathe it.

Dear God, but she was nigh on to being besotted with the man. And he, her enemy!

That thought sobered her, but it did little to douse the wicked flame that burned unrepentant within her. Shuddering at her own perversion, she pushed away from the wall. He'd said to wait for him in their chamber—*their* chamber. Did that mean he intended for her to share it with him always? Even her father, who'd adored her mother, had kept separate chambers.

But then, she should not expect her husband to be anything like her father.

She straightened her skirts as best she could and took a

deep breath. It did nothing to calm her, but it did get her going. As she made her way down the ladder, however, she was conscious with every step of the chain's movement against her. Oh, but the man was truly perverse. Between the burning feel of his gift upon her skin, the lingering aftereffect of what he'd just done to her, and the anticipation of what he intended to do next, she was so preoccupied that she did not notice the several stares and sidelong looks that followed her. Only when she rounded the first flight of stairs in the keep and came into the antechamber, was she forced out of her unsettling thoughts.

"Peter," she gasped as she skidded to a halt.

Her husband's brother looked up from where he sat, his back against a newly hung tapestry that depicted William the Conqueror's crossing of the English Channel. The monstrous animal he called a pet lay between his legs, its own legs opened and relaxed while its master groomed him.

"Well, 'tis my brother's wife. How like you his robust manner?" he taunted her.

Shame stained her cheeks with burning color, while a cold lump choked her throat. She could not spar with this boy right now, not and hold her own with him.

"That robust, eh?" He laughed at her discomfiture. But when she bowed her head and hastened past him, intent only on gaining the privacy of her chamber and the protection of the stout plank door, he pushed to his feet. The dog leaped up too, but it promptly sat down and scratched at some vermin behind its ragged ear.

"What have we here?" the boy jested. "No dire looks? No threats to poison either me or Moor? Don't tell me Axton has burned all the fire out of you." He blocked her way with a hand on the iron door latch. "If you are made meek, what entertainment shall I find to divert me from the utter boredom of this place?"

She should have bristled at the bratling's haughty tone. But Linnea simply could not. Mayhap he was right. Axton had burned all the fire from her—or at least he had diverted it into other areas.

She blushed all the harder. "Let me pass."

He studied her, then frowned a little at her subdued tone. "Art tired? Ah, but of course. He has worn you down with his attentions."

He chortled in the crude way of all young men, but even that was not enough to rouse Linnea's temper. She had other troubles far more serious than this boy's unpleasant humor.

"Let me pass," she repeated. She grabbed his wrist and flung his hand aside, then pulled open the door and hurried in.

Unfortunately, Peter followed right behind her.

"Go away! Leave me be!"

But he was as stubborn as his brother, it seemed, for he only crossed his arms and stared at her. "What is wrong?"

Linnea let out a hysterical laugh. "What is wrong? What is wrong? Better to ask what is right, for I can answer that with one word. Nothing. Nothing is right anymore. Everything is wrong, wrong, *wrong!*"

She spun away from him—as if that might disguise her agitation. But that brought her face-to-face with the bed. And the bear pelt.

She felt every single link of the chain against her skin. Every individual stone.

"Gloat, if you must. Then leave," she muttered. "But hurry, for Axton comes."

She heard the shifting of his stance. "He has sent you here to await him? Again?" His voice rose in awe of his brother's obvious prowess.

Linnea did not deign to answer. The fact was, she too was in awe of his brother's damnable prowess.

" 'Tis said you stabbed him."

Linnea jerked around to face him. How did he know?

"So, 'tis true." His face settled into a scowl that was a fair imitation of Axton's. "I hope he beat you for the offense, for if he has not, I will."

Once more Linnea laughed, but this time she was perilously close to tears. "Beat me? Yes, he has. But not in the manner you suggest. If you wish details, you should ask him, not me. He will boast and gloat and tell you all you would hear. Then you may both have a hearty laugh at my expense. Two big, strong men who have bested a girl. How proud you must be!"

Peter wanted to respond with some biting remark, some witty rejoinder. But he could not. Two big, strong men . . . They *had* bested her, hadn't they? So why did he suddenly feel no joy of it? Why did he feel cruel and mean-spirited?

He stared at her in confusion. She no longer appeared the intimidating witch who'd threatened to poison Moor. Even his rage that she would raise a weapon to his brother—her husband, now—unaccountably dissipated in the face of her misery.

He stood there, inside her chamber, his legs wooden and his mind blank of any words, either of torment or comfort. Though she was nearly his height, at that moment she appeared small and slight, a sapling brought low in the violence of the storm around her. She had not caused the storm, he realized. She was merely trying to survive within it.

He cleared his throat and shifted from one foot to the other. "Lady Beatrix—"

"Just leave me be!" She glared at him and he was relieved to see that she retained at least some portion of her temper. "Go away from here. Leave me at least one moment's peace before I must face my husband."

Peter backed out of the opened door and she slammed it closed. But he did not leave right away. Moor approached him and nosed in his hand, searching, no doubt, for a treat. Peter reached mindlessly into a pouch tied at his girdle and gave his pet a hard baked roll of flavored dough. While the hound crunched the morsel, Peter stared at the door to the lord's private chamber.

He stood there still when his brother burst into the antechamber.

"What do you here?"

"I . . . I was, ah, grooming Moor." Peter glanced from his brother to the closed door, then back to Axton. "She is . . . I mean, well . . . What is—"

Axton cut him off with a sharp gesture. "If you can find no better task than to linger here with that overgrown hound, then I will find one for you. Begone."

He did not bother to see if Peter complied, but with an impatient stride, crossed the room, threw open the door, then entered and slammed it shut.

Peter stood as he had before, staring at the door in shock. But it was worse this time. For when the door had been pulled wide, he'd seen something he'd rather he hadn't. He'd had a clear view of the bed and the enormous bear pelt that draped it. On the pelt, however, lying there without a stitch of clothing to cover her, had been Beatrix.

It had lasted less than a moment, yet the image was burned forever in his head. She'd been naked, her milky white skin and golden hair a startling contrast on the huge black pelt. And she'd been lying on her stomach. He'd seen her tiny waist, the gentle curve to her hips and the twin mounds of her derriere. Beyond that, the endless length of her legs had stretched, to the bare soles of her delicate feet.

He'd heard of pagan sacrifices and to his mind, she looked disturbingly like one. The fact that she lay on her stomach bothered him even more, for it was clear to him that she had been terrified.

What in God's name had Axton done to her? What was he doing to her this very minute?

He advanced to the door, then halted. No shouts came from within. No sounds, either of anger or violence.

He hesitated. She was his brother's wife. Axton was her husband, and as such, he had the right to do with her as he wanted—short of killing her or maiming her, of course. And Axton would never do either of those, he told himself, recovering his filial loyalty.

He thought of his parents and the love they'd shared until his father had been killed in a battle near Caen. But his death had not killed his mother's love for her husband. Though Peter never thought about the wife he would someday take, he knew now, with an unshakable conviction, that when he wed, it must be for love. He would not have a wife cower from him in their bed.

To think of his parents sharing such intimacies brought a flush of embarrassment to his cheeks. But he was nevertheless certain that on the few occasions they'd lain together, they'd done so in love, not in anger and fear as Axton and his bride now did.

Still, it was none of his concern. Axton would not welcome his interference, and Beatrix had made her mind clear in that matter as well. However, when he turned away, taking Moor by the collar as he quit the antechamber and trudged down the stairs, Peter was heavy of heart.

They'd come home to Maidenstone Castle, but it felt nothing like a home to him. Nothing at all.

Chapter 10

When she awoke she was alone. She knew it as surely as she knew night had fallen. Her eyes told her it was dark; some other sense—one without a name or a source, but an innate sense just the same—told her that Axton was gone.

Linnea rolled onto her back. She was naked, of course, and cocooned within the heavy bear pelt. The thick fur slid over her skin in a caress only one step removed from that of the man who'd wrapped it around her.

He'd killed the bear in a place called Gisors. He'd told her that in one of the brief moments of calm, as they'd lain there recovering their breath and their strength until they could begin again.

Linnea closed her eyes in utter dismay. A small cry of despair slipped past her lips into the shadowed silence of the chamber. She could not count all the times they'd come together in the way of husbands and wives—in the way of lovers.

She'd understood little enough of the goings-on between men and women before her marriage, but she knew that some women enjoyed it, while others dreaded it. Marriage gave no promise of enjoyment, so Linnea had assumed that love must be the factor that brought pleasure to the act, at least for women.

But now she knew that was not true. She had enjoyed it. She enjoyed it far too much. She did not love the man—how could she? He was her enemy, and besides, she hardly knew him. But she had cavorted with him as if he were her lover. She knew things about him now that she wished she did not know. And he knew things about her . . .

He knew she was ticklish. She knew he was not. She knew the scar on his chest came from the bear who comforted her now. He knew the mark on her leg was a birthmark. She knew he was twenty-eight and had been born at Maidenstone Castle, in this very chamber. He knew she was ten years younger and had been birthed in the room just across from this one.

But he didn't know she had a sister. He didn't know her name was Linnea. And he didn't know how close she'd come to revealing the truth to him tonight.

Linnea clutched the bearskin to her chin, feeling for all the world as if she were a pagan from the far-gone past. The fur slid like rough silk against her flesh, rousing a faint blush on her sensitive skin. He'd touched her in all those same places. He'd kissed her there and licked her there too, and tasted every portion of her body, it had seemed.

And she'd reveled in it.

She'd been so afraid at first—and so angry she thought she'd explode from it. He'd been angry too, though *why* she could not fathom. He'd been the one to humiliate her out there on the wall-walk where anyone might see them. The fact that no one had seen was no solace at all. They *might* have. But when he'd come to their chamber he'd been angry nonetheless, and she had expected the worst. That was why she'd done as he'd ordered, hoping to appease him in some small way.

Once she'd sent Peter away she'd torn off her clothes and lain facedown on the bearskin. She'd prepared herself to be beaten. She could have withstood it too, for she'd long ago taught herself not to react to pain. It gave the person who inflicted it too much pleasure. So she'd steeled herself for the weight of his angry hand on her vulnerable flesh.

That hand that had fallen on her had not inflicted pain, though. He'd been rough, but he'd not hurt her.

But he had made it clear that he possessed her, that he owned her and that she was his. Just as he'd defeated the bear and now took his pleasure of its silken fur, so had he defeated her. Then he'd taken his pleasure of her in ways that still boggled her mind.

He'd lain on top of her that first time, kissing and biting her, from the bottoms of her feet, up the tender backs of her legs, to her derriere and waist and back and neck. Then he'd raised her to her knees, spread her legs, and entered her that way.

And she had cried out from the pleasure of it.

"St. Jude," she whispered now to the cool night air. She had loved every moment of it, every touch and every stroke.

They'd slept afterward, a violent, collapsed sort of exhaustion. He'd roused first and found new ways to excite her. He'd kissed the chain he'd given her, following it wherever it lay against her skin, and then other places too. It was the ultimate kiss of intimacy, he'd told her when she'd started to object.

She'd been scandalized at his boldness. She'd even tried to stop him. But he had prevailed. He was stronger and older, and he knew what he was doing, he'd told her. She would like it very much.

He'd been right, of course. It had been an unthinkable act, and yet when she'd yielded, it had been exquisite beyond the telling. Even now she quivered to remember. Her very insides seemed to purr like a contented cat—an obscenely satiated cat.

But even that had not been an end of it. They'd slept again and this time she'd been the first one to awaken. She should have taken that opportunity to escape from him, at least for a little while. Instead, she'd studied him, sprawled upon the bed in his naked, masculine glory.

He was a magnificent specimen of a man. She might be naive and innocent of men, but she knew that much. Long and strong of limb. Solid and thick in the chest; stomach flat and rippling with muscles. And everywhere dusted with dark hair.

She'd touched him then, marveling at the different textures of him. Hard; soft. Rough with hair; smooth. Her fingers had explored lightly. Stroking and investigating.

That's when he had awakened. That's when he had discovered that she was ticklish and tortured her almost to tears. Then without warning he had entered her, and within a matter of seconds he'd brought her to stunning completion. She'd almost died in that moment. At least it had seemed so at the time. Now Linnea didn't know what to think.

At least he was not here now, and she had time to clear her head and try to reason things out. But a part of her would rather have not needed to think. It was easier simply to react, to surrender and go where he would take her.

But he was not here and Linnea knew she should be glad of it.

With a heavy sigh she threw back the pelt and lay there, allowing the chill of night to settle upon her. She was hungry. Starving. Had she gone the whole day through without eating? Had he? Or was he in the kitchen this very moment gathering a feast for them, that they might regain their strength and continue on in this mad orgy of physical pleasure?

It was that thought which pushed her to her feet. She could not spend every moment of her wedded life in bed with him, even if he was her husband. She needed to . . . needed to . . . She needed to do something else, but she was not sure what.

She found her kirtle, twisted and slightly ripped, but still serviceable. Her sister's clothes had been moved into the chamber, so she hastily donned the first gown she laid hands on. It was a simple teal-blue fitted tunic, with narrow sleeves laced tight at the wrist, and a strip of sheared white rabbit fur edging the neckline. She knotted a pair of plain wool stockings above her knees and stepped into a pair of everyday leather slippers.

Her hopeless hair she caught in one hand and after tying it back with a bit of cording, covered it with a wispy length of gauze veiling, anchored in place with a carved, bone hairpin.

It would have to do, she decided, tucking the slackened wrist cords up into the sleeves. Her girdle—the one with the key Axton had given her—went around her hips. Then she hurried from the empty room and into the antechamber.

She listened at the door to the stairwell. A voice or two sounded quietly from the hall, just murmurs that she could not put a name to. She did not want to run into Axton, but she would have to go down the stairs and take her chances if she was to find something to eat.

But with every step she knew she did but delude herself to think she was somehow escaping him. There was no escape from him. The chain that burned against her inner thighs was a constant reminder of that fact, as was the damp soreness that went much deeper.

The hall was dark. All the torches had burned down save the one beside the door to the bailey. Opposite that the fire that softly hissed in the big hearth cast a small half-circle of light, an eerie, red glow in the dark cavern of the empty hall. A brace of candles flickered at one end of the table that had not been put away, and it was there a few men gathered still.

One of them lay on his back upon the bench beside the table, his arms crossed over his chest. He seemed to be asleep, and his snores rose in a soft, regular rhythm. Another man sat head down, his elbows bent on the table, studying his heavy mug of ale—or else asleep sitting up, she speculated. It was the man with the red beard, she realized. Axton's man, Sir Reynold.

But where was Axton?

"I would be better rid of them."

Linnea nearly leaped out of her skin. Though not loud, the words caught her unaware, and she pressed a hand to her chest, above her pounding heart. The man at the table lifted his head and looked to his right. Linnea followed his gaze only to find precisely what she'd not wanted to find. Her new husband sat in the lord's chair. She'd not spied him before because the chair was turned to face the fire. But only the lord of Maidenstone would dare sit in that chair.

Her heart did an odd sort of dance, a thumping response to him that she would prefer to think was caused of agitation rather than anticipation. She could not possibly want to do any of *that* again. Only a complete wanton could desire even more of such shameful behavior!

"I would like to be rid of them all," he repeated. "Father, son, and crone, as well."

"But you would keep the daughter." It was not a question, Sir Reynold made, but a statement.

Axton let out a snort that sounded like derision. But he did not answer.

That seemed to goad Sir Reynold on, however. "I take it the minx suits you. 'Tis the talk of the castle, how you have bedded her the whole day long." He laughed. "Was the wedding night inadequate, that you needed the entire day to prove you could do better? Or is she simply a slow learner?"

Linnea's ears turned hot with shame. Axton de la Manse had no need to prove his prowess. But she . . . she knew nothing. Did he consider her a slow learner? Was he disappointed in her?

Axton pushed himself out of the chair and moved to stand before the fire. He'd donned plain braies and a loose chainse. He wore neither weapon nor even a girdle. Even his boots were low and ordinary. But there was nothing ordinary about him, she saw at once. Even garbed little better than a squire, he was every inch the lord. It should have angered her to no end, but instead Linnea felt a foolish prickle of pride. This was her husband. She was married to him.

"The son and father will remain my prisoners until

Henry orders otherwise. The old crone, however, can go to Romsey Abbey," Axton said.

"Romsey Abbey, you say. Well, then, it is too bad you did not decide this sooner. The priest has already departed for there. She might have accompanied him, had I known that was your intent."

Axton turned toward his captain. "The priest is gone from the castle? Why? And why there? Who authorized his travel?"

"You did." A slow grin broke over the other man's face. "As I recall, however, you were staring at your bride when we spoke on it. Never say you were distracted at the time?" he added, laughter in his voice.

Axton thrust both of his hands through his hair. "Apparently I was. When did he leave?"

"Before first light. Why? Does it matter?"

Linnea held her breath. The real Beatrix had traveled with Father Martin. Did Axton suspect anything? Did he know how they plotted against him? Did he know who she really was?

Axton shrugged. " 'Tis in my nature to be suspicious. Arrange a small band to deliver the old woman to the abbey—the sooner the better. Keep two men at watch over de Valcourt, and one on his son."

"What of the daughter? Who will keep a watch over her?" the bearded fellow asked, not bothering to hide his mirth.

But Axton was not annoyed by the man's humor. There was a bond between those two, Linnea noted. Axton did not appear the sort to suffer the jesting of just anyone.

"I will manage my wife—"

Axton broke off, and Linnea at once knew why. He'd seen her, though she yet stood in the shadows of the wall. She felt the touch of his eyes and it was like a familiar shock to her system.

"I will manage my wife," he repeated, but this time the words were spoken directly to her, not to his man. Sir Reynold must have recognized the change in his voice, for he looked around and grinned when he spied her.

"Ho, Maurice. Come greet your mistress, man. Do not offend her with your stinking breath and worse manners." Sir Reynold kicked the bench that held the third fellow, and with a muffled curse, the man landed on the floor.

"Whoreson bastard!" the fellow sputtered, springing instantly to his feet. His hand went to the hilt of the dagger sheathed at his waist, but he did not draw it. Indeed, he seemed to forget why he'd reached for it and now stood there befuddled. Swaying on his feet.

Drunk.

Was Axton drunk too? Linnea's eyes darted back to her new husband. Had he been down here, drinking with his friends, telling them every aspect of what had occurred between him and his wife—his wife who was his enemy? Her face flamed with humiliation to even think it. But she would not allow him to dominate her here as he did in their bedchamber. Now was not a time to emulate the yielding Beatrix. She must be more like her grandmother, proud and aggressive. But restrained too.

She stepped forward into the light, her initial hunger forgotten. "If it please you, husband, I would keep my grandmother with me. There is no need to send such an old woman away from her home."

She broke off when his head jerked up. "Maidenstone is not her home." He bit the words out, sounding not so much drunk, as angry.

Linnea stifled a groan and gnawed her lower lip. How stupid of her. What a poor choice of words. She should have known that to defend her family would infuriate him. But the damage was done. "She is an old woman," she repeated, in a soft, pleading voice. "This is the only home she has left."

She could not see his expression, for the fire was behind him. But she did not miss the tension that wrapped around him like another blanket of darkness. It showed in the slow, loose-limbed way he strolled toward her. It was there in the precise way he set his pewter chalice down as he passed by the plain trestle table. She felt it in the very air she breathed, cold and fiery, like hell must be.

144

She should not have pressed the point, she realized too late.

"The fate of every de Valcourt lies entirely in my hands." He leaned forward so that his face was but inches from hers, hard and terrifyingly cold. "They live, die—or sprawl naked upon my bed—as I will it."

So vicious were his quietly uttered words that Linnea stumbled backward, stunned and scarcely able to believe her ears. This was the man who'd caressed her and aroused her so easily she'd felt herself a wanton. But he could just as easily slash her to pieces, she now saw. He could just as happily crush her like chalk beneath his heel. Why had she ever imagined that he might be different?

She gathered her wits and her courage and bound them to her with fury. She could not bear to look at his two men, for fear she'd see their snickering leers. But *him* . . . She glared at him, made brave by her hatred and her utter contempt for him.

"How brave a man is my husband. He bests women and old men and gravely injured ones as well."

One of his brows raised in black, mocking humor. "He was not gravely injured when first I encountered him."

Had Linnea been possessed of a weapon, she would have attacked him for that. How dare he boast of so loathsome an act to her! How dare he nearly murder her brother, imprison her father, send her grandmother away, and then bed her as if she should be grateful to him!

"I despise you!" she swore, shaking from the force of her feelings. "I despise you and . . ." Her mind searched for a way to cut him as he so easily cut her. "And I *cringe* to think that I must submit to your disgusting touch—your revolting attentions. You make me want to retch!"

She had the fleeting pleasure of watching the smugness drain from his face. But the fury that replaced it banished her pleasure before it could take hold. She flinched when he raised a knotted fist. He would hit her; he would kill her with the power of one angry blow.

One of his men gasped. The other grabbed for his liege lord's arm before he could lash out.

"Get away from here." It was Sir Reynold who growled the order at her.

Linnea did not have to be told twice. She backed up, but all the while her eyes were fastened to her husband's face. There was murder in his eyes and she felt a slow, sinking fear rise up to swallow her whole. He would kill her now. And even if he should not, her grandmother would. This was not how she was supposed to deal with her husband. It was her role to make him content, to lull him into complacency. Instead she had only fired him to new heights of rage.

Axton threw off Sir Reynold's hold. The man knew better than to intercede a second time, however. When Axton strode furiously toward Linnea, Sir Reynold watched but did not interfere.

"Whether you despise my touch or ache to feel it, 'tis no care of mine, madam. You are my wife and you are mine to do with what I please. 'Tis *my* pleasure that I care for, not yours." His eyes bored into hers, ice-cold. Granite hard. "Now, get you to my chamber and await my return. Wife," he added, making of that single word the cruelest slur she'd ever heard.

Linnea wanted to oppose him. After all, what worse punishment would that earn her than whatever he already planned for her? But she could not. She was too afraid to do anything but duck her head, turn, and flee, just as he'd wanted her to do. She hated herself for being such a coward. Maynard was not a coward, nor should she be. But she was, and as she shrank into the shadows of the stairs, she knew she was too afraid to return to the solar and await him and his wrath.

It was not the need to oppose him which made her slink back down the stairs and wait until he faced the fire once more. It was not foolish bravery but unadulterated fear. She did not know where her grandmother was housed, but she knew she must find her. Lady Harriet would be furious with her too, but she, at least, would help her figure out what to do. Linnea dreaded facing her grandmother, but she was the only ally she had. Better to deal with the Lady

Harriet's fiery temper, than the ice-cold fury of her husband.

Axton burst into the room, then could hardly believe his eyes. He was drunk; he did not pretend otherwise. But it was not too much red wine that deceived his eyes. She was not here! The coldhearted little bitch was not here!

He strode across the room, flung the bear pelt aside, then ripped the luxurious down mattress from the bed and threw it across the room. A cupboard crashed down, dumping his clothes and personal belongings across the floor. He shoved over her trunk and tore a tapestry from its anchors. She was not here!

He would kill her when he found her. By God and all the saints, he would kill her!

He kicked the heavy bed then, when it did not budge, threw his entire weight against one of the posts, as if he could shove the massive piece of furniture through the very walls of the chamber.

Something cracked, and the bed sagged. But it did not give, and that enraged him further. He spun around, searching for his sword. He would find her and she would be sorry—

The room swam and he grabbed the bedpost. She was a conniving witch and she'd waited until he was drunk to make her move. He clung to the post, blinking hard as he tried to clear his head. She'd waited until he was drunk with the want of her—and drunk from too many toasts on his amazing good fortune to have wed a woman of such a passionate nature. She'd lulled him and then cut him down as surely as if she'd gutted him with his own dagger.

She was revolted by him. Disgusted.

He wanted to howl with fury, to find her and force her to take it back. To prove that she was wrong. But she wasn't there.

He stared around the solar, at the shambles he'd made of the place, and as quickly as his temper had exploded, so now did it drain away. It was better that she was not here. If he'd burst in and found her here, whether cowed or belligerent, she would only have angered him more. There was something in her that pushed him to extremes. Extremes of passion. Extremes of anger.

His knees began to fold beneath him and he slid to the floor. She'd inspired him to extremes of passion, but he'd inspired only disgust in her.

And now everyone knew.

He groaned and his head fell forward into his hands. He had his home back. He held his enemies in his hands. But his wife spurned him. She said he made her want to retch.

His stomach knotted and roiled. At the moment *he* wanted to retch. But he would not. He was no woman to gnash his teeth and become sick from his emotions. She was his wife. He was her husband. She would obey him and conform to his wishes whether she retched the whole night long from it.

Tomorrow he would tell her that very thing. But right now . . . right now he would just lie down and think how best to proceed with her.

Peter peered cautiously into the lord's chamber. He'd heard the ruckus, the oaths and smashing furniture and furious cries. It had to be that woman. No one else could anger Axton so; no one else had the ability to. Even her father, whom Axton had hated since forever, did not rouse his temper to such furious outburst. Edgar de Valcourt inspired cold vengeance in Axton; Beatrix, however, made him boil over with emotion.

But much as Peter wanted to blame her for his brother's current condition, that image of her, naked on the bed, continued to haunt him. She was much too small to withstand Axton's rage, whether it be a rage of temper or sexual in nature. She was too vulnerable.

That's why he'd lingered in the keep tonight, finding a place to sleep in the pantler's cabinet. He'd heard every word that had passed in the hall. He'd heard his brother's cryptic responses to his men about his wife, but he'd also heard the pride and satisfaction in his voice. Then he'd heard Linnea's foolish defense of her family followed by

Axton's insults and her own. He'd seen his brother raise his fist, and Reynold grab for his arm. He'd witnessed Beatrix's hasty departure, then watched as his brother drank himself into a deeper and blacker rage.

He'd watched and he'd waited and he'd worried. He hadn't wanted to follow Axton above stairs, but the image of that slender, naked body at the mercy of Axton's uncertain temper had forced him to it. He'd been more than relieved to find her absent from the chamber, even though the repercussions on the morrow would be harsh.

But tomorrow Axton would be sober. Tomorrow there would be witnesses. And mayhap their mother would arrive soon. Surely she would be able to talk sense into her eldest son, Peter hoped as he spied Axton sprawled beside the remnants of his broken bed.

He held the small torch he carried higher and surveyed the brother he'd always worshipped. He frowned in confusion. Never had he seen Axton as angry as he'd been this night. Never had he seen him in such a drunken state. And all on account of *her*.

He shook his head in bewilderment. He'd better go find her. God help them all if the wench was stupid enough to flee the castle itself. If tonight's display were any indication, Peter feared his brother would turn the entire countryside upside down to find her.

Chapter 11

Linnea's eyes watered and her cheek burned. But she did not flinch away from her grandmother's stinging slap. Though this time she knew her grandmother's wrath was deserved, the habit of stoic resistance was too ingrained for Linnea to cringe.

"I *knew* you were unfit for this task! I knew you would fail your family! One thing only have I asked of you and what is the result? Failure. You are the ruination of this family!"

Linnea stood miserably before her grandmother's onslaught. She would have preferred further physical punishment; she was more inured to that. But this . . . Every curse and every accusation fell like a vicious blow upon her, hurting her in ways no mere slap could ever do.

It was true, all of it. She'd let her temper and her foolishness hold sway where reason and cunning should have reigned. And now she feared she would never be able to regain the ground she'd lost with her enemy husband. He would send her grandmother away, imprison her father, and do God knew what to poor Maynard. And it was all her fault.

Her grandmother paced the small chamber given to her. It was mean housing, the cook's chamber behind the kitchen. Her father was under guard with Maynard in the priest's chamber. Of them all, only she yet resided in the keep. All four chambers had Axton kept empty to afford them privacy. But instead of using that to her advantage, in one fit of temper Linnea feared she had wasted it all.

"Did he say what he would do with Maynard and Edgar?" The old woman bit out the words, glaring at Linnea.

"He said . . . he said they would remain his prisoners until Henry, Duke of Normandy, comes."

"He comes here? Henry of Anjou here?"

"So he said." Linnea peered warily at her grandmother. "And he wouldst see me confined at Romsey Abbey." The old woman continued her agitated pacing, her stick a sharp click against the stone floor. Then she turned with a start, her black skirt belling out around her. "Mayhap is for the best. These be uncertain days. There is not a nobleman in England who does not hope to gain Henry's goodwill. The right position . . . The right loyalties . . . Father Martin is not wily enough to represent the de Valcourt family's best interests. But once I am at the abbey, I can better solicit the right husband for her. You—" Her eyes lost their speculative look and fastened once more in dislike upon Linnea. "You will remain here and approach your husband as the meek and obedient bride you are meant to be. You will grovel and beg for his forgiveness, if that proves necessary to appease him. Wilt barter thy body to ensure the continuing safety of your father and brother—understand me, girl? Beatrix?" she added, with threatening emphasis.

As he crept toward the door, Peter heard only the last of the old crone's words. He gritted his teeth against the epithets that rose in his throat. So that was the way of it. The young bitch was to deceive his brother at the behest of the old bitch. He wanted to wring both their necks. At least men fought face-to-face. But women . . . Women slunk around in the shadows, smiling on the surface while they plotted behind your back.

Well, not all women, he amended, thinking of his mother and her complete devotion to his father. But these de Valcourt women, they were nothing like his mother.

He pulled back into the black shadow of the wall. It was a moonless night and easy to hide. But it had also been hard to find his brother's new wife. He'd only come upon her just in time to hear her grandmother's orders.

Barter her body to ensure the safety of her brother and father. He would have to tell Axton.

Then he frowned. Axton would not like to hear this. He would be furious, both at her and at anyone—like his younger brother—who knew the truth of his pretty wife's opinion of her husband. He would wonder what had prompted Peter to follow her, and he would guess what his little brother had overheard earlier in the hall.

Peter rubbed his hand over the top of his head. Axton would not appreciate his brother knowing what Beatrix the Bitch had thought about his skills in the bedroom.

And yet, what could he expect when he did frighten the foolish wench right out of her wits?

Remembering how she'd huddled terrified on the bear skin when Axton had slammed into the lord's chamber, he was amazed she'd faced Axton in the hall later. If nothing else, she was a brave one, he grudgingly conceded. Brave, or exceedingly stupid. Jesu, but this had become so confusing. Loyalty demanded that he tell his brother what his wife did plot. But another sort of loyalty—that of loyalty between men—demanded that he remove himself completely from such goings-on and let his brother deal with his wife as he would. It was not as if the women's plotting would actually come to aught. The fate of Edgar de Valcourt and his son rested entirely in Henry Plantagenet's hands. Beatrix's pretty little tricks would not influence anything.

Besides, in time she might come to accept Axton's attentions. Some women were hot-blooded, he'd heard. Others were cold as a witch's teat. Maybe this was something Axton should work out for himself. Most assuredly he would not welcome his younger brother's interference in matters of this sort.

Maybe the best thing would be for him to simply keep an eye on his brother's wife. Once the old woman was gone, Beatrix the Bitch might soften a bit.

And even if she did not, he reasoned, she was only a woman. She might enrage his brother, but that would eventually pass. In the greater scheme of things, she was really of no consequence at all.

Linnea crept slowly up the stairs. In the great hall servants had begun to stir, building up the fire, pulling out the many tables, beginning the day's routine. Above stairs, however, all was still as death.

She'd left her grandmother under strict orders to return to her husband, ashamed, repentant, and willing to do anything to earn his forgiveness.

It would not precisely be an act for her to portray those emotions. She was ashamed of how easily she'd forgotten her role as Beatrix. She was repentant of her quick temper and willing to do whatever she must to save her family, even if she must barter her body, as her grandmother had ordered. Hadn't Maynard done much the same every time he went out in defense of Maidenstone? Didn't he even now pay a dear price with his body?

She could do no less.

Yet as Linnea peered into the antechamber and toward

the door that led into the lord's private chamber, her insides were quaking. She was too terrified of what Axton would do when he saw her, terrified of his anger and the punishment he most assuredly would mete out. But she was just as terrified of the other reactions he could rouse in her if he put his mind to it. That was when she felt most in his power and most vulnerable to him.

It would probably be better for her if he had struck her last night. It would harden her resolve against him. But he hadn't struck her. His man had grabbed his arm, true. She wondered now, though, whether he would actually have hit her. After all, he'd been so tender before, rough and tender and passionate, all at the same time.

She edged into the antechamber and felt the disturbing slide of the ruby chain between her thighs. A shiver of remembered passion stirred deep inside her.

What manner of man had she been wed to, that he could be such a bewildering combination of warrior and lover, husband and foe? Would it ever be this way between them?

At that foolish thought she shook her head. Was she already forgetting that this was only a role she played? He and she would not be wed long enough to know what he truly was like. Nor was it wise for her to wonder or care. She was here to placate him, to beg his forgiveness and make him content. That was all.

Best that she got on with it.

Drawing a deep breath, she straightened to her full height, then walked across the room, measuring every pace. Not too fast and bold, but neither would she slink in fear. Well, maybe a little fear was appropriate. And she *was* afraid.

The door stuck a little, then creaked when she shoved it open. She caught her breath in alarm, but when nothing stirred, she peeked inside.

The entire chamber was a shambles. The hairs rose up on the nape of Linnea's neck. Oh, but he must have been furious beyond her wildest imagination to tumble the cupboard over and fling everything about. His shirts, her

153

gowns—Beatrix's gowns, actually. And the bed! It did list to one side, while the mattress lay against the far wall—

And Axton sprawled on it!

She almost slammed the door shut and ran away at the sight. But she knew that would gain her naught. When he did not move—when she heard only the sound of his light snoring, a slow, steady rhythm—she gathered her courage, pushed into the room, and warily studied her sleeping husband.

He did not look nearly so threatening asleep, she decided as she picked her way across the littered floor. He'd thrown his tantrum and tired himself out, like a spoiled child might. Like Maynard had so often done.

He'd also been helped along by a considerable quantity of wine, she surmised when she caught a whiff of his breath. Just like her father was wont.

Linnea sighed. Men were so alike in such matters: great roaring beasts, prone to swearing and stamping about, but made tame by too much drink. And women were always left to clean up after them.

Feeling a trifle more confident, she surveyed the room once more. She could pick up the clothing and smaller items. But she would need help to right the cupboard and repair the bed.

As for Axton . . . he would need a bath, she decided, remembering his instructions to her. He obviously valued cleanliness. She would also have a plain breakfast of good bread and cold meat brought for him. She would provide every comfort she could think of, for men were like grouchy children after drinking and raging about. He would want to be soothed, she hoped.

Perhaps if she simply behaved as if last night had never happened . . . perhaps the drink would make him forget how she had angered him—and the truly awful things she had said. How she prayed it was so.

Linnea swung into action. It was good to have something to do. Inactivity and uncertainty were unbearable. She hurried back to the hall and gave a maid orders to have a bathing tub brought up into the antechamber along with lots of hot water and the best soap from the storerooms. Another she instructed to prepare a breakfast tray and leave it also in the antechamber. She would first deal with Axton alone in their private chambers. Should he turn out to be an unpleasant drunk, she did not want everyone in the castle to witness her humiliation.

She returned to the chamber and packed her scattered clothing back into the trunk. Then she stacked his as neatly as possible on the carved top of her trunk. She gathered the bedding and folded it, and generally tried to put the chamber back in order, as much as she was able.

Then it was time to awaken him.

Linnea had tried to ignore her husband's slumbering form while she busied herself with the other tasks. Now she had no choice but to face him.

He was sprawled on his side up against the wall, as if he'd slid down the stone surface into a sitting position, then toppled over in a stupor. Yet even in so ignominious a pose, the man was formidable. Powerfully built, tall, lean, and solid muscle, his body showed the evidence of the years he'd spent honing himself with the tools of war. But there was also something of the boy in him.

Grimacing at the foolishness of that thought, she opened one narrow window and let the beginnings of dawn's light into the silent chamber. In the faint, golden haze, she saw how his ebony hair tumbled over his brow. His hard mouth was relaxed too, and there was no frown to mar his forehead, nor scowl to crease his cheeks. He was exceedingly handsome, in fact. But only because he slept, she reminded herself. Only because too much drink had stolen his sour disposition.

Oh, but he would have a terrible headache, she speculated, and she was glad of it. He deserved to suffer as he made everyone around him suffer.

On that thought she nudged one of his large, booted feet with her smaller, slippered one.

"My lord. My lord, 'tis morning. You've many a task awaiting you this day. Axton!" she added more forcefully when he did not make any response.

At the sound of his name he shifted and snorted. But then he resumed the slow, easy breathing of before. Linnea glared at him. "Great lummox," she muttered. "What would you do if the castle came under siege? Sleep right through the battle?"

She studied him a moment. Then her eyes fastened on the sheathed dagger still strapped to his side. To disarm him in his sleep would be a great coup and it would go far toward restoring her sense of confidence. He would be furious when he learned of it. But he would have to respect her, she told herself. Especially if she told him where she'd put the weapon—for safekeeping, of course.

She crept nearer, though she feared to come within reach of his hands. But he was so far gone as to be deaf to everything, she decided, even the roof capsizing over his head, should it so happen.

As she leaned over him she was intensely conscious of how much larger and stronger he was than she. He was every inch the warrior. Then the chain brushed her left thigh and she unwillingly admitted that he was every inch the lover also. The same power that stood him in such good stead when he pitted himself against his enemies served him equally well with his wife—who was *also* his enemy, she sternly reminded herself.

With an effort she quashed all the disturbing sensations his nearness roused in her and focused instead on the dagger he wore. She reached for the hilt, just beneath his elbow. It was a bigger weapon than the one she'd found in his cupboard that night, and when she slid it from the sheath, it bumped against his arm.

He shifted suddenly. His arm fell over her hand, pressing it against his hip, and Linnea sucked in her breath. St. Jude, but she was in for it now!

But instead of opening his eyes and pinning her with an accusing gaze, he mumbled something incoherent, then sighed and smiled. While her heart raced in panic, he was having sweet dreams!

She set her lips in determination. She would have his dagger and then she would wake him for his bath. He would see that she was a sweet and docile wife whom he could trust, and he would be lulled into complacency if it killed her—or him!

That thought gave her pause. Whatever happened in the coming days or weeks, she did not want Axton killed. She wanted Beatrix to find a suitable husband and to reclaim Maidenstone for the de Valcourt family. But she did not want Axton de la Manse to die in the process.

What if he chose to fight against Beatrix's husband, though?

Linnea shook her head, banishing that thought. She had no control over that. Most certainly she had no control over Axton de la Manse. Why, she could not even awaken the man!

She shoved his arm roughly aside and drew the dagger all the way out, then hastily stepped away from him. It was fortunate that she did. No sooner was she beyond his reach than he lurched upright, swinging one of his arms in a wide, arcing blow. The fact that he met with nothing but air seemed to jolt him finally awake.

" 'Tis only I, your wife," Linnea said, backing as far away from him as she could. "Remember me?" she added, when he stared wildly about. He was not fully alert, though he stood upright now, tensed and ready for battle.

She saw as his eyes cleared, and as they did, his expression changed. The creases of his frown returned his face to its more normal appearance. To her shame, Linnea regretted that, and not because of her need to deceive him. There was a tiny, wicked part of her that longed for his full, relaxed smile directed at her. But he only smiled like that when he dreamed.

She forced an apologetic expression to her face. "I tried to wake you for your bath," she explained. She set the dagger down on a small table. "You slept in your clothes, my lord. Here, let me remove your shoes."

She moved right up to him, though she trembled with fear for his reaction. Would he remember what she'd said about being repulsed by him? Would he remember how angry he'd been? She decided that forthrightness would sit better with him than anything else.

"We quarreled last eve and I thought to mend things between us this morning." She reached for his girdle and began to unbuckle it, staring at the golden clasp, not into his face. Her fingers shook so that she could hardly manage, but she was determined and he did not resist her.

"I hope . . . I hope you will not destroy our bedchamber every time I anger you," she continued, praying her woman's chatter would calm him. "While you bathe in the antechamber I will have the bed repaired and the cupboard put upright—"

"I hope you do not intend to anger me often."

Linnea swallowed and pulled the girdle free. "I will try not to, my lord."

With a finger beneath her chin, he tilted her face up, then stared down into her wide eyes. He had come wide awake, but as to his mood, she could not determine it at all. "Where did you go last night?"

"To my grandmother. I was afraid of you," she added, unable to hide the accusation in her tone.

He seemed to consider that, all the while studying her face as if he could see well beyond its surface and all the way into her mind. Then he sighed and his hand fell to his side. "In the future I will try to control my temper better. You must not argue with me, however, especially in matters pertaining to your family."

"I fear then, that we have a problem, my lord. For I can no more abandon my family than you can abandon yours."

For one long jangling moment she feared she'd really done it, for his brow lowered, first in disbelief, then in anger.

But just as she expected an outburst of furious temper, he threw back his head and laughed—and immediately groaned and gripped his head with both hands. He grimaced, then gave her a pained look. "Have I married me a warrior woman, then? A shrew who would battle me with her waspish tongue and beautiful face as her only weapons and yet expect still to hold her own against me?"

He groaned again and rubbed his eyes. But there was no outburst and Linnea sagged in relief. Confronting her husband head-on *was* the safest way to deal with him, it seemed.

She did not have to try hard to force a smile. "I called for a bath and meal for you, if you are so inclined."

He tilted his head back and forth, as if testing whether it was still well attached to his shoulders, then gave her a wry grin. "I put myself in your hands, madam. Pray, impress me with your wifely skills, for I am sore in need of them. But know this," he added, speaking in a huskier tone. "You have impressed me in other of your skills already." He glanced at the bed in its tilted state, then back at her. "Once this chamber is put back to rights, we may well make a shambles of it again." Then he frowned as if something had only just occurred to him. His gray eyes narrowed. "Or perhaps you do retch at the very idea."

Linnea's mouth went dry. She'd hoped he'd forgotten her hateful words. What was she to do now?

"I . . . I should not have said that," she stammered. She wove her fingers nervously together.

"That does not answer my question. Do I disgust you? Do I make you want to retch?"

"No. No," she repeated. "I was . . . angry. You had said cruel things to me and I . . . I wanted to hurt you as you had hurt me."

They stared at one another, a long, unsettling look that did not ease her mind. She could not sense the direction of his thoughts behind the carved granite mask that was his face. Had she thought him boyish but minutes before? There was nothing of the boy in him now, only battle-hardened warrior, inflexible and distrustful.

"Perhaps," she began, mindful of her grandmother's instructions. "Perhaps we should begin this day anew, with neither grudges nor suspicions to darken it."

His lips curved in a mirthless smile. " 'Twould certainly be better for you, would it not?" Then he sighed and she felt a faint glimmer of hope. "I will have my bath, wife, and we will see where this day leads us. Pray that it ends better than did the last."

Linnea let out a shaky little breath. *Thank you, St. Jude.* "I will check on the water."

"No. Stay." He caught her hand before she could slip away. "Leave the servants to their work. Your duty is only to me. And I would have a proper morning greeting from my wife," he added, slipping a hand around her waist and drawing her up hard against him.

Linnea's breath left her in a rush. She had thought the remnants of his drink would put an end to that, at least for a while. But it appeared not. Most certainly the rigid length of flesh pressing against her belly did say otherwise.

"Please, my lord," she murmured, trying to grab his wandering hands. "The servants are just without—"

"So?" One of his fingers rubbed the length of the chain lying across her derriere, which sent a fiery shiver through her. "Tell me, my sweet Beatrix. Does my gift keep you ever in mind of me?"

Beatrix. In that moment of near surrender, Linnea wanted to throw off her sister's shadow and stand before him as the woman she truly was. As Linnea. She wanted to forget her grandmother's words and her sister's name. Like some perverse demon, that insane urge gripped her, body and soul.

But what would that gain her? Or more importantly, what would it *lose* her?

The answer was easy. Everything.

The cold reality of that fact chased away any thoughts of surrender. She twisted out of his embrace. "I did not take it to be a gift, but rather a threat," she answered him in a voice that trembled with anger. That the anger was directed more at herself than at him did not matter. He assumed it was for him, for once more his eyes narrowed and his lips turned up in grim humor.

"You may make of it what you will, but again, that is not an answer to my questions. Does it keep you in mind of me?"

Linnea glowered at him, then caught herself. She was

supposed to be compliant. She was supposed to barter her body if necessary.

She swallowed the bitter lump of emotion that caught in her throat. "Yes, my lord. It keeps you ever in my mind."

That pleased him, if his smug smile was any indication. "I would see again how it lays against your skin." He gripped the tail end of his soiled chainse and tugged it over his head, then tossed it aside. Clad only in his russet braies and black leather boots, he stared at her. "Come bathe with me, wife, and we will scrub each other very well."

At her stunned expression he began to laugh, but Linnea could not marshal her features to either acquiescence *or* opposition. She was shocked by his preposterous suggestion and unable to pretend otherwise. It would have been hard enough not to stand slack jawed at the sight of his magnificent body. But to be told in the same moment that she must join him in his bath was more than her naive senses could cope with. Did he actually mean for her to bare herself as unashamedly as he did? To step into the water with him as naked as the day of her birth? Despite every intimate act they had already done together, this one seemed somehow even more intimate.

"The tub . . . the tub is . . . is too small," she stammered. She picked up his shirt and began nervously to fold it.

At just that moment, the door fortuitously creaked open and Norma poked her head inside. She met Linnea's anxious look with an anxious one of her own. "Milady, the bath is ready."

Norma. Thanks be to the Holy Mother. At least Norma was on her side. "Come, my lord." Linnea sidled toward the door, taking what advantage she could of the interruption. "Come while the water is still warm."

He came without comment and Linnea held out the hope that maybe she had thwarted him for once. While she knew she must be agreeable to him, she also knew that she could never be so bold as to bathe with the man.

In the antechamber two young pages poured the last buckets of steaming water into a large, wooden tub. A

161

maid entered with a heavily laden tray of bread and meats, while another carried a silver ewer and two goblets. Norma directed where all was to go, while Axton crossed without comment to the tub and tested the water. Then he sat on the edge and looked over at Linnea.

"Send the servants away. We have no further need of them."

"But . . . but . . ." Linnea sputtered. She stopped when he raised one dark and imperious brow, however. If she was to be docile and sweet—and obedient—then she must begin now. With a strange knot of both dread and anticipation twisting in her gut, she slowly nodded her head.

"I will attend my lord Axton. Norma, see to the hall and any tasks that yet remain unattended. But do not stray too far," she continued impulsively. "I will wish to confer with you once I am finished here. If it pleases you, my lord," she added, staring back at Axton.

When he only met her gaze one long moment, she had to force herself not to bite her lower lip. Finally he gave a short nod, though, and she felt a rush of relief. Perhaps today she might find some bit of normalcy in her castle routine.

She watched the servants file out, conscious of the curious glances. Once again her husband kept all the upper floors of the keep for their exclusive use. She had no doubt that everyone knew precisely what sort of use he intended for it. And for her.

When she eventually did resume her daily routine, would they all continue to stare and speculate as they did now?

She did not want to think about it.

But while she could shove that unpleasant thought away, at least for a while, she could not avoid the impending bath ordeal. The antechamber had emptied save for the two of them. Despite the fact that there was no door to close off the stairwell, and the faint sounds of activity in the great hall drifted up to them, they were in every sense alone. No one would dare venture above stairs uninvited, not when the lord of the castle made his intentions regarding his new wife so clear.

Linnea took a deep breath and slowly let it out. Since he seemed to value forthrightness, she would be forthright. She would express her feelings and her opinions and be as honest as was possible with him.

But not in all things. Not when it came to her true name.

"What do you wish, milord? To bathe first or to break your fast?" she began. Her words were those of a coddling wife, but her tone was that of an efficient housekeeper. She waited expectantly, but still a safe distance across the room.

"No food," he muttered, rubbing his head, then grimacing as if it pained him even to touch it. "I would bathe first."

"I can have an infusion of lavender, pennyroyal, and sweet woodruff prepared to ease your pains," she suggested.

He eyed her warily. "Would it mend my head *and* soothe this unease in my gut?"

Linnea shrugged. "It manages both. I have prepared it many a time for—" She broke off. Any mention of her family members seemed to enrage him; to rouse his temper now was not her intent.

But he must have sensed her thoughts, for he studied her closely. "For your father?"

She met his gaze. "And my brother."

Their eyes held a long moment. But it was a different sort of look than they'd shared before. For once he was not the predator and she was not his prey. It was as if his temporary weakness had made of them equals, and she could not let her opportunity pass.

"When the men of Maidenstone have overindulged themselves with drink, my preparations have ever seen them more quickly recovered. Shall I make it for you?"

He nodded, but she detected a puzzled expression in his eyes. She decided to answer his question before he asked it. "It is my intention for there to be peace between us."

"Peace," he repeated. "Tell me true, Beatrix. Is it your

hope that through this peace I shall keep your grand-mother here with you at Maidenstone?"

That gave her pause. Last night she would have said yes. But the Lady Harriet would rather be gone from the castle—so that she could better see to Axton's inevitable defeat. Linnea searched for the right words.

"In the light of a new day I see that it might be better for everyone if she were settled at Romsey Abbey. She would never be content here. But what do you plan for . . . for the other members of my family?"

"The men of your family await Henry Plantagenet's pleasure. Do not ask me for their freedom," he warned. "For 'tis not mine to give."

Linnea looked down at the floor. "I understand. But I would plead with you, Axton, to consider your vengeance done. You have achieved your aim. Do not heap further suffering upon them who cannot defend themselves any longer."

"In case you have not noticed, wife, 'tis you who have of late suffered the worst brunt of my temper."

Linnea looked up, startled by his blunt words. He was much nearer now, and his expression was not so much of pain as it was of undisguised desire. She sidled around the back of the tub. "You have not always seemed angry when we . . . when we came together."

A faint grin of amusement curved one side of his face. "Nor have you, else I would sport more than one fresh scar," he said, rubbing the ragged scab on his shoulder. Then his expression sobered. "I cannot promise you a mild-tempered husband any more than you can promise to be a meek wife to me. But we shall manage one way or another."

He removed his boots one at a time, then reached for the ties at the waist of his braies. Linnea was once more made uncomfortably aware of the raw beauty of the man. "I would bathe now," he said. "Then retire to bed."

The ties came loose. The russet caddis cloth dipped low on his lean belly, and Linnea could not help but stare. Only at the last moment, when he tugged the garment down past his hips and stepped out of them gloriously naked, did she jerk her eyes away.

"We . . . we cannot . . . The bed is broken."

"Call someone to fix it then." She heard his step on the floor, then the soft ripple of water as he eased into the steaming tub, followed by a slow, heartfelt sigh.

Fix the bed. Easier to tend to that task than to the naked male body that awaited her attention. So Linnea took him at his word. She backed away from him, staring at the wide, muscular chest and its sprinkling of curls with a dark fascination she could not hide. Call someone to fix the bed. Yes, she would do that. And she would prepare the decoction for him as well.

"Soak you a while," she said, angling toward the arched opening to the stairs. "I will see to . . . to other things," she finished in a mumble.

"Wait. Beatrix!"

But Linnea did not heed his call. Once again logic had succumbed to emotion. As always, the potent combination of his masculine threat and magnetic appeal conspired to scare her to death. She backed out of the chamber, nearly tumbling down the steps at the last glimpse she had of him. He'd stood up in the tub, with water sheeting down his body, every inch a man—a man who was her husband. Despite the intimacies they'd shared, she was not accustomed to his casual nudity. She did not think she ever would be.

She would have to face him again, of course. And soon. But maybe by then she would be better composed. Maybe she would be in control of herself, she prayed, as she hurried to her tasks.

But she feared that somewhere along the way she'd lost all control to this man. And she feared also that even St. Jude could not help her recover it.

Chapter 12

Linnea sent an army of workers in ahead of her. Axton would be annoyed, she feared. But the infusion would appease him. And mayhap he would begin to see her as more than merely a convenient female body.

But why should she have such a foolish notion? she asked herself. Why should she care that he appreciate her housewifely skills? If her grandmother's plan came to pass, he would soon be gone from Maidenstone, replaced by her sister's husband, whoever he might be. How Axton felt about her wifely skills would be completely buried beneath the pure hatred he would feel for her deception.

Unfortunately, that bit of logic did her no good at all. The fact was, there were those aspects of Axton de la Manse that appealed to her. He might be a fierce warrior and possessed of a lethal temper, but he was still better tempered than her brother, Maynard. Even ignoring the incredible intimacies they'd shared, she could not entirely hate him. For the most part he treated her decently and she, perversely, wanted him to appreciate her.

Of course, he thought she was Beatrix, she reminded herself. Even Maynard treated Beatrix decently. If Axton knew she was not Beatrix, he would not be nearly so decent. Indeed, his temper would very likely become uncontrollable.

He had not struck her last night, but when he learned the truth . . . She shuddered to even think of his reaction.

But that day was a long way off, she told herself. A long way. Meanwhile, whether she liked him or hated him, she must play the part given to her. She must appear to be a dutiful and loving wife to him, and thereby prove her worth to her family.

"Does Ida go to Romsey with the Lady Harriet?" she asked Norma as they started up the stairs.

"Yes, milady. They depart very soon with a small guard to escort them."

Linnea grimaced. Truth be told, a part of her was relieved to have her grandmother's dour presence gone. But it created problems as well. "I pray her absence does not hasten my father's decline."

Norma shook her head. " 'Tis a sad thing, but not unknown. His father was the same. One day a strong man; the next crushed by adversity and robbed of his senses."

"Did he never recover?"

Norma's answer was a grim shake of the head.

Linnea digested that in silence. She'd known her father would offer her little help. To know he could offer her none, however, was bitter indeed. She sighed. "I hope my grandmother does not have to endure the journey to Romsey on horseback."

"She travels in a horse litter. Milord Axton did order it so."

Linnea paused on the steps and stared at Norma. A horse litter? Her husband had ordered a horse litter to make the journey easier for an old woman who did hate him and conspire against him? Not that he knew she conspired. But he did know she hated him. No one could mistake that. Even so, he'd ordered a horse litter for her.

The news of her father had depressed her, but this knowledge of Axton's kindness unaccountably lifted her spirits. When Linnea entered the antechamber and he scowled at her and the several carpenters who headed into the bedchamber, she met his frown with a sincere smile.

"They will not be overlong, my lord. They do but repair the bed . . ." She trailed off. The bed they would very quickly retire to. She might have avoided an escapade in the bathtub with him, but she could not avoid him for very long.

He watched her as she approached with the pewter goblet that held her remedy. He sprawled back in the huge tub, his hair wet and slicked back, his shoulders bare and gleaming in the strengthening morning light. The water covered the lower half of his torso and all of his legs except

167

the tops of his bent knees. But those portions of him that showed—the powerful chest and well-shaped arms—were enough to unnerve any woman alive. Even feeling as wretched as he must, he looked the perfect image of glorious manhood.

"What is in this vile brew?" he asked, sniffing suspiciously at the dark liquid she held out to him.

"Lavender, pennyroyal, and sweet woodruff," she answered. "I will drink of it first if it please you."

His hand closed around hers and lifted the chalice to his own lips. Cool metal and warm flesh cupped her hand and Linnea felt a frisson of heat. Against her thigh his chain of ruby and gold did seem to sear her skin.

"That's not necessary," Axton murmured. "Methinks you anticipate the reward too well to strike down he who would give it to you." So saying, he drank deeply. But he kept his eyes locked upon her face.

For her part, Linnea wanted nothing more than to escape his smug confidence. She jerked her hand from his hold, sloshing a goodly portion of the infusion into the bathwater. The fact that he only chuckled riled her further.

"Do you deny the pleasure you find in our joining?" he asked, not the least concerned by the several servants and workmen who labored within the sound of his voice. "Answer me, wife. Your coyness is unnecessary now."

"I would rather have this conversation in the great hall," she snapped. "That way the *entire* populace of Maidenstone Castle can hear of what we speak. 'Tis what you want, is it not?"

His silent chuckles started a series of waves within the tub, soft, fragrant lapping that was at odds with the intensity of her feelings. "Never let it be said of me that I do not honor my ladywife's delicate sensibilities. Come, my lovely little shrew. While the carpenters repair one part of what my temper has wrought, you can repair the other part."

When she hesitated to approach him, unsure exactly what he meant, he extended a hand to her. "Do not fear. I shall harness my base nature and ask only that you scrub my skin while the carpenters labor."

Linnea looked away from him. Why was she always so easily unsettled by him? How could she be one moment pleased by his thoughtfulness toward her grandmother, the next minute unnerved by his masculine beauty then, like lightning, outraged by his innuendo and unnerved all over again. It was perverse. *She* was perverse.

She swallowed hard and willed herself to a self-possession she did not truly feel. "As you wish," she murmured, edging toward the tray of soaps and bathing cloths.

He did not move when she came up beside him. His eyes followed her, watching her with a burning gaze she felt even when she did not look at him. But his arms remained stretched along the sides of the tub and his head relaxed against the high back.

She dipped the cloths in the hot water and rubbed it with the castile soap her grandmother had purchased at the last fair at Chichester. Once she'd worked up a lather, however, it was time to actually scrub him. But how to begin? And where?

As if he knew her dilemma, Axton raised one foot out of the water. She began there.

His feet were large and well shaped. His ankles strong, and his calves muscular. As she soaped them, first one leg and then the other, she knew she scrubbed harder than necessary. But he did not rebuke her.

His hands and arms were next, long fingers, square palms, and well-formed arms, like hard, living steel. Under the touch of those clever hands of his she might forget everything but him.

"Shall I stand for the rest?"

Linnea dropped the cloth with a soggy plunk. Conversely some wanton part of her seemed to leap. "No. Not . . . not yet," she managed to get out. She pulled her gaze away from his face, with its planes made sharper by the wet gleam of light on it, and stared instead at the soapy surface of the water. The washcloth was down there, somewhere near his hips, she suspected. And now she had to get it.

She closed her eyes and plunged her hand in. Slippery skin that was nonetheless hard and firm as the oaken beams that held up the roof rubbed against her hand. Coarse hair, then no hair. Her heart began to thud an almost painful rhythm. Then she felt the cloth, and her fingers clutched it as fiercely as if it were the Bacon of Flitch prize that she'd grabbed from a pike.

Before she could right herself, however, one of Axton's hands caught her at the nape of her neck. "Come in here with me," he whispered in a husky tone. "I would do to you what you have done to me."

"I . . . I can bathe myself without aid of—"

" 'Tis not the bathing I speak of," he interrupted her. His other hand caught her wrist and drew it back down beneath the water, pressing it against the thickened arousal hidden beneath the fragrant suds.

Their eyes met and held, and Linnea knew he must see the way he affected her. She might protest with words and evasive actions. But when they were this close, when her fingers felt every inch of his desire and her eyes could not close away the answering desire she felt, she knew he recognized the truth. Time and circumstance might make of him her enemy, but there was a will in her that ignored everything but the way he made her feel.

She wanted to be in the tub with him. And he knew it.

"What of the bed linens, milady? Shall we change them—" At the sight of them, Norma halted in the doorway to the bedchamber. "Beg pardon, milord. I did not . . . um . . . that is . . ."

Linnea jerked her hand out with a splash that wet her skirt. The soggy washcloth dripped all over her shoes and the floor, but she was too dismayed to notice. Her cheeks had turned to scarlet and she wanted nothing more than to slink away in shame.

Axton, however, seemed entirely unperturbed. "Leave the bed linens as they are. And get those carpenters out of there now."

"Yes, milord." Norma backed away, bowing as she went. "They are nearly finished, milord. They'll be gone at once."

Linnea stared down at Axton. She should dread what was coming, but she could not. She could not.

Lord help me, she prayed. *St. Jude. Mother Mary.* Afraid to even think about what she was doing, she circled behind Axton. "Dunk your head," she quietly ordered as she took up the soap once more. To her relief, he complied, and when he surfaced, she applied the soap to his head and began to scrub his raven black hair.

The carpenters were noisy as they approached the antechamber, as if to give fair warning of their presence. They were completely silent as they marched through, however. Norma was the last to leave. She hesitated a moment at the top of the stairs. But when Linnea shook her head, then turned her attention back to Axton, the older woman left too.

It was only Linnea and her husband now. Her husband who had been kind to her grandmother and in his own way, kind to her as well.

"Dunk again," she told him. When he came up sputtering and wiping streams of water from his eyes, she had moved back a pace from the tub.

He raked his gleaming hair back from his brow and looked around for her. "Come here, wife."

"I am removing my shoes, my lord."

He watched as she pulled her skirt up and slipped first one, then the other shoe off. "Am I really your lord, then? Your esteemed lord and husband whom you do wish to please in every way?"

The chain burned against her thigh and she shifted restlessly from one bare foot to the other. "Yes."

"Come here."

Linnea edged a little nearer. "Shouldn't I . . . well, remove my gown first?" she asked, fumbling with the ties at her wrists.

"No." He sat up straighter and caught one of her hands, then pulled until she was off balanced and had to brace herself on the far edge of the bathtub.

"But how . . . I mean, the gown—"

"The gown is of no consequence, no consequence what-

171

soever," he murmured, pulling her other wrist too. In a trice she tumbled over into the tub of frothy water, falling onto his chest with her legs flailing in the air.

Amidst her frantic efforts to right herself, she only sank more fully into the bathtub. Water sloshed over the edges, splashing across the floor as he pulled her down over him. His hands caught her around the waist and in less than the blink of an eye, she found herself straddling his hips, with her skirt floating around her waist, settling like a wet tent around them both.

"Ah. Much better," Axton murmured, tugging her a little closer to him. "Now, my troublesome little wife, finish the task you have begun."

It was preposterous and outrageous, but every part of Linnea that was a woman thrilled to it. The gown was a sodden hindrance. The tub was far too small for what he intended. But somehow they managed. He settled her over his impatient shaft and as if they were of one mind, they began the tandem rhythm, the offering and acceptance. The taking and giving.

"God, woman," Axton groaned. His hands gripped her waist, digging into her skin, burning the chain he'd given her into her flesh. He drove her down on him, over and over, until Linnea felt the shuddering rush of it, the molten heat of it welling up. She cried out and tried to pull away, but he held her and forced her to more and more. Longer and stronger. Then he cried out too, a hoarse shout that was both a victory over her, and a surrender to her.

That fast was it over, and they collapsed into the much diminished bathwater. The side of Linnea's face pressed into his wet shoulder. His arms circled her back and the appeased flesh of his manhood rested deeply within her.

In the quiet aftermath, when the only sound was their labored breathing, Linnea admitted to herself that this was not as she pictured marriage to be. She'd expected love and not thought at all about the physical part of it. She'd imagined a man who was gentle and kind, more a friend to her than anything else.

Instead, she'd wed a man she must fear and hate, and

172

had discovered a physical joy she could neither understand nor explain. The fact that every least soul in the castle must know what she did with him and how she reveled in it only confounded things further.

Yet for all her mental debate, Linnea remained just as she was. She rested in Axton's arms, limp from their lovemaking, and still wearing the drenched dress which would no doubt be discussed in whispers for days to come—or at least until he involved her in another such escapade.

God only knew what that might be, but Linnea would not deny that she could hardly wait to find out.

Axton watched his bride as she walked away.

The wench was truly amazing.

She was not at all what he would have expected. Not her beauty, nor her fire. Neither had he expected the powerful reaction he had to her whenever he saw her—or even thought about her.

He'd known he would have no difficulty responding to her vibrant beauty. Such a sweetly formed woman would heat any man's blood. But the desire he felt for her burned with an intensity he was beginning to find disturbing. The plain truth was that he could not get enough of her.

He trailed behind her, down the stairs to the main hall, keeping his eyes on the rounded hips that swayed so enticingly beneath the softly draped gown she'd changed into. The woman was a temptress without even trying to be. At times she made him so angry—so angry that he wanted to throttle her.

He frowned to think how close he'd come to striking her last night, and all because she'd challenged him on account of her family. That she was loyal was commendable. But the fact was, *he* wanted to command that same level of loyalty from her. He wanted her world to center around *him*, not around her family. He wanted to create a new family with her.

It was a need he could never have foreseen.

At the foot of the stairs he halted and watched her walk away. Though it was foolish, he wanted her to look back.

She knew he was here. So look back, he silently commanded her.

When she paused near the hearth and did just that, he couldn't prevent the pleased smile that lifted his lips. She smiled back, a surprised half-smile that revealed more of her feelings for him than she probably knew. She was as confused by the unexpected attraction between them as he. That knowledge pleased him almost as much as anything else. She could not hide her feelings from him. A good trait in a wife. Though he would never have thought it possible between them, he found himself eager for honesty in their dealings together.

"What say you, brother?" Peter's taunting voice interrupted Axton's drifting thoughts. "The last I saw of you, you were not nearly so hale and hearty as this."

Axton stifled a grimace. So Peter knew about last night. No doubt everyone did. Nevertheless, he shot the boy a tolerant smile, then returned his gaze to his wife.

The boy followed his gaze. "Talk is that you were not nearly so well pleased with her last night."

Axton's jaw tightened. His brother's tone was not one of brotherly teasing; in truth, he sounded more angry than jovial. Axton turned to face Peter. "Last night I was drunk. Today I am sober."

"I take it she has forgiven you."

Axton frowned. "Not two days ago you despised Beatrix. Yet now I detect an air of protectiveness in you. I hope you do not imply that she needs be protected from her own husband."

He glowered at his brother, daring him to push the matter any further. But with a mulish light in his eye and a belligerent set to his jaw, Peter pressed on. "If that husband would strike her, then destroy his own possessions when she is not completely submissive to him, then yes—"

"I did not hurt her!"

"But you would have!" Peter hissed. "Had Reynold not prevented it, you would have struck her down. Had she not hidden, you would have trapped her in your chambers and punished her last night."

174

"My wife is mine own affair." Axton bit the words out, cold and clipped. When Peter did not flinch, however, his fury grew even greater. " 'Tis a man's right to discipline his wife. 'Tis his duty. To cuff her when she has erred is no great sin."

"I never once saw our father strike Mother."

Axton could not believe his ears. It was not his brother's words that were so shocking. Axton knew as well as Peter—better even—that their father had never raised a hand to their mother. He had honored her and respected her and loved her. What Axton could not believe was that Peter would bring up such a thing to him, when the circumstances of his marriage were so vastly different from their parents'. He'd wed his enemy's daughter, not his childhood sweetheart. And the fact remained that he had not actually struck the troublesome wench!

"Your concern is touching, little brother. But Beatrix is my wife and I will deal with her as I see fit. You have only to look at her to see she is well pleased with the role fate has given her."

"Is she?" Peter asked, giving him a cold smile. "Or is she simply playing the role she believes will keep her safe?"

"Damn you! That is not the way of it. If you value your place here, you will leave this matter alone!"

Under Axton's blistering glare Peter finally looked away, across the hall to the paired oaken doors through which Beatrix had departed. "I assume she goes to bid her grandmother farewell."

Axton felt a modicum of satisfaction that his brother had decided to let the subject go—and a considerable relief. Despite his defense of his actions last night, Axton was uncomfortable with Peter's accusation. He had overreacted. To himself, at least, he would not deny it. But that was over and done with. He would not allow himself to be so provoked again. He answered Peter, "The crone's departure is for the best."

"What of Sir Edgar and his injured son?"

Axton sighed. His new wife's family was a wearisome burden. Most of his life he'd lived hating them and wanting revenge against them. Now he only wanted them to go away. "Henry comes soon. Once he has dispensed his justice, we shall be relieved of the de Valcourt family once and for all. Peace and prosperity will finally be ours and you will not have to worry over my treatment of my wife."

"Your wife *is* a de Valcourt. That you can so easily forget that fact surprises me."

"In that you are wrong, brother. She is no longer a de Valcourt, not from the moment of her wedding oath. She is a de la Manse, now. Beatrix de la Manse. My wife and lady of Maidenstone. You need not doubt her loyalty to me, nor mine to her."

Then spying Sir Maurice, Axton gave his brother a curt nod, turned, and departed. But Peter's words left him with an uneasy feeling. He had embarked on his marriage to de Valcourt's daughter, intending to bind her to him on the strength of her passionate nature. He'd behaved like an idiot last night—he could admit that much to himself. But he'd mended that this morning. That Beatrix had been so willing to forget about last night had only assured him that he was succeeding with his plan to gain her loyalty—all her loyalty.

But Peter's doubt about the girl's acceptance of their marriage had set him to wondering.

As the day passed, filled with the business of reacquainting himself with his home and making myriad decisions, he had little time to dwell on his wife. But like a persistent bell ringer, just waiting for a quiet moment to peal forth a memorable tune, Beatrix remained in his mind.

When he accompanied Maurice to inspect the burned storehouses and decide on the rebuilding of them, he wondered if she'd ever visited those storehouses. At the house of Wascom the Weaver, unofficial mayor of the village, they were given cheese and ale as they discussed the possibility of holding a village fair. But all the time Axton wondered whether Beatrix would like a bolt of velvet cloth from the cloth dealer who would surely attend such a fair. Something rich and green, to match the startling color of her eyes when they made love.

By the time dusk approached and he and Maurice were homeward bound, he was resolved. If she were not completely in thrall to him—as Peter seemed to imply—she soon would be. He would bind her to him, using her own fiery passions to do so.

He kicked his mount to a faster pace, anticipating the moment when he would once again have her to himself. The grandmother was gone; the father and brother soon would be. Then she would be entirely his.

Chapter 13

If Maynard dies, you are our only hope.

Throughout the day, her grandmother's final words to her before departing for Romsey Abbey had echoed in Linnea's head. *If Maynard dies . . .*

Linnea had gone to him directly after her grandmother had left Maidenstone. Once a day their father visited with him, but he went away each time more shrunken and lost within his own thoughts than ever. Maynard no longer had a guard set on him, only a series of servants to feed him broth and give him the medicines Linnea prepared. But now, as she sat beside him in the priest's shadowed lodgings, Linnea feared her medicines were not enough.

Maynard lay on the priest's bed, his skin as pale as the sun-bleached bed linens, only grayer. His breath came slowly, in shallow, irregular rattles. His face was clammy, his eyes sunken shadows, and his cheeks peppered with thin scruff. He had not spoken since the morning before.

Linnea heaved a great sigh and prayed fervently for his recovery. She did not want him to die. She did not want to be the only hope of her family.

She did not want to be Beatrix anymore.

Her face creased with the intensity of her prayers. *St. Jude, I was wrong to do this. Wrong to deceive Axton.*

But if she had not, the real Beatrix would have become his wife. Her sister would be the one sharing his bed, not her. In retrospect it seemed she'd not saved Beatrix from so very dreadful a fate.

A slight noise drew her attention. "What do *you* want?" she hissed when she spied Peter de la Manse lurking within the open doorway.

The boy stepped into the narrow room. In the scant light of the solitary candle his young face was solemn, with none of the cockiness she'd come to expect of him. At least he'd not come to gloat over her fallen brother.

"I hoped to have a word with you," he answered. He stood on the opposite side of Maynard, studying her across the shrunken form of her brother. How fitting that seemed.

"What is it you want to know?" She was in no mood to fight with him. So long as he was civil she could behave the same.

He shifted from one foot to the other and passed the Phrygian cap he held from his left hand to his right and back again. "I, well, after last night and . . . and then this morning . . . well, 'tis not my wont to pry, but you . . . and Axton. Well, I wondered . . . that is . . ."

"Everything is mended between us, if that is what you ask," Linnea responded more curtly than was strictly necessary. Heat stained her face with faint color and she was sorry she'd invited him to speak. Was her personal relationship with her husband always to attract so much attention? She was embarrassed and aggravated all at the same time.

"Well, I am glad of that," he said. Then his expression turned him from awkward boy to knowing young man. "The furnishings cannot bear much more of such abuse."

Linnea's face turned scarlet. "What do you mean?" she gasped.

"The bed, of course. Axton broke it— Oh!" His brows lifted and a grin curved his mouth. For a moment he looked very like his brother—a fact that did nothing to endear him to her.

"Oh," he continued, the grin firmly in place. "I assumed *he'd* broken it in a fit of rage. Mayhap it was the *two* of you in a fit of passion who did cause the carpenters nearly to despair of ever setting the piece to rights again."

Linnea's palm fairly itched to slap him. Every time he seemed close to becoming reasonably pleasant, he reverted to the crude behavior that seemed to be at the core of all young men.

"You do concern yourself overly much with your brother's personal affairs. And mine."

He shrugged, but his smile faded. He looked down at Maynard a long moment before returning his gaze to her. "If everything is mended between you and him, then that is good. But what if your brother dies? Will everything splinter apart once more?"

As if a cloud had passed unexpectedly over her, Linnea shivered. "I . . . I pray that he will recover."

"Will he?"

Linnea bowed her head and closed her eyes. This boy was not the person she wished to confide her fears in. Yet the need to speak honestly with someone—anyone—was simply too overpowering to resist.

"I fear he is not long for this world," she answered, all her fear trembling within her voice.

After a short silence he said, "I have lost two brothers to war. And my father as well. I am sorry for the grief you will endure."

Linnea nodded. The lump that had risen in her throat made it impossible to speak. She'd lost far more than merely this brother who had never spared a thought for her feelings. Peter did not know that, of course, nevertheless his plain words were a comfort.

"But I must ask," he continued. "How you will feel toward Axton when—if—your brother dies? Will everything remain mended between you, as you termed it? Or will the carpenters have to be summoned once more?"

Linnea raised a stricken face to him. His expression was serious. He wanted there to be peace at Maidenstone, she realized in that moment. He wanted her to be content in her marriage, and for the union of the de la Manse family with the de Valcourts to be successful.

How she wished it could be so!

But it could not. Not now. If only she had not interfered. If she had allowed Beatrix to marry Axton as he wished, the two families might have achieved a grudging peace. But that was impossible now. To confess her lie to Axton . . . She shuddered even to imagine his rage. What anger he did not take out on her he would surely transfer to poor Beatrix, were he ever given the chance. And beyond that, the perverse truth was that she could not now bear the thought of Axton sharing the same relations with Beatrix he'd shared with her. Had there ever been a woman so disloyal as she?

She compressed her lips tightly. No, there was no going back. And there could be no peace between her family and Axton's.

"You do not answer," Peter cut into her dismal thoughts. "Will your brother's death destroy the fragile peace between you and Axton?"

Linnea looked at him—really looked at him. He was not yet a man, but the day fast approached when he would be as formidable as Axton. He would be as fierce a foe also, and as loyal to his family.

She swallowed down all her regrets and forced herself to remember the role she had elected to play. "It will not be . . . easy to bury him, should it come to that. It will not be easy to forget who did strike the blow that felled him."

"I do not ask if you will forget, only if you will be able to put it in the past."

"You mean forgive, don't you? Can I forgive Axton for murdering my brother?" she said, becoming emotional despite her best effort not to be. She should not be in this terrible predicament. It was not fair.

"It was not murder, only the unfortunate realities of war. Can you forgive him?" he persisted, pushing her further.

Linnea turned abruptly away. To stay here with him as he explored and poked at the troubling emotions she'd rather keep hidden was to invite disaster. "I will find a way to cope. 'Tis what women have always done best, you know. Cope with the life that others choose for them."

She paused at the opening in the heavy stone wall and looked back at Peter. He was strong and straight, and when compared to the dying Maynard, so incredibly alive. "Were it women who controlled the land, there would not be war. There would not be this eternal struggle for power and control and land and soldiers—"

She broke off when her voice began to tremble. But before she could escape the boy's presence, he caught her by the arm. He might be no taller than she, but his grip was strong and determined.

"I searched you out for a reason."

"Then state it and leave me to . . . to mourn my brother in whatever peace I can find."

"My mother arrives."

Linnea went still. From struggling to control her churning emotions, she veered abruptly into a complete dearth of them.

Their mother, Axton's and Peter's. If she had been unsure of herself before, Linnea was tenfold more so now. Would the woman despise her on sight as her own family had despised Axton? Would she plot against her son's wife in the same way the de Valcourt family plotted against their son-by-marriage?

"She is a good and kind woman."

Linnea stared at Peter. "Good and kind enough to forgive the unfortunate realities of war?"

Peter frowned at her use of his own words. "This will not be an easy homecoming for her. But if you will resolve yourself to be patient and allow her time to settle her disquieting emotions . . ."

"Time to grieve for all that she has lost since she was last here. Is that what you mean?" Linnea shrugged off the hand he'd laid on her arm and stared blindly toward the deep window and the narrow slice of sky beyond it. The sky was gray, hiding the sun from view. It was better than if the sky were brilliant and the sun cheerful. This was not a day for cheer. No doubt she and Axton's mother would agree on that one thing, if nothing else.

She took a steadying breath. "She is here now?"

"Her party arrives within the hour." Then he added, "She will not treat you unkindly, Beatrix."

As always, the use of her sister's name jolted her into reality. She swallowed and straightened up. "I must see to her chamber and call for a tray—" She stopped and stared at him. "You don't think Axton means also to deny *her* a room in the keep, do you?"

Peter grinned. "Axton may tower over her, but he knows better than to deny the Lady Mildred her due. If you like, I will relay a message to him that you do prepare your new mother-by-marriage a suitable welcome."

Linnea nodded. She had known the woman was coming eventually. She should have been better prepared. She wasn't though, and she doubted now whether she ever could have been adequately prepared to face her.

She owed Peter her gratitude for taking the time to forewarn her.

"Thank you," she said to him, frowning a little, for she did not quite understand this boy. She'd hated him on sight, and he'd felt the same toward her, she was certain. But perversely enough, there were times when he seemed to be her only ally. "Thank you for giving me time to prepare myself."

He stepped back a pace and turned so that she saw only his profile. "I did not do it for you, but for her," he replied in a gruffer tone than before. Then he tilted his head and pinned her with a stare disturbingly similar to his brother's. "I would not have her arrival made any harder than it necessarily will be. I would not want you to meet her as an adversary."

We are adversaries, though. Adversaries in a battle none of you yet recognize. But Linnea could not say that. Though it roiled like a sick knot in her stomach, she forced herself to nod acquiescence. "I will try to make myself agreeable to her."

But she feared, as she hurried away, that making herself agreeable was a worse affront than clashing with the woman outright. No matter what she did now, there was wrong in it. She'd been wrong to start this terrible plan going and she made it worse with every turn she took.

The chain slid along her thigh, but this time she felt more clearly the small thickened birthmark on her calf. The sign of her sin, her grandmother had always called it.

Today it seemed to throb and remind her of that truth. She'd begun this terrible deception. Whether she abhorred the path she'd chosen could not matter to her. She must do as she'd promised, though it made her feel far worse a sinner than she'd ever felt before.

Where was he? Linnea scanned the bailey, searching for Axton. His tall, imposing form was generally easy to spot, but not this afternoon. He must be elsewhere, perhaps in the village. That left her with the full responsibility of welcoming his mother.

A chamber was already prepared. Fresh linens, a warm fire, and a fragrant bath even now awaited Lady Mildred. Pray God that she would prefer to retire to her chambers, rather than reacquaint herself with the castle or visit with her younger son in the hall, for good manners would demand that Linnea accompany her in those activities. Though Linnea had no experience whatsoever as lady of the castle, she'd observed her grandmother and also her sister. In the lord's absence, all responsibility for a castle fell to his wife. Even if the duty was unpleasant, Linnea must rise to it.

Her eyes swept the bailey once more. Where was Peter?

Before she could locate him, the rattle of metal-shod horse hooves sounded from the bridge, and in a moment the yard filled with over a dozen mounted men and two stout wagons. The muddy yard was churned by the weary, circling cattle. One wagon forged on, separating from the others and only halting before the steps that led up into the keep.

Linnea sucked in a bracing breath. A hand parted the stretched canvas cover on the wagon and a woman's face peered out.

She looked sad and exhausted. That was what first registered in Linnea's mind. She had expected the woman to arrive triumphant and condescending. To see the apprehension on her face made Linnea reconsider, and in that moment she resolved to extend every kindness she could to this woman. No matter the troubling future that loomed so threateningly, Lady Mildred was a woman who had suffered much loss in her life. That she must lay the blame for it on Linnea and her family was not of primary importance now. This homecoming must be hard for her. Painful. Linnea would try not to add any further to that pain.

She moved down the steps, forcing a pleasant expression to her face, though her knees shook beneath her skirts. The woman's eyes caught hers, just for an instant, and Linnea recognized the depths of the woman's traumatic feelings. Then a shout diverted both their gazes, and Peter dashed around the front of the wagon.

"Mother! Welcome! Was your journey difficult? Are you weary or hungry or in need of anything—"

His excited greeting was muffled when Lady Mildred stepped down and enveloped him in a tight embrace.

"Peter," she whispered, barely loud enough for Linnea to hear. But that one word roused a storm of emotion in Linnea. Lady Mildred loved her sons. She'd already lost two of them. During these past months of Henry's campaign against King Stephen, she must have been sick with worry for the remaining two.

Pray God that she herself only bore daughters, Linnea thought. No sons to send to war, only daughters whom she would see wed to men they did care deeply for.

"I am hale and hearty, Mother. Not a scratch upon me— save those Axton did inflict." Peter wriggled out of Lady Mildred's warm hold. But his chagrin at being treated like a child was tempered by his obvious delight in his mother's presence.

Only when he glanced up and spied Linnea did his wide grin fade somewhat. "Mother, since Axton is not present to perform the honors, it needs must fall to me to introduce you to . . . to Lady Beatrix of Maidenstone." He paused a moment when his mother's gaze darted from him to Linnea and back again. "She is Axton's wife," he finished.

When Lady Mildred's eyes grew round and fastened once more upon Linnea, it became shockingly clear that she hadn't known of her son's marriage. "His wife?" she repeated, suddenly looking even more exhausted than before. "His wife? A de Valcourt?" She stared disbelievingly at Linnea.

"She is Beatrix de la Manse now. Axton is well pleased with her," Peter added in a gentle tone. "But come, Mother. Beatrix has prepared a comfortable chamber for you."

With a pointed look and a subtle twist of his head, Peter roused Linnea from her inertia. As he led his mother up the steps, Linnea gave her a tentative smile. "You are most welcome to Maidenstone Castle—"

"Thank you," Lady Mildred murmured. Then she pulled her pained gaze from the unexpected sight of her son's wife and leaned heavily on Peter's arm. "I am tired and would lie myself down for a while."

Linnea let them pass, then followed them up the steps, through the hall, and up two more flights toward the third floor chambers. Lady Mildred seemed to droop even more as they progressed past the second floor lord's chamber. Linnea had decided to put her on the top floor for that very reason, to save her the pain of remembering the time when she'd shared that chamber with her husband. Now, however, she worried that the older woman had not the stamina to make so hard a climb.

They had reached the antechamber on the third floor when Axton's call wafted up to them.

"Mother! You are arrived!"

With a clatter of heavy leather boots on the stone stairs he was quickly upon them, and once more Linnea witnessed the emotional reunion of mother and son. Axton was still dressed for riding. Mud clung to his boots and sweat to his brow. But that seemed only to make him more masculine, more vital, and more beautiful in Linnea's eyes.

His mother too seemed to drink in the sight of him and be revived by what she saw.

"I have prayed more hours than I can say . . ." The rest of her words were lost when he wrapped her in his arms.

"You are home now. Your prayers have been answered."

They drew apart and the Lady Mildred stared up at her warrior son. " 'Twas not for Maidenstone that I prayed, but for you and Peter. Never forget that." Then her eyes turned to Linnea, and in the awkward silence both Axton and Peter followed her gaze.

Linnea stared back at the woman who she knew must detest the thought that her son had wed a daughter of de Valcourt. The fact that she would detest even more the deception that daughter played brought an unpalatable lump of shame into Linnea's throat.

"I take it you have met Lady Beatrix," Axton said.

Lady Mildred nodded. She looked up at her son without speaking, but Linnea heard all her unspoken questions. So, apparently, did Axton, for he gestured for Linnea to approach them.

"I know my hasty marriage has come as a surprise to you. But there will be no question of property ownership now. No matter the agreement Stephen and Henry ultimately make, Maidenstone will remain ours. My marriage to Beatrix ensures it." He caught Linnea's hand in his and drew her even nearer. "I am well pleased with her as my wife. When you have time to know her, I hope you will be equally pleased for me."

To her credit, the Lady Mildred gave Linnea a strained smile. But she did not move to greet her more warmly. She had passed on to Peter his blue eyes, Linnea saw. And to Axton his straight, proud nose. She was not a beautiful woman, but no doubt she'd been very handsome in her youth. Now, though, her face was tired and lined, and she looked beaten down as much by the unsettling news of her son's marriage as by anything else that had happened to her in the past eighteen years.

Linnea tried to smile. "If I can provide you with anything else—"

"There is no need." Lady Mildred forestalled any further offers from Linnea. "This chamber is quite adequate." The older woman drew a deep breath, as if she did marshal her energy. "Ah, here are my maid and my trunk. If I may be allowed a few hours respite?"

Linnea took her cue and backed away. Though Axton and Peter did not linger above stairs much longer than she, Linnea was nonetheless aware that she was excluded from the most important discussions within the de la Manse family. No doubt Axton had much to answer for to his mother. Despite her restraint, it was plain she did not approve of the woman he'd wed, and for some perverse reason, that troubled Linnea mightily. It should not. But it did.

But then, everything was perverse about her situation, most especially her own reaction to it. To try to make sense of it only muddled things worse, for the fact was, she wanted her enemies to approve of her, while at the same time, she was beginning not to care whether her own family did or not . . . If it were not for her sister—

The thought of Beatrix stopped her cold. It always came back to her. Beatrix was the one person in the world who loved Linnea and always had. Axton and Peter might be coming to accept her presence in their lives. Their mother might conceivably do so as well someday. But it was Beatrix who actually loved her, and whom she loved.

She stared across the great hall that bustled now with dinner preparations. The tables were being assembled and the benches put in place. Two boys filled dozens of ewers with wine and centered them, two to a table.

As children she and Beatrix had played and teased each other and daydreamed in this room. They'd huddled beneath the tables and chased one another between them. As they'd grown, they'd carried their adventures into the bailey and further, into every crack and crevice of the castle. There was no escaping the fact that she was half of Beatrix and Beatrix was half of her—and also that after Maynard, Maidenstone Castle should go to Beatrix.

It would have been best if the real Beatrix had married

Axton. Linnea could see that now. But it was too late for that. She must protect Beatrix and allow her to make a marriage that would win back her birthright for her, even if that birthright conflicted with the birthright Axton felt he held.

But she could not care about Axton, not when it came to Beatrix. This was all about Beatrix, she reminded herself, and she must keep that uppermost in her mind.

It was all about Beatrix, the sister she loved.

Chapter 14

Linnea sought out her father. Beatrix and Lady Harriet were gone. Maynard clung but barely to life. That left Sir Edgar, changed though he was, as her only link to the de Valcourt line.

She found him in the stables watching the farrier tend to the shoeing of the great destriers the knights rode in battle. In the scant week since they'd been overrun by Axton and the de la Manse forces, her father had seemed to become another man entirely. He was shrunken somehow, much like Maynard. She knew that Sir Edgar's affliction was not of the body, however, but rather of the soul. Maynard fought to live, only his body betrayed him. But her father had somehow lost his will to live, and his body was succumbing to the inner sickness of it.

She steeled herself to be strong, as much for him as for herself. "Father, I have been looking for you. I would talk with you a while."

At first he seemed not to hear. He only stared at the farrier, watching as the man steadied one massive forefoot between his thighs and picked out pebbles and flint and any other debris that might cause injury to the beast. When the farrier paused and slanted her an understanding look, however, Sir Edgar seemed to come out of his trance.

"Beatrix?" He peered at her, squinting from beneath his bushy gray brows. "Beatrix?" he repeated, as if he were enormously relieved to see her. "Something is wrong. Derek will not saddle Vasterling for me. I would ride but he says I may not."

"I'm certain he is only following orders," Linnea murmured, shooting Derek a concerned glance.

"But I order him to let me ride," her father retorted petulantly. "I *order* him to saddle my horse."

"But Derek's orders from Lord Axton are to keep you within the castle." Linnea took his arm and steered him away from the farrier's sympathetic gaze. She'd come to her father for comfort, but she knew now that it was only foolish hope that had brought her here. He did not have the means to comfort her when it was he himself who needed comfort. Still, she would not abandon him to his increasing confusion, nor allow it to make of him a public spectacle.

"But I am lord here!" he argued, jerking his arm from her hold. "My word is law at Maidenstone!"

Several servants in the yard turned at the sound of his angry voice. Linnea grabbed him again, and this time she made him face her.

"You are no longer lord here, Father. Try to remember," she pleaded. "Axton de la Manse has reclaimed his childhood home and I am now wed with him—"

"Beatrix? You are Beatrix?"

Linnea caught her breath in sudden terror. Her father was staring at her in renewed confusion, while beyond him the farrier watched the exchange. The alewife and her helper paused in the yard at the commotion and two knights and several squires were watching them also. Linnea could not think, she was so unnerved by his unexpected words.

"You are my daughter—"

"Of course I am," Linnea interrupted him. "I am Beatrix. This is Maidenstone Castle, and—" Her mind raced for a way to divert him. "And Maynard, your son, is sorely wounded. Don't you remember, Father?"

Linnea's heart pounded an uneven rhythm as he stared at her. She was causing him pain, she knew. Reminding

189

him of everything he'd lost, most especially his beloved son and heir. But she simply could not risk him blurting out the truth about who she was. Still, it cut her to the core to see his confusion give way to painful remembrance. The anguish that came over his face was as grievous as a mortal blow might be.

"Beatrix," he mumbled, and his eyes clouded as he tried to remember everything. "For a moment I thought you were—"

"She is gone away," Linnea interrupted him before he could say her true name out loud. "She left before . . . before the castle was besieged. I am Beatrix," she lied to her father, whispering now, so none of the onlookers could hear. "I am Beatrix. You and I and Maynard must cling to one another now, for we are all we have left of our family."

The resistance left him like red wine gushing from a ripped wineskin. He deflated. His chest sagged and his head sank deeper between his shoulders. "We've lost everything, haven't we?" He looked up at her like a child might, searching for comfort and reassurance. Only she had none to offer.

The same despair that had turned him from a blustering lord with a proud history of accomplishments, into a broken old man, bereft of all hope, swept over her now, robbing her of what little confidence she had. She'd come to him, needy in spirit, only to find him far more needy than she.

"Come along, Father," she murmured, past the knot of emotions in her throat. "Let us go and sit with Maynard. He needs our prayers, I fear. Come along."

He followed her without resistance, like a forlorn child would. Linnea guided him toward the keep, beyond which was the priest's chamber where Maynard lay. But as they mounted the steps, the door swung open and they came face-to-face with Axton.

His eyes caught with hers and held for one long, fleeting moment. Then his gaze switched to her father, and Linnea saw them darken with dislike. Not dislike, she immediately amended. Hatred.

"Where are you going?" He crossed his arms and stared down at them, his body rigid and his expression grim.

Linnea felt her father's arm tense beneath her hand. He might not have recalled their circumstances just moments ago, but it was clear he was remembering now. "We are going to see my brother," she answered Axton, hoping to get past him before her father said anything.

Axton studied her a moment. "He may no longer have the freedom of the castle," he stated, indicating her father with a jerk of his head.

She stared at him incredulously. "Are you saying he may not visit his own son?"

"I would not have my mother upset by the sight of the man who did rob her of her home and husband and sons."

The sharp retort she wanted to make died unsaid. What argument was she to make against that? That his mother should not blame her father for the disruption of her life? That the woman should simply have adjusted to her circumstances? That she should not hate him and be forever pained by the very sight of him?

It was the sad state of the human race to always covet what others had and to hate those who coveted what you had. Axton had taken Maidenstone from her father. Her father had taken it from Axton's father. No doubt Axton's father had taken it from someone else—

"How did your family come by this castle?"

He frowned at her unexpected question and his eyes narrowed suspiciously. "My grandfather received it from William Rufus."

"As a reward?"

"He saved his life during the campaigns in Normandy before the First Crusade."

"Who was lord here before him? Before your grandfather?"

He nodded then, as if he understood the direction of her thoughts. His expression lifted into a faint smile, but he was plainly not amused. "This castle was but a motte and bailey fortress then."

"But it had a lord, did it not? A man with a family who claimed it as his home."

"He was a traitorous fool. But that is of no moment. Maidenstone is mine, and my word is law. Keep him *away* from my mother, for if he upsets her, I will have no choice but to confine him in the donjon!"

Her father had not said a word during the exchange between the two. But at Axton's icy threat, Sir Edgar fell back a step.

"What *do* you here? I hold the demesne in the name of my liege lord, Stephen of Blois, King of England—"

"He won't be king for long!" Axton advanced on Sir Edgar as if he meant to murder him right there.

Without pausing to think, Linnea stepped between them, pressing her hands against Axton's chest. He grabbed her by the upper arms as if to thrust her aside. But she clung to him, demanding he hear her out.

"Please, Axton. Do not punish him. I beg you!"

His hands gripped her with bruising strength as he glared over her head at her father. To his credit, however, he did not push her aside or advance any farther toward Sir Edgar.

"Henry will be king of England soon enough. I suggest you bow to the inevitable, old man. Henry holds England and I hold Maidenstone. And your daughter," he added. He drew Linnea up against him, encircling her in a familiar and intimate embrace.

Caught as she was in Axton's unyielding hold, Linnea could not see her father's reaction. But even she could not have imagined the violence of it.

"Unhand her!" Sir Edgar roared. "Remove your foul hand from my daughter!"

"No!" Linnea clung to Axton, certain he would strike her father down. "He's not right in his mind. He doesn't understand—"

It was her father who flung her aside. She stumbled and fell down the several steps to the ground. But she was oblivious to the sharp pain in her knee or the burning scrape to the heel of her hand. She had to save her father from Axton.

"I will strike you down!" Sir Edgar screamed his challenge. "I will skewer you—have you drawn and quartered! Mount your head on a pike!"

Linnea scrambled up only to be lifted upright by Axton. "Are you all right?" he asked in a taut voice. His eyes scanned her swiftly.

"Don't you touch her!" Sir Edgar shrieked.

One of Axton's men came up, hand on the hilt of his sword. Everyone in the bailey had halted their activities and stared now in morbid fascination at the confrontation between the old lord and the new one.

Axton handed Linnea into his man's care, then turned to face the ranting man behind him. Linnea saw his lethal calm, and she knew her father was in the greatest danger of his life. What did she achieve to save Maidenstone for Beatrix if she could not save her father's very life?

She jerked away from the man who tried to support her and reached Axton on the fourth step. Her father was one step up, but Axton's greater height put their faces on the same level.

"Don't hurt him!"

"Stay out of this," Axton ordered.

"He doesn't understand!"

"He issued a challenge to me. And I am more than ready to meet it."

"I am lord here!" Sir Edgar bellowed, adding more fuel to the fire. His face had turned an ugly color; his eyes bulged and the veins stood out on his neck.

He had gone mad, Linnea realized. He must have, to confront Axton so. Still, she could not abandon him to her husband's furious temper.

"Axton. Listen to me. I beg you!"

The two men were but inches apart. Only her arm across Axton's chest stood between them, and it was little enough barrier. She could feel the tension in him, the stiffness, the taut readiness to strike out at his enemy.

"Begone, daughter—"

"Be quiet, Father!" she snapped back at him. With her other hand she pushed him back from Axton, and to her surprise, he did not resist. She squeezed between them once more. "Father, do you forget that Sir Axton is lord here now? That he is my husband? I cannot have you quarreling with my husband—" She broke off when she saw his scowl give way to confusion and then to a terrible sort of sadness. The very hopelessness of it hurt her to look at. He was her father, and though she'd always known she was the most insignificant of his children, she owed him her life—both the creation of it and the preservation of it. She'd heard the stories of her birth—how her grandmother had demanded that the second babe be killed and her father had prevented it.

She blinked back tears. It was hard to witness his terrible decline now. "Father, this does none of us any good. Let me take you to your chambers."

He was trembling, his whole body quivering as if at any moment he would shatter apart. The violent anger of before seemed to have become instead a violent sort of sorrow, a self-consuming misery that she could not save him from. He turned toward the keep as if to mount the steps and go to the lord's chamber.

"This way, Father," she whispered, past the emotions that seized her chest and caught in her throat. She caught his hand in hers. "This way."

She guided him to go down the steps. As they passed Axton, she paused and looked up at him. His expression was hard, like hewn granite, and terrifyingly easy to read. He'd wanted to fight her father. He still did. He wanted his enemy dead.

"Axton," she murmured, meeting the awful opaqueness of his pale eyes. She started to place her palm on his chest, but her father pulled on her other hand and the moment passed. At least he'd spared her father's life, she thought as she proceeded with her father to the chapel and the priest's chamber. He could have had him killed but he did not.

Someone called out for everyone to disperse. Sir Reynold, she thought. The clusters of onlookers began to break up, though the stunned castlefolk stared as she and her father passed.

Where Axton went she did not know. What he did, how he felt—all those things she could only wonder about as she settled her father in a corner of the chapel. He leaned heavily against one of the stone pillars and covered his face with his hands. If he cried, he did it silently.

Linnea did not face the altar. She went instead to the wall niche that held a painted wood statue of the Holy Mother, knelt before it, and began to pray.

I don't know what to do. Please guide me. Help me. Tell me what to do about my father—and about my husband, who is not truly my husband at all.

Axton strode to the tilting yard. No one spoke to him or hailed him or came anywhere near him. Fury emanated from him in waves—steaming, frigid—and no one would dare come near it.

He had needed to strike someone down, to spill blood and find a release for his rage in raw, brutal battle. But he had no battle, save with an old man he could not justify killing, no matter how desperately he wanted to. He had no opponent to face this day, to vent his seething anger upon. Even in his fury he knew better than to call for one of his men to practice with him. He might not be able to control himself.

He shoved into the storage room and grabbed the first sword he spied. It was a heavy, bastard sword, meant to be wielded with both hands. Before the door to the shed had time to even close behind him, he stormed back out into the yard.

The tilting dummy had no chance. He charged it, envisioning Edgar de Valcourt, only twenty years younger than he now was. Chopping, hacking, swinging with every bit of the rage that was in him, Axton made swift work of his mute enemy.

If anyone witnessed his display of deadly skill and murderous temper, they did it from afar. No one came near the tilting yard. The entire bailey seemed too vacant and too empty for a summer afternoon; the alewife, the armorer, and the beekeeper should all be out of doors with their work.

Did no one in this damnable place have any sense of duty or responsibility? Axton raged. Must he force every one of them to know their place and do the work assigned to them?

With one final, mighty swing, he severed the dummy from the frame it hung upon. It landed with a dull thump and a cloud of dust. Axton stared at the slaughtered remains of the tilting dummy. His arms trembled from their exertion, his chest heaved as he gasped for breath. But he felt no real satisfaction.

Beatrix should not have interfered.

Then he shook his head. No. Even he must admit that she could not have stood aside and watched as her husband destroyed her father. But she should not have gone off with that ruined old man and left *him* alone in the bailey. She was his wife now. Her loyalty must be to *him*.

He shoved the bastard sword into the dummy, as he might into a downed enemy, then left the weapon standing upright in the inert sack of fustian and wheat chaff. She had much to answer to, he decided as his narrowed gaze scanned the deserted yard. If she would protect her father and show him the attention she should turn on her husband, then she had much to learn about being wife to Axton de la Manse.

It was Peter who found her, and Peter who told her what she already knew.

"Go to him and undo his anger before it erupts and burns us all."

Linnea glanced at her father, but he did not seem to hear. He sat now on a crude bench, not praying, not doing anything. She sighed and without reply to Peter moved toward the door. She was so weary, so tired of all this tumult and tension, this hatred and lying.

But it was *her* lie that was the greatest, and it was the truth she hid which would cause the greatest tumult of all.

"Where is he?"

"In the tilting yard." Peter held the door open, then fell into step beside her. Linnea felt everyone's eyes following her. The feeling that everyone's future depended on her settled like a gruesome burden upon her shoulders. And yet, what choice had she but to take up that burden, to carry it until . . . until she could lay it down.

She didn't want to think about that.

She looked sidelong at Peter. "Is he taking out his anger on one of his hapless men?"

The boy grimaced. "No one would dare cross swords with Axton when his temper flares this high."

Linnea shivered to think how furious he must be. Yet she could not escape the irony of the situation. "The most powerful of his men fear to approach him and so you send for me?"

They went down the steps that led to the bailey. "He will not hurt *you*."

Linnea thought that was true. She *hoped* it was true. But when she saw the deserted yard, she was not so sure. Not a soul was visible in the bailey. The laundry kettles stood abandoned; the steam that rose from them was the only indication that someone had been there not so very long before. No one rummaged in the kitchen garden, though a small handcart stood within the gate, half-filled with weeds. Only one hound—an old one—lay in a patch of sun. He thumped his tail three times when they passed him. Otherwise, nothing moved.

Axton was not moving either. He stood over a sack, from which protruded a long sword. Linnea hesitated and glanced at Peter. But he only shrugged and stepped back, letting her proceed alone.

Then Axton looked up and spied her. His gaze narrowed as his anger found a new focus in her, but in that moment everything Linnea had worried about seemed to fade into the background. What she saw in him went deeper than the anger wrapped so tautly around him. He mourned his

197

father and brothers. The rage and frustration that he wanted to take out on her father had been thwarted, however, and he'd been left with no one to punish but the blameless sack lying inert at his feet. He would take that frustration out on her, of course. But then, she'd willingly become her family's sacrificial lamb, hadn't she? Why fear playing that same role for *his* family?

Besides, he was hurting. Deep down in his soul, where he didn't want anyone to see, he was still hurting.

She walked right up to him until only the fallen dummy separated them. The fallen dummy and the forbidding sword.

"Would you walk with me?" she began, saying the first words that popped into her head.

"Walk?" His face was dark with barely suppressed emotion. Mutilating the poor tilting dummy had clearly afforded him no great comfort.

"Well . . ." Linnea hesitated. "If you would prefer other . . . another sort of . . . activity . . ." She trailed off, knowing her face had heated with color. But she did not look away from his intense stare.

To her surprise, her offer seemed somehow to confuse him. His gaze shifted briefly to his brother who stood across the yard still, then came back to her. "Does my dear brother throw you at me that I will vent my rage on you and spare him and the rest of my men? Do you come to me, wife, with the offer of your body at his behest? To sacrifice yourself to me—"

"I would have come to you of my own choice anyway, without his prodding. I did but wish to see my father settled—"

It was the wrong thing to say, and she broke off when she saw him stiffen. But the subject of her father would not go away, and so she decided to confront it head-on. She always fared better when she confronted Axton head-on. She lifted her skirts and stepped over the dummy and past the sword, so that she and Axton were but inches apart.

"Walk with me, Axton. Outside the walls of this place that brings you such pain. We will talk of my father and his sins against you, and see if we can find some way to a peacefulness between us."

She reached up one hand and rested it against his chest, imploring him with her eyes to do this with her. In that moment she was not thinking of her family or of any plots to recover Maidenstone Castle for the de Valcourts. She was not thinking that he believed she was Beatrix, or that they had no real future as man and wife. Her mind was filled only with the wish to see him let go of the past that caused him so much sorrow. She wanted to see him smile at her, and perhaps even to laugh.

"Come walk with me," she repeated, not flinching from the terrible intensity of his eyes.

Without warning he caught both of her arms in his hands, as if he meant to haul her up against him, to initiate the explosive passion that existed between them, here and now. She wasn't sure if she wanted him to do that or not. But he only stared at her with eyes darkened by too many emotions to name.

He was a man of war. Everything about him bespoke it, most especially now. He was damp with his maddened exercise with his sword. He trembled with lingering need to see his enemy's blood spill into the dirt and gravel beneath his feet. But he did not see her as his enemy. Not anymore. She felt that about him most clearly.

She leaned into him and rested her cheek against his chest. "Walk with me, Axton. 'Twould do us both a world of good."

Lady Mildred had wept as she watched her oldest son hack so violently at the tilting dummy. She knew what he felt, for she felt it too.

Edgar de Valcourt had no right to be here. He never had. A part of her had wanted to see Axton slay him. She would have happily watched the man's head be severed from his shoulders and tumble down the steps, leaving a trail of blood as it went.

But de Valcourt's daughter had protected him from Axton. Though Lady Mildred knew the girl had done the right thing—the only thing she could have done—she resented it. Now, though, the girl was standing before Axton, speaking quietly to him did seemwhile the sword swayed slightly between them.

Lady Mildred leaned nearer the open window, not wishing to be seen, but unable to turn away either. The couple in the tilting yard had no eyes for her, however, nor for any of the myriad other eyes that surely watched in secret.

Then the girl stepped closer to him, and Axton grasped her arms.

Tears blurred Lady Mildred's vision once more and a sadness unlike any previous one seemed to press in on her, making it almost impossible to breathe. He was going off with her. Her son, who'd sworn to avenge the deaths of his father and two older brothers, had turned away from his sword and moved now with his wife toward the gate that opened to the moat and the village beyond.

She turned her back to the view as a sob rose then broke free. She leaned against the well of her third floor solar and wept the most painful tears of her long and painful life. Coming back to Maidenstone was supposed to have been her triumph. A bittersweet triumph, perhaps, but ultimately satisfying as her enemies were dispossessed of all they'd stolen from her.

But instead they'd stolen from her anew, something even more precious. Something she'd not realized could ever be taken from her. They'd taken Axton's heart. She could see that as clearly as ever she'd seen anything before.

She sagged against the solid wall and wept the hard, hot tears she'd not thought she could still possess. They'd taken Axton too, on top of William, Ives, and her beloved Allan.

She didn't think she could survive this new loss. She didn't think she wanted to.

Chapter 15

They walked in silence. Yet once they crossed the narrow bridge, the dusty thud of their feet led them to a world filled with sound. It was as if they'd departed the mythical castle of the sleeping princess, a tale Norma had often related to Beatrix and Linnea. Though the castle was oppressed by a terrible curse, the countryside outside its walls brimmed still with life. Bright, noisy, wonderful life.

Linnea was acutely aware of Axton's presence beside her. They did not touch, but only walked side by side, not speaking, not looking at one another. But there was a communication between them. She knew that without a doubt.

She followed the flight of a pair of goosanders as they dipped and swayed, darted and dove. An otter plunged off a rock and into the water as they passed. A golden oriole cried down in agitation at their invasion of its domain, while a startled duck and her string of downy young scurried from a stand of blue flag, parting the irises and their stately spears, and leaving a trail of Vs as they swam.

Linnea had forgotten how beautiful the month of April could be. The past several days had been dark and grim, in spirit at least. More like January than April. But spring was nigh, she was a married woman, and her husband did walk at her side.

"I am glad to be away from there," she began, as they turned off the rutted road and onto a narrow path that led toward St. Catherine's Beck. "Perhaps I will pick flowers for the table. Or for your mother's chamber. Would she accept them from me?" she added in an uncertain voice.

She thought he did not mean to answer, for he was silent so long. Then he sighed and she heard in that release of his breath, a release also of some portion of his rage.

"She will accept them. You will not find in my mother the outward opposition that your grandmother did show.

She will not send you killing looks nor curse you when your back is but half the way turned."

"But in the privacy of her room, will she shred the flowers I send to her?"

He finally looked at her. "Perhaps. Does it matter so much to you?"

Linnea looked away. " 'Tis not my wish to inflict further pain on her. Yet I fear that by my very presence I do that. She would have you wed to any other woman but myself."

He made a sound, as if he intended to speak but then thought better of it. Linnea stopped in the shade of a towering sycamore tree that marked the narrow strip of forest lining the riverbank. "You also would rather be wed to any other woman."

He faced her and their eyes met and held. "I did not wish to marry you any more than you wished to marry me. But now that it is done, I am not sorry for my lot."

"But because I am a de Valcourt, you can never be content." Linnea knew she spoke the truth, but it brought her a pain she could hardly bear.

"You view it that way, but I would rather say that I am not sorry to have you to wife in spite of your name."

A small enough thing it was, but Linnea was comforted by his words.

"But what of you?" he continued. "How much pain does it bring you to be wed to me, the man who has struck down your brother and reduced your father to the crumpled old man he has become?"

When she would have looked away, he caught her chin and tilted her face up so that she must meet his gaze. "I was . . . reluctant," she answered him honestly. "But . . . you have proven to be not so terrible a husband as I did fear."

That drew the faintest hint of a smile from him. A slight easing of the lines in his brow; a subtle curve of one side of his mouth. " 'Twould have been easier to have met in a neutral court," he admitted. His hand cupped her cheek, a warm, callused caress, and Linnea's heart rate increased. This was what she'd wanted, to divert him from his rage, to lull him into a more peaceful state. Yet now, in this dappled place where birds trilled, insects went busily about their routine, and the wind blew the heady scents of verdant life all around them, she found herself unable to let go of the castle and everything it symbolized.

"You asked me once about the suitors that did call at the castle. What of the maidens you did court? Was there not one you did think to make your wife?" She did not want to hear his answer, so she could not fathom why she had asked the question. But she stood there waiting for it just the same.

"I have been too engrossed in avenging the wrongs done to my family to have entertained the subject of a wife. My mother has had better success planning Peter's marriage than my own."

Linnea felt her relief in every portion of her being. There had been no particular woman in his life. Yet her foolish relief was just as swiftly undone by an intruding reality. "But you know everything about what happens between a man and—" She broke off when she realized she'd spoken her thoughts aloud. Though she prayed he did not understand what she'd started to say, it was clear he did.

A rueful grin curved his lips up farther. "A man need not entertain thoughts of marriage to become skilled in . . . certain activities."

Though it was an idiotic reaction, Linnea was nonetheless crushed. "You have done . . . done *that* with other women. Many other women," she forced herself to add.

His grin faded. "It counts for nothing. Much as a knight's exercise counts for nothing if he does not acquit himself well on the battlefield."

Linnea did not like that argument, though she could not quite verbalize why. He had practiced with other women so that he could perform well for his wife? "Such practice is forbidden to women," she muttered.

"There is no need for the woman to be well practiced in the bedroom so long as her groom is." He caught one of her hands and brought it up to his lips. He kissed each knuckle slowly, all the while holding her gaze captive in his. "We did very well together. Indeed, my knowledge and your innocence together did seem to ignite the very air around us."

Linnea gulped hard. She felt as if the air around them *now* had begun to burn.

" 'Tis foolish to dwell on the past," he continued. "Only you have I wed. Only you have I gifted with a chain of gold and rubies." His free hand moved to her waist, then slid lower, to where his wedding gift rested warm and telling against her bare flesh. "I have no regrets, Beatrix. Do you?"

Beatrix. Linnea stiffened at his use of her sister's name. For a very few minutes she'd allowed herself to forget.

Then his expression altered and she knew he'd felt her reaction. His hands fell away from her and he took a step back from her.

"A foolish question, it would appear. I forget that your brother yet suffers from the blow I struck him, and that your family is torn apart because I am returned to Maidenstone."

Linnea could not manage a reply. Why must she be Beatrix? Why? All he spoke was true—Maynard lay near death and her family was torn apart even more so than he suspected. Still, that did not lay so heavily upon her as did the ugly reality of the deception she did play. She stared up at him, wanting more than anything to tell him the truth.

"Axton, I . . . I must confess to you—"

"No. Do not speak of your family to me. 'Tis not a matter we are ready to make peace over. It will take more time than we yet have had." He raked both his hands through his hair and let his gaze roam the edge of the wooded riverbank. "But that day will come, I hope. For now, pick you the flowers you seek. Let us wander awhile and not think on those matters that await us in the castle."

His eyes met hers once more and for once she saw him as a man only, not as a warrior or the lord of the castle. Not as a vengeful son or a harsh conqueror.

If he was willing to abandon those roles for a little while, then perhaps she could put aside Beatrix—not entirely as she'd very nearly done, but in her mind, at least. To confess the complete truth to him would destroy any hope for peace between them, even this temporary peace. Although she knew she did but postpone the inevitable, there was something in her that longed to meet him shed of the difficult truth. She wanted to pretend, if only for a very few hours, that theirs could be a good and joyful union.

The truth was, she wanted to pretend that he loved her, because she . . . Once more she stiffened, though this time it was shock. She wanted to pretend that he loved her, because she was beginning to love him.

Sweet Mary, but she was more foolish than even her grandmother could have imagined!

A sudden sting of tears made her avert her eyes to the partially tamed path. Beneath her feet string-of-pearls fern swept the hem of her gown. Beatrix's gown.

Go away, Beatrix! Leave me be, for just a little while!

"Yes," she mumbled, hoping she sounded coherent. "Yes, I would . . . I would leave those troubles behind us for now."

So saying, she bent and plucked a stalk of rue, then lifted the bright yellow flower to him. "Herb-of-grace. 'Tis good to expel worms."

He met her gaze with a face devoid of expression. "Are there any among these weeds that erase memory?"

Linnea's heart went out to him. "Valerian is said to ease bad dreams. But memories . . ." Her eyes searched his face as if she'd never truly seen him before. "I think only time can ease that sort of pain."

"What of hunger?"

"Hunger? Well, if you are hungry, there may be wild strawberries or blueberries. Perhaps fiddle ferns—"

"Not that sort of hunger, Beatrix."

Linnea firmly blotted out her sister's name and focused instead on his other words. A physical hunger, but not for food. The chain burned against her tender flesh as the hunger grew inside her too.

"There are those herbs which can curb that . . . that sort of hunger."

"I would not curb it, but rather would assuage it." He moved nearer. She backed farther into the shaded place. "Is there anything within this sheltered woodland upon which I might feast? My need is great," he added, following her ever deeper in the stand of sycamores and beech trees.

A shiver of longing and anticipation swelled to encompass Linnea's entire being. She'd often thought of him as some great, dark predator, the bear that adorned his coat of arms and his bed. *Their* bed. At those times, though, she'd always considered herself his hapless prey, and she'd feared for herself. Now, though, she found a thrilling excitement in it.

She backed into the deep shade of the towering beeches and the understory of fern and holly. The castle walls were blocked from view by the forest's mantle of spring greenery. Scolding squirrels and a pair of competing jayhawks drowned out any sounds from the nearby village. She was truly alone with him as he stalked her toward the river's edge.

Her heart began to pound with anticipation. Surely she could not want *that* to happen between them. Not here! But she kept backing away, all the while hoping he would catch her soon, for she felt very much like kindling must, smoldering and about to burst into flame.

Axton trapped his pretty, flushed wife against a yew tree, an ancient, gnarled specimen that must have seen a thousand lovers pass beneath its heavy limbs. But never had it seen a man so powerfully driven as was he, he vowed. Whether a lad giddy with his first love, or a halé fellow intent on wooing his lady fair with well-rehearsed words and knowing caresses, none among them could match the depths of his feelings for this woman before him, neither his desire for her nor his love.

Love.

As Axton pressed her against the yew with a hand on either side of her—as he stared into the depthless green of her wide eyes, and drowned in the fiery sea of her emotions—he could not quite trust his own emotions.

Love? No, only an understandable lust, combined with a new need for peace in his life. He wanted the joy and comfort of a sweet and willing wife. That was all.

And as he took her against the sturdy, patient tree, as he filled himself with her taste and scent, and even the sounds of her as she found her own pleasure, he told himself it was no more than that. She offered him a new sort of peace while at the same time letting him exhaust his body upon her. Any man in his right mind would feel the same. Love had nothing to do with anything, most especially not with him and de Valcourt's daughter.

But as he spilled himself deep inside her, he admitted that he could learn to care for her. If she proved her loyalty to him, if she behaved as a good wife should . . . If she gave him a child and continued to please him . . .

Maybe he could someday come to love her. Maybe.

They returned as dusk settled gray and purple over Maidenstone. An early moon floated low on the horizon, huge and luminous. A good sign, Linnea hoped.

Most certainly it had presaged a very good day.

She pushed back a loose tendril of her hopelessly tangled hair. Her feet were damp, as was her hem, and no doubt twigs and bracken and green stains on her skirt would proclaim to all precisely how she and Axton had spent the last several hours.

But she was content, and so was he, if his tender considerations were any indication. His arm circled her waist and his hand rested comfortably on her hip. As they came out of the woods and onto the road that led to the castle, and spied the twin torches that marked the gate, she impulsively slipped her arm around his waist too.

"Are you afraid to return?" he asked her.

"Afraid?" she echoed. Afraid did not begin to describe her feelings about their return to the castle and all the troubles, deception, and responsibilities it harbored. "I wish . . . I wish that for once there could be peace at Maidenstone."

"For once? Was there not peace there before I arrived?"

He stopped and turned her to face him. "What was life like here before I came?"

Empty, she wanted to say. Before you came into my life it was empty, hollow, and lonely.

But that was not entirely true. She hadn't felt those things then, because she hadn't known what else there could be for her. Now, though, she knew. Thanks to him and the way her heart was filled with only him, she knew exactly how terrible her life used to be. How aimless and without purpose.

"It was simple and uneventful," she finally answered.

"But not peaceful?"

When she only shrugged, he went on. "The day will come, Beatrix, when it shall be simple and peaceful again."

"But not uneventful," she said, only because, as always, her sister's name had jolted her and she could think of nothing else to say.

He cupped her face in both his hands then, and kissed her. His mouth met hers, parting her lips and devouring her whole, it seemed. But not so much with passion as with . . . as with something else, her dizzied mind vaguely noted.

He'd kissed her very seldom, she realized when he slowly drew back from her. At the wedding ceremony, but not otherwise. Not even when they'd made love before.

But he'd kissed her today up against that tree, and when he'd laid her down in the bed of ferns.

And now again.

Something had altered between them today. Did he sense it? Did he realize she loved him? Had she revealed that in something she'd said or done?

She searched his face, fearful and hopeful all in the same moment. Then a cry drew his attention away and, to her dismay, she saw a trio of riders bearing down on them, followed by a dog. Peter's dog, she saw as they drew nearer. It was Peter and Sir Maurice and another knight.

"What ho, brother?" Peter's horse danced an excited circle around them. While the other men held back, Peter continued. "We did begin to think some wood ogre had made mischief with you. I see, however, that it was no ogre, but rather a wood nymph who has distracted you so long."

"Perhaps," Axton replied, pulling Linnea closer into the shelter of his arms. "I am touched by your concern," he added dryly.

" 'Twas the Lady Mildred who did bid us—" Sir Maurice broke off when Linnea stiffened and Axton frowned. "She feared the evening meal would be delayed," the man finished lamely.

"Would you ride?" Peter offered a hand to Linnea. He stared at her curiously, as if to ask how she had dealt with Axton's terrible temper. In answer she leaned her head against Axton's shoulder, though she worried it was too bold a gesture.

But Axton did not shrug her off, and Peter's face lit with an unsubtle grin.

"We will walk," Axton stated. "Be off with you and allow us to return at our own pace. We will arrive in sufficient time to dine as ever."

Sir Maurice and the other knight nodded, wheeled their anxious beasts, and rode off at once. But Peter circled them once more, handling his massive steed with an admirable ease while Moor scratched his ear, chasing some unseen pest.

"Shall I announce to your men that they should no longer fear being summoned by you to practice with sword or lance, or any other weapon?"

Axton eyed his younger brother warningly. "Tell them this. Should I desire to strike anyone low this evening, 'tis my promise that the first one I summon shall be you."

But Axton's threat had little effect on the boy's exuberant mood, for he laughed then spun his spirited animal and charged back toward the gate with Moor behind him, sprinting through the lowering light like a dark and silent wraith.

Peter had every right to be jubilant, Linnea thought as she and Axton started forward again along the wide, dusty roadway. The boy thought matters were easing at Maidenstone. The fact was, in spite of the rude reminder of the Lady Mildred and her disapproval of his marriage, even Axton was not nearly so tense and frustrated as he'd been after the confrontation with Sir Edgar. Their interlude in the forest had done much to ease his mood. Peter had been right to send her to him.

But the new peace between her and Axton, perversely enough, made Linnea's situation worse than ever. She loved him. There was no longer any doubt in her mind. But she was bound to betray him—she'd betrayed him the moment she'd made her vow before the priest. There was no way for her to undo the lie and the damage it would wreak.

Loving him only made it that much worse.

Chapter 16

The mood surrounding the evening meal was strange. The de la Manse soldiers, led by Peter, did seem to celebrate. Lady Mildred's return to her home was the culmination of their long struggle and the symbol of their ultimate victory. Lady Mildred herself tried hard to participate in their gaiety. But Linnea was seated near enough to her to see the effort it took. The woman's smile was forced; her hands trembled; and not once did she look directly at her new daughter-in-law.

Axton, likewise, did not seem as caught up in the mood. He sat between his mother and his wife, with his predecessor, Sir Edgar, nowhere to be seen. Linnea had made certain her father was kept content in his new quarters tonight, and well out of sight. Still, for all his appearance of calm, Linnea knew that Axton could not be entirely satisfied until Maynard and Sir Edgar were dealt with by the young duke, Henry.

So the dinner progressed through twelve courses of suckling pig, blackbird pie, stuffed swan, grilled eel, and prodigious amounts of roasted and stewed vegetables and fruits, as well as oysters, meat pasties, and breads. They were entertained by minstrels, musicians, and tumblers, and even a man who ate fire.

But while the rest of the castle folk ate and drank themselves into a happy oblivion, at the head table a somberness prevailed.

Lady Mildred retired first, and Axton escorted her to her chamber. Linnea waited for his return before bidding him a good-night. It was Peter who escorted her upstairs, a grinning, drunken Peter who looked more the boy than the man in his foolish state. As ever, his dog followed at his heels.

"I have told my mother that you and Axton are well suited. After this day, there is none who can doubt it." He tripped over the edge of the carpet that stretched across the antechamber on the second floor, only catching himself on Moor. He rubbed the dog's ears affectionately and gave Linnea a sheepish grin. " 'Tis a good day to be a de la Manse."

Linnea glanced up the stairwell toward the third floor where Peter and Axton's mother now resided. "I don't think everyone in your family feels as you do."

"She will thaw toward you. You must only give her time. My mother is a good person. The fineth . . . *finest* lady I have ever known." Holding on to Moor's leather collar with one hand he made a reasonably credible bow. "I bid you good night, milady. I must return now to the hall, for we are laying bets—"

He broke off with a shame-faced expression that would have been comical had she not immediately suspected that the wager had something to do with her. Her and Axton, she realized with dismay.

"Peter?" she said warningly. "What sort of bet?"

He was backing away though, his face red, but his eyes sparkling nonetheless with drunken mischief. "I give him no more than a half-tankard downed before he is back up here with you."

"Peter!" she exclaimed again. But he was gone. She heard a clatter, as if he'd stumbled and fallen on the stairs, and she hoped he had. She hoped he'd fallen and dented his thick head!

But the secret truth was, she too wondered how long it would be before Axton joined her.

She was ready when he came, and he was ready too. Linnea did not think about the older woman upstairs when she welcomed Axton into their bed. She did not think of her grandmother or father, nor sister or brother, as he and she together sank into that dark, private oblivion. This would not last for long, this blissful feeling of loving someone and receiving his love in return—or at least his affection.

She had no control over what was to come. But she had some control over now, and she meant to squeeze whatever joy she could from this brief, ill-fated marriage. She meant to take a lifetime's joy of it. For the memory of their time together was all she would ever have in the empty years to come.

The week that followed was peaceable enough. A new routine settled over Maidenstone, though it was not so very different than the routine of before. But it was Linnea who did direct the castle servants now, not her grandmother. It was Linnea who decided on the menu and dispensed the herbs and spices; she who supervised the inside workers and the kitchen staff. She'd expected the Lady Mildred to assert her authority, but she had not done so. Axton's mother spent most of each day in her solar, accompanied only by her maid, and visited each day by both of her sons.

She did join the family for the midday meal, and of course for the morning mass. When she and Linnea had occasion to interact, it was cordial, but brief, and usually initiated by Linnea. Was her chamber comfortable? Did she have sufficient candles to sew by? Were the dishes seasoned to her liking?

To these questions Lady Mildred always gave the answer which least required any further response from Linnea. Yes, her chamber was comfortable. No, she needed no extra candles. Yes, the food was well seasoned.

If Axton noticed the awkwardness between his mother and his wife, he did not speak of it. Most certainly Linnea did not bring the subject up to him. But she felt a deep sorrow for the aging woman. Lady Mildred was home again, but she could take no true joy from it.

But Linnea was taking a joy from Maidenstone, despite the dark sword of truth that hung always over her head. Maynard shrank into a pitiful semblance of himself; her father was silent and lost somewhere in his thoughts; and Lady Mildred was a sad specter of a long-ago past. But Linnea had Axton and everything else faded beneath the light he brought into her life.

Whether it was his hard embrace as he drew her nightly to their bed, or merely the caress of his eyes from across the bailey, the effect he had on her was profound. She lived for those looks, for the casual touches. Even his hand at her elbow set tremors alive deep inside her. Though she knew it would not last—that it was in fact a fantasy that she lived—the more she had of Axton, the more she wanted.

Foolish as it was, the idea of bearing his child had begun to obsess her. Not a fortnight had she known the man—a man who'd begun as her enemy—and now she had no more fervent desire than to give him a child that would forge an enduring peace for Maidenstone—and for them.

Except that, of course, it would not. If anything, it would make matters worse, for the babe would ultimately be termed a bastard—if the Lady Harriet even allowed it to survive.

Linnea shivered and pressed a hand to her flat stomach. One thing she knew, she would not let her grandmother near her child. She would fight heaven and earth to protect any child of hers.

But she tried to put the idea of having Axton's child out of her mind, for to worry on that would have spoiled what little time she did have with him. She was determined not to do that.

Then on a Friday, the feast of St. Theodore, Maynard died, and she could no longer ignore reality or the awful implications of her only brother's death.

"He is gone," her father muttered helplessly as he stood in a corner while Linnea supervised the preparations of Maynard's body for burial. "He is gone. He is gone."

"He has been gone all along," Linnea whispered, though she knew her father was too caught up in his grief to hear her. She shaved Maynard's cold, shrunken cheeks, while Norma bathed his arms and legs. There was a scent of death about him, though in truth it had permeated the room a week and more. Perhaps it would have been kinder of her to have let him die that very first day.

Her trembling hand slipped and she nicked his cheek with the razor-sharp knife. He did not bleed, though, and that fact made her hands tremble all the worse.

"I cannot do this." She stared helplessly at Norma. "I cannot do it."

Norma took the blade from her. "Fetch his clothing. I will finish this task."

"He is gone. He is gone," Sir Edgar mumbled in the background, like a chant he must repeat to hold himself together.

Somehow they made Maynard ready, though Linnea feared at every moment that she would go mad from her father's incessant words. Why must he keep reminding her? She knew Maynard was gone, and she knew that it meant everything now fell to her. All the responsibility for her father and sister and grandmother.

Still, if she thought about that she would fall to pieces, and she didn't have that luxury. Clasping her arms around herself, she looked at her father. "Pray take him away from here, Norma. Entertain him somewhere else. Frayne can help you."

"What of Sir Maynard? Where will he be buried?"

Linnea wiped her hands with a length of toweling, though cleansing this sense of doom from herself was proving impossible. "I go now to speak to Lord Axton about that very subject. Be sure to keep my father away from my husband," she added.

She found Axton in the hall presiding over the morning court. She'd not personally observed him in his dealings with the various problems within his demesne, but she'd heard enough to know the people of Maidenstone would not suffer for his return. According to Norma, he'd thrown the tanner in the stocks for drunkenness and for beating his wife, Norma's niece. Frayne reported that Lord Axton had donated the timber beams and posts needed to reconstruct the storehouses that he'd had burned. And the entire castle fairly buzzed with the news that they would celebrate the planting of the spring crops with a grand feast and a day of sports and games, sometime before St. Dympna's Day.

The man certainly knew how to win the loyalty of his people—and his wife, she thought as she paused in the open door and studied him.

He sat in the lord's chair, the table before him, the day's petitioners arrayed in a short line across the hall. He was listening attentively to a grizzled man who was dusted with a powdery substance. The miller, she realized. Behind him stood a buxom young woman and a glum-faced young man. The miller was speaking with his hands, gesturing toward the silent couple. Curious, Linnea moved nearer.

". . . lazy and a spendthrift. He has not the wherewithal to pay the marriage fee," the miller complained, glaring at the silent fellow.

Axton leaned back in his chair and rubbed one finger along his chin. "I take it *you* will not pay the fee for your daughter and her bridegroom."

"If he cannot pay, he is not prepared to wed!" the man exclaimed, his face going red with the intensity of his outrage.

"But, Papa—" the girl began. She broke off, however, at a sharp gesture from her father. Linnea was near enough to see tears well in the girl's eyes and spill over onto her cheeks. The young man placed an arm around her for comfort, drawing a further frown from the miller. But the instinctive movement touched Linnea's heart. Two lovers separated by a disapproving father and, apparently, the cost of the marriage fee which must be paid to their lord.

She turned her gaze back to Axton only to find him

looking at her. If he was surprised to see her here, he gave no indication in his clear gray perusal. After only a brief moment he turned back to the miller and his unhappy daughter.

"If they have preceded the marriage with the consummation and yet cannot pay the fee to wed, there is only one solution. They will both spend a day in the stocks—tomorrow—as an example to those who contemplate such a sin, and again when her belly has swollen with the child, as a reminder to others who might behave so. Of course, the babe must be sent away once it is born. A bastard child must not—"

The poor girl's anguished wail drowned out whatever else Axton said.

"No! Not my child! You cannot mean to take my child!" Had her young man not caught her, the girl would have collapsed on the floor. Linnea was nearly as stricken as the prostrate woman. She stared at her husband, crushed by his callous decision.

He, however, was watching the miller, not the man's grieving daughter. When Linnea looked also at the burly fellow, she saw that his face had gone gray.

"Well, miller? Will you deliver her to the stocks?" Axton asked. "Not today, for 'tis midmorning already. Bring her tomorrow so that she may serve the full day as an example to other unmarried maidens who might be tempted to sin."

The miller could not respond. Whatever judgment he'd expected of his liege lord, this was clearly not it. "But . . . but, milord . . ." He sputtered to a halt. In the absence of any further discussion, the girl's weeping filled the hushed hall until Linnea could no longer bear it.

She started forward, but Axton's sharp gaze stopped her in her tracks. Then, before she could speak out, the miller let out a great sigh. "I will pay it," he muttered.

Though quietly spoken, all the principals in the drama heard him well. His daughter looked up, her face wet and red with her weeping. The hasty bridegroom's pale face showed a spark of hope.

Axton smiled. "Only half, miller. You shall pay but half the fee. The groom shall toil extra hours to pay the rest."

"Oh, thank you, milord. Thank you," the young man repeated. He drew his sweetheart to her feet, all the while bowing to Axton. "Thank you."

"Do not thank me yet, for I will order that only the most noxious of tasks be given to you. Best you learn from them the value of hard work and of a man's responsibility. You do bring a child into this world. If you will not yourself set a good example to it, then I needs must make sure you do so." He paused a long moment. "See that such will not be required of me."

Then Axton signaled to the seneschal and with many a bow and a promise, the trio backed away.

Linnea stared at her husband in unabashed amazement. He'd been stern—threatening, even—at least to the young man. But he'd not been unjust. He'd forced the self-righteous miller to loosen his notoriously tight pursestrings and made it clear to an aimless young man that he must rise to his responsibilities. She realized now that he'd never had any intentions of putting a breeding woman in the stocks.

Was ever a man so perfect? she wondered with a glad burst of feeling. No wonder she loved him.

When he waved her forward, she was filled with hope that the same sense of fairness would influence his judgment when she presented her case to him.

Axton was unaccountably pleased by his wife's appearance in the morning court. Well enough that the stingy miller had made this small gesture for his youngest child. Better yet that the slackard bridegroom would clean out the castle's cesspool and thereby learn the value of honest labor. But knowing his wife had witnessed this particular triumph gave him an unexpected yet undeniable satisfaction. She'd sensed at once what he'd done, and she'd been impressed, if her softly colored cheeks and round, wondering eyes were any indication.

"Would you sit?" He gestured to the chair beside him.

"No, my lord. I have not come here to intrude upon your business."

"There is no intrusion. Is there something I can do for you?" Besides what I would like to do, he thought, shifting to the left at the arousal that rose so quickly from just the sight of her. It was his good fortune that the heavy table hid his discomfort.

She approached the table hesitantly and lowered her eyes from his. She had woven her fingers together in a knot at her waist and he sensed her sudden nervousness. Was it because she knew how intensely he wanted her? Or perhaps because she wanted him just as much? He felt a deep satisfaction as he leaned forward, resting his elbows on the oak tabletop.

"I . . . I bring you news, my lord. And I make a request which . . . which I hope you will consider with the same fairness you have shown to other of your petitioners."

Axton smiled indulgently. "What news do you bear? And what request?"

She drew a slow breath as if she did prepare herself for his reaction, and in that moment he suddenly knew he would not like what she had to say. "I would bury my brother beneath the altar as befits a noble son of Maidenstone who did die in its defense—"

"No!"

The denial came out before he had rationally even considered her request. But then, he did not need a lengthy consideration to make that decision.

"No," he snapped once more. He rose to his feet, shoving the heavy chair back with a screech of wooden legs on the stone floor. His wife's cheeks had gone pale in the wake of his violent reaction, and a small part of him regretted that. But by damn, had the wench no sense at all? Maynard de Valcourt had been his enemy! The man had fought as hard to kill Axton as Axton had fought to kill him. He had been the son of a usurper, and a usurper himself. And he'd contributed to the deaths of Axton's father and two brothers. Now that he was dead . . . Now that he was dead, Axton felt only a vague sort of relief, not the satisfaction he'd expected. But that only increased his anger. Would these damnable de Valcourts forever thwart

218

him? Although there was no longer anyone who could dispute the de la Manse claim to Maidenstone now, that did not change the past. Axton would not honor his enemy with a burial in Maidenstone's chapel.

He leaned forward over the table, his entire being rigid with hatred for his wife's family—and in that moment, for her as well. Would she forever align herself against him? Would she never realize that her future rested in his hands?

"If you would mourn him, do not do so in my presence. If you would bury him, find some mean plot of ground that has no other use—not for crops, nor grazing, nor even foraging. But do not think to inter him in the place where my father should now rest, and my two brothers as well!"

He was shaking with rage when he finished. Every eye in the hall had fastened upon him, but it was only Beatrix he fixed his furious glare upon. "Do not speak to me of this matter. Not ever again."

Then, although other petitioners awaited him, he spun on his heel and stormed out of the hall.

From a sheltered spot near the pantler's cabinet, Lady Mildred watched her son's violent departure. The massive oak door shuddered closed with a heavy thud. A satisfying sound, she thought as her fingers knotted around the curtain beside her. Had there been a door between the hall and the pantler's cabinet, she would have slammed it herself.

Imagine! A de Valcourt buried at Maidenstone. It was too much to bear!

Yet for all her outrage at the girl's insolent request, Lady Mildred could not drag her eyes away from her. She stood yet in the same place, slender in her green gown and pretty golden hair. Yet distressingly vulnerable in the great, cavernous hall.

The others drifted away—the servants and villagers and castle folk—sidling along the walls on silent feet. No one approached her to offer comfort, neither for her brother's death nor her husband's terrible rebuke. She simply stood there while those who had been her people, but were now her husband's people, deserted her. Then the girl swayed a little, and her vivid green eyes welled with tears.

It was more than Lady Mildred could bear. Her fingers tightened on the figured cloth curtain, as if she might somehow prevent herself. But in the end she could not. She hated the weeping woman out there and everything she symbolized. But she had felt that same sort of pain before, and she knew how deeply it cut.

With a soft imprecation at her own perverseness, Lady Mildred stepped out of the pantler's cabinet and into the hall proper. The silence was so oppressive that the padded soles of her slippers sounded like warning signals. The girl looked up at her approach and stiffened, as if she expected even more pain from this new source. But to her credit, she did not turn away. She did not attempt to hide the hurt and anguish in her face either. Nor the tears.

That she could be both vulnerable and brave all in the same moment was what most affected Lady Mildred. By the time she'd reached her son's young wife, she found herself truly sympathetic to the girl's plight.

"Shall I take you to your private chambers?" Lady Mildred asked. Up close she could see that the girl did tremble with the ferocity of her grief. "I am sorry . . ." She hesitated, for she did not wish to lie. But in the face of Beatrix's grief, Lady Mildred realized it would not be a lie. "I am sorry for the pain visited upon your family by our return to Maidenstone. It would have been so much easier if there had been no need for war. If you and Axton had been wed in peace instead of . . ." She trailed off with a helpless shrug.

The girl stared at her warily, as if she did not believe a word being said to her. Suddenly it seemed very important to Lady Mildred that she did believe her. "My sister Anne was sent as a token of peace to be the bride of a man she did not know. She was the eldest, and so the responsibility did fall to her. I was younger and I wed a man I already had a care for. But I suffered for Anne. Her life was hard, whereas mine brought me much joy." She paused, wondering at her own perversity at dredging up her youth for this girl who must hate her. Still, she forced herself on. "I would not have your union with Axton be based on hatred."

As quickly as that, the wariness left Beatrix's eyes, chased away, unfortunately, by hopelessness. "How can it not be based on hatred?"

Lady Mildred restlessly tucked her hands into her pendant sleeves. "To hate your husband because your brother fell to him in battle gains you nothing—"

"*I* do not hate *him!*"

Lady Mildred frowned in confusion. "Then . . . then what is the difficulty?"

"He hates *me!*" she cried. "He hates me and all of my family!"

"No—" Lady Mildred caught herself and her mind spun. Axton *had* hated the de Valcourt family a long time—as had they all. But he did not hate his wife; that she knew instinctively. He might *want* to hate her, but he could not bring himself to do so.

That sudden intuition took her aback, and for a long moment she could do no more than stare at the young woman before her. That Axton, her own son, could harbor deep feelings for this woman, this daughter of his enemy, was a bitter dose to swallow. And yet, if he did . . .

In the uncomfortable silence the girl started to turn away. But Lady Mildred stayed her with a hand on her arm. "Wait. Wait. I would . . . I would walk with you awhile. There is much we ought to speak about."

At her new daughter-in-law's hesitant and fearful glance, Lady Mildred mustered a smile. It was not nearly so hard as she expected. "He does not hate you. Of that I am certain. And if you do not hate him . . . Well, that is a beginning, is it not?"

Chapter 17

Maynard was buried in the same crypt as his mother and brother, beneath a stone in the floor beside the altar. How the Lady Mildred had achieved such a thing, Linnea feared to ask. It was sufficient that the deed was done. The fact that only she, her father, Norma, and Frayne attended the simple service was of no consequence.

It was Peter who had delivered the news to her. A solemn and subdued Peter. He'd found her in the chapel and related his mother's message.

"Axton had agreed to this?" Linnea had questioned him.

Peter had given a one-sided shrug. "He does not oppose it."

"That's not the same thing, though. Is it?"

"Why should you care?" He'd flung the words back at her.

But Linnea had not wished to argue with Peter, so she'd not responded to him. She had permission to bury Maynard properly. That was more than she could have hoped for. Nonetheless, she'd been more than a little nervous about her next meeting with Axton.

But he'd not returned, either for the evening meal or to their bedchamber later. He stayed away the entire night as well as the day of the burial too. It was only after the long summer twilight had begun to fail that the seneschal brought word that Axton did approach the castle.

Linnea looked up from her discussion with the alewife, relieved and yet alarmed as well. Everyone else looked up too and stared at her, for they'd all heard about his outburst and they all knew about the burial. Linnea sought out Lady Mildred's eye, however, and took a small comfort from the woman's steady gaze.

The two of them had shared no real discourse since their conversation the day before. When Linnea had tried to thank her for her intercession, the woman had waved her thanks away. "Do not thank me for seeing to my son's happiness. 'Tis a mother's duty. 'Tis her nature. Some day you will understand that."

Linnea was not sure how Maynard's burial at Maidenstone could possibly contribute to Axton's happiness, but she was glad to have this matter behind them. It remained, however, for her to face Axton. She had no intention though of doing so before so avid an audience as presently filled the hall.

"I shall be in my chamber," she said in a voice she meant to carry throughout the capacious place. "Norma, pray convey to my lord husband that I await his pleasure there. Have a bath prepared for him," she added. "I will attend him myself."

That started a faint buzz of whispers in the far reaches of the torch-lit hall. When Linnea glanced again at the Lady Mildred, however—seeking her approval, if the truth be told—the older woman's face reflected more pain than reassurance. There was more regret than anything else in her aging eyes.

Deflated, Linnea nevertheless had no choice but to go forward as she'd planned. Norma hurried after her as the hum of speculation rose in the smoky atmosphere behind them.

"P'rhaps I should stay with you, milady." Norma huffed along the curving stairwell.

"That will not be necessary."

"But he may be sore angry—"

"No." Linnea reached the second floor antechamber and turned to face the worried maid. "No, he won't be angry. Nothing has happened here that he did not permit to happen. I cannot guess why he has allowed Maynard to be buried with all the honor of any son of Maidenstone, but I know it was he who said yea. He will not be angry." *Only perhaps grieving someplace on the inside.* Linnea vowed to ease that grief of his no matter what it took. She welcomed the chance to do it.

Norma patted her arm, drawing Linnea's thoughts back to the moment. "Your grandmother would be proud of you—and rightly so—were she to see you now. Mark my words, milady, I shall convey to her how well you have played your part."

It was the last thing Linnea wanted to hear—how well she did dupe her so-called husband and the rest of his family, when all they wished was to live a life of peace. Though Norma left with an encouraging nod, it was all Linnea could do not to dissolve into tears.

Axton was coming, a man she'd grown to love—yes, love!—in just two short weeks. But she had committed herself to a path that must bring him down, to a lie which must strike him down when he was most unaware.

A step on the stair caused her to gasp in alarm. But it was not Axton. Not yet. The servants filed in with the tub and all the other accoutrements of his bath. She let down her hair and sat watching at the window, combing the red-gold tresses until no knot or tangle marred their length. Her life was a hopeless tangle—hers and Axton's. But her hair was smooth and silky for him, just the way he liked it. And she would be eager and waiting for him, as he also liked. She would show him her love in every way she could, she told herself. With every pull of the carved bone comb through her waist-length hair, she vowed to make him certain of her feelings for him, for she knew the day would eventually come when he would question everything that had ever occurred between them. Though she doubted anything she did now could change the way he would feel once he learned who she really was—or rather, who she wasn't—that didn't stop her from needing to try.

When a commotion at the gatehouse heralded his return, she leaned out the window, watching for her first glimpse of him. When he cantered into the yard with neither hood nor helm to cover his hair, when the orange glow of the torches showed him clearly to her—the dark glint of his hair, the white gleam of his teeth—she felt a swell of a painful joy in her chest.

Then he looked up at her, at the window of the chamber they shared, and she knew in that moment that he could love her too. If she let him. Mayhap he already did.

It was a thought that should have brought her to the pinnacle of happiness, and for the long moment that their gazes met and clung, it did. But then Sir John approached him and Axton looked away, and Linnea's happiness became a hell.

If he loved her, then her betrayal would be all the worse. Norma had said that the Lady Harriet would be proud of her for the role she did play. But, oh, Norma did not know even the beginning of it. Yes, Lady Harriet would be proud. Everyone of de la Manse would be proud, and she would have at last redeemed herself of the taint her birth had given her. But at what a cost . . .

"Leave me," she snapped to the two maids who yet fussed over the arrangements of towels and soaps. In a moment she was alone, and in almost as short a space of time, she heard Axton's footfall.

Moor bounded first into the room, followed by a frowning Axton and an anxious Peter.

"Get that hound from here," Axton barked when the dog gave an interested sniff to the black bear pelt that covered the high bed.

"Mother had hoped to have an audience with you," Peter replied.

"Tomorrow." Axton stared steadily at Linnea who stood silently before the window. Her hair hung in rippling streamers against the dark green of her gown. Her feet were bare and she'd shed all the complicated portions of her daily wear. "Tomorrow I will see her." Then he seemed to relent and sent his brother a patient glance. "But convey to her, little brother, that no one need fear for my temper, nor for my lady wife's well-being."

Peter's tense posture relaxed and the crease in his young brow eased. He slapped his thigh, clearly content by what he'd heard. "Come, Moor. There is nothing for us here."

He sent a wink to Linnea, but she could not share his mood. That no one should fear for her well-being with Axton was no surprise to her. But it brought its own peculiar sorrow with it. Peter left; Axton shut the door firmly behind him. Then he faced Linnea.

"Are you satisfied, woman?"

"Satisfied?" Linnea repeated.

"I have let my enemy be buried within the walls of mine own home. It remains for you to tell me whether or not you also have buried the remains of your animosity toward me."

"Yes. Oh, yes," Linnea answered, without pausing even an instant to think. She moved forward until she stood just inches from him. Once before she had undressed him, though that night it had been a game to him, a hunter proving his power over his hapless prey. This, however, would be different, she vowed.

Without speaking, at least not with words, she began to disrobe him. Hauberk, chainse. Chausses and braies. She removed all the trappings of the warrior from his beautiful warrior's body until he was only a man—a husband—come home to his wife.

She bathed him, slowly and reverentially. It was not playful this time. He did not drag her into the steaming waters with him. Instead it was a silent communion, a silent commitment between them.

When they at last met, skin to skin upon the luxurious black fur, it became the union she could only have dreamed of—had she even known all those long, lonely years to dream of such a thing. She knew now, though. They came together in the hot, sweet violence of lovers who love with the completeness of their entire beings.

One thing only marred the perfection of it. In the finest moment of his passion he cried out her name. Only it was not her name. How could it be? Though she refused to let that spoil the deep joy she found in him, this husband of hers whom she loved, that one word lingered afterward in her mind.

They collapsed in a passionate exhaustion that encompassed both their bodies and their spirits. They rolled beneath the massive fur and burrowed into the quiet depths of a satiated sleep, tangled together in the perfect knot of marital bliss.

But Linnea slipped into sleep with a single thought circling in her head. To hear Axton call out her name—her name, not her sister's—was what she desired above all the many pleasures the wide world might offer. That one cry, in the moment of completion, that single utterance. It would mean both heaven and earth to her if he could just one time breathe out, "Linnea."

She awoke with the firm resolve to tell him.

But Axton was not there. Not in the bed nor in their chamber. Linnea raked her hair back from her sleep-flushed face, and stared blearily about the bedchamber. It was well into morning, she realized by the bright spark of light that fell through the window glass, long past time for the morning mass and all the daily responsibilities that fell to the lady of any castle. She must order the meals and measure the spices. Today was the day to inventory the storerooms and plan for all the sacks and barrels that would be needed for next fall's harvest.

But first she must speak to Axton.

After the hastiest of ablutions she dressed herself, only wondering for a moment why Norma had not come to her once Axton had descended into the hall. Though it was not important, she would have preferred to have her hair better dressed when she met with him.

But then, the state of her hair or garments, or anything else was inconsequential, she told herself. What she had to tell him could not be made easier by the way she appeared to him. Truth be, she did court disaster this sunny morning. He might hate her—No, he *would* hate her, as would Peter, the Lady Mildred, and even that hound Moor. Their hatred, however, would be insignificant when compared to her grandmother's.

Still, her grandmother no longer mattered to Linnea. Even Beatrix, who was her beloved sister, her other, better half, could not compete with Axton when it came to Linnea's deepest feelings. She was not betraying Beatrix, she told herself. She was only being honest with Axton. Wherever that might lead her, it must be better than this lie she'd been living.

She found him in the hall. Only it was not the hall as it should be on a late morning in the spring. It was an empty cavern with no fire burning in the massive hearth and no servants busy with the myriad tasks necessary to maintaining a castle like Maidenstone.

Her brow creased in concern. Something was not right, she thought as she stared across the wide plank floor to where Axton sat in the lord's chair. He had pushed it back from the table and stared blankly at the de la Manse banner that hung down behind the dais. When she approached him on hesitant feet, however, his attention turned sharply to her.

Something was wrong, terribly wrong. Then she spied a creased length of parchment in his left hand, and a quick comprehension sent her heart plummeting to her feet.

He knew!

"Axton," she whispered. She did not know where to begin or how to explain, but she knew she must somehow make him understand. But he cut her off with a glare of such pure and frigid contempt that she stumbled backward. Had he struck her hard and with the full weight of his considerable strength behind the blow, he could not have hurt her more cruelly.

"I have a correspondence from Duke Henry. It contains news that you will find most interesting."

"Axton . . ." She stepped forward, her hands upturned in entreaty.

"No! You will be silent and hear me out!" He lurched out of his chair and stood, tall and forbidding. The lord of Maidenstone, standing in terrible judgment over the lowliest of his people.

He raised the parchment. "England's king does yield to the young duke. Stephen yields demesne by demesne, county by county to Henry. Soon enough it will be the entire country, and then the crown itself. The prediction is that Stephen is defeated in spirit as well as body, and that he will not long reign over this isle he has stolen."

Axton folded the parchment along its existing creases and laid it down on the table. Then he stepped down from the dais. In the intervening moments he had mastered his rage, it seemed. But the cold stone mask he had made of his face chilled Linnea even more so than did his temper.

With slow, measured tread he approached her, then just as slowly circled her, as if he did examine her from every angle, or else did wish to view each aspect of her reaction to his words. "There is more to Henry's correspondence," he said in her left ear. When she turned to face him, however, he had already circled behind her, a dangerous, taunting beast of prey, playing with her before he pounced.

Linnea resolved not to play the role of hapless victim. Since he was behind her, she stared instead at the de la Manse banner. "He has told you news of my family," she said.

With the lightest of touches he stroked the length of her unbound hair. "Your family," he murmured. "Yes, your family, which I thought I already knew more than enough about. Your family, which I thought would grieve me no more. Your accursed family which I have shown considerably more mercy to than ever they have shown to me and mine!" he finished in a voice that again shook with rage.

With a rough movement he jerked her around, then held her within the crushing grip of his powerful hands. "Tell me of your *family*," he demanded, stretching out the word so that it sounded like the vilest entity, a cancer upon the earth. "Tell me about your *sister!*"

Her sister. She'd known already that he had found out the truth. All of it. But still, the actuality of it hit her with renewed force.

"My sister," she whispered, echoing his words while her jumbled brain struggled for some direction to go, some words to explain, some way to negate the awful betrayal that consumed every portion of his being.

"Yes. Your sister, Beatrix. The elder of twins. The one who has petitioned to wed Sir Eustace de Montfort, one of Duke Henry's men who does now make claim to Maidenstone by virtue of his impending marriage to Edgar de Valcourt's eldest daughter and heir!"

Axton's eyes were as dark as storm-lashed granite, only

infinitely harder. If there was a pain in them, it was buried too deep for her to see, somewhere lost within the catacombs of his heart.

But the pain in Linnea's eyes was not so buried. It was there, raw and bleeding, in plain view. Only he did not care about her pain. He cared about his home, his mother, his family, and his heritage. He cared that he had been duped by a woman he had come briefly to care for.

How could she ever hope to undo the damage she had wrought?

"Perhaps . . . perhaps Duke Henry will still honor your claim—"

"He is not a man given to fairness. He will enjoy the sport that pits me against Eustace." He drew her inexorably closer, devouring her with his hard hunter's gaze. "What is your name?"

Linnea's heart hammered in wild panic. "I am . . . I am Linnea—"

"Twin to the real Beatrix. Younger of the two."

She nodded.

"What a bond must be between you, that you would sacrifice yourself to your enemy for her—"

" 'Twas no sacrifice!" Linnea exclaimed. She gripped the front of his tunic, holding onto the pewter-colored wool with all the strength she possessed. "I have not been disappointed with my choice—"

"You have whored for her!" He thrust her away, as if he tainted himself by the very touch of her. "You have whored for her and for everyone in your accursed family!" His handsome face was twisted with rage, and his words thundered through the empty hall. "That they could ask it of you sickens me. That you would agree—" He broke off, shaking with the power of his violent emotion. His nostrils flared as he drew a deep breath. His body quivered; his hands clenched.

Then he stepped back again, as if he must distance himself from her or lose control entirely.

"You wed yourself to me in the guise of another, in the

hopes of denying me my birthright. Admit the truth to me. *Linnea.*"

Linnea. Finally he had said her true name. But it was not as she had dreamed of. Indeed, it was the complete antithesis of her dream. It was the worst nightmare she could imagine. But it was far worse even than a nightmare, for she could not awaken from this horror and have it end. The sneer in his voice as he mouthed her true name was real. The contempt in his eyes would not fade away in the light of dawn. She was awake and all of this was horribly, horribly real.

"I . . ." She swallowed hard, fighting down a sudden wave of nausea that left her light-headed. "I feared for my sister. For Beatrix," she added in a whisper. "I love her and would do anything to save her—"

"Even whore for her," he broke in. When she shook her head against so ugly an accusation he let out a hollow laugh. "Such a display of loyalty even I would not demand of my sister, had I one."

"I love her!" Linnea repeated, for she could think of no other explanation which he might understand.

Once again he laughed, but it was an awful sound in the deserted hall. "Your love has earned you naught but the contempt and disdain of everyone. You have failed in your mission, Linnea. For our bonds are severed by the existence of your lie. We are not wed, not in the eyes of the Church. But your sister—"

He broke off, but she knew at once what he meant to say. Somehow she knew. She flinched away when he continued, however, for she could not bear to hear the words out loud.

"Your grandmother is shrewd enough not to fight Henry. To choose de Montfort, who has Henry's ear, was canny indeed. But Henry had not yet granted them permission to wed. They come here, all of them, to hear my argument."

He stalked her as she fell back, step by awful step. "I will challenge de Montfort for her hand. I have been wed to a false Beatrix, but I will make that aright. I will have the real Beatrix, though I must fight Henry's entire retinue to

231

have her. I know Henry, and I know that is his plan. His sport. And he, likewise, knows me well enough to be certain I will cooperate.

"I have had you as whore for your sister. Now I will have her. You have failed, *Linnea*. You have failed!"

She came up hard against a wall. He loomed over her, before her, around her, while his terrible words stabbed her through the heart. This was not the man she had loved last night. It could not be!

But that denial gained her nothing, for she could not escape the truth any longer. Having seen the best of him, to see now the worst was very nearly a killing blow. But she deserved it. She deserved it. Every word he spoke was true. She could not lie either to him or herself any longer. She had goaded him to this and left him no other way to turn but against her.

Yet as he pulled himself away from her, leaving her a boneless heap supported only by the cold, unyielding wall, she felt not hatred for him, nor sorrow for herself. What she felt was a monstrous envy of her sister. Her beloved sister, Beatrix, would have this man for her husband—for Linnea had no doubt that Axton's rage would win him a victory over any man, be he a giant or a wizard, or possessed of unearthly powers. Axton would defeat this Sir Eustace de Montfort and he would wed Beatrix. Once his rage was exhausted, he and Beatrix would make a family together, while she . . .

Slowly she slid down the wall until she was no more than a puddle, a morass of misery at its base.

They would make a family together while she would be outcast from the only two people she had ever loved. Beatrix and Axton.

The loss of her dear sister, she believed she could survive.

But to lose Axton . . . to lose Axton was to lose the heart right out of her chest. And everyone knew a person could not live without a heart.

Equynoxial

"I crowned her with blisse, and she me with
   thorne . . .
I did her reverence, and she me vilanye."

—unknown

Chapter 18

It rained. Starting just before the midday meal, continuing through the afternoon and on into the early dusk and dreary night, the sky seemed to weep for Maidenstone Castle, for its betrayed lord and its uneasy people. But it did not weep for the woman he had cast out of the keep. It could not, Axton told himself, for she deserved no pity, not from him nor the forces of nature. Nor even from God.

He stood at an open window in the third story chamber opposite his mother's. The rain misted in, cold against his skin, but it could not cool his raging mood. Beyond him stretched a portion of the yard, then the kitchens, the herb garden, the stable and outer walls, and then the black countryside beyond. He could make out little, only the struggling glow from the wet torches at the gate, and an occasional window or door outlined by lamplight. But in his mind's eye he saw it. It was the home of his childhood—the home where he meant to raise his own children.

At the moment, though, it was an ugly place, a hard and unaccepting place that harbored betrayal at every turn. He leaned into the window alcove until the rain fell upon his face. Why had no one revealed to him that there were two daughters? Why had the younger been so willing to whore for the elder? Damnation! What sick and perverted sort of family had held Maidenstone all these years?

And now, what new and twisted entanglement did he

pursue so recklessly? He'd had the one daughter, false-hearted jezebel that she was. Did he truly wish to have children of the other faithless bitch?

A streak of light split the sky, illuminating for just one unearthly moment the view beyond the wet window frame. All was a cold white, a harsh world of unyielding stone and unrelenting storm.

Why had he thought he could again find a home here?

He snatched an ewer that sat on a three-legged table, but it was empty. With a cry of frustration, he flung the innocent vessel across the room.

Damn the bitch! Damn the lying little bitch! And damn her all the more for having made him think that peace and happiness were finally within his grasp!

He braced himself against the window frame, his arms stiff, his head sagged forward, while his breath came hard and irregular. Damn the bitch, he cursed her once more. But the heat he would have mustered, petered out in his dark and solitary vigil.

She had sucked him in and he had flung himself head-long into her arms. He had not meant ever to trust any offspring of de Valcourt. But he'd let down his guard and now he did pay the price.

But never again, he vowed. Never again would he let a woman deceive him. This Beatrix—the real Beatrix—would warm his bed when he desired her. And no doubt if she were twin to the other, he would desire her. But aside from that necessary intimacy, there would be no warmer sentiment between them. He would fight for her, win her, and wed her. And he would keep her thick with child until she had populated the nursery to his satisfaction and was no longer of any use to him.

But what was he to do with her sister?

A tentative knock at the door saved him the misery of contemplating that question. "Who is it?" he barked.

"Your brother." The door swung open with a reluctant squeal of its wrought-iron hinges.

The last thing Axton wanted was to discuss this newest of disasters, yet he did not want to send Peter away either.

Peter, at least, he could trust. Peter and their mother were the only people who suffered as much loss as he from Beatrix's—no, she was Linnea. From Linnea's betrayal.

He slanted a look at his brother. "You warned me ere I wed her that she was not to be trusted. It seems the younger son is wiser than the elder."

Peter did not smile at Axton's dark jest. "I had rather I had been mistaken," he replied. "In truth, I had come to like her. And trust her," he added more quietly.

"Then we have the both of us been duped." Axton turned back to the bleak view beyond the narrow stone window.

Peter picked up the battered ewer and placed it on a slab of stone that protruded from the wall, creating a narrow shelf. "What do you plan?"

What indeed? "To challenge de Montfort. To defeat him."

"What of Beatrix?"

"Which one?"

"Well, both of them."

Axton felt a surge of anger so intense he could not at first answer. "I would like to strangle them both." He drew a long breath. "But I won't. One I will wed. The other . . ."

The other would torment him all the days of his life, he feared. "The other I will send to a convent. She will never wed, for she is ruined and no decent man would have her."

An image of her flashed into his mind, of her last night, welcoming him so gladly to their bed. He spun away from the dreary view without and the dangerous one in his head. "Mayhap I should send her to a stewholder. Or better yet, sell her to him. She would fetch a goodly price. But no," he continued sarcastically. "That would be no punishment at all for her. She would enjoy it far too well."

At Peter's look of consternation Axton let out an ugly laugh. "Do not worry yourself for that one—that Linnea. She does not warrant any of your concern."

"I worry more for you, brother. I would help you did I but know a way."

237

Axton tensed. He did not want Peter's help. Most especially he did not want his pity. But then, everyone would pity him now. Pity him or mock him. He stiffened in resolve. He would not be pitied. Anything but!

Axton faced his brother with a determination forged of both pain and rage. "If you would help me, then go and find me a woman. Two women," he amended. "Then arrange a practice tomorrow, to begin at dawn's light. I would wrestle Odo, face Reynold with the long sword, and meet Roger with the short. Have the stable master prepare the two best horses, for I would meet Hugh with the lance."

"All of that? In one day?" Peter exclaimed. His eyes were round and his expression doubtful.

"I will not lose to de Montfort," Axton stated in a deadly tone.

Peter stepped back, but he nodded his understanding. "If I may suggest—" He raised his hands when Axton frowned. "Only that you forgo the women if you do intend so intense a practice on the morrow."

"Send me two women," Axton reiterated in a tone that brooked no further interference. "And pray that they do their jobs well and take the edge off my mood, else on the morrow I will leave a trail of broken heads and bleeding bodies."

Peter left without further comment, and Axton was relieved. His brother was not the source of his rage, but he had come perilously near to becoming the focus of it. Better to exhaust himself upon two nameless women, and then his well-armored men, than to lash out at a lad who did but wish him the best.

Of course, the one who most deserved his wrath was the best protected from it.

He glanced at the door and for a moment contemplated seeking her out. He'd had her locked within a storeroom behind the kitchen. But the door and lock which did confine her, instead protected her, he realized. He'd meant for it to be a punishment, but in truth it saved her from the fury of his temper.

238

He started quickly for the door, intent on confronting her once more. But the unexpected appearance of a shadowed figure in the antechamber took him aback.

"Linnea?" He stopped short, unaware he'd even spoken. How was she here? Had Peter released her?

Then the woman came into the meager light of a guttering candle and he recognized his mother. The quick disappointment he felt, however, only roused his anger to new heights. How could one woman be so devious as to draw this perverse response from him? Had the witch entranced him? Placed a spell upon him? If she had, by damn, then he would break it!

"What do you here, Mother?"

"I have just spoken to Peter." She moved farther into the room and her eyes seemed to miss nothing. Not the dented ewer, the open window with rain now pouring in, or his own disheveled appearance. She looked small and old in the flickering light, but she did not look frail. Even in his distracted mood he could appreciate that.

"You will not bring any women into this keep," she said, staring sternly at him.

That was the last thing Axton had expected to hear, and his jaw sagged open in disbelief.

"If you would fornicate with loose women, then do so elsewhere, not under the same roof with your mother. But I caution you," she added in a gentler tone. "What you think will bring you relief will not do so. You must settle this matter with Linnea, my son, not with some other poor substitutes."

"There is nothing to settle. Nothing that *can* be settled."

"I know she has hurt you with this betrayal—"

"I am not hurt," he countered. "Only enraged that once again a de Valcourt has tried to weaken our claim to Maidenstone. But she will not succeed—neither she nor her sister."

"You will fight Sir Eustace." She said it with a quiet resignation that he knew hid the ever constant fear she felt for her sons. But her fear was not reason enough to stop him, and they both knew it.

"Seek your rest, Mother. Tomorrow I train for de Montfort. He will not steal our home from us, though the de Valcourts and even Duke Henry do lend him their support. By damn, but I should have let that whelp drown in the Risle when I had the chance!"

She nodded but she did not leave, and when she spoke, it was not of the young Henry. "I expected to hate her, but I can not. And now . . . now though I hate what she has done, I think I can understand why she did it."

"You can understand?" he exploded.

"And I believe could she undo this tangle, she would willingly do so."

Axton snorted his disgust. " 'Tis a foolish point to speculate upon, since she cannot undo it. Go, Mother," he said, "go and say your prayers that I best de Montfort."

She gave him a steady look. "I will pray for you, my son. I will pray that you best Eustace de Montfort and pray that you find your peace. But I will also pray that you do not seek to bury your pain in the wicked embrace of some loose woman—or two."

Axton could hardly believe his gentle mother was discussing such a matter with him. He bristled. "You do not understand a man's needs."

"And you do not understand a woman's heart," she replied.

Whether she referred to her own heart or obliquely to Linnea's, Axton did not know. Nor, when she turned and glided silently back to her own chamber, did he call out to ask her. Linnea's heart mattered nothing to him. How could it when his mattered nothing to her?

Peter sent the women to his brother's chamber together. One was a saucy thing, young and sweet and amazingly adept, as he had already learned. For a bit of shiny coin she would do the most astounding things to a man. The other was an older woman, possessed of the largest and most impressive bosom he'd ever seen. Gossip held that Reynold had nearly smothered between that pair of quivering white mounds.

But even as Peter sent the women up the stairs, he was consumed with guilt. He knew little enough of the doings between a man and his wife, but somehow he knew what Axton did was wrong. Though Linnea—how hard it was to think of her by that name—though Linnea had duped Axton and deserved not even a shred of his loyalty, there yet lurked in Peter's mind a sense that this was wrong.

But his own anger at her betrayal yet seethed, and it was a strong enough emotion to drown out any guilt he felt. Did *she* feel any guilt as she lay in her comfortable prison? Did she give a second thought to the man she had wed and seduced—for there was no doubt she'd seduced Axton, body and soul. Otherwise he would not be so heartsore. Ah, but she was a cunning little bitch.

So he sent the two women up to his brother. But his lingering unease kept him awake in the hall, wrapped in a rug, leaning against a wall near the base of the stairs.

They were not above stairs very long. They came down together, clearly disheveled, both grinning and whispering. They flashed him the gold coins they'd earned, then disappeared into the night.

Peter could not help but be awed by his brother's swift performance. Perhaps it was for the best. Perhaps now Axton would feel some relief for his anguish.

Shedding his rug, he made his way up the stairs once more. He found Axton on the second floor, in the lord's chamber. He lay facedown on the huge bearskin, sprawled across the bed still fully clothed.

For an instant Peter stood there just staring. Once he'd seen Linnea in just such a pose—though she'd been Beatrix then. She'd lain naked and waiting, filled with fear and anguish upon that same black fur. Now Axton lay there, and though he was fully dressed, his emotions were every bit as naked and raw as hers had been.

He grieved for her. For the loss of her. He had not used those women—Peter was certain of it. He might have tried, but he'd not succeeded. He'd not had the stomach for it.

God in heaven, did he feel so deeply for the deceitful wench? Did he love her?

Linnea had not even the strength to pace the length of her narrow prison. It was a dark, cold place, blessed with neither a window nor even a grate. But then, the milled flour kept better in such surroundings. So she endured the endless hours of her imprisonment in the company of a week's worth of flour. Coarse flour, dark and fragrant. Fine flour, powdery and pale. The sacks lined one long wall, and muffled even more what little castle noises drifted to her ears.

Norma came once in the evening, bearing plain fare and bedding for the night. She came again in the early morn, and while two serving men retrieved flour for the day's baking, the old maid tried to comfort her.

"Do not despair, child. Henry is to arrive soon, mayhap e'en this day. You will be freed and returned to the bosom of your family. I am certain of it."

Unfortunately that was not a comforting thought to Linnea. She ignored the tray of food. "What of my father? Is he well? Is he the worse treated for what I have done?"

Norma heaved a great sigh. "He is confined to the priest's chambers as before. No better, no worse. As to his well-being . . ." She shook her head. " 'Tis hard to tell. He eats what is set before him. He has been told of the new lord's mistreatment of you, but . . . he does not respond." Again she sighed.

"Axton does not mistreat me," Linnea whispered, turning away from her loyal maid to stare at the dark end of her storage prison. The two serving men passed her with their second loads.

"Time to lock up," the older one murmured, not unkindly, to Norma.

Before Norma could follow them, however, Linnea caught her by the arm. "How is he? Axton," she clarified when Norma did not at once respond.

"Him?" The old woman frowned. "He is hale and hearty, and as full of himself as ever," she muttered. She glanced at the men who waited outside the small storage chamber. "He is not deserving of your concern," she said in the barest of whispers. "Already he fills his bed with other women. *Women,*" she repeated, emphasizing the plural.

In the silence that resounded after that awful revelation—after Norma shuffled out, the door thudded closed, and the key turned to lock her once again in darkness—Linnea could not move. She remained where she was, frozen in her pose with her hands laced together at her waist.

Women. He'd taken other women into the chamber they'd shared. Onto the high bed, and upon the luxurious bear pelt.

She'd tortured herself with the knowledge that when he wed Beatrix he would take her to his bed. But she had not considered, even for a moment, that he would take other women as well. *Women.* Women he did not care about and yet would share such intimacy with—

"Oh, God!" The involuntary cry was wrenched from the deepest part of her being. From her heart. From her soul. From that part of her which was her truest self—and which loved him completely, she now knew. Oh, God, could it be that one woman was no different than another to him? Had she been of as little consequence as the women he already took to his bed? And what of Beatrix? Would she be the same, just one more meal to satisfy his robust sexual appetite?

She did not want to weep, but that's what she did. She fell to her knees upon the floury plank floor and tried to pray. But all she could do was weep. She had been nothing to him, nothing at all, while he'd become the center of her world.

But that world had cracked and was shattering all around her. Where she would end up no longer mattered, for she knew that hovel or castle, wilderness or town, emptiness would forevermore be the place in which she dwelled. Emptiness. Solitude. Darkness.

She might as well live out her days in this storage room as anywhere else.

Then she thought of her sister. She thought of Beatrix, sweet, generous Beatrix, who deserved better than to marry a man who hated her and who would make a mockery of his vows to her.

With the back of her hands she wiped the tears from her eyes, then scrubbed her face dry with her sleeve.

She would save Beatrix from him. That had been her original goal and so it must be again. But how?

That she did not know, but as she rose to her feet she felt the slide of Axton's chain against her thigh and her desolation turned to a furious resolve. With a cry of outrage, she pulled up her skirt, grabbed the delicate jewelry and yanked. It came free with a sharp, cutting snap and she flung it as far from her as she could.

She'd been wrong to let herself love Axton and to think he could ever care for her in return. She'd been wrong to be jealous of Beatrix and Axton's wish to wed her.

Beatrix was the only one who'd ever loved her and now she must fight harder than ever to protect her beloved sister. Eventually she must be released from this prison. Then she must be clearheaded and ready to do whatever it took. Axton must not have Beatrix, though he win Maidenstone from Eustace de Montfort and Duke Henry.

It seemed an impossible goal to achieve, and perhaps it was. But as she sank down onto the flour sacks, consumed by both misery and outrage, she found it easier to focus on that unlikely future than on the unbearable present. Worrying for her sister muted, at least a little, the pain of her uncertain future.

And the absolute devastation of losing the man she still loved.

Chapter 19

On the third day Norma came to her, excited, agitated, hardly able to speak.

"They come. All of them. We must prepare you."

"Who comes? Duke Henry?"

"Yes! And Beatrix and Sir Eustace. Even my Lady Harriet accompanies them. Come, milady, we needs must make haste," she added, tugging on Linnea's arm.

Despite her desperate need to be free of her dreary dungeon, Linnea felt an awful dread. "Haste to do what? Where do we go? What plan does Axton make to use me to hurt my family?"

Norma stared at her sorrowfully. Her round face was creased with concern. "Ah, child, 'tis not Lord Axton who does command your removal from this closet, but rather that good dame, his mother. She would not have you appear disheveled." Her faded eyes swept over Linnea. "Nor dusted with the miller's best efforts. Come along," she prompted, pulling Linnea toward the door. "There's not time to be wasting, for milord Axton is expected to return very soon. You must be within Lady Mildred's chamber before he arrives."

Linnea followed Norma's lead because it would be foolish not to. The light of day hurt her eyes and her confinement seemed to have made her clumsy. But for all her relief to be rid of that storage closet, a tiny part of her wished to return back to the place. There she lived only with her *fears* for the future. Out here she must face that unknown.

All eyes followed her as she crossed the hall. The servants were out in force, preparing the castle for the imminent arrival of the visitors. But they slowed in their tasks as she threaded her way through them. They stared at the sister, Linnea, who had deceived their new lord—and themselves as well. One and all they'd thought her to be the Lady Beatrix, and now that was Linnea's only comfort. She'd fooled them all. Willing herself to a courage she was not sure she possessed, she stiffened to a haughty posture and raised her chin to a regal angle.

Somehow she made it across the hall then up the winding stairs. At the second level she paused and though it was the last thing she wanted to see, she stared past the antechamber to the door that led into the lord's chamber. It stood ajar and as she watched, a woman pushed through the opening, her arms filled with soiled bed linens.

245

Linnea must have gasped or made some other horrified sound, for the maid looked up and abruptly halted. Norma looked back, then made her way back down the stairs.

"Not her!" the old woman hissed, understanding Linnea's thoughts. " 'Twas not *her.*"

The young woman's face went scarlet at Norma's words, while Linnea's went pale. Though her relief was huge to know this maid was not one of the women Axton had taken to his bed, there was still the fact that the maid obviously knew what Norma meant. She knew what Axton had done. Everyone must know.

Norma grabbed her hand and together they made their way to the third level. Lady Mildred's chamber was warm and well lit, with two wall sconces and a brace of candles beside a tub. The tub was filled with fragrant, steaming water and sat before the small wall hearth. A delicate gown of salmon-dyed linen and other necessary women's garments were laid out on the bed.

The lady herself sat on an upholstered bench before the window.

She dismissed Norma with one raised eyebrow and the faintest gesture of her hand. "Do you need assistance with your bath?" she asked Linnea once they were alone.

"No."

Baring herself before this woman was not something Linnea desired to do. But the chance to thoroughly cleanse herself was something she could not forgo. She approached the tub while watching Lady Mildred warily.

"Why have you summoned me here? Does your son know?"

"I have my reasons," the woman replied. "And no, he is not aware that you are with me now."

"You know my family returns with Henry of Anjou."

The woman's eyes narrowed, but she did not respond directly to Linnea's comment. "Go on. Bathe while you may. Once Axton returns to the castle, he may seek you out. When you are not there he will rage the length and breadth of Maidenstone to find you. Unless you wish him to find you at your bath—and mayhap you do—I suggest you get on with it."

Linnea's jaw tensed. "I assure you, that is the last thing I desire!" She began to unlace her gown.

Her words drew an amused chuckle from the older woman. "I wonder if you will tell me the true extent of your feelings for my son."

Linnea sent her a sidelong glance but did not pause at her task of removing shoes and stockings, and gown and kirtle. "I like Peter very well," she sarcastically replied.

Lady Mildred smiled. "And he likes you. What of Axton?"

Linnea sternly ignored the sudden lurch of her heart. "Axton does *not* like me. In fact, he despises the sight of me, the sound of me, and the very thought of me."

This time the woman shook her head and smiled. "Judging from your evasive answers one would think you are avoiding my question." The smile faded. "What are your feelings for my son Axton?"

Linnea did not at once respond. She did not want to respond. To purchase more time, she clutched a length of towel to her and stepped into the hot water, then let the towel fall to the floor as she sank into the soothing broth.

"Ahh." The exclamation escaped her lips unexpectedly. She released her hair from its fitful chignon, shook it loose, then sank completely under the water before rising to face the question that yet lingered between her and this woman. Indeed, what were her feelings for Axton?

"We have been as man and wife," she began in a tone far less forceful than she might have wished.

"You deceived him apurpose."

"To save my sister from a man . . . from a man we feared would treat her cruelly."

"But you would willingly suffer that cruelty for her."

Linnea had been staring blankly at the uneven wooden edge of the foot end of the tub. But now she glanced sharply at Axton's mother. The woman knew more than she ought. She had been talking to Norma!

"I love my sister. I would do anything for her," she said curtly.

"You are the second twin." When Linnea did not bother to respond to that obvious fact, the woman continued. "'Tis an old and foolish belief, that the second babe is accursed. I comprehend now that you have done all this to prove yourself worthwhile to your family. And I suppose in that you have succeeded. But you do not appear much gladdened for your success."

She pushed up from the bench and approached the tub. She offered Linnea a bowl of shaved soap. "You have achieved all you hoped for. You lulled us into complacency while your family did mount a challenge to our position at Maidenstone. And you have made a fool of my son—a man who came, against the opposition of his family and all logic, to have a deep and abiding care for you—"

"He did not care for me! He could not—not when he brings other women so swiftly to his bed!"

"Men are not known for their fidelity. It does not mean they do not care—"

"My father loved my mother. Once my mother was gone he did not—"

"And my husband loved me!" She broke in, leaning down until their faces were very near. "My husband loved me and I loved him and I have been faithful to his memory. But we speak of you and your husband, and he is his father's son—"

She broke off and drew back. But Linnea had heard what the woman started to say, and though she did not believe it, oh, she wanted to.

"What . . . what is that supposed to mean?"

Lady Mildred's lips pursed thoughtfully. "Your husband—though I suppose he is not truly your husband, since you married him under a false name. Axton is not a man of inconstant affection. His loyalties run deep. Likewise, betrayal strikes him to the heart. Such a betrayal as you have dealt him will be a hard thing for him to forgive."

Linnea stared at her in amazement. "Forgive? Surely

you do not think—No. He will never forgive me. He cannot, not and have Maidenstone too."

At that, Lady Mildred frowned. "That is the only thing."

Linnea sank down to her chin in the water. "Yes, for him this place has always been the *only* thing."

Lady Mildred moved restlessly around the room, silent for a while, and Linnea took that opportunity to scrub herself. Arms, legs, face, hair. When she finally rinsed the lavender-scented suds from her heavy hair, the Lady Mildred once again was studying her.

"Tell me of your sister."

Linnea eyed her warily. "She is sweet and guileless and easily intimidated. She does not deserve your enmity—nor his. This deception was of my own making, not hers. I would beg you to intercede for her, should Axton be inclined to treat her cruelly."

"Does she look like you?" the woman asked, ignoring Linnea's plea.

Linnea pondered her reply only a moment. Then she sighed. "We are identical in every way. Save one." She raised her leg. "This birthmark is the only thing that distinguishes us from one another."

Lady Mildred stared at the mark, then back at Linnea's face. Then she turned away and went to the window. In the silence that fell, Linnea felt a shiver run through her. The water was growing chill. She should finish her bath and prepare herself for the coming unpleasantness. As she dried herself and dressed, the Lady Mildred remained quiet. Only when Linnea sat before the fire and began to comb and dry her hair did the woman rouse from her deep thoughts.

"So, Axton shall be as pleased with the real Beatrix as he was with the false one."

The color drained out of Linnea's face. It was no more than she could have expected from the woman. After all, Lady Mildred's one goal was to gain what was best for her son. Still, she'd seemed to imply that Axton might somehow forgive Linnea—or else Linnea had misread her intentions. Now, though, it seemed she was content to see Axton wed again—only this time to the true Beatrix.

"Does that thought displease you?" the woman continued, eyeing Linnea shrewdly. "Would you rather remain wed to him?"

Linnea pulled the bone comb through her hair, unmindful of the painful tug as the carved teeth found a knot, then broke through it. "To remain wed to him would be . . . it would be impossible. He despises me."

"But *you* do not despise *him.*"

That said, the woman pushed to her feet. "I must go. There are tasks I must supervise. You, however, should stay here. Dry your hair and dress it. Nap, if you will. I will have a tray sent to you if you would eat. But I caution you to remain in this chamber until I send for you. Or Axton does."

Then she left and Linnea was alone to ponder her fate. There was no understanding this strange interview—most especially the emotion that drove Lady Mildred so unexpectedly. One thing Linnea knew, however: Axton would not send for her. She doubted he ever wanted to lay eyes on her again.

"Where is she!"

Peter trailed after Axton as he stormed across the crowded bailey. The people fell away—guards and servants, peasants and children—as the lord strode angrily past them. His brother struggled to keep up. "She cannot have escaped. It is impossible!"

"Then where in God's name is she!" Axton roared, slamming into the great hall.

All activity ceased. Every eye turned askance to him. Lady Mildred paused in conversation with one of the castle women, but she did not flinch. She caught her son's gaze. "She is in my chamber."

Anything she might have added was lost when he let out an exceedingly foul oath, then strode purposefully for the stairs.

Linnea heard him coming. A deaf woman would have

heard him. In the short minute it took for him to reach the third floor, she positioned herself near the window—as far from the door as she could get, if the truth be told. Her hair was neat, her dress impeccable. But she trembled like a sapling willow before a spring storm and her palms were damp with perspiration.

The door flew open, crashing against the wall. Then he was there, in the room with her, and she forgot to be afraid. He was there, tall and formidable, weary and streaked with the sweat of his day's work, yet powerful as only a man can be powerful. He glared at her, and she knew he hated her. But she could not hate him in return. She had betrayed him; she understood that he had every right to hate her. But she was so glad to see him, so deprived of any sight of him, that all she could feel was an absurd sort of joy, an insane surge in the vicinity of her chest, as if her life force had abruptly been renewed and her heart and lungs and everything else worked better and faster than they had before.

He stared a long angry minute at her. Emotion seethed in the silent chamber, burning the very air with its blistering intensity. But like all fire did, it burned hot and then sputtered low, until they were standing facing one another without the buffer of anger between them.

Axton stepped back, as if he suddenly would flee her presence. But Linnea raised a hand to him, palm up and pleading.

"I . . . I had *hoped* to see you again, but I had not expected to." She swallowed as the reality of this moment washed unwelcome over her. "Shall this, then, be our farewell?"

Axton stiffened as a longing so vivid, so powerful that he feared he could not withstand it, struck him with cruel force. He'd been furious to find her released from the prison he'd put her in. Furious and panicked too. But having found her, the fire and need of those two emotions had merged into something far worse.

He wanted her. He wanted her physically, but he also wanted her yielding and sweet, welcoming him home every day when he returned to her. He wanted her to care for him as he had come to care so desperately for her.

"By Lucifer and Judas!" he swore, shuddering at his perverse reaction to her. She was his own personal Judas, sworn to him yet betraying him. And still he would clasp her to his bosom and suffer the consequences!

Again he stepped back.

He struggled for composure, to control the hard pounding of his heart and the urgent force of his desire for her. "Duke Henry comes, along with your sister and her doomed bridegroom. While the outcome of that dispute is already foretold, what will become of you is not."

He stopped short. What was he saying? What did he intend for her, the sole cause of this madness—to allow her to choose her own fate?

He thrust his damp hair back from his brow and steeled himself against any weakness. "Have you anything you wish to say before I decide your fate?"

She shook her head no, but her eyes, dark as the sea at storm, shimmering with what he feared were tears, communicated more than words could. He forced himself to be cruel, as cruel as she had been to him.

"Do not think to turn that sorrowful look upon Henry. Likewise, do not delude yourself with the hope that he will offer you his protection or find you a suitable husband among the many who court his favor. You have no value now," he continued, growing angrier with every word. "You have no dowry and now you have not even the value of virtue. You can be only one thing to Henry—or to any other man!"

He broke off as the idea sprang full-blown into his head. It was insane—and yet it was the only solution he could find in this insanity that was caused of her machinations.

He crossed the room and grabbed her by the arms. The tears that had shimmered in her eyes before had swelled and spilled over, and now left damp, glimmering tracks down her cheeks. It must be his own peculiar perversion that even still, he could not bear to see her cry.

"I will keep you," he muttered, staring down into her

great, luminous eyes. "I will keep you locked away, in a place where no man but I can have you."

He pulled her up against him, so that he could feel the sweet warmth of her belly, the full softness of her breasts. He could breathe her in. She was his for the tasting and for the taking. And he would take her, he swore an oath to himself.

His mind made up, he wrapped his arms around her and lifted her off her feet. The bed was nearby and convenient, and though she struggled against him, she was no match for him.

"Be still," he growled. He pressed her down into the bed, holding her there with his greater weight.

"No, I will not be . . . I will not be your *whore*." She whispered the word as though it was foul to even speak it.

But her opposition only roused his anger and stiffened his resolve. "You assumed that role when you took on your sister's name. You have whored for your family—and liked it very well," he added. He pressed his aching loins into the yielding softness of her belly and at the same time forced her legs apart with one knee. "There is no honest life left open to you. You have not the virtue to demand marriage, nor the dowry to buy a place in the abbey."

"No! No, you're wrong—"

"There is no other place for you but in my care," he insisted. Beneath him he felt her resistance falter. Her hands pressed against his chest, but they weakened. Her lips, pressed tautly together in anger and other emotions, now trembled.

Though he knew he was striking her where she was most vulnerable, he buried any twinge of guilt. He meant to win this battle of wills. He meant to keep her for his own, whether he hated her or—No!

He shook his head against the beginnings of an insane thought. No matter what other perverse emotions he felt for her, it did not matter. She had no other options, so he would keep her.

One sister to wed, the other to bed.

"You have no other choice, save to whore for any man

who will have you for the coin. You should be grateful I save you from such a fate."

Linnea heard his every word and she understood them. She knew he spoke the truth. Yet she could not resign herself to what was happening to her. To what he intended to do. She loved him. She had not wanted to hurt him.

But she had hurt him, and now he was hurting her.

He leaned on one elbow and unfastened the front of his braies. Then he pulled up her skirt until they were pressed, flesh to flesh. He was hard and ready, and she . . . she, God help her, was ready too. She loved him despite all the madness that lay between them. She would not fight him.

He entered her and she closed her eyes. But not fast enough to mistake the slight softening of his intent features. He knew she was ready for him, and so he must know that she desired him yet. And if he knew she desired him, he might know, also, that she felt even more. Had his mother revealed her suspicions, or had she, herself, somehow revealed it to him?

He began to move in an erotic rhythm that took her out of herself. He took control of her, body and soul, with that age-old rhythm, with the connection it forged between them. In the hot, rousing pace he set, Linnea ceased to care. He possessed her body, and she gladly accepted everything he offered her. Then he groaned and a shudder wracked his magnificent warrior's body.

Linnea lost the last of her shattered control. For one violent, lightning moment they were joined in the most perfect union God could ever have conceived between a man and a woman.

Then it was over and they were only two people on a bed, gasping for breath. Tears started afresh in her eyes, for the reality was too cruel for her to accept.

Axton drew back, frowning. "Are you hurt?"

She shook her head. He meant physically of course, and she was not hurt physically.

He rolled off her and lay on his back, staring at the painted roof of his mother's bed until his breathing became more normal. "Tears will not change your fate. Better that you save them to use upon another. Though they will not sway Henry either," he added cuttingly.

Linnea rolled away from him. She could not bear this. It was too hard.

She yanked at her skirt, trying to cover her naked thighs. At the same time, Axton shifted on the bed. Suddenly he let out a curt oath and caught her wrist. He jerked her skirts all the way up to her waist.

"Where is the ruby chain?"

Chapter 20

He dragged her down the stairs, through the hall, and across the bailey. He'd made a spectacle of every aspect of their dealings together, but this . . . For Linnea, this was by far the worst.

Her protestations were useless. Her struggles, of no moment whatsoever. Like a recalcitrant child, she was hauled past every staring eye, back to the flour closet. He had snatched a small torchère and lit it on the laundry fire. Now he pushed her into the closet and followed close behind.

"Find it!"

Linnea caught herself on a pile of burlap sacks. A cloud of fine white powder rose from where she'd landed.

"Find it!" he thundered. He advanced on her, holding the torch high so that the narrow chamber shivered with an unaccustomed light. "Find it, damn you. You will not leave this place until you wear it again. So help me God, Linnea, I swear you will not leave here!"

It pushed her beyond the edge of reason.

Although he appeared the very devil at that moment, a furious specter filled with malice, with not a shred of mercy to show, Linnea was past caring. The light quivered, red and ugly, casting awful shadows, but she saw only Axton. With a cry that mingled pain and rage and more frustration than she could restrain, she charged him.

It was like hitting the stone wall itself. He did not budge. But she had caught him unaware, for he dropped the torch. It sputtered and flared, but Linnea ignored it. Axton was her target. Axton and his hateful, hurtful ways.

She punched his stomach with both fists, though it jarred her all the way up to her shoulders. But she would not stop. She could not stop hitting him until his arms caught her in a bear hold.

"Stop this. Damn you, Linnea. Stop this, I say!"

But she couldn't, not until she was exhausted and simply could not fight his superior strength any longer.

He held her in a smothering embrace. Somehow he'd stamped out the fallen flame before it could ignite any of the burlap sacks. Now they stood in the dark, caught in this angry embrace that was no true embrace at all.

Tears wet her cheeks, but they were tears of anger, at least. She had no intention of crying for him ever again, except, perhaps, in anger.

She tried to pull away, for to rest in his arms seemed somehow the very worst thing she could do right now. But he held her fast.

"If you want that accursed chain, then let me go," she muttered into the smooth kersey of his tunic.

He shifted, and a fresh panic assailed her. He was aroused! Worse, in that moment of instant recognition, she became aroused too.

No. No! Her mind shouted the words. She tried again to break free of him. To her surprise and relief, however, this time he let her go.

She backed away from him until she came up against a tower of flour sacks. She stared warily at him as she fought to regain her breath. He stared too, and though the dim chamber cast them both in shadows, she sensed some change in his temper.

"Go ahead, then. Find it," he prodded in a voice devoid of discernible emotion.

Without responding, she shoved herself away from the wall of flour and moved deeper into the storage closet. She'd flung it all the way to the back of her prison, and though it took a few minutes feeling around, she located it without any real trouble. Then she turned to face Axton.

"Here." She flung it at him.

It hit his chest then fell to the dusty floor at his feet.

"Since we are no longer wed—not in the eyes of the Church anyway—you can have back your disgusting *gift.*" Emboldened by his silence, she added, "I hated wearing it."

Still silent, he bent low and scooped it up in one hand. Even in the dim room, Linnea saw the glint of golden chain and bloodred stones, and their winking was like a mocking torment. She hadn't entirely hated it.

Axton played a moment with the perverse length of jewelry. Then he advanced on her. But this time she did not retreat. When they were but inches apart, he halted and raised the chain until it dangled between them.

"You hated it," he repeated her words in clipped tones. "Perhaps. Perhaps not. In any event, it has served its purpose with you. We shall see if it works so easily upon your sister," he added.

Had he struck her fully across the face, he could not have hurt her more. Stunned, Linnea fell back a step, unaware she'd gasped. Unaware of the stark pain that covered her face.

But Axton saw it. He saw it and he was ashamed. St. Jude, would this madness between them never end?

Unable to face her a minute longer, he spun on his heel and stalked away. But with every step he felt the coward. In the face of her bravery and her pain, he felt like the lowliest of knaves.

In the ward he felt everyone's eyes upon him. But with one sweep of his threatening glare, they all turned instantly back to their work. A silence preceded him like a wave as he stalked back to the great hall. In his wake, however, he knew the buzz would start again. He'd been made a fool of by the most improbable woman, by the least important member of his enemy's family. By a younger daughter!

His fist clenched around the chain, tightening until the

delicate stone settings cut into his flesh. Damn her! Damn her to hell!

He stormed into the hall and up the stairs, taking them three at a time. He slammed the door to the lord's chamber, then spying the towering bed, started toward it, intent on smashing it fully to pieces this time.

But the chain in his hand stopped him. Like the winds of a storm, cut off in mid-gale, he halted just short of his objective and stared instead at the delicate jewelry. The fact was, he'd given it to her as a form of torment. Could he be angry now that she'd hated wearing it? He'd wanted her to hate it.

With a groan Axton turned away from the bed. In the beginning he'd wanted her to hate it and yet have to yield to it—and to him. But too quickly he'd abandoned his vendetta. He'd wanted her to want him. Only she hadn't. It had all been a plot, a ruse.

So, what was he to do now?

He knew he must challenge Eustace de Montfort and win the real Beatrix to be his wife. That part was easy and he had no doubt he would succeed, though it galled him to be forced once more to win back what was rightfully his.

But what of Linnea? What was he to do with her? It was a question he had no answer for. He feared he never would.

More than anything Linnea wished to flee her hated prison. No door barred her way. No lock or guard stood between her and the inner ward. Should she wish to flee the very castle itself, she suspected that she could do so. Just walk away and disappear into the forest and never again speak nor hear nor even think the name of Maidenstone Castle. Or of its lord, Axton de la Manse.

If only there was a way, she mourned. But how could she abandon her sister? And anyway, where would she go? What would she do?

For a long, dark while she remained in the storage room. She needed to regain her composure. She needed to know where she would proceed when she finally emerged.

With an effort she controlled her frantic breathing and slowed her heart's violent race. She battled tears too, but that struggle was harder to win. She was never going to cry over him again, she vowed. But then she would remember some tender word, or some exquisitely thrilling moment they'd shared, and tears once again would threaten.

"Fool!" she accused herself. "You are an utter fool!" But that knowledge offered her no solace.

When finally she forced herself to move, she decided to seek out her father. He was her only ally, though Axton's mother—She stopped short on that thought. She could no more decipher the Lady Mildred's intentions than she could decipher her son's.

Determined to leave the flour closet with her head high and her dignity intact, she started forward again. Near the door her foot kicked something small and hard. It ricocheted against the wall and came to rest just beyond the doorway. A tiny, glinting jewel.

Linnea stared at it with a mixture of horror and fascination. It was one of the rubies, one of the jewels that had adorned the chain. It must have come loose when she flung the awful thing at his chest.

But it had not been entirely awful, some part of her countered. Not entirely.

She sent a furtive glance around to see if anyone else had seen it. Her hand trembled as she reached for the tiny ruby. Her fingers shook so badly she almost dropped it. Just the feel of it, small and sharp in her fist, was enough to make her dissolve all over again. But she forced herself to be stalwart.

Axton would miss it, she knew. When he gave the chain to Beatrix he would notice the gold setting missing its stone.

But he would not find the jewel, she vowed. Not ever! She would hide it and keep it and . . . and use it as a way to escape, she decided. It would provide her with the means to leave this place forever—and Beatrix with her, she thought, elaborating her plan. She and Beatrix would use this ruby to buy themselves a place in a convent.

It was a pitiful plan, she knew. But at least it gave her some goal, some future to focus upon. Meanwhile, however, she must go to her father and await the arrival of the young duke Henry, and the rest of her scattered family.

Peter sat upon the parapet. His feet hung over the edge as he stared out at the village of Maidenstone. He had found a seam of loosened mortar, and now he tossed the pebbles, one by one, out into the void, watching them plunge silently into the dark moat. A perfect circle of ripples was all that marked each pebble's entry into the still water. He was too high to hear the sound of water yielding to stone. But he saw the results.

Not that it mattered. Not that it signified anything. Not that it was even particularly entertaining. He tossed out another bit of stone. It was just something to do.

"There you are."

He turned his head at the sound of his mother's voice. "You should not have climbed up here," he admonished her when he spied her flushed cheeks. "You could have sent your maid to seek me out."

"I may be old, but I am not yet so infirm that I cannot roam any portion of Maidenstone that I wish." She leaned against the merlon on his left, silent a moment. "I remember how pleased your father was when the walls of this castle were finally completed. This was the last section," she said, sliding her hand along the top edge of the rough stone, as if it somehow comforted her. "How dearly he loved this place."

Peter sighed. His father's memory was not strong in his mind. He'd been but a little child when Allan de la Manse had fallen. In truth, Axton had been more father to him than had his true sire.

"Axton loves Maidenstone as well as did our father."

Lady Mildred looked a long moment at him. "Do you imply that you do not?"

Peter shrugged. "It is a fine fortress. I do not deny that. It would seem, however, that it is not a place destined to bring happiness to our family. I much prefer our stronghold in Caen."

His mother smiled. " 'Tis just as well then, for Castell de la Manse shall be yours when you are of an age."

"Mine?" Peter leaped to his feet, unmindful of his precarious perch. "In truth, Mother?" Then he paused. "What has Axton to say on this matter?"

"He agrees. He knows you see it as your true home, as he sees this place as his."

Peter grimaced. "He may see it as his home, but as of yet it does not bring him any happiness. I wonder if it ever shall."

He did not have to elaborate, for she clearly knew what he meant. His mother turned to look down into the bailey. "I confess this only to you, my son, but I am torn. I do not wish him to fight this Sir Eustace, and if he is hurt—" She broke off and he could see her chin quiver. "If he is hurt, I shall never forgive her. But I fear also, that even a victory over Eustace will not bring him ease."

"He loves her," Peter stated, taken aback that he and his mother had come to the same unbelievable conclusion.

"I believe he does."

Peter lowered himself from the parapet. "Mayhap he will come to love the other sister as well. They are said to be the very image of one another."

At that his mother smiled. "Identical in their appearance they may well be. But it is not the face that sustains love. It is something far deeper. If that is what he has found with this girl . . ." She trailed off, no longer smiling.

For a long moment they stayed silent upon the castle wall. Somewhere in the distance thunder rumbled its ill-tempered threat. The sky hung low and gray, and the wind had begun a fitful assault upon them. Then in the distance, they spied a rider galloping full tilt toward the castle.

"Young Henry comes," Lady Mildred murmured. "I think I will visit the chapel before the duke arrives."

Peter watched her turn and slowly depart. She was old, he realized, and she'd suffered much loss in her life. But still she was a lady, gracious even to her enemies, which Linnea most assuredly was.

He frowned. If he ever wed—*when* he wed, he amended. As a landed knight which he now was—or would be, when he was knighted—he would have to wed in order to beget an heir. When he wed, he hoped he could find a woman as noble and refined as his mother.

Even as he thought of his mother, he spied Linnea across the castle yard, darting from the kitchen storage rooms toward the barracks. He'd heard she was no longer confined. She probably was seeking her father to tell him of the coming confrontation.

He frowned at that. She was ever the warrior wench, it seemed. Though she was without argument a beauty, she was nonetheless too bold for his tastes. She could learn much by emulating his mother, he decided. How to be a proper lady. How to know her place. How to care for her husband and create order all around her, though the world beyond be in total chaos.

The wind thrust his hair into his eyes and he turned against it to watch Linnea disappear around a corner of the chapel. For a short while she'd seemed content to be Axton's wife. Now they all knew the farce she'd played.

Peter shook his head. Poor Axton. He'd seemed to have tamed her, only to learn, to his humiliation, that he'd done no such thing. Now he must do the same with the other sister.

God help this other de Valcourt bitch if she were anything like her devious sister!

Chapter 21

Henry Plantagenet, Duke of Normandy, entered Maidenstone with all the pomp of a king. But then, it was king he claimed to be, king of England and heir to all the lands his grandfather, Henry I, had ruled a score of years before. His mother, Matilda, had fought Stephen to regain her lands. But it was her youthful son, a brilliant strategist though only nineteen years old, who was succeeding already. He'd stormed Britain, fanned across the entire countryside in his march toward London, and with an astounding lack of bloodshed, had claimed the land his own.

But he seemed intent on seeing blood shed at Maidenstone, Axton brooded. In the guise of sport he would allow two of his nobles to settle their opposing claims by spilling their blood before him. It was Henry's greatest strength: He assembled powerful nobles around him but kept them at odds with one another and, therefore, loyal only to him.

Axton steeled himself for the coming hours. Maintaining a semblance of civility would be his hardest test. Entertaining Eustace and Beatrix under Henry's amused observation would strain every bit of his patience. What he wanted was to draw out the other man now. This very minute. Challenge him. Fight him. Defeat him. Then get on with things.

But Henry would never allow the game to be played under any rules but his own. And as Axton's liege lord, his word was law.

So Axton waited on the stairs to the great hall, then descended when Henry's milk-white stallion pranced forward.

"Welcome to Maidenstone Castle, my lord," Axton said, taking his liege's hand in the required show of obeisance.

Henry looked around the bailey, missing nothing with his quick gaze. "I was wont to see this noble assembly of Hampshire stone, which two of my ablest nobles would both claim." He shrugged then looked down at Axton from his lofty mount. " 'Tis a sturdy place, but grim. Nothing like the Tower in London, where Stephen does yet reside," he added with a wolfish grin. "Come, show me to your table, for I am famished."

Henry dismounted. Behind him a tall knight urged his steed nearer, then dismounted as well. "De la Manse," the man muttered his greeting with a grudging nod and an assessing stare.

"De Montfort," Axton returned. But before he could turn away from the man de Montfort spoke again.

"You have not yet met the Lady Beatrix de Valcourt. My fiancée," he added in a taunting tone.

Axton had spied the slender figure on the cream-colored palfrey. Her pale golden cloak and hood had blended with the pretty animal so that she appeared a golden creature, a mythical centaur, half winsome maid, half prancing steed. But he had not looked longer than that first glance. Something in him did not want to see her, this woman he was prepared to kill a man to possess.

Now, though, he must see her.

"Come, my love," Eustace commanded, holding a gloved hand out to her. A page led both woman and horse right up to the steps. Her back was turned to Axton and he saw only her slender arms and hands as she reached down to Eustace for his aid. But then she looked over her shoulder, just for a fraction of a second. Still, it was long enough for Axton to be stunned.

Though he'd known they were twins and shared the same face and eyes and hair, he was nevertheless completely stunned.

It was Linnea. It was Beatrix, he knew, but it was Linnea too. He was momentarily speechless, a state Duke Henry was quick to note.

"Ah, but she is a beauty, is she not, Axton? Fair and innocent. And the prize that you and Eustace do compete over. But where is her sister? I would see the lively wench who has fooled my most able lord." He laughed out loud and it took all of Axton's self-discipline not to react to the insult implied. Instead he smiled.

"I dare to speculate that even you, my lord, would be hard-pressed to discern which of them is which."

Henry gave him a shrewd look. "Ah, but there is one way, is there not? But, alas, only you—or else Eustace—will ever be able to tell which is the virgin. So, where is this unnatural creature who would whore for her sister? I am fain to reward her for her extreme loyalty to her family, misguided though it may be."

Of all the things Henry said that were meant to goad Axton's famous temper, this mention of reward was the most galling. For Axton knew what he implied. To grace the bed of the Duke of Normandy, Count of Anjou, and soon-to-be King of England, would of course seem a generous reward to one as self-involved as the youthful Henry. He was a man come too young to such a success as he had already found. He was a man who placed no limits on himself—or on his desires. And clearly he would take Linnea to his bed, unless someone stopped him.

Someone. Himself?

Axton kept his face impassive. Though Henry watched him with a mocking gaze, he kept his outrage hidden and his sudden confusion buried. Why should he care what happened to her? Why should he imagine, even for a moment, that he must save her from Henry's lusty attentions?

"She is most fair," Axton conceded, though he knew his tone implied no compliment. He faced the maiden, the sister who warranted so great a sacrifice from Linnea, and couldn't prevent himself from studying her. In truth, he was searching for some difference between them. Some mark or sign that would set her apart from Linnea.

But there was none. Her skin was as creamy and soft, though at this moment, a trifle pale. The downcast fringe of lashes was as thick as her sister's, her nose as slender, and her lips as lushly formed. Even the tendrils of golden hair that escaped the confines of her hood looked as silky and fine as Linnea's.

As the moment lengthened, Eustace's arm circled the girl, pulling her possessively against his side. Startled, her gaze flew up to Axton, then darted over to Sir Eustace, whose dark glower was directed at his foe.

"Do not think you shall gain more than the honor of gazing upon her," the other man growled the warning.

But Axton ignored Eustace's threat and stared still at Beatrix. There was a difference in the eyes! He'd seen it though their gazes had locked little more than a moment. Her wide-set eyes were the same variable blue as Linnea's, but this sister—this Beatrix—was terrified of him. He'd

seen it in her eyes and he knew instinctively that she would
dissolve in the face of his anger or at the assault of his body
upon hers.

But Linnea had not dissolved. Nor had he ever once
expected her to. She'd met him with mutiny in her eyes and
opposition at every turn, even when she was terrified. He
flexed the muscles of his right shoulder, conscious of the
tender skin yet healing from the cut she'd inflicted on him.
This Beatrix would never have hidden a knife in the bed.
She would never have fought him as her younger sister
had.

But though this one distinction between the two sisters
satisfied some part of him, it nevertheless solved nothing.

He shifted his gaze to meet Eustace's ferocious glare.
"To wed this woman is no honor at all, but a curse I must
endure if I am to regain my home. And I *will* regain it," he
promised.

Beatrix gasped and fell back—pushed when Eustace
lunged forward. But Henry stepped in with a sharp rebuke,
preventing the men from coming to blows.

"Hold! 'Tis not a brawl will resolve this dual claim!"
Then he laughed and clapped Axton on the shoulder.
"Come, show me this heap of stones you have spoken of
since I was but a babe in arms. Show me its wonders and
show me its defenses. But first show me to its alewife.
Show me its table, for I am famished and would feast and
drink and relive all our triumphs with the prompting of
your best ale and dearest wine. There is time enough to
morrow to settle this dispute between you."

From her perch in a chapel window Linnea watched the
meeting between Axton and Beatrix with dread. Poor Bea
trix.

Poor Axton!

She frowned at such a perverse thought. Poor Axton
indeed! He deserved no pity, or sympathy, or any other
soft emotion from her. That did not prevent her, however,
from straining forward in the window, striving in vain to
hear some word of what passed between the foursome. I

did not stop her from trying to decipher something of their mood or intention.

She'd identified the young duke at once, as much by his haughty bearing as by his purple cloak and silver helm. Beatrix she spied immediately as well, arrayed in cream and gold and as radiant as one of God's angels come brilliantly to earth. The hulking knight who'd helped Beatrix dismount Linnea assumed was the man promised to marry her. The man Axton must defeat.

Then the man lunged forward, Beatrix fell back, and Linnea gasped in alarm. But the duke interceded and after a moment they all proceeded into the keep.

Linnea slumped back in the small, cold chapel. What would happen next? When would Axton meet his rival in battle? When would she be able to see her sister?

Then a slight figure was handed down from a horse litter and a new fear gripped Linnea. It was her grandmother. The stooped figure with the ever present cane could be no one else. And like some dark, yet regal witch who knew every inch of her damnable domain and precisely where her victims cowered in fear, she looked up, right at the chapel window and straight into Linnea's heart—or at least that's how it felt to Linnea. For the Lady Harriet smiled, a cracked and ancient smile of malicious triumph, and Linnea fancied the old woman knew every emotion she felt: her love for Axton as well as her love for Beatrix.

With a cry of despair, she spun away from the window. She wrapped her arms around herself, as if somehow she could contain her desperate, dangerous emotions, as if she could stop herself from being shredded into a thousand pieces by them.

"Are they here?" her father asked in a voice flat and weary. That he was even aware of what was going on was an improvement, but Linnea could take little joy of it. If this Sir Eustace won the coming battle, her father might very well regain his old vigor and confidence. Most certainly his mother would be overjoyed. But Linnea would be crushed. Whether Eustace or Axton won, her life was over.

"They are here," she finally answered, steeling herself to

express no emotion. "The Duke of Normandy, grand-mother, Beatrix, and . . . and the man who would wed her."

She expected that news to cheer him, but it did not. If anything, he drooped further still. He had lost weight in the past weeks, and the deep blue tunic he wore hung loose on his frame. The skin on his face seemed too loose also. It sagged in tired folds. Aged folds.

An unaccountable anger leaped in her chest. "Shouldn't you be rejoicing? Isn't this what you wanted, a champion to avenge all the wrongs Axton de la Manse has done you, even though that champion is Henry's man as much as Axton is? But then, 'tis Axton who has killed your son, ruined one daughter, and would wed the other. But worst of all, he has fought to regain the home you took from him. You should be happy, Father. You should be rubbing your hands in glee and anticipating the moment when his blood is spilled in yon bailey!"

Under the barrage of her emotional outburst, he seemed somehow to shrink even further. Only when he raised tear-ful eyes to her did she stop, suddenly ashamed of herself. He was beyond defending himself against her. She of all people should know better than to take advantage of someone so vulnerable.

She started toward him, unsure of herself, but knowing that she must somehow try to comfort him. But he shook his head and held his hands up as if to ward her off. His hands trembled as he spoke.

" 'Tis all . . . all as it should be." He blinked and one tear spilled onto his lined cheek. "If only my Ella was here."

Ella? Linnea felt a shiver up her spine. He hadn't spo-ken of his wife in years. To hear him invoke her mother's name now filled Linnea with a nameless dread.

"I miss her too, Father." She stared at his damp eyes and the unkind cut of years upon his face.

"She should not have left me," he whispered, his old face as crushed as a child's. "She didn't want to go, but . . . but God took her from me." He shook his head as if bewildered. "I tried to do right. I did. But I . . ." His chin quivered and more tears streaked down his pale cheeks. "I broke too many of his commandments."

He looked past her toward one of the murals that adorned the chapel's plastered walls. Linnea twisted her head to see that it was Moses he stared at. Moses with the tablet of commandments clutched unbroken in his arms.

"I have killed. I have lied. I have coveted the possessions of my neighbor—"

His voice broke so piteously that Linnea's own eyes filled with tears. "Father, it does no good to dredge up every mistake you've ever made."

But he was staring at Moses and seemed not even to hear her. "I have coveted the wife of my neighbor," he choked out. "Even my own mother have I dishonored." His eyes came back to her. "She wanted you killed but—" He broke off. His chest heaved with the force of his emotions.

Linnea knew her grandmother had wanted her killed on the day of her birth. The old woman had never kept that a secret. But she'd never known why she had been spared.

"Ella pleaded for you," her father said, as if sensing her thoughts. "She pleaded, and I would do anything for my Ella.

"But it was not enough," he continued, growing more agitated. "I spared you but I marked you. I burned you, and Ella—" This time he broke off completely.

He'd burned her? But where—Linnea gasped. The birthmark. Only it was no birthmark at all but, rather, his mark, a brand given to her by her own father!

The small raised scar on her calf began to throb as if to say, "He did it. He did it."

She fell back a step. "You did that to . . . to me? *You* did it?" She echoed the accusing voice in her head.

"To please my mother. To honor her." His face crumpled and his shoulders heaved in huge, awful sobs.

It should not matter, Linnea told herself. It should not, for the pain of that mark had been no pain at all, not like the other pains she'd suffered growing up so unloved.

But it did matter. He'd scarred his own child, an innocent babe who'd done no sin save to be born second. Second! As if that signified anything!

She might have suffered her rage in silence. But at that very moment the chapel door creaked open and the sharp click of a metal-tipped walking cane announced the Lady Harriet's presence. Linnea whirled around, her every sense instantly tuned to the old woman's presence. Her heart thundered; her muscles tensed. The very hairs on the back of her neck stood on end. It was as if she'd come face-to-face with her enemy—and verily she had. For this woman had hated her from the moment of her birth. She'd despised her, tortured her, and never missed an opportunity to make her life miserable.

That she'd caused Linnea's father to scar his innocent child was, in truth, the least of her many crimes. But it was the one that pushed Linnea beyond her limits.

She glared at the Lady Harriet, but the old woman only smiled. "You have done a commendable job, girl. Against all odds, most commendable. I freely admit I had my doubts," she said. "But I will be the first to speak your praise. Though but a maiden, you have been brave and true, and you have provided your family the means to a victory over our enemy."

The cane clicked as the old woman advanced. "Come girl. Let me kiss you, the kiss of peace between us. For you are proven worthy. Let no one say you are not."

Linnea could not move. From the terrible heights of a rage fueled by a complete hatred, she was flung to the depths of a dreadful despair.

She was worthy. At last her grandmother smiled upon her and would kiss her as one proven to be worthy. But when Lady Harriet grasped her shoulder with one bony hand, Linnea recoiled in horror.

"No," she mumbled, wrenching free of the old woman's hold. "No," she repeated more stridently.

She stumbled back until she came up against the wall and the brilliant likeness of Moses.

Lady Harriet's eyes narrowed and Linnea was reminded

of a lizard or a snake. She shuddered at the cold, reptilian look. "What ails you?" the old woman snapped. Then her expression grew more cunning. "Aha. Methinks I know. 'Tis that overlarge appendage he has attacked you with. Methinks you did enjoy the surrender too well." Her face cracked in an ugly laugh. "Don't worry, girl. One is very like another. Is it not, Edgar?"

Sir Edgar had moved closer to Linnea, as if he might protect her from his mother's cruelty. But his mother stilled him in his tracks.

"One man can substitute for any other much as one woman can take the place of another, isn't that so?" Lady Harriet continued, staring coldly at him. Daring him to contradict her.

When his head bowed in silent defeat, the old woman turned her triumphant gaze on Linnea. "You see, girl? Whatever he felt for Ella, it did not prevent him from sampling wherever he chose. So it will be with that bear of a man you so foolishly think you love. 'Tis not love!" she snapped. Her mood turned from ugly amusement to sudden anger. "They do not love, nor should we! Nor should *you*," she amended after a brief pause.

"So." She took a slow breath. "You have bested him with your cunning. Now Eustace will best him with steel." She approached Linnea again until their faces were but inches apart. "He is no longer your ally—not that he ever was. Your future lies in the fold of your family. With me and Edgar and Beatrix. And Eustace," she added. "Now. Give me the kiss of peace."

She grabbed Linnea's shoulder and kissed her, first on one cheek, then the other. Linnea could not kiss her back, however. She simply could not.

But if Lady Harriet noticed or cared, it did not show. She only stared at Linnea afterward, the workings of her twisted mind buried in the opaqueness of her old eyes. For one moment Linnea fancied she saw fear in them. Fear, of all things. But that ludicrous thought quickly vanished. What had Lady Harriet to fear of her ruined granddaughter?

The old woman stamped her cane on the floor. "Come, the both of you. Duke Henry would see the girl who has deceived one of his mightiest knights. He considers it a huge jest that a man all others fear could have been duped by a woman with no other weapon but a face that looks like her sister's. Come," she repeated. "He awaits."

Sir Edgar moved forward like an obedient child—which he was and always had been, Linnea realized. Linnea pushed away from the wall. Anything to get away from this place and away from her hateful grandmother. But Lady Harriet stopped her at the door. This time her eyes were bright with a shrewd avidity.

"Are you with child?" She stared at Linnea like a vulture might, waiting to dissect her brain, and thereby know all her secrets. Her bony fingers bit into Linnea's arm. "Answer me truthfully, girl. Are you?"

In that moment Linnea would have given anything to say yes. Anything. Her reasons were confused and perverse, but her desire was very clear. She wished she could say yes. But she couldn't.

"I don't know," she answered honestly. Miserably.

Whether Lady Harriet was pleased or displeased, Linnea could not tell. As for herself, however, she was crushed. Despairing. Heartbroken.

She'd had her chance to have a husband and bear his children. No other chance would come again, for no other man would want her now.

But that was not the worst of it. The worst was that she would never want any other man.

Chapter 22

They were assembled like actors in a farce, like mimes or tumblers or minstrels come to perform their given roles and then depart. Linnea feared, however, that she would not be entertained.

Henry Plantagenet, Count of Anjou and Duke of Normandy, sat in the lord's chair, as did befit the liege lord of Maidenstone Castle. To his right sat the handsome knight Eustace de Montfort. To his left, Axton, joined by his mother and then Peter. Lady Mildred's face was drawn. She feared for the impending battle. Peter's face was set in a scowl, as if he, himself, would gladly take on Sir Eustace. Arrayed beyond Sir Eustace were Beatrix and two empty chairs. Obviously for Linnea's father and grandmother.

But where was she to sit?

Nowhere, it seemed, for with a flick of his bejeweled hand, the duke signaled her to approach him.

She had no ally here, she realized. Or no ally with any power, she amended. For Beatrix was with her. That was plain by the look in her sister's dear, worried face. Their eyes connected and held, and Linnea felt a reviving spurt of strength. Beatrix still loved her and that meant she was really no worse off than she'd ever been.

She took a hard breath and tilted her chin up another notch. Only then did she look directly at Axton.

He might have been a statue carved of unyielding stone, so rigidly set were his features. Even his eyes—his clear gray eyes that could vary from hot as steam to cold as ice— even they appeared like stone as they met hers. Hard, opaque, and brittle.

A sharp nudge from her grandmother forced her toward the high table. The rest of the hall was empty, save for the trio of servants who did scuttle about, anxious to please the man who would soon be their king.

Linnea advanced slowly toward the table. "My lord." She curtsied to the hearty young man who did toy with all their futures. Better to gaze upon his half-amused countenance than to face Axton's condemning stare.

The young duke's bright blue gaze ran over her appreciatively. "Well, and well again. It is as I was told. She is every bit as fair as Lady Beatrix. No wonder you did not question her more closely, de la Manse." He grinned then, and shrugged. "But of course, she is sadly lacking in those qualities which make of sweet Beatrix the bone which two of my ablest nobles do snarl over. For this sister is the younger, not the elder." He paused and Linnea felt the unpleasant rake of his gaze once more. "And she has already been despoiled."

Someone gasped. Beatrix? Or had she done it herself? In either event, his cruel words cut Linnea to the quick. She hated Henry Plantagenet instantly. She'd feared him before. Now she hated him as well.

"I have no doubt, however, that some man . . ." Henry paused once more, as if musing. "Some man will find a place for her in his . . . household."

Linnea's cheeks turned scarlet with the implication. Before she could speak, however, Axton pushed upright. "You insult me to allude that I have despoiled this woman."

Henry looked up at Axton. If he was unsettled to find a man of Axton's fierce reputation towering over him, fists knotted and muscles tensed, he did not indicate it by so much as a raised eyebrow. "There is no insult intended to you, my ever loyal friend. I only observe the results to her of her own deception."

The hall fairly shivered with the frosty exchange. It was into this perilous conversation that Linnea thrust herself. "The insult, I believe, is for me." She stared at the powerful young man and saw with relief the amusement return to his eyes. Axton did not need him as an enemy. She, however, had nothing at all to lose.

"As you will it," Henry answered. Linnea knew, though, that her will had nothing whatsoever to do with it. It never had. Then he leaned forward, his eyes as sharp as a frigid winter sky. "You were pure when you wed him?"

Linnea nodded, hating him more with every word he uttered. He arched one russet brow. "I assume that in the fortnight of your false marriage he did claim his husbandly rights."

She did not respond, at least not in words. But her cheeks again burned with the intensity of her shame. Not shame that she'd given herself to Axton. She could never be sorry or ashamed for that. But ashamed that they should be made into such a public spectacle. What would Henry want next, a recounting of every detail?

Henry laughed at her obstinate silence. "I know well enough Axton's appetite. Safe to say she can well instruct her sister on her wedding night—no matter who shall ultimately be her husband."

He laughed again, but when no one else did, he looked about with a tolerant expression. "Come, come. Let us not be somber. If either of you would not fight, you have only to say the word. The last thing I want is to lose either of my most loyal men."

Axton had remained on his feet during the exchange between Linnea and Henry. Now he spoke up. "When will this matter be resolved? I see no reason to delay—"

"Tomorrow will have to be soon enough." Henry turned a benign smile on him. "Sit down, Axton. Sit down and play the gracious host, for tomorrow—well, who knows what tomorrow shall bring?"

He waited until Axton had reclaimed his chair. Then Henry picked up an ornately bejeweled goblet which he must have brought with him. Linnea knew it was not from Maidenstone's plate. A servant filled the goblet with a deep red wine. Then Henry smiled at the tense company. "A toast to . . . to Maidenstone. May its lord and lady reside here in peace, and long pledge their loyalty to England—and to me!"

Everyone drank, despite the ambiguous meaning of the toast. Everyone, that is, except Linnea, for she had no cup. But even that circumstance Henry used for his own perverse amusement. He gestured to her with one finely manicured hand.

"Come. Sip from my cup, fair Linnea. 'Tis only right that one so willing to sacrifice herself for the honor of her family should share my cup. I have spent my entire life sacrificing for the honor of my own family. And look now where it has taken me. I am poised on the brink of my triumph. You too are poised on the brink of triumph—if Sir Eustace can defeat Sir Axton. If not . . ." He shrugged. "Come, drink from my cup," he commanded.

Linnea edged toward the table, toward the man who would soon rule all of England. He already ruled everyone in this grim and silent chamber. She halted before the raised table and stared into his smooth, grinning face. He extended the heavy goblet to her. When she grasped it, however, he did not release it. She was forced to lean forward to take her sip, and when his fingers circled hers, to suffer his touch without recoiling, no matter how repulsed she was.

Once she'd had her damning taste of his wine, she tried to release the goblet. It wobbled and nearly fell. But Henry's clutch tightened around it and caught it. Then he very deliberately turned the handsome vessel, placed his lips where hers had been, and quaffed the remainder of the wine.

A chair scraped back and Axton was once more on his feet. "I would fight de Montfort now. This very minute!"

"Tomorrow," Henry answered. He glared at Axton, then he turned his gaze again on Linnea. "I would sate my appetite first. My appetites," he amended, emphasizing the pluralized word.

Linnea did not wait another moment. Without asking his pardon to leave, she gave a trembling curtsy, then backed away. She refused to look at Henry and see the leer she was certain was there. She could not bear to look at Axton and see the contempt in his eyes. She looked, instead, to Beatrix.

But Beatrix's stricken expression provided Linnea with no comfort, save for the knowledge that someone, at least, sympathized with her plight. It was equally plain, however, that the innocent Beatrix did not understand what the young duke implied. How could she? She knew nothing of men and their carnal desires. Everyone else did, though. Her father and grandmother. Even Lady Mildred and Peter. But none of them cared. Not one of them.

Linnea hastened from the hall, nearly colliding with the seneschal and his wife, who waited just beyond the door.

"Does he wish to be served now?" Sir John nervously asked.

"Yes," Linnea responded, knowing there was only one "he" when Henry was in residence. "He is ready to be served."

And he would be served, she feared. He would be served anything he asked for, including a despoiled and terrified young woman whose loyalty he publicly proclaimed, but whose honor he meant privately to steal.

Axton watched Linnea depart with a growing sense of outrage. Henry meant to have her in his bed. In Axton's own bed, in fact. He threw back the last of his wine and thumped the pewter vessel down. Immediately it was filled by a page and immediately he downed the contents again.

The serving boy hesitated, then at Axton's impatient glare, hastily filled the goblet a third time. Before Axton could lift it to drink, however, he was stayed by his mother's hand on his arm.

"You will win nothing this way," she murmured lowly, so that Henry could not hear. "Not this battle, nor tomorrow's."

But Axton did not want to hear that or any other advice. "Give me credit for knowing how to deal with any knave who would stand between me and my rightful heritage."

" 'Tis not the knave I worry for so much as the maiden."

He turned an incredulous gaze on her. "You worry for that . . . for that bitch?"

She met his stare with one so sad that it made him feel guilty. "I do not worry for her, but for you. For what she has done to you. I wish we were still at Caen," she added lower still.

Axton did not respond to her. What was there he could say that would give her any comfort? The meat platters came and he accepted whatever the server offered. He ate, he drank. He responded as little to Henry as was still not insulting to the young man he'd known all his life. He had never deluded himself about Henry in the past, and he did not do so now. Henry was his friend up to a point. Beyond that he was strictly Matilda's son and King Henry's grandson. Destined to be king of England. Nothing else interfered with that, not childhood friendships nor lifelong loyalties.

Henry quickly tired of Axton's sullen mood and turned his attention on Eustace. Eustace preened and swelled under Henry's interest and sent Axton many a smug glance as the meal progressed past the roasted piglets, poached oysters, and stewed starlings to cheese and herrings, then pears and pastries. But Henry did but set the man up for a fall, Axton suspected.

"I would have a word with Lady Beatrix. A private word," Axton pronounced when the three musicians he'd brought in had exhausted their repertoire. He made certain his voice carried to one and all.

Henry shifted in the lord's chair so that his back was now turned to Eustace. The assessing smirk on his face confirmed Axton's suspicions. Henry loved nothing better than to bait and tease those most loyal to him. Earlier he'd baited Axton. Now it was Eustace's turn.

Sure enough, Henry tapped a finger thoughtfully on his chin as if considering Axton's request. In truth, though, Axton knew he'd already decided. The young duke shifted and leaned forward on his elbows to look past Eustace to the pale-faced Lady Beatrix.

"Methinks that a reasonable enough request," he said.

Eustace's face darkened in a scowl. He opened his mouth as if to object, but just as quickly closed it. Axton did not have to see Henry's expression to know the warning it held.

When Eustace's angry gaze switched to him, he could not resist a smug grin. He would take a complete pleasure in laying low this man who thought to wrest Maidenstone from him. A satisfying, unmerciful pleasure.

"I am weary," Henry announced into the waiting silence. When he stood, so did everyone else. "Have your word with Lady Beatrix," he told Axton with a negligent wave of his hand. "Her grandmother will ensure no impropriety," he added, which implication deepened Eustace's scowl even further.

They filed from the hall. Eustace, the Lady Mildred, and

Peter followed Henry up the stairs to the better chambers, while Edgar de Valcourt wandered away as if confused about where he was to go. Only Beatrix and the old woman lingered at the table. Even the few servants Axton gestured off. He would have no distractions, he decided as he considered the young woman he meant to have, even at the risk of his own life.

The fire in the huge hearth burned low, sending lonely shadows jumping across the empty hall. Neither of the women spoke as he scraped back his chair then moved toward them. The young one stared at him with eyes round with dread. The old one glared her loathing and disdain. A perverse thought occurred to him. Could he merge those two into one, he would have Linnea.

That ludicrous idea stopped him in his tracks, but he knew nevertheless that it was truth. The breathtaking beauty of one coupled with the unquenchable spirit of the other. Without that spirit, this Beatrix was nothing like the woman he'd wed.

And yet, this pale, frightened creature was the one he *must* have.

Ruthlessly he quashed any memory of Linnea. "Will you be a faithful wife, standing with me, though it be against the rest of your family?"

" 'Tis a question with no point," the old woman snapped. "She will not have to stand with you against—"

"I asked her," Axton bit out. "Can you not speak for yourself?" he taunted the trembling girl. He held her terrified gaze with the force of his stare and took a stark satisfaction when her eyes misted with tears. "Have you no voice of your own?" he persisted.

"Who . . . whomsoever I am wed to," she said in a thin, faltering voice. "I shall endeavor to be a worthy wife to."

At least she did not weep, Axton thought. Still, if he'd pressed Linnea for the same answer, there would have been both challenge and warning in her answer, though the words themselves be exactly the same as her sister's.

"You are not like your sister."

Now why had he said that? She blinked at what must have seemed a very odd observation on his part, for the likeness they shared was uncanny. And yet there was something . . .

For a moment he thought to press the issue, to push it further and discover precisely what the differences between them were. But he stopped himself before he could begin. It was not the differences between them that mattered—save that this wench not be so devious as her sister. No, it was their similarities.

With an abrupt motion he drew her to her feet. In the background the old woman objected, demanding that he unhand her, threatening him with every manner of punishment. But her shrill complaints were no more than an annoyance grating like the threatening roll of thunder that could do no real harm.

Axton held Beatrix before him, her arms small in his hands, her body as easy to overpower as ever her sister's had been.

But she was not her sister. Something he could not name—she was softer, not as strong; she smelled different; she gave off a different level of heat. Whatever it was, the difference was there.

"By God's bones!" he swore. Then he let out a low growl of frustration, hauled her up to him, and kissed her.

He was not easy with her. He devoured her mouth and forced his tongue in. He tasted her with the ferocity of a man who could take whatever he wanted, whenever he wanted it.

Only when he tasted the salt of her tears did he finally thrust her away.

"Baseborn brute! Spineless cur! Villain!" the old woman shrieked. She struck out at him with her stick, but the blow was as ineffectual as her curses. Axton stared at the girl, at her sobbing form, clutched now in her grandmother's skinny embrace.

That he was almost as despairing as she, he quashed with brutal determination. He could take her, yes. And tomorrow, once he'd felled that fool de Montfort, he would take her. Henry would have to concede then that both woman and castle were rightfully his.

Fists clenched, he turned and strode from the hall. But he was acutely conscious of the weeping girl and the shrill old woman behind him. Once in the darkened yard he was beyond hearing them. But he could not so easily escape his thoughts.

The feel of her was all wrong. But he would grow accustomed to it, he told himself. He would learn to rouse to the touch of her. She was not so different from her sister as all that. Besides, one woman was much the same as the next. He'd thought so all his life. No reason to believe otherwise now.

But even as he told himself that, he knew still that he must find Linnea. He must find her now and decide what to do with her before the morrow came.

And before Henry found her first.

Chapter 23

Linnea slipped from shadow to shadow. Thank God and all the saints that it was a moonless night. As it was, her heart thundered so violently she feared anyone might hear it and thereby detect her presence.

A voice drifted down from the ramparts; a step sounded just beyond the stable. Duke Henry's men were everywhere, as were Axton's. Eustace de Montfort's entourage had been forced to camp beyond the moat. But that only increased the feeling of an armed camp ready to erupt. As much as she already despised Henry Plantagenet, she nonetheless prayed he could maintain peace on the morrow.

Meanwhile, however, she must cope with tonight, and manage somehow to avoid Henry and yet find Beatrix. She had no doubts about the young duke's intentions toward her, but even the threat of landing in his bed could not overcome her need to be with her sister.

How long would Beatrix be detained in the hall?

The wait seemed interminable, though in truth it was not so very long. The watchman nearest her whistled a broken tune only three times through. He spoke briefly to another man and they shared a crude laugh at the expense of some woman they referred to as Creamy. Then he began again to whistle.

On the fourth verse Axton stormed down the steps and into the yard.

He paused as if to get his bearings, and with an impatient gesture thrust both hands through his hair. She could see very little of him, only his silhouette dimly rimmed by the wall torch next to the oak doors. But she could sense his frustration—and his seething anger.

I'm sorry. So very sorry. More than anything, she wanted to run to him, to beg his forgiveness and to offer him some comfort. But that would be madness. He would never forgive her for making a fool of him, nor could he possibly feel any comfort in her presence. She was the thorn that had pricked him, then festered, and on the morrow she might very well prove to be the instrument of his downfall.

She almost cried out on that thought. He could not die. He must not! But what could *she* do about it?

With a mighty effort she tried to make herself as small as possible, to shrink into the rough wall of the alehouse and disappear forever into the stones that made up Maidenstone.

When he finally moved on, headed she knew not where, instead of relief, she felt a devastating sense of loss. I love you, she sent the message silently to him. *Though you see only my betrayal, what I feel most for you is love.*

After another bleak span of time one of the tall doors creaked open and a head ventured out. Then two women crept past the door and down the steps—one with a walking stick nearly as tall as she—and Linnea's aching heart leaped with joy. Beatrix! At last her beloved sister was come to her!

She joined them at the base of the steps, only to find

Beatrix violently weeping. "I cannot!" she sobbed. "I cannot wed him. I will kill myself first!"

"Do not be stupid!" Lady Harriet hissed. Then spying Linnea, she thrust Beatrix at her. "Talk some sense into her!" she snapped. "The man does not walk this earth who is worth dying over!"

Beatrix fell into Linnea's arms with a grateful sob. "You are here! You have survived! Oh, but I should not have been such a coward as to see you sacrificed to that . . . that—" Again she burst into sobs.

Half-supporting her distraught sister, Linnea managed somehow to guide her into the shadows where the outer wall met with the eaves of the alehouse. There she hugged her sister hard, offering her the only comfort she had, just as Beatrix had so many times hugged and comforted her.

"Shh. Do not weep, sister. You do but make yourself sick." She held the shuddering girl as if she'd never let her go. "Shh. Just listen to me. Listen to me!"

"Oh, Linnea, I have prayed and prayed for you," Beatrix whispered against Linnea's neck. "But it has been for naught."

"No," Linnea retorted. "Not for naught. If you prayed for me, then you see now that I am well. No harm has come to me. Nor will it come to you. Axton is not a cruel man. He—"

"He will die on the morrow, so it matters not," their grandmother broke in. Despite her harsh pronouncement, however, she looked small and beaten. She leaned heavily on her stick as a sudden fit of coughing shook her frail form.

Linnea glared her fury at the old woman. "What matter to you if it be Axton or this Sir Eustace who marries her? They are both Henry's men—"

"Do you so easily forget your brother?" Lady Harriet spat back at her. "Are you that ungrateful to him who did sacrifice his very life for you?"

Not for me, Linnea wanted to say. She chose instead to ignore her grandmother and turn back to her sister. "Whatever shall come tomorrow, Beatrix, you shall not suffer for it. I do not know this Sir Eustace as do you, but I know Axton."

Beatrix drew back, just enough to look into her sister's face. Though the darkness shrouded them, there was yet that sense that they could see one another very well.

"Do not defend him to her," Lady Harriet croaked. "She has experienced already his cruelty." She moved nearer to them and fastened her bony hand on Beatrix's arm. "Tell her how he mauled you just now. How he forced himself on you. Tell her!" The old woman shook with the vehemence of her emotions. "Tell her 'ere she conspires with him to destroy Eustace and your only remaining hope for happiness!"

"He would be a good husband to her," Linnea countered, frowning at her grandmother. "You do not know him like I do."

The old woman snorted at that. "No. You *do* have a particular knowledge of him that I do not. A carnal knowledge that I would save your sister from!" she finished shrilly.

Loyalty and selfishness fought a terrible battle in Linnea's heart: loyalty to Axton and Beatrix—both of whom she loved better than herself—against a selfishness she could not defend. She did not want to share Axton with anyone, not even her sister. She wanted to keep Axton all for herself.

She let out a laugh that was half sob. Even if she could keep him, he would never agree. He hated her now. There was nothing she could do for Axton—save to help him retain this home he'd fought so long and hard to possess. And even that was not within her means.

She pressed her cheek to Beatrix's damp one and felt her sister's trembling fear. "Do not be afraid of him," she whispered. "In time you will see that I am right in this."

But Beatrix twisted away. "I will pray the whole night long that Eustace defeats him. I will keep vigil on my knees," she swore with a fierceness Linnea had never seen in her mild-mannered sister. But when Beatrix spied Linnea's stricken expression, her angry expression relented. "I do not wish him ill. But . . . but I cannot be wed to him. I cannot!"

She began once more to weep, but this time Linnea did not have the words to comfort her. How had this happened? How had it come to this between them, that one could want a man she could not have, while the other could spurn that same man who, meanwhile, was set on possessing her?

"If you love your sister," Lady Harriet broke in, "you will do whatever it takes to ensure that man falls on the morrow. Weaken him with some potion. Sap his strength in another fashion, if it so suits you. But do not betray us now when you have almost succeeded." Her voice had altered and now she reached out a hand to Linnea's face.

Linnea flinched, but the old woman only made a grimace of a smile and patted her cheek. "You have done well, Linnea. Do you wish to prove your worthiness, you will not falter now."

Linnea tried to swallow but something hard lodged in her throat, a lump of emotions that threatened to choke her no matter what answer she made. She stared at Beatrix who huddled now in her grandmother's embrace, but she could not reply. Her heart was breaking; her world was collapsing in ruin about her. The future loomed forbidding and grim. But Linnea could not reply.

Distraught, she spun around, disoriented, but desperate to escape. But escape was no real solution to her plight, and anyway, even escape was denied her. For a sturdy figure blocked her way, a figure she recognized even in the dark. It was Peter and it was plain he'd come for her. It was equally plain the contempt he felt for her.

"Do the three of you meet still to plot against my family? Do you gather here to gloat and anticipate your triumph?" He advanced on them, his fists knotted, his expression cold.

Beatrix and Lady Harriet fell back a pace. But he looked so much like Axton that Linnea could do nothing but stare. When he stood just before her he sneered, "Are you indeed Linnea, brave but stupid, or are you the cowardly sister, Beatrix?"

"I . . . I am Linnea."

He glared at her, then past her at Beatrix. His eyes narrowed suspiciously. "Prove it. I have heard that the first sister is unmarked, but the second one sports the devil's own mark."

" 'Tis not the devil's mark," Beatrix cried from behind Linnea.

"So you are Linnea!" Peter accused her.

"No, I am the one you seek," Linnea countered. She stayed him with a hand on his arm when he would have advanced on Beatrix. "I am Linnea. See?" She raised her skirt to display the red welt on her calf. "I carry the mark, not she."

He looked at her, then over at Beatrix. When his gaze came back to her, however, some of the belligerence had been replaced by confusion. He studied Linnea's face as if searching for some other difference between them, some indication—the shape of her lips, the arch of a brow—that would set them apart. When he could not find one, he frowned at her.

"Come with me."

To Henry, Linnea assumed. To Henry's bed, for Henry's pleasure. She thought she would be ill.

He grabbed her above the elbow and steered her back toward the hall. But Beatrix unexpectedly tore herself from her grandmother's arms.

"No! You can't take her. Hasn't your family done enough! Haven't you taken our home, our brother. Even my father—" Beatrix burst into tears. But even unfinished, her words seemed to affect Peter. Or perhaps it was *because* she'd been unable to finish, for Peter's stern expression faltered and Linnea saw him swallow hard. Then he rallied and his grip on Linnea's arm stiffened.

"You forget that I have lost two brothers and a father to your family. We owe you nothing." Then with a rude jerk he hauled Linnea off. But Beatrix's sobs were not silenced until the stout doors of the keep thudded closed behind them.

In the hall all was quiet save for the grumbles of sleeping servants. The hearth glowed but dully with embers of the banked fire. One torch yet gave a faint dying glow. There were no signs in the hall of the terrible tension that gripped the castle, only their own harsh breathing.

Peter's fingers tightened even more as he steered her toward the stairs. Before Linnea had been too numb to object. Besides, she'd known it would be pointless. Now, though, pointless or not, she could not bring herself to cooperate. To be given over to Henry was unthinkable. Impossible. She dug her heels in and grabbed at a corner of the wall.

Peter swung around. "Bitch you may be, but don't be a stupid bitch also," he snapped. Then with a rough jerk he yanked her up the stairs.

"No! I won't go! You can't make me—"

"Shut up!" he hissed, clamping his hand over her mouth. "Do you want to wake up the whole castle?"

But Linnea was far beyond caring about waking up anyone. Instead she fought him as violently as if he did plan to murder her. For to her mind, sending her to Henry was tantamount to murder, for it would forever kill something in her soul.

"Bloody hell!" he swore when she bit his hand. He shoved her so hard against the wall that her head cracked painfully against it and the breath was knocked out of her. "Damn you!" he swore, shaking the hand she'd bitten. "I'm trying to help you! My mother is fool enough to wish to protect you—"

"That role is better filled by me," a voice from behind them broke in.

Axton's voice.

But no, Linnea could not believe it. It must be her imagination and the dizzying spin of her head.

But then another hand curved around her arm. A bigger hand, equally harsh, equally stern. Peter released her and stepped back.

"Mother instructed me to fetch her—"

"Her involvement in this matter will not be necessary," Axton retorted. Without giving Linnea the time even to look up at him, he steered her ahead of him up the stairs.

Linnea was too confused to resist. Peter had been bringing her to the Lady Mildred, not the young duke? That was difficult enough to comprehend. But Axton's appearance was even more difficult, for he'd said that protecting her was his responsibility.

"What do you intend to do with her?" Peter whispered as he followed behind them.

"Exactly as I please," Axton bit back. His words were meant less for Peter though, and more for her, Linnea feared.

She balked as they came into the antechamber, but her lack of cooperation was of no moment to him at all. He merely clasped her to his side with one brawny arm, and pressed her face into his shoulder. Muffled against his wool tunic, Linnea could neither cry out nor object. He hustled her past the lord's chamber where Henry waited, past the several sleeping men who made up Henry's personal staff, and into the smaller chamber he was occupying. She vaguely spied Sir Reynold before Axton slammed the door shut. Only then did he release her.

Only then did she realize the danger she was in.

He bolted the door. For a moment he just stood there, facing the door. Breathing hard. Then he turned and without looking at her, he began to undress. Weapons he set carefully aside. His boots he placed beside a low table. His tunic and chainse, then stockings and braies, he laid across the table.

He was deliberate in every movement he made, as if she were not there, and he prepared for bed in the normal fashion. But she was there and he knew it, and Linnea turned cold inside.

She circled around him then backed up to the door, though she knew escape was not possible. He clearly knew it too, for though he straightened to face her, he did not advance on her. Instead he fixed her with his wintry gaze.

"Choose, Linnea. Will you warm Henry's bed tonight or mine?" Like a double-edged blade, sunk to the hilt in her chest, those harsh, unfeeling words cut her. Linnea sucked in a hard breath. This was her punishment then—or the beginning of it. To choose Axton over Henry Plantagenet was not so hard. But to have him take her without any feeling whatsoever—it would be worse even than in his mother's chamber. She did not think she could bear it.

He looked at her, a long, unendurable stare that stripped away all the layers of what they'd each done and why they'd done it. He faced her, naked, virile—a man who wanted no words or excuses from her, only the use of her body.

Linnea began to tremble.

"Take off your clothes."

She must have shaken her head, or perhaps it was only her lack of response that revealed her opposition.

"Take them off, then come here and work your wiles on me."

"Axton, no . . ."

"You played the whore when I did not recognize the role. The only difference now is that I know you for who you are. Take off your clothes," he demanded in a deadly tone.

She pressed back into the door, but there was no relief there, only rough wood and the nubby protuberance of bolts and hinges keeping her inside with him. She tore her eyes from his unflinching gaze. But scanning the room brought no promise of escape. Simple furnishings and unadorned stone walls. And on a peg on the far wall hung the chain.

Her eyes froze on it. Its gold links and red stones winked in the erratic firelight. It was the sight of that chain that finally defeated her.

So it was come to this. She would be raped by the man she loved. The man who might have grown to love her had she not forced him to hate her.

She turned her face back to him, then slowly pushed off from the door.

First she removed her veil and the circlet that held it in place. Her hair came undone from its simple looping with little effort. She unlaced her sleeves, then the waist slits of her gown. But she kept her eyes on him and he kept his on her.

She removed the gown though her fingers shook with every task. She stepped out of her low-heeled shoes then stood before him, hesitant. Only her kirtle covered her and it was so thin as to be nearly transparent.

When Axton only stared at her, however, she knew it too must go. She slid it off her shoulders then freed her arms and pushed it past her hips until it fell to the floor.

He had not moved as she'd disrobed. He'd not even watched really, for his smoldering gaze had remained locked with hers. But now, as he waited for her to come to him, she saw one change in him. He was aroused. Fully and completely aroused.

That part of him she'd once feared, then grown to love, she now feared again.

She glanced away, toward the weapons he'd so casually discarded. Could she move fast enough to grab one of them? Could she then fight him off? She feared not.

Once before she'd tried to fight him when he'd begun to take her in anger. She'd fought back. Then . . . then somehow everything had turned around. A spark of sudden hope flared as she recalled what had happened. He'd pulled her on top of him and let her control everything.

Perhaps if she took charge . . . Perhaps if she made love to him, he would be unable to make it into something hateful and ugly.

Linnea took a steadying breath. When his eyes moved to her breasts and her bared, puckered nipples, she felt both chagrin and another tiny shiver of hope. She took another breath.

"Lie on the bed," she ordered, forcing herself to stare straight at him. When he raised his gaze back to her face, his eyes narrowed.

"Lie on the bed," she repeated, before he could reply. " 'Tis what you want, is it not? For me to give you pleasure.

For me to play the part you have assigned me," she added bitterly.

" 'Tis a part you willingly embraced," he countered. But she saw his manhood stiffen further.

"Well, then. Let me perform my part. Lie on the bed."

This time he complied. He lay on his back on the bearskin, his strong body framed by the black fur. He was like the bear, she fancied. Dangerous to approach. Deadly to touch. Yet she was too ensnared by his fearful beauty to be careful.

She came to the bed and for a moment she simply stared down at him. He was all muscle and smooth skin, marred occasionally by the scars of his profession. But that only magnified his appeal. He was like a battle-scarred bear that had fought many times to protect its territory. Even the hair on his legs and chest and loins was the black of the bear.

A frisson of erotic heat shivered its way up from her belly. If only he loved her . . .

His viselike grip trapped her wrist, then pulled her hand rudely to his groin. She felt the hard heat of him, the angry demand, and she almost faltered. He hated her. She did not think she could bear to make love to him when he despised her so.

He moved her hand up and down on him and she had to steel herself not to snatch it away. When she glanced wildly at his face, however, her near panic vanished. There was such torture in his eyes. His face was impassive, but his eyes . . .

Without pausing to think, Linnea bent down and kissed him fully on the mouth. She felt him stiffen; he had not expected that. But that only prodded her on. She kissed him again, so fervently that she feared he would sense all her emotions. All her love.

Of all the intimacies they'd shared, kissing seemed somehow the most personal. Other than their wedding kiss, he'd not kissed her until that day in the woods alongside the river. She'd taken it, if not a declaration of love, then a declaration of caring. And now, she was declaring

291

the depths of her caring to him—of her love, if he was listening.

She heard a growl, as if he objected. But when she ran the tip of her tongue along the seam of his lips, he parted them. And when she delved deeper, and he met her tongue with his own, she felt the bittersweet pang of her triumph.

She kissed him and he kissed her back, and suddenly he tumbled her onto the bed. Onto him.

It was a frantic coupling, hasty and intense, marked as fiercely by the melding of their mouths and tongues as by the joining of their bodies. She rode him and possessed him, and in some subtle way, she knew that he was aware of it. He'd thought to possess her, but she possessed him.

When it was over—when he grabbed her and pumped all he had into her, and she clenched and seemed to die upon him—they lay in one sweaty heap, a sprawl of trembling limbs and tangled hair and exhausted bodies.

Only then did Linnea end their kiss and turn her face into the strong curve of his neck.

They gasped for breath in unison. One of his hands clasped her bottom. The other spread across the small of her back. As they calmed, he began to move it, sliding it up her spine, letting his fingertips trace the rhythmic bumps of her spine.

Linnea would happily have died just then, sated by their lovemaking, held yet in the warm embrace of the man she loved.

But then his light stroking stopped and Linnea felt the change in him. It was as if he'd just surfaced from a fog and realized where he was. And with whom. A north wind blowing icy across their overheated bodies could not have chilled her so swiftly as did the renewed tension that filled his body.

She rolled off him at once, but he did not let her escape. Instead he caught her hair in his fist and forced her to face him. What she saw in his eyes tore her heart to shreds.

"What is it you have, that you can so easily bewitch me? What sorcerer's spell? What devil's evil?" His darkened gaze bored into hers. "Is it the devil who has taught you

292

these tricks? Is it he who has given you this dark magic, this ability to seduce a man's body and his soul?"

With his free hand he grabbed her leg and roughly thumbed her birthmark. "Is this his mark? Has he sent you here to torment me with a living hell?"

"And what of you?" she cried out in despair. "Are you no less cruel to me?"

But he was too angry to listen. With a curse he drew back from her. "Begone from here, witch! Get out of my sight!" That there was a bleakness in his eyes as he said it was no salve to Linnea's pain.

Burying any show of emotion, she snatched up her kirtle and gown. "Now that you are sated, shall I go to Henry? 'Tis said the sign of a good lord is ever to please his liege. To share your whore with him is only good manners." She had struggled into her clothes. Now she faced him with blazing eyes. "But tell me this, my *lord.* Shall I clean away the leavings of our joining before I go to him—or does he prefer a woman wet from the man before him?"

Then without allowing him the chance to answer, she fled.

Chapter 24

She did not warm Henry's bed. That much Axton knew, for when he would have stormed half-garbed into Henry's chamber, Reynold had barred the way. "She is not there," he'd said, and gestured toward the stair with his head.

Where she'd gone—where else she might have hidden herself for the night—he did not know. Nor did he care, he told himself. He would not share her with any man, most of all Henry. Beyond that, however, he did not care what she did with herself.

He repeated that to himself in myriad versions through the endless hours of the night. He did not care if she wept. He did not care if she was sorry for deceiving him. He did not care if she slept huddled in some cold corner or within her sister's cowardly embrace. He only cared that she be available to him whenever he desired her.

Only that would not be as easy as it had been when he'd thought her his wife.

Christ, but he wished he could kill this insane desire he had for her!

But it was more than desire, and he knew it. Were it only desire, another woman would suffice. But he had no taste for other women, not her sister nor the wenches Peter had sent to him. He wanted only Linnea, the woman who was the source of all his pain and yet, was the only one he would turn to for comfort.

God save him from such perversity!

But even God could not help him in this, and as the night progressed and he fell at last into a fitful slumber, it was to dream of battle and slaughter, and the enticing smile of Linnea waiting for him. It was not Beatrix. He could see well enough the difference twixt the two. No, it was Linnea who waited for him.

And Linnea who always disappeared before he could reach her.

He awoke in a foul mood. Fitting for battle, he acknowledged as he made his brief ablutions. Peter appeared to help him dress, then together they proceeded to the chapel to pray. By then the entire castle was roused and in motion, and everywhere he went, everyone's eyes followed.

They knew what this day held, though they could not predict the outcome. From lowliest kitchen drudge to knights from three different entourages, they all anticipated the coming confrontation with morbid fascination. More lives than his own hung in the balance, but Axton knew better than to dwell on that. His focus must be on Eustace de Montfort, on the man's strengths, but most especially, his weaknesses. And the foremost of his weaknesses was his arrogance.

Axton had seen Eustace fight, both on the battlefield and in tournament play. He had a strong arm and considerable endurance. But once shaken, he quickly unraveled. Unnerve the man, and he would swiftly flounder.

It was Axton's intent to goad him, taunt him, and then make swift work of him. But that simple plan was sorely tested over the next several hours.

Henry arose late. He bathed leisurely. By the time he came downstairs to break his fast, the kitchen did already prepare the midday repast.

"He does but prolong the sport," Peter groused when Henry settled in the lord's chair. "*His* sport."

But Axton only shrugged. Henry was not his enemy this day, no matter what torment he presented. No, it was Eustace whom Axton awaited. He could put up with Henry so long as he ultimately confronted Eustace.

When Henry caught his eye, Axton made his way directly to him. "Perhaps it is only that you are newly settled here," the young duke began. "But you have much to learn of hosting a monarch. My bed was cold." He smiled, showing his even teeth. "And lonely."

Although Axton heard the chastisement in Henry's tone and knew the man did yet lust over Linnea, he refused to be baited. "Perhaps you should send for Eleanor. No doubt she pines for your presence as you do for hers."

Henry's grin only broadened. "To pine for one woman when so many others are available—" He shrugged, then he looked around. "But where are the other participants in today's little drama? Never tell me that Eustace has absconded in the night."

Axton shifted and rested his hand on the hilt of his sword. "I would not allow him to escape me so easily."

Henry's eyes glinted in anticipation. "Good. That is good. I trust today's confrontation will be entertaining—and that no one will die," he added.

This time Axton could not restrain his feelings. "You cannot set us like dogs upon one another and not expect to see blood flow!"

"Oh, but I can." Then his easy smile faded and he leaned forward. "No one will die. I need all my nobles. Your reward should be adequate—the beauteous Beatrix de Valcourt and all this," he added with a sweep of his hand to indicate the castle and demesne beyond. "By the by, where is she—and her equally beauteous sister?"

Linnea dressed with haste and not an iota of care for how she looked. Beatrix delayed, finding every excuse to reject this gown or that one. She wanted different slippers, a new veil, and her other kirtle. Even the Lady Harriet, who'd been unusually patient, could take no more.

"Be done with it!" the old woman ordered, stamping her stick upon the floor. "To delay changes nothing. Even your sister realizes that."

Indeed, Linnea did. Nothing any of them did would delay or change anything of what this day might hold. Beatrix would be the reward to one of the men who did vie for her. As for the other man, the one who lost—

She turned to her grandmother. "Do they fight to the death?"

"Of course," she snapped. "Blood must be drawn and quarter asked."

"But if one of them begs quarter, then why . . ." But Linnea knew the answer before her grandmother gave it.

"Neither of them will ask quarter," Lady Harriet said. "They are men of war, come fresh from battle these recent months. To think they will stop short of a killing blow . . ." She trailed off when Linnea paled. "Do you yet fear for his safety? Ah, but I forget. Even last night you did whore for him—"

Linnea cut off the vicious old woman with a stinging slap. She had not planned it; she only reacted to her grandmother's cruel words. But as her grandmother staggered back and caught herself on the window ledge, Linnea felt not a moment of regret. She advanced on her grandmother, consumed by a cold rage.

"Every day of my life have you belittled me. And every day have I struggled to earn some crumb of your approval. But not anymore. Not anymore! What I have done has been for my sister, no one else. Most certainly not for you! I am no whore and you will not call me such ever again!"

Linnea glared down at her grandmother, daring her to

oppose her. How she expected the bitter old woman to react, she did not know. To her utter surprise, however, Lady Harriet's eyes flickered with fear. She rubbed her cheek then slowly drew herself up.

"You have performed your role . . . well," she finally conceded. "I will not hold it against you," she added more grudgingly.

Linnea stared at her grandmother, and suddenly she could not understand why she'd feared her so long. What, truly, was there to fear? That quickly she felt her anger fade, like a pennant capsizing when the wind ceases. But there was neither joy nor triumph to fill the empty space it left. To have intimidated her formidable grandmother should have been immensely satisfying. To at last have gained her approval should have brought her some level of contentment. She'd struggled for it so long. But it meant nothing to her now. It gained her naught, she finally saw.

She turned away from the wizened old crone and faced her terrified sister instead. "Come, Beatrix. You must be brave and face whatever this day holds."

"I don't want to marry him. He will kill me," she whispered tearfully. "He will."

Linnea took her sister by both arms and stared intently into her eyes. "He will not. He is angry now—but at me, not you. He is a fair man. Given time, you will discover that."

But her words clearly carried no weight with Beatrix. "Perhaps with you he is so. But with me—" She shuddered and broke off, then wiped her eyes with the back of her hand. "How I pray that Eustace defeats him!"

Linnea drew back shaking her head. "No, Axton should be lord here. His family has lived here longer than ours and—"

"Then *you* marry him!" Beatrix shouted. "You marry him. 'Tis plain enough you crave his touch!"

I would marry him, would he have me. But he does not want me, at least not for his wife. "He . . . he wants you." Linnea barely choked out the words. Then she gathered all her resources. "If Axton de la Manse defeats Eustace de

Montfort, you will marry him and be a good wife to him."
She glared at Beatrix, at the sister she loved but who had
never learned to face adversity. "You are a de Valcourt.
Never forget it. You will meet your obligations with dignity.
And you will make your husband proud to have you as his
wife!"

Beatrix shrank back at Linnea's strident words. When
Linnea finished, Beatrix stared sullenly at her. "I still hope
he loses," she muttered.

"But he won't," Linnea vowed. Then she turned and
strode from the solar.

On the other side of the door, however, her certainty
faltered and her shoulders slumped. She hoped Axton
won. She prayed he did. Her family had already taken
enough from him. Despite the untenable situation between
them, she could not hate him. Indeed, she could not stop
loving him.

But what if Eustace won? What if he wounded Axton?
Or killed him? Though the idea was inconceivable,
still . . .

She would stay long enough to be sure he was not
harmed. If he was wounded, she would stay to nurse him.
Beyond that, however, she could not linger at Maidenstone. She could not bear to see him wed to Beatrix. She
could not stay a minute in this place while he took her
sister to his marriage bed. Once she was certain he was all
right, she would leave.

She thrust her hand into her cloth pocket and felt for the
tiny ruby. She would take it as her one memento of Axton.

Then her hand moved of its own will to her stomach.
Was it the only memento she had? She could not be certain, but she prayed it was not.

The bailey was crammed to overflowing. Axton walked into
the yard and swiftly scanned the crowd. Castle folk, villagers, his men and Eustace's spread among the crowd. And
everywhere that the soldiers of de la Manse and de Montfort appeared, so also were Henry's men dispersed. At
least the violence between him and Eustace would not ig-

nite the entire castle to warfare. Henry was being very wise on that point.

"There will be but three passes. If no one is unhorsed, then the competition will be moved to hand-to-hand combat," Peter said, hurrying along at Axton's side. It was not information Axton hadn't already heard, but his brother was nervous. He'd talked incessantly while assisting Axton with his armor, and he'd been muttering all the way out to the yard. Axton paused now and stayed his brother with one hand. He waved Reynold and Maurice on.

"I do not intend to lose, however . . . however in the event I do, you must not react foolishly."

"You will not lose. Why—"

"Hear me out, Peter!" He fixed his brother with a firm look. The boy was tall, nearly a man, he realized. It would be natural for Peter to seek revenge for a fallen brother. Hadn't he wanted revenge when his father and brothers had fallen in battle? But there were other considerations.

"There will be no quarter given this day, at least not for me, for there will be no quarter asked. I fight to win. But should I lose, then you become patriarch of our family. Take our mother back to Castell de la Manse. It will be yours anyway, and methinks she prefers it there." He stared at the boy until Peter reluctantly nodded. Then he went on, but more lowly.

"I would make one other request of you." He stopped and looked away, toward the pavillion that had been erected for Henry and the other important guests: his mother, the de Valcourt family.

Linnea.

He turned back to his brother. "Do not let Linnea fall into Henry's clutches."

"What?" Peter's face creased in a scowl. "She is hardly *your* concern."

"Do as I say, brother. Protect her as you would our mother. It is my last request of you."

He watched as Peter's face changed from anger to bewilderment, and then to a dawning comprehension. "You do love her—"

But Axton cut him off. "What she has done has been for her family, and I cannot fault her loyalty. 'Tis a rare thing . . ." He trailed off and looked again toward the pavillion, searching for the slender figure with the brilliantly golden hair that was Linnea, not the pallid copy that was her sister.

"To receive that sort of loyalty from anyone—brother, comrade, wife—is a rare thing indeed."

He turned away from Peter then. "Time for it to begin. Time for it finally to end."

.

Linnea spied Axton as soon as he entered the bailey. Had her eyes been blinded, she still would have known he was there. She could feel his very presence.

At his entrance a small cheer went up—his men and some of Maidenstone's people. That did not surprise Linnea, for he'd been fair and even-handed with his people—something Maynard would never have been.

A hard lump formed in her throat. Please don't let him die, she prayed. *Dear Lord, blessed Mother, St. Jude, please keep him safe!*

Sir Eustace appeared and another ripple of support sounded, though not as strong. Beside her Beatrix clapped her hands.

"There he is. Just look at him. He will defeat this de la Manse. Just see if he doesn't."

Linnea swung around to face her twin. "You go on and on about defeating Axton, but have you thought at all on what will happen if de Montfort wins? Are you so eager to wed with him, or do you simply fear to wed Axton?"

Beatrix started to reply, then abruptly turned away. But Linnea saw her chin tremble. For once, however, Beatrix's tender feelings did not deter her. She pressed on without mercy. "Shall Eustace's kiss be any gentler? Shall his demands of you be any less coarse? He looks as wont to kill you with his husbandly demands as Axton."

Without warning, Beatrix burst into tears. Even that, however, could not soften Linnea's feelings. Beatrix wanted Axton to die! "Axton is a lusty man," she continued, so consumed with jealousy for Beatrix's fate that she could not stop. "He will demand much of you, much of your body for his pleasure. But he will give it back tenfold. A hundredfold! He will—"

"Enough!" Lady Harriet interrupted, pinching Linnea hard on the arm. "Enough of this! Henry comes," she hissed.

Somehow Linnea swallowed all the invective that burned for release. Somehow Beatrix managed to stifle her sobs and surreptitiously dry her tears. By the time the young Henry stepped up onto the raised dais and approached them, the three de Valcourt women were outwardly composed.

But Linnea seethed still with anger. How long had all her resentments been buried beneath a patient and compliant facade? All her life, she realized. But over the past two weeks the layers of that facade had slowly been peeled back until now the burning center of her feelings felt exposed for anyone's casual perusal. How dare they think her feelings less important than their own. Her father. Her grandmother. Even Beatrix, it seemed.

And Axton was not exempt either. If anything, he was the most guilty, for he'd made her love him, then thrown her love away. The fact that he was justified in his suspicions about her did not matter at that moment. He should have recognized the depths of her love for him!

But Axton was not there with her, and so, as Henry turned to greet them, it was he who became the focus of all Linnea's ire. For he was the least involved of all the participants in this dreadful drama. The least affected. Yet it was he who wielded all the power.

His sharp blue gaze flitted between her and Beatrix. When he spied her belligerent expression, however, it settled upon her. "Lady Linnea?"

She curtsied as required, but there was no other sign of greeting. That only made him smile, however. He studied her with undisguised interest, letting his gaze rake her body with a thoroughness meant to flatter, or else fluster her. It only made her more furious.

"Have you thought on your future beyond this day's doings?" he asked. "I am certain my esteemed wife would be pleased to have so lovely an addition to her personal retinue."

At that moment a commotion drew his attention, and before Linnea could respond to him, the white, fluttering canvas parted, and Lady Mildred entered the open tent.

Axton's mother was robed in a fine gown of wine-colored silk. Her hair was dressed and covered with a sheer veil shot through with gold that shimmered and caught the light. Her carriage would have befitted the queen Henry spoke so blithely of as she acknowledged Linnea with a nod. She gave Beatrix a curious look, but the Lady Harriet she ignored entirely. Then she turned to Henry, and it was clear that while everyone else deferred to the young man who soon would be king, Lady Mildred was of a different mettle.

"Good morning, my lord. Have you come to see Axton fell yet another of your hapless men?"

Henry straightened up in his tall chair. It occurred to Linnea that the Lady Mildred had probably known him all his life. She had very likely dandled him on her knee when he was a babe. No doubt he commanded the same sort of respect from him as did his own mother.

" 'Tis but men's sport," Henry replied, rising to seat the older woman himself.

"Yes. Sport," she repeated. Then she turned to look at Linnea, a stare so serious it seemed almost to demand a reply from Linnea. "I could not help but overhear your question to the Lady Linnea," Lady Mildred continued. "I believe, however, that she will stay with me as my companion."

Linnea's heart lurched. Stay with Lady Mildred? Though she was drawn to the woman and knew the offer of such a position was a godsend to one in her precarious situation, she could never accept. Never. For she could not bear to be so near to Axton and yet not be his wife. She started to shake her head, but an intent look from Lady Mildred gave her pause.

"I will not stay long at Maidenstone," the woman went on. "I plan to leave for Caen once Axton is settled here."

Henry twisted to look over at Linnea, a wry smile lifting his handsome face. "Caen. How nice. I am often there. My wife periodically resides at Argentan, but a day's ride away. Mayhap we will have occasion to . . . to visit upon my return to the continent."

Linnea somehow managed a tight smile. "Mayhap we will, milord." *But only if I am not forewarned that you are coming.*

A blast of a horn and the thunder of a heavy horse approaching the pavillion put an end to that dangerous conversation. Everyone turned to watch Sir Eustace's approach astride a magnificent gray destrier. He was resplendent in gleaming mail and half-armor, and his steed was as handsomely draped in the yellow and green of de Montfort. He saluted the young Duke of Normandy, then everyone else, save for Lady Mildred and Linnea. When Henry rose to accept his man's salute of honor, Axton's mother smiled at Linnea, and in that smile was all the reassurance in the world. Win or lose, Linnea had an ally in Lady Mildred. As unlikely as that seemed, she knew it was true.

Then a second horse cantered up and both women turned to watch Axton's approach.

He was dressed in heavy mail and a solid breastplate and had a square-topped helmet perched in his lap. His only ornament was the scarlet bristle that adorned his helmet, that and his weapons. The lances they would use were blunted in the hopes that neither man would be mortally wounded in the joust. But even so, Linnea knew the risk was great.

He saluted Henry, raising the lance up a long moment before lowering it, then did as much to his mother. The women of de Valcourt, however, he did not favor so generously. Instead he stared at Linnea so fiercely she was unnerved.

He must think she was Beatrix, she reasoned. He must. After all, it was Beatrix he fought for. That's why he stared at her. When he turned away and cantered to his end of the jousting run, however, she was not so sure.

Though the yard was not large and the combatants were not far removed from the viewers, Linnea felt, nevertheless, that Axton was as far away from her as he could ever be. He was near enough that she could detect the rhythmic rise and fall of his chest, and yet he might as well have been far across the sea, so completely separated were they now.

Then there was no time for such dismal speculation, for with another brilliant sounding of the horn, the first deadly contest was announced.

The crowd of onlookers quieted. People circled the yard, perched on walls, and leaned precariously from every window opening. Two boys swung like red squirrels from a mason's scaffold. Even the castle hounds stood at alert, as if they knew the import of the coming conflict.

But while all else stilled, Linnea felt as if she'd begun to rattle apart. Her heart hammered; her blood roared in her ears; and her breathing came hard and labored.

Then, as if at some unheard signal, the two destriers charged, and Linnea forgot to breathe.

Dust rose in a cloud beneath the animals' fierce attack. Like maddened bulls they charged one another. Then with a crash they came together.

One of the horses screamed and veered off. Both men teetered in their saddles, rocked by the force of the impact. But somehow they held on.

Linnea let out a gasp of relief; so did all the others in the pavillion, except for Henry. He only grinned at the women arrayed around him. "Good show. Good show!" he exclaimed.

A sharp reply lodged in Linnea's throat. In her opinion it would be a better show to see the callous young duke drawn and quartered. But there was no time to confront Henry, for at the end of the run, the two knights turned and adjusted their armor. Then with fresh lances in hand, they again urged their steeds forward.

Linnea caught her breath. The earth fairly shuddered

beneath the heavy animals' hooves and she closed her eyes in terror for Axton. Then again came the crash, and her eyes sprang open.

A lance splintered. A man toppled and fell. Linnea bit down on her knuckles and a muffled cry escaped her lips. Then one of the destriers broke out of the dust storm and Axton emerged unscathed from the fray!

This time it was Lady Mildred who cried out in relief. But both women caught their breath in renewed fear. For Axton flung himself from his mount before it came fully to a halt and turned to confront Eustace again.

Stay down, Linnea silently cried out to the fallen knight. Stay down, you fool! But with the help of two of his men, Eustace was set upright and handed a short sword.

By that time Peter had run forward with a sword for Axton. The two knights then faced one another swathed in steel, yet nevertheless vulnerable to the slicing power of a well-aimed sword.

Eustace was slower. Linnea saw that at once. He favored one leg and shook his head as if he were not yet clear-headed. He'd taken a hard fall and it clearly left him at a disadvantage.

Please, God, let this end quickly, she prayed. *I will not interfere in Axton's life again. I will wish him well, and my sister too, if You will but spare his life.*

"Don't let that beast kill him!" Beatrix cried, and for one foolish moment Linnea thought her sister gave voice to her own thoughts. But in the next moment she knew her error. Beatrix feared for Sir Eustace, not for Axton.

"Never fear," Henry remarked. "I have given Axton strict orders not to make a fatal blow."

"And have you given Sir Eustace the same instructions?" Lady Mildred demanded to know. Despite her show of composure, the woman's knuckles were white, she clenched her fists so tightly.

Henry shifted in his seat. "Would it be a sporting match if I had? Eustace must have some advantage. God knows, Axton has enough of them."

As much as Linnea wanted to strangle the conscienceless young man who could set two men upon each other, simply for the sport, she nonetheless knew whereof he spoke. She'd never seen Axton do battle, save against the hapless tilting dummy. But it had been clear to her, from Peter as well as the other men's attitudes, that he was a warrior of uncommon skill.

Still, Sir Eustace was not without his own skill, and as the men began their dangerous dance, it was obvious his head had cleared. He attacked Axton, wielding his sword with no sign of restraint, slicing the air with deadly force. Axton parried every strike, but he fell back under the onslaught. The men's grunts and curses as they fought carried to the silent crowd. Steel rang on steel, an awful clamor that sliced Linnea's heart to shreds. No, she chanted the prayer with every awful blow that landed. *No, no, no!*

Then Eustace lunged and everyone gasped—only Axton was no longer in the path of his blade! He'd spun aside and with the flat of his blade, he struck Eustace hard on the back of his helmeted head.

Sir Eustace went sprawling and a small cheer went up. But the man scrambled swiftly to his feet and whirled around to once more face his foe. He had clearly lost his momentum, however. He charged as fiercely as before. His blows were as cruel, his advancement as determined. While he struggled to land a killing blow, however, he wielded the lethal blade in wilder and more erratic strokes.

But Axton repelled each blow, never striking back, only fielding Eustace's weakening attack. The ugly clang of steel on steel rang across the yard.

Then without warning, Axton lunged and Eustace went down on one knee.

A gasp went up and Henry leaped to his feet. As if Axton sensed his liege lord's presence, he tensed, his sword held just beneath Sir Eustace's chin, where his throat was exposed between his helmet and breastplate. Axton's blade dripped blood. Linnea saw that plainly enough. But though Eustace grasped his right shoulder and his groan of pain was clear to all, he had not released his own weapon.

He held it up, pointed at Axton, though it wavered from

the pain of his wounded shoulder. Linnea knew Axton would not strike the man down. Henry had seen to that. But Eustace might still inflict damage on Axton.

Then to Linnea's horror, Axton flung his sword aside, stepped within thrusting range of his enemy's weapon, and grabbed the sword right out of the man's hand.

An elated cry went up—Peter's voice, she recognized. At once the whole castle erupted. Cheers from some, curses from others, and the dusty roar of a hundred people rushing the victor and his fallen foe.

Linnea lost sight of Axton. In the first moments of her enormous relief, she lost sight also of what his victory actually meant. But when she turned, weak with elation, it was to face her distraught sister—Axton's intended bride.

Beatrix had collapsed in her grandmother's arms. Even Lady Harriet looked shaken by this final defeat of her hopes and plans. But the old woman was rescued by the core of iron which was such a part of her. Beatrix possessed no such core, and now, Lady Harriet showed no sympathy for her plight.

"Do not shame us!" she hissed at Beatrix, shoving her back and forcing the girl to stand alone. "Your sister showed a better mettle than this! Would you do any less?"

Lady Harriet met Linnea's gaze, and though she did not reveal her feelings by either smile or scowl, there was yet an understanding between them. They were, the two of them, made of the same stern stuff. They were fighters and survivors. But Linnea would never let herself turn as sour as her grandmother had. No matter what her future held, she would not become cruel and inflexible.

"My congratulations, madam."

Linnea turned at the sound of Henry's voice. He did not address her though, but rather Lady Mildred, who was trying very hard to rein in her joy, but not succeeding. Relief and happiness exuded from her like heat from the sun. It brightened the interior of the tented pavillion, casting away all shadows, even the one that still haunted Linnea.

Lady Mildred murmured her thanks to Henry. When he turned back to the field, however, her happy gaze moved to

Linnea. Circling Henry, she came up to Linnea and took her hand.

"I meant what I said." Her voice was pitched low. "I would gladly have you accompany me to Caen. Peter shall journey there as well."

The shadow returned to Linnea's world. "I . . . I cannot. I think I must be farther separated from Axton than that." She shook her head at the hopelessness of it all.

Then the sound of the crowd changed and when they both looked up, Axton strode directly toward the pavillion. He halted before Henry, his eyes steady on his liege lord. Not until a hush fell over the bailey did he speak.

"I have bested my rival and, as you requested, I have spared his life. I submit to you now, Henry Plantagenet, Count of Anjou, Duke of Normandy, and rightful king to all of Britain that I seek permission to wed with the daughter of Edgar de Valcourt."

Linnea could see his chest still heaving from his exertion. She saw the sweat trickle down his brow and the strains of the battle in the lines of his face. She saw also the triumphant light of victory in his deep gray eyes.

At least he was getting his due. He would have his home, secured through both his line and his wife's. If only she could be that wife. But she had prayed for his victory and now she must hold to the promise she'd made. She must leave him and his bride in peace.

Henry stared down at Axton. "She is yours," he finally said. "I only hope you can keep straight this time which one is the wife and which one the sister."

For an instant Axton's eyes flickered to Linnea. Then as quickly they moved to the weeping Beatrix. Linnea saw his jaw clench. "I know well which is which."

"Very well then. I shall depart within the hour, for duty calls me to Salisbury." He grimaced. "It appears there will be many such disputes of ownership and I must resolve them all." He turned, then spying Linnea, he paused. "Shall I take de Valcourt and his other womenfolk with me?"

Linnea held her breath. Before Axton could respond,

however, the Lady Mildred stepped forward. "De Valcourt and his mother would be better served at Romsey Abbey. She is old and he is no longer right in his head. They will be well tended there."

"And the Lady Linnea?" the young duke asked with one brow arched.

"As I said, my lord. I would have her accompany me to Caen. If that is not to her liking, then, by your leave, I will find her a place in a good household."

"A place?" Henry repeated in a mocking tone.

"A *good* place, my lord." Her voice was stern and motherly.

Henry shrugged then, and with a casual gesture, conceded to his mother's longtime friend. Lady Mildred gave him a small smile while Linnea at last released the breath she'd been holding.

Was it over? Was her father to receive no further punishment than that? Would life at Maidenstone at last return to some semblance of order, though without the presence of the de Valcourt family?

It appeared it would, for now that the entertainment was done, Henry seemed more than ready to depart. As the crowd began slowly to disperse, the wounded Eustace was carted off to the surgeon, the duke's entourage was rounded up, and the early tension of the day dissolved. The cook returned to his kitchen. The mason shooed the boys down from the scaffold and took up his trowel and mortar. An army of small boys hauled water to the kitchen garden.

Everyone's lives went back to their prescribed order, save for hers and Beatrix's. And perhaps Axton's, she thought as she watched him stride away beside Henry. Would he have any regrets about marrying Beatrix?

At once she admonished herself for such foolish maunderings. Why would he regret it when it did gain him his most fervent desire? Hadn't he just risked his life to that very end?

Remembering Beatrix, Linnea turned with a heavy heart to face her sister. She was seated on a chair, a stricken expression on her pale face. Despite her own grief, Linnea felt a spasm of pain for her sister.

She knelt before Beatrix and took her hands in her own. "It will be all right. A week from now you will wonder that you did shed a tear over this."

Beatrix swallowed hard, and though it was clear she was not convinced of Linnea's words, she nodded ever so slightly. Linnea managed a bitter smile. Then, spying Peter, she pulled Beatrix to her feet. "You will have an ally in Peter. He will be here awhile, should you need a friend."

"But I want you to stay. Please, Linnea," she begged. "For I will have no one if you go."

Linnea could feel herself succumbing to the desperation in her sister's voice. But on this point she could not waver. "I cannot stay. I cannot stay here . . ."

She trailed off. Her future was unclear, but to remain at Maidenstone or go to Caen were both impossible. "Perhaps I will travel with Father and Grandmother to Romsey. They'll need someone to care for them. You will have Norma. And Peter—" She turned to Axton's brother who stood now watching them both. "Peter, please help me to ease her fears."

When Linnea beckoned, Peter came nearer. He'd meant to gloat, to taunt these two devious sisters and their witchy grandmother about their family's complete fall—and his family's triumph. But as the twin faces turned up to him, the one with wet and frightened eyes, the other pale with her own private despair, he could not do it. They were so alike, and yet so different.

He cleared his throat. "My brother . . . my brother is a fair man. He will treat you better than you deserve," he added more gruffly.

"He hates me. He will punish me and I—" The damp-faced Beatrix broke into tears again.

He let out a sharp oath and stepped nearer. Linnea stepped back. "He is angry now, but it will not last. Linnea knows whereof she speaks. If you would but withstand his temper awhile, it will eventually wear itself out."

But even as he spoke the reassuring words to her, he

questioned their validity. Linnea had been able to withstand Axton's temper. But could this other, gentler sister? More importantly, though, were Axton's feelings. If he loved Linnea, as Peter suspected, would he ever find a peace with this meek and teary-eyed Beatrix?

His gaze swept over his brother's new bride, noting her pretty face, her heavy golden tresses, the delicate line of her throat and the fullness of her breasts.

"By the rood!" he swore, raking one hand through his already disheveled hair. When Beatrix cast him a damp, imploring look, he swore again. He didn't care how lovely she was nor how miserable, he told himself. He didn't! His brother's bride was none of his concern and he refused to involve himself in their affairs.

"I cannot help her." He bit the words out to Linnea. "I will be in Caen. She must make her own way with my brother!" Then he turned on his heel and beat a hasty retreat.

But even as he did so, he knew with a sinking despair that he did but lie. He could no more see his brother's new bride abandoned to Axton's famous temper than he could the last one. Worse, this time he feared Axton's fury would not be so easily tempered. The fact was, Axton had lost his heart to Linnea, the wrong sister. Peter feared that as long as Axton was married to Beatrix, he would always remain angry and discontented.

Chapter 25

It was Peter who brought the news. "The wedding will be tomorrow morning."

The entire de Valcourt family had gathered in the chamber given to Axton's bride, the chamber opposite the lord's chamber. Edgar de Valcourt sat at the window, staring out at nothing. The other three were equally silent.

"For now he wishes to sup privately with his bride," Peter continued. He turned to Linnea. "Afterward he would speak to you, Lady Linnea."

Linnea's father did not move, as if words no longer registered in his mind. But Beatrix and Lady Harriet both turned to Linnea. On Beatrix's face was a mixture of fear and resignation. On Lady Harriet's a sad sort of defeat. Linnea knew somehow that her grandmother's days were numbered. Without any power to wield, she would have no reason to live.

But that eventuality was not Linnea's most pressing problem. Peter's message was.

She cleared her throat and stared at him. "Why does he wish to speak to me?"

Her grandmother snorted at the word *speak,* and Linnea felt color rush into her cheeks. Even Peter blushed. It was painfully clear what Axton wanted of her. No doubt he thought it the perfect punishment. He would sup with his bride, then sleep with her sister. Or so he thought.

She steeled herself to feel neither longing nor pain. "I must tend to my family tonight, my aging grandmother and my father, who is ill."

When Peter started to protest, she stood up. "I am firm in this."

He frowned at that, then pulled her rudely toward the door. "He will come for you," he whispered.

"I will go to your mother then. She, at least, will protect me from his improper advances!"

"He won't care!" Peter hissed. "He will come for you anyway. Anywhere. You haven't seen him since Henry and Eustace left. You don't know how angry he is!"

"Angry?" This time it was Linnea who drew him away, out the door and into the antechamber. "What in the name of God has he to be angry about?"

"I don't know!" he shouted back. "I only know that if you do not come there will be hell to show for it!"

She did not respond to that but stormed back into the room and shoved the door closed in his face. Inside, though, with all eyes turned on her, she knew she was well and truly caught. She could not stay, yet she feared he

312

would not let her go. He would keep her and torment her, and she would die from a broken heart. Already she could hardly breathe or think, so excruciatingly painful was her fate.

"It appears I taught you well." Lady Harriet approached her, click by metallic click. "Whatever it is you did—go willingly or fight—he cannot get enough." She stood just before Linnea, her face crafty again, her voice lowered to a cracking whisper. "If you would just advise your sister as to his desires—"

"No. No!" Linnea recoiled from the old woman. "I will not be a part of any more schemes against him!" Then she jerked open the door and fled, oblivious to her grandmother's call or her sister's.

She had to get away! She could not wait another day—not even another minute! She must flee this place even though it be on foot with no plan or direction or coin. She must run from Axton, else she would surely fling herself into his arms.

He was irritated. He was angry.

No, he was nervous. Axton had planned to sup privately with his bride so that he might determine what sort of woman she was—beyond the mask of fear she always wore in his presence. But he just wanted to be done with this supper with her, and move on to his meeting with her sister. With Linnea.

It was the thought of dealing with Linnea again that had him so restless, with palms sweating and his gut in a knot.

She would fight him, and she would have many allies—his mother and brother, primarily. And, no doubt, his soon-to-be-wife.

Christ, but he was a madman to even think he could wed the one and bed the other! But he was not prepared to let her go. Not yet.

The curtain to the pantler's closet parted and Peter poked his head in. "She will be here soon."

Axton stood, scraping the chair backward. He'd chosen to meet with Beatrix in the castle offices, to allow them

313

privacy from the many curious eyes of staff and servants, and prying family. Of a sudden, however, he wished he'd not done so. With Linnea he preferred the privacy. With Beatrix—

"Christ," he swore, raking his close-cropped hair with one hand. "Just show the wench in."

Peter frowned at his words. "She is to be your wife. To call her wench is to begin the union in a less than hopeful manner."

"I started my union with her sister in a less than hopeful fashion," Axton snapped. "Look how that turned out."

"Disastrous?" Peter retorted sarcastically.

"No, damn you! With her more than content! With her melting beneath my hand! So shall it be with this sister. They look alike. They will respond alike!"

"They are not the same woman!" Peter pounded the air with his knotted fist. "Linnea fights you—and wins," he caustically added. "But Beatrix will not be able to withstand your foul temper."

"What do you mean, she wins? She has not—"

"She has won your heart! She has lied to you, deceived you, and brought you to the brink of defeat," he pointed out, ticking the items off on his fingers. "Yet she nonetheless has won your heart." Peter's strident voice had softened at the last point. Now his young face creased in a frown as he stared at his brother. "You cared what became of her should you fall to de Montfort. But now that you have won, what do you intend to do with her?"

Axton was shaking with rage. But it was not his brother who deserved that anger, he recognized. It was himself. He was a fool to let a mere woman affect him so. Why couldn't he be content with the sister, especially since she was just as fair, just as comely, and no doubt could warm his bed just as well on a cold night?

Because she was not Linnea, and he could tell the difference between them in every aspect of their bearing.

Still, in the dark one woman was much the same as another, he told himself. Hadn't he always thought that? Hadn't he proven it true innumerable times?

"What do you intend to do with her?" Peter demanded to know.

"I shall keep her," Axton snapped. He glared at his brother. "I shall keep her as long as I want her," he added, goading the boy, though he knew it was pointless.

"You cannot do that!"

"I can and I will."

"You would take a vow to one woman—before God, your family, and hers. You would take that vow, knowing all the while you intend to break it?"

"Didn't Linnea do as much to me? She took the same vows, but she lied."

But Peter was obstinate. He shook his head. "Beatrix is not Linnea, Axton. She is not a part of your anger at Linnea."

"She's at the very center of it! She's what this is all about. Linnea loves her so much she whored for her!"

With a furious cry Peter launched himself at Axton. Though smaller by half, his attack was nonetheless hard enough to set Axton back on his heels. But he recovered quickly and with a rough shove sent Peter sprawling.

That, however, did not stop the boy. He rose to his feet, his fists clenched in rage. " 'Twas but a few hours ago that you lauded her loyalty. You said it was a rare thing. Now you would berate her for it?"

Axton winced under Peter's painful accusation. It was true, all of it. Worst of all, however, was the bitter knowledge that it was not so much Linnea's loyalty to her sister which did bedevil him as it was her disloyalty to him. He could never command that same sort of loyalty, that same sort of love from her as did her family members.

But he could not admit as much to anyone, not even his own brother. He glared at Peter. "She made a fool of me. I am entitled to my anger. Besides, we speak here not of Linnea, but of Beatrix."

"Yes, Beatrix, who is so sweet and so mild-tempered that she did inspire her sister to make the ultimate sacrifice for her. Did you ever think, great lummox that you are, that

Beatrix might just be worth that sacrifice? That Linnea loves her so fiercely for a reason?"

Axton gritted his teeth. "What I think is that you are as easily coerced by that wilting wench as is her sister."

"And what am I to do, stand by and watch you torment the defenseless creature? She will not survive so well as did Linnea—"

"Do not speak to me of Linnea!"

"Very well! Then let us speak of Beatrix. You must not take your anger out on her when 'tis Linnea who has you so besotted!"

It was the last straw. With a string of the worst curses he could think of, Axton exploded. "Besotted! Besotted? 'Tis not I who is besotted, but you! If this damnable Beatrix is so sweet and good as you would have her then . . . then by all that is holy, *you* marry her!"

Axton did not remain in the castle office for his interview with Beatrix. Instead he retreated to the only place where he could be alone with his thoughts, and that was the chapel. No one interrupted him. No sound penetrated the thick stone walls or narrow glass-paned windows as he sat on a bench slumped forward in despair.

You marry her.

His final words to Peter echoed in his head, whipping him with their barbs, taunting him with an idea that was insane.

The words had been borne in anger, but they tempted him now with visions of a peace he'd thought vanished since the moment he'd received Henry's devastating missive.

If Peter would marry the Lady Beatrix, then he . . .

He shook his head and let it fall forward into his palms. How could he even consider marrying a woman who had done everything in her power to deter him from his goal?

Because he could not help but admire her courage, her spirit, and her deep sense of loyalty. To have such a wife standing beside him . . .

Again he shook his head. Who was the besotted fool

now? Linnea would never agree to it. He'd treated her too cruelly too many times. And then there was Peter to consider, and Beatrix.

He took a slow breath, then raised his head. He was in a holy place. Perhaps if he prayed for guidance. Then he had a quick thought and he felt the first glimmer of hope. Perhaps the saint that Linnea was forever invoking, St. Jude, patron saint of hopeless causes, would come to his aid.

He made a swift but fervent prayer. Then he quit the chapel and went in search of his brother.

He'd made many promises to St. Jude in the chapel, and he meant to honor them all. But most of all he meant to keep Linnea with him, though he must fight her and his entire family for that privilege.

Linnea slipped from the castle in the company of four village women and six or seven children. She'd dressed in her own clothes, an old but serviceable gray gown over a plain wool kirtle. She'd wrapped her hair in a couvrechef and clutched a sack to her chest. Though it was warm, she also wore a nondescript cloak and hood, and walked with an uneven gait, slightly stooped over. With her face averted, she could have been any aging matron returning home after a long day's service at the castle.

Only she wasn't returning to her home. She was fleeing it.

Once out of the castle, her deliberate pace let her fall farther and farther behind the other women. Though they sent her several curious looks, they thankfully did not approach her.

As they neared the village, Linnea veered away, toward the fringe of woods that lay along the river. Only when she was well away from this place would she feel safe, although she doubted she could ever feel happy.

Where she would go and how she would get there were two questions she could not yet answer. Even though the abbey was the only logical destination she could think of, she worried that she could easily be tracked there—assuming Axton tried to find her. Even without him in pursuit, however, the fact remained that she had no idea where the abbey was. And she didn't dare ask anyone in Maidenstone village.

She paused in the shelter of an ancient yew, its trunk twisted and gray. It seemed to be crying out in a silent agony—much as she was crying silently inside. A magpie called down in scolding tones. A flock of blackbirds rose up indignantly at her rude invasion of their territory.

Coward, coward, their raucous calls seemed to mock her. Coward to flee. Coward to abandon her sister. Coward to remember even now the pleasure she and Axton had taken of one another in this very woodland.

She moved away from the tortured yew and pushed farther into the shadowed forest. No longer did she worry about disguising herself. On impulse she decided simply to follow the river against the flow. Eventually she would find another village. Eventually she would find someone who would direct her to the abbey, or perhaps an even more likely place. Meanwhile, she must travel as quickly and quietly as she could.

An hour passed without incident. She saw no one as the afternoon wore on into the long lavender dusk of summer, although once she did hear a distant whistle, as if someone did signal their dog. Where the riverbank was clear, she traveled easily. Through bracken and hip-high fern, the going was slower. Her cloak was a hindrance; she took it off. Her skirts were equally awkward, but she could do no more than hike them up over her arm, freeing her lower legs to stride more freely.

Still, she was beginning to feel the first bit of confidence that she might succeed. Her heart no longer pounded a fearful rhythm, but rather an exhausted one. But though tired, she meant to travel through the night, at least until she found another village.

She reached for a bit of brown bread she'd hastily stuffed in her sack. But before she could bring it up for a bite, the whicker of a horse froze her in her tracks.

She shrank down into a bed of queen fern. The ground was damp here, and she felt the moisture seep into her sturdy shoes. A cricket leaped off a nodding frond, landed briefly on her arm, then whirred off, indignant to be disturbed thus. But Linnea remained frozen in place. Someone was coming—she could not precisely determine his direction. But whoever it was, he boded ill for her. She had no friends, not on this precipitous flight; therefore whoever it was, he must be her foe.

She twisted her head, trying to hear past the river's constant rush and the disparate songs of woodlark and lapwings, to the crash of heavy hooves in the forest undergrowth. But the horse was still. There was no sound.

She peered cautiously about. Where was he? *Who* was he? Or had she, perhaps, only imagined the sound? Perhaps it had not been a horse at all. Perhaps it had been the huff of a stray sheep. Or of a wild boar.

"St. Jude!" she muttered under her breath. Wild boars were fearful creatures, aggressive and mean. She'd once helped tend a woodsman who'd been gored by a boar in rut. He'd not survived.

The birds suddenly went silent. When something rustled behind her, Linnea reacted in panic. She sprang upright, and without pausing to look around, sprinted for the nearest tree.

Up she went, cloak and bundle falling where they might. She scrambled up the rough-barked ash, grabbing for a handhold, scrabbling with her feet for extra purchase. Her skirt caught, held, then ripped when she hauled herself over a sturdy branch. Was she high enough? Could a boar rear up and reach her still?

Holding another branch, she stood up, balancing herself as she scanned the area around her leafy oasis. She spied her bundle, fallen in a patch of blueberries. But her cloak was nowhere to be seen. Neither was the boar.

Then a sound came from beyond the tree's thick trunk, and she muttered another oath. How was she to escape if some wild creature had her trapped in a tree? "St. Jude!"

When she peeped fearfully through the budding foliage, however, the sight that greeted her was so shocking she almost lost her hold and fell. For it was Axton—Axton sitting tall and grim-faced on one of his warhorses. Axton, who could reach up and pluck her down as easily as if she were a pear or an apple.

Axton, who'd come for her after all.

She didn't know whether to exult with joy, or weep with frustration. She chose to climb higher.

With an imperceptible movement he directed the horse closer to the tree, circling it so that he had a clearer view of her in her green bower. Her green prison.

"Will you climb all the way to the top in order to escape me?" he taunted her. "Do you think it will do you any good?"

"Go away!" Linnea meant it to come out an imperious order. It was, rather, closer to an ineffectual plea. In any event, he did not heed it.

"Come down, Linnea. Before you fall and hurt yourself."

"Go away. Begone from here," she replied, more fiercely.

"Damnation, woman. It's for your own good. Get down here so that we can talk—"

"Talk! Talk? Is that what you call it?" Though she was trembling with too many conflicting emotions, Linnea managed to take hold of a higher limb and pull herself farther out of his reach. She wedged herself into a fork in two branches and glared down at him. "If you truly want only to talk, then you may do so. As for me, I shall stay right where I am."

She saw his jaw clench in irritation, but instead of scowling at her, his face took on an assessing look. Then he smiled.

"As you wish, Linnea. We will talk as we are—you up there, me down here. I came to bring you news of your sister."

Something seemed to break inside Linnea at his reference to Beatrix. Although she feared for Beatrix and worried over her—and loved her dearly—she did not want to discuss her with him. Especially not with him.

320

When she did not respond, he continued. "Her wedding has been delayed."

Linnea blinked at that. She bent down a little, the better to see him through the ash's dense summer foliage. "Delayed?"

He shrugged. "Yes. Until Peter has been knighted."

"Knighted?" she repeated blankly. What had Peter's knighting to do with Beatrix?

"They will reside at our castle in Caen. He prefers Normandy to Britain. But 'tis only one day's journey by ship and two more over land. You can visit her as often as you like. And, of course, she is welcome to visit you."

Linnea frowned and shook her head. Nothing he said made sense. He would wed Beatrix after Peter was knighted. Then he would send her with Peter to live at Caen?

Then another possibility occurred to her—another meaning to his words—and she sucked in a sudden breath.

"Watch out!"

She grabbed for a limb just in time to prevent herself from slipping right out of the tree.

"Damnation, Linnea! I'm coming up to bring you down," Axton growled.

"Wait!" she cried, clutching the tree tighter than ever. She didn't want to get her hopes up, but still . . . "Why must Beatrix not wed until . . . until Peter is knighted?"

He urged the destrier nearer until he was just beneath her. If he reached a hand up he could probably have touched her foot. But he didn't do that. He simply sat there staring up at her. He'd been wearing a half-smile as he'd revealed the little details about Beatrix but it had disappeared, and now his expression was solemn. Worried, even.

" 'Tis you I wish to wed, Linnea, not your sister."

"But . . . but . . ." She heard the words but could scarcely believe them. He wanted to wed her, the second sister? "But you fought to win Beatrix. To win Maidenstone."

He nodded. His face was creased in a frown. "And now I am fighting to win you."

"But . . ." Linnea paused, trying to understand, wanting to believe. "But what of Maidenstone Castle?"

"It is in de la Manse hands now and it will remain so. For my father's two sons to marry your father's two daughters cannot weaken the claim." It was his turn to pause. "Marry me, Linnea, but as Linnea, this time. As the woman I must have if I am ever to be content."

He meant it. He really did! Emotions rose in her chest, so hard, so violent, that Linnea could not answer him. Tears made his image swim before her and she could do no more than hold tight to the tree and struggle for the breath to speak.

When she did not respond right away, however, his frown deepened and he went on. "I know you have no reason to believe I will make you a good husband. I have berated you. I have raged at you. I have forced myself on you in both anger and in the grips of a desire I sometimes hated."

"You hated it?" she asked, her elation sinking.

He shook his head. "No, that's not what I meant. I hated myself for wanting you so badly."

"Mayhap that is all you feel for me," she whispered, though the idea made her despair. "Mayhap it is only the physical wanting between us—"

"No! I swear to you, Linnea, that it is more than that."

"You say that now," she replied as all her initial joy faded into the ugly reality of the situation. "When we lie together you forget how I deceived you. How I played the whore," she added, though the word fairly choked her.

"St. Jude!" he swore. "I was but a fool—an angry, stupid fool to have ever said that. But I know better now, and I beg you to forgive me."

"How do you mean, know better?"

"I know about you, about the curse your grandmother said you bore. The curse of the second twin. I know how much you love your sister and how much she loves you. I know," he added more slowly, "why you were driven to sacrifice yourself for Beatrix, and how desperately you longed to be accepted and loved."

He reached up and she felt his hand on her foot, then circling her ankle, not demandingly nor threateningly, but gently. Sweetly.

"Know this, Linnea de Valcourt. You are loved. Your sister loves you. But more than she can ever love you, I love you. With every part of me, I love you. And I would have you as my wife, to put before all other women, to love and honor all the days of my life and beyond."

Linnea could hardly comprehend his words, so startling and unexpected were they. Added to that, the maelstrom of her own emotions made the entire world seem to spin.

With the back of one hand she wiped vainly at her teary eyes. Beneath her he sat on his steed, his face turned earnestly up to her. He'd ridden out without helm or hood, and his close-cropped hair ruffled now in the evening breeze.

More than anything she needed to reach down and touch his face, to say yes, even though there were so many questions yet unanswered. She moved as if to come down, but he held her ankle still.

"Will you?" he asked, and she heard the uncertainty in his voice. Did he honestly fear after such a soul-baring proposal that she might refuse?

But he must have, for with a sudden move he grasped a branch and pulled himself up into the tree. In a moment he was before her, sharing the same branch, bending through the leaves to draw her into his arms.

"I love you, Linnea. 'Tis more than the pleasure we find in the bed. 'Tis—" He broke off, shaking his head. "Your sister is not you. She could never be you, not to me. And I know now that—" Again he broke off. "Maidenstone can bring me no joy if you are not there at my side."

Linnea cut off his words with a kiss; she could not restrain herself any longer. She pressed into his embrace, and for a dangerous moment they teetered on the swaying branch. Somehow Axton lowered them both, and without

323

her quite knowing how, they were on his startled horse as it danced a circle beneath the ancient ash.

"You will do it? You will marry me again?" he asked, forcing her to look at him.

From her position settled sideways across his lap, Linnea gazed up into the face of the man she loved. "Yes, if you are certain."

"I am certain." He cut her off with a kiss that made the world tilt beneath them. Linnea melted into that kiss and into the knowledge that he loved her.

He loved *her.*

They drew away from one another and she stared wonderingly up at him. "How can you tell us apart? How can you choose me when Beatrix—"

"She is not you. I cannot say how I know, but it takes no more than a glance for me to see the difference. To see you." His eyes ran over her face and she could feel the full force of his love shining from his eyes.

"You are certain in this," she persisted.

"I am certain." Once more he paused. "Are you?"

Linnea smiled, and when she did, she felt the last edge of his tension recede. "I am certain. I love you, Axton." She shook her head, unable to speak past the lump of emotion in her throat. For so long she had been the second sister, unloved by anyone, save Beatrix. And now this man, who should want Beatrix, wanted her. He loved *her.*

As if he sensed and understood her feelings, his arms tightened around her. For a moment there were no words between them. Then without warning he kicked the horse forward and they were flying through the forest, up the road, then on toward Maidenstone.

She had not gone so very far, she realized, for beyond the fringe of trees the towers of the castle were plainly visible. But even had she run forever, she knew now she could never have escaped the hold this one man had on her.

As if he read her thoughts, he spoke in her ear. "Where were you running to?"

"I wasn't running *to* any place. I was running . . . I was

running away from you. No, not from you," she amended. "From the thought of you and Beatrix together."

At her whispered admission, Axton felt a deep pang of guilt. He'd caused her such pain. He didn't deserve her love, but by God, he was grateful to have it.

He reined in the horse. They were on the crest of a low hill. Below them spread the fields that radiated from Maidenstone village and from the castle beyond. The last light of day glinted on the crenellated walls. The sky loomed a deep purple, ready to creep dark and quiet across the entire valley.

This was his home. And this was his woman. He buried his face in her loosened hair, breathing in the very essence of her. "I'm sorry, Linnea, sorry for every cruel and selfish thing I did."

"No. No. 'Tis I who deceived you. If I had not pretended to be my sister—"

He cut her off with another kiss. "Never say that. Never wish that you had not done that brave and foolish deed, my love. For had you not, I never would have found you."

She conceded that point with the sweetest, sexiest smile he'd ever seen. Then her expression grew grave. "What of your mother?"

"She approves."

"And Peter?"

"He is in agreement."

She placed a hand on his chest. "But what of Beatrix?"

He chuckled. "Your sister is so relieved not to marry me, I believe she would agree to marry the lowliest stableboy at Maidenstone, if that was the price of her freedom."

"More the fool she," Linnea murmured, snuggling into his arms.

It was just an off-handed comment, said under her breath. But it brought Axton a happiness he never would have believed possible. She loved him. He had the woman he loved as well as the home he'd fought so long and hard for.

The truth, though, was that the home was not half so

valuable as the woman. He could be happy with Maiden-stone, now that he had Linnea. But without Linnea . . .

He shook his head and hugged her tighter to him. Thank God he would never have to be without Linnea. Thank God and thank St. Jude.

Author's Note

Medieval attitudes toward twin births varied from place to place and century to century. There were those who believed multiple births only occurred if the mother had been intimate with more than one man, or with the devil. In those cases the mother was often put to death immediately upon the birth, along with her innocent babes. Other cultures revered twins, believing them the children of a god, and therefore a blessing upon their village or town.

Another belief was that they were the symbol of good and evil, that they fought within the womb to be born first. It was also believed that they shared one soul, and that the first born received all the goodness of that one soul, while the second received all the evil. In such cases, as in the one I have depicted in THE MAIDEN BRIDE, the second child was put to death. Or at least she was supposed to be . . .

Shy Eliza Thoroughgood is traveling to Madeira with her frail young cousin Aubrey when they find themselves held captive on the ship of Cyprian Dare. Desperate to save herself and her innocent ward, Eliza will do anything.

Full of bitterness, Cyprian intends to wreak revenge on Aubrey's father—the man who years before abandoned his mother and made him a bastard. And Cyprian is confident he can tame the lovely Eliza in the dark, seaswept night...until her heart challenges him to a choice he could never have foreseen.

Heart of the Storm

REXANNE BECNEL

HEART OF THE STORM
Rexanne Becnel
_____ 95608-8 $5.99 U.S./$6.99 CAN.

Publishers Book and Audio Mailing Service
P.O. Box 070059, Staten Island, NY 10307
Please send me the book(s) I have checked above. I am enclosing $_____ (please add $1.50 for the first book, and $.50 for each additional book to cover postage and handling. Send check or money order only—no CODs) or charge my VISA, MASTERCARD, DISCOVER or AMERICAN EXPRESS card.

Card Number_____

Expiration date_____Signature_____

Name_____

Address_____

City_____State/Zip _____
Please allow six weeks for delivery. Prices subject to change without notice. Payment in U.S. funds only. New York residents add applicable sales tax.   HS 3/97